# Sultana's Legacy

Lisa J. Yarde

SULTANA'S LEGACY


ISBN-10 1456487779

ISBN-13 978-1456487775



www.lisajyarde.com

Cover Artwork
*Femme Orientale*, Jean Francois Portaels, 1877
File source: Creative Commons, Attributions License
http://nl.wikipedia.org/wiki/Bestand:Jeanfrancois-portaels-Femme_Orientale.jpg

Background courtesy of Fotolia, Royalty-Free License

Cover arrangement and title font by Lance Ganey

# *Dedication*

To Jeanne, who inspired my love of historical fiction and honors me with her friendship.

For my dear mother, devoted to her family and generous in her love, much like my heroine Fatima.

# Acknowledgments

I remain grateful for the support of everyone who read and assisted with various drafts of this novel, the members of my critique groups, especially Anita Davison, Mandy Ducrot, Jennifer Haymore, Laura Hogg, Mirella Patzer, Rosemary Rach, Ginger Simpson, Devorah Stone, Richard Warren Field, and Anne Whitfield.

To my beta readers, Victoria Dixon, Mirella Patzer, Lindsay Townsend and Kristen Wood, thank you for your continued support and encouragement with this novel and its prequel. To my editor, Candice S. Watkins, thanks for your attention to detail.

As always, to my loving family, thank you for imparting the values of patience and perseverance. Without your guidance, my work would not be possible.

# *Foreword*

Dear Reader,

The events in this book take place in the kingdom of Granada during a turbulent period for thirteenth-century Moorish Spain. Historians have referred to the rulers of Granada as Muslim princes (*emirs*) or kings, but I have used the title Sultan. While the first four Sultans of Granada are members of the Banu'l-Ahmar and other clans were the Banu Marin and Banu Zayyan, I have chosen the more commonly accepted names, e.g. the Nasrids for the Banu'l-Ahmar, then the Marinids and Zayyanids.

Many of the male historical figures bore the same name. I have distinguished between them with reference to their titles or familial connections where possible. There were six key characters named Muhammad, whom I have mentioned in the narrative. In addition to my protagonist Faraj, there was also Faraj, the son of Muhammad II, Faraj, the paternal grandson of my protagonist and another Faraj, who conspired with his brothers in the murder of a Sultan of Granada. There were also three historical figures named Ismail, two of them cousins.

I have also used Arabic words for Moorish cities, regions and certain terms. While the correct title of chief minister in Granada was *'Dhu l-wizaratayn'* in various periods, I have kept the usage of *Hajib* throughout the novel. The chronology of events differs in a variety of sources, but the narrative follows the best-documented dates in the Moorish period.

I remain indebted to invaluable research materials for an understanding of thirteenth-century Spain and its inhabitants, including Shirley Guthrie's *Arab Women in the Middle Ages* and L.P. Harvey's *Islamic Spain 1250 to 1500.* Other vital sources of information on the detailed history of the Alhambra and Moorish architectural achievements came from Antonio Fernandez Puertas' masterwork, *The Alhambra: Volume 1 from the Ninth Century to Yusuf I* and Michael Jacobs' *Alhambra.*

# *Months of the Hijri Calendar*

Dates approximate the equivalent periods of the Hijri and Gregorian calendars. The sighting of the crescent moon determines dates in the Hijri calendar. The term AH refers to events occurring in numbered periods after the year of the Hijra or the emigration of the Prophet Muhammad from Mecca to Medina in September AD 622.

| **Months** |
| --- |
| Muharram: the first Islamic month |
| Safar: the second Islamic month |
| Rabi al-Awwal: the third Islamic month |
| Rabi al-Thani: the fourth Islamic month |
| Jumada al-Ula: the fifth Islamic month |
| Jumada al-Thani: the sixth Islamic month |
| Rajab: the seventh Islamic month |
| Sha`ban: the eighth Islamic month |
| Ramadan: the ninth Islamic month, a venerated period of abstinence and fasting from sunrise to sunset |
| Shawwal: the tenth Islamic month |
| Dhu al-Qa`da: the eleventh Islamic month |
| Dhu al-Hijja: the twelfth Islamic month, a period of pilgrimage to Saudi Arabia |

# Characters

*The Nasrids*

**Fatima bint Muhammad,** daughter of Abu Abdallah Muhammad II of Gharnatah

**Abu Abdallah Muhammad II of Gharnatah,** the second Sultan of Gharnatah (r. 671-702 AH), Fatima's father

**Abu Abdallah Muhammad III of Gharnatah,** the third Sultan of Gharnatah (r. 702-709 AH), Fatima's elder brother

**Abu'l-Juyush Nasr I of Gharnatah,** the fourth Sultan of Gharnatah (r. 709-714 AH), Fatima's younger brother, only son of Abu Abdallah Muhammad II of Gharnatah and Nur al-Sabah

**Abu Said Faraj ibn Ismail,** Fatima's husband, Raïs of Malaka

**Abu'l-Walid Ismail I ibn Faraj,** Fatima and Faraj's eldest son

**Arub bint Muhammad,** second wife of Abu'l-Walid Ismail I ibn Faraj

**Abu Abdallah Muhammad IV ibn Ismail,** eldest son of Abu'l-Walid Ismail I ibn Faraj and Arub bint Muhammad

**Moraima bint Ismail,** eldest daughter of Abu'l-Walid Ismail I ibn Faraj and Arub bint Muhammad

**Zubaidah bint Ismail,** second daughter of Abu'l-Walid Ismail I ibn Faraj and Arub bint Muhammad

**Ismail ibn Ismail,** second son of Abu'l-Walid Ismail I ibn Faraj and Arub bint Muhammad

**Sahar bint Ismail,** third daughter of Abu'l-Walid Ismail I ibn Faraj and Arub bint Muhammad

**Jamila bint Ali,** third wife of Abu'l-Walid Ismail I ibn Faraj
**Faraj ibn Ismail,** son of Abu'l-Walid Ismail I ibn Faraj and Jamila bint Ali
**Hamda bint Ismail,** eldest daughter of Abu'l-Walid Ismail I ibn Faraj and Jamila bint Ali
**Muna bint Ismail,** second daughter of Abu'l-Walid Ismail I ibn Faraj and Jamila bint Ali

**Safa bint Yusuf,** fourth wife of Abu'l-Walid Ismail I ibn Faraj
**Yusuf ibn Ismail,** son of Abu'l-Walid Ismail I ibn Faraj and Safa bint Yusuf
**Tarub bint Ismail,** eldest daughter of Abu'l-Walid Ismail I ibn Faraj and Safa bint Yusuf
**Khalida bint Ismail,** second daughter of Abu'l-Walid Ismail I ibn Faraj and Safa bint Yusuf

**Leila bint Ismail,** eldest daughter of Abu'l-Walid Ismail I ibn Faraj

**Fatimah bint Ismail,** second daughter of Abu'l-Walid Ismail I ibn Faraj

**Aisha bint Faraj,** Fatima and Faraj's second daughter
**Faridah bint Faraj,** Fatima and Faraj's third daughter
**Muhammad ibn Faraj,** Fatima and Faraj's second son
**Qamar bint Faraj,** Fatima and Faraj's fourth daughter
**Mumina bint Faraj,** Fatima and Faraj's fifth daughter
**Qabiha bint Faraj,** Fatima and Faraj's sixth daughter
**Saliha bint Faraj,** Fatima and Faraj's seventh daughter

**Muhammad ibn Ismail,** Faraj's brother, *Raïs* of Qumarich
**Soraya bint Samir,** wife of Muhammad ibn Ismail
**Ismail ibn Muhammad,** son of Muhammad ibn Ismail and Soraya bint Samir, Faraj's nephew, *Raïs* of al-Jazirah al-Khadra
**Leila bint Faraj,** Fatima and Faraj's first daughter, wife of her first cousin Ismail ibn Muhammad
**Muhammad ibn Ismail,** first son of Ismail ibn Muhammad and Leila bint Faraj, Fatima and Faraj's first grandson

**Faraj ibn Ismail,** second son of Ismail ibn Muhammad and Leila bint Faraj
**Ali ibn Ismail,** third son of Ismail ibn Muhammad and Leila bint Faraj

**Alimah bint Muhammad,** Fatima's second sister, widow of Abu Umar of al-Hakam

**Faraj ibn Muhammad,** Fatima's younger brother, only son of Abu Abdallah Muhammad II of Gharnatah and Shams ed-Duna

*The Marinids*

**Shams ed-Duna,** second wife of Abu Abdallah Muhammad II of Gharnatah, aunt of Abu Ya'qub Yusuf el-Nasir al-Marini ibn Abu Yusuf Ya'qub

**Abd al-Haqq,** a prince of the Marinids

**Hammu,** a prince of the Marinids, cousin to Abd al-Haqq

**Uthman ibn Abi'l-Ula,** the *Shaykh al-Ghuzat* in the service of Abu al-Rabi Suleiman and Abu Said Uthman of the Marinid Dynasty

*The Ashqilula*

**Abdallah ibn Ibrahim,** Fatima's maternal uncle

*The Courtiers of Castilla-Leon*

**Prince Juan de Castilla, Senor de Valencia,** brother of King Sancho IV of Castilla-Leon

**Doñ Alonso Perez de Guzman,** the defender of Tarifa, a Leonese knight in the service of King Sancho IV of Castilla-Leon

**Doña Maria Coronel,** the wife of Doñ Alonso Perez de Guzman

**Doñ Fernan Alonso,** eldest son of Doñ Alonso Perez de Guzman and Doña Maria Coronel

*Retainers, Slaves and Others*

**Ibn al-Hakim al-Rundi,** the *Hajib* (chief minister) to Abu Abdallah Muhammad II of Gharnatah and Abu Abdallah Muhammad III of Gharnatah, head of the Sultan's chancery

**Ali ibn al-Jayyab,** the *Hajib* (chief minister) to Abu Abdallah Muhammad II of Gharnatah, Abu Abdallah Muhammad III of Gharnatah, Abu'l-Juyush Nasr I and Abu'l-Walid Ismail I ibn Faraj, head of the Sultan's chancery

**Ibn Safwan,** the *Hajib* (chief minister) to Abu'l-Juyush Nasr I, head of the Sultan's chancery

**Ibn al-Mahruq,** minister to Abu'l-Walid Ismail I ibn Faraj and Abu Abdallah Muhammad IV ibn Ismail

**Nur al-Sabah,** Galician favorite of Abu Abdallah Muhammad II of Gharnatah

**Khalid of al-Hakam,** the *Shaykh Khassa* (captain of the guard) of Malaka. Alimah bint Muhammad's brother in-law

**Adulfo,** the captain of the Galician guard of Abu'l-Juyush Nasr I

**Abu'l-Qasim of Bannigash,** chief eunuch of Abu'l-Walid Ismail I ibn Faraj and Abu Abdallah Muhammad IV ibn Ismail

**Niranjan al-Kadim,** Fatima's eunuch-guard

**Marzuq,** Faraj's chief steward
**Leeta,** Fatima's maidservant, Marzuq's wife, Niranjan's first sister

**Amoda,** governess of Fatima's children, Niranjan's second sister and twin of Leeta

**Faisal,** chief eunuch of Shams ed-Duna
**Haniya,** Fatima's maidservant, Faisal's third sister
**Basma,** Fatima's maidservant, Faisal's fourth sister
**Asiya,** Fatima's maidservant, illegitimate daughter of Khalid of al-Hakam and Haniya

**Sabela,** a Galician slave in the service of Nur al-Sabah

**Amud,** a Tuareg in Faraj's service
**Bazu,** a Tuareg in Faraj's service, Amud's brother

**Baraka,** Faraj's Genoese concubine
**Hayfa,** Faraj's Nubian concubine
**Samara,** Faraj's Provençal concubine

**Sitt al-Tujjar,** a Jewish merchant

**Musa ibn Qaysi,** a hashish seller
**Ali ibn Musa,** Musa's son

**Jumaana,** a Castillan concubine of Abu'l-Walid Ismail I ibn Faraj

# Chapter 1
# Fathers and Sons

## Prince Faraj

Tarif, Al-Andalus: Dhu al-Qa`da 693 AH (Tarifa, Andalusia: October AD 1294)

Faraj stood on the white, sandy shores of Tarif. His legs spread apart, dark red leather boots encased his feet. Dawn's pale pink glow illuminated the sandblasted, stone battlements of Tarif's citadel. The tides surged and brought an autumnal breeze ashore from the White Sea. The tangy scent of salt spray wafted through the cool air. The aroma mingled with lingering smoke from the previous night's cooking fires. Atop the weathered ramparts of the citadel, Castillan banners unfurled, caught in the whip-like motion of the wind.

The camp at the beachhead on Tarif's eastern coast stirred to life under the rising sun. Men readied themselves for war and death after the observance of the first prayer, *Salat al-Fajr*. Birds squawked and weaved a dizzying pattern of flight over the camp, before the flock raced across the Straits of Jabal Tarik.

Faraj imagined the majestic Arif Mountains of al-Maghrib el-Aska dominating the opposite shore. Yet the coastal landscape remained obscure behind a thick, morning mist that rose to the height of the billowing, white clouds. Hundreds of black hulking shapes, barely visible in the haze, bobbed on the water. Marinid ships hugged the coastal waters of the White Sea, their captains undaunted by Castillan bowmen aligned along the ramparts.

Faraj crouched and grasped a rough stone. He rolled it between his palms. It remained cool to the touch.

He stood and scratched his wiry beard. "The Nasrids would bring honor to our family today, if our Marinid allies from al-Maghrib el-Aska would let us. Why do we wait? Why hasn't Sultan Abu Ya'qub Yusuf ordered the attack?"

He spoke to no one in particular, not even among his personal guardsmen standing at his back, but an answer soon followed. "Are you so eager to die, brother?"

Faraj glared across the encampment as his brother Muhammad ibn Ismail emerged from a cluster of green silken tents. The wind whipped thinning strands of graying hair back from the glistening pate of Muhammad's egg-shaped head. Time had not been kind to him.

Both men were in their forty-eighth year, one of a few similarities that remained between them. Muhammad's face mirrored Faraj's own, though fleshier with jowls of dark olive skin and the same hawkish nose of most males in their family. Streaks of gray lined each remaining strand on Muhammad's head.

Faraj twirled a lock of his own dark, silky hair at the nape. His brother displayed a sizable paunch beneath the folds of his tunic. His belt hung low beneath his ponderous belly rather than encircling his waist. Faraj straightened at the sight of his bandy-legged gait and patted the trim stomach beneath his own chainmail tunic.

He said, "How brave of you to leave the comforts of your fortress at Qumarich to attend our master's wishes."

Muhammad chuckled and halted beside him. "You would know more about comfort than I could guess. You still hold the prize of Malaka, a pearl compared to the rocky outcropping of *Al-Hisn* Qumarich. The Sultan's warriors ravaged the city when he took it from our Ashqilula enemies."

Faraj clamped his jaws shut and glared at Muhammad before he spoke again. "Yet, fifteen years after we defeated the Ashqilula, you would have me believe Qumarich has not recovered?"

"It is not a rich territory like Malaka."

When Muhammad fell silent, Faraj ground his teeth together. "Nothing is like Malaka."

"True, for you are well-protected at your harbor and inland."

Faraj rolled his eyes heavenward.

"Does the promontory of *Al-Hisn* Qumarich offer you so little security?" He moved closer and bent toward Muhammad's ear. "Does it require a worthy defender?"

His brother sneered at him. "I hold what is mine. I do not need anyone's help."

Muhammad glanced behind him. "The Marinid Sultan has not appeared. Do you think he has decided the terms we should offer the Castillans?"

Faraj shook his head. "Terms? We have besieged King Sancho of Castilla-Leon for three months. What do you think the defenders intend to do? They shall fight to the death for control of this citadel. Terms, indeed."

"Do you doubt the resolve of our Marinid friends?"

"I doubt any ally who shifts loyalties like the Marinids have in the past. Even worse, they fight with the support of the rebel Prince Juan, whose only aim in life is to steal the throne of Castilla-Leon. The greatest danger for us lies in the unpredictability of Prince Juan. He can be foolhardy and rash, as when he first ordered our initial attacks without the benefit of siege weapons. I have also heard his tactics are brutal. He gains advantage by means of subterfuge and secrecy. It is the coward's way."

Muhammad nodded, but his face took on a haunted, gray pallor. Faraj wondered why his brother suddenly seemed so pensive and silent, his eyes fixed on the tableau before them. Faraj's hands tightened into fists before he sighed.

"You disagree with my view? Speak what is in your heart, Muhammad."

"I do not disagree with you, but your answer surprises me. It would seem the rumors are true. You have changed. You did not always disclaim ruthless and mercenary means in the achievement of any goal."

Though he hated the reminders of his history, Faraj nodded. "In my past, I was a selfish man. I have learned there are other values that mean more to me. The blessing of fine daughters and strong, proud sons. The heart of my beloved Fatima."

Faraj grinned at the mention of his wife's name. Her beautiful visage stirred into clear view within his mind. To think, he had once feared life with her would bring no joy or contentment. The image of her dark waves of hair beckoned him, silken strands slipping through his fingers, as vivid as the last day he had beheld her. He recalled her pale olive brow, which had remained smooth even as they parted. Yet, he knew her well, as he knew himself. She had concealed her concerns from him and their family.

In the long months since his departure from Malaka, Fatima and their children remained ever-present in his thoughts. His grasp tightened around the pebble. He closed his eyes for a moment. He sighed with longing for the prospect of holding his family close. He would kiss the dark brown and red curls on his children's heads and inhale the jasmine scent in his wife's hair soon enough, if Allah the Compassionate, the Merciful willed it.

He met his brother's gaze again and found him aghast, his lower jaw drooping. Muhammad blinked rapidly before looking away. "Then your family prospers? The Sultana Fatima is happy?"

"My wife and children are happy and safe at Malaka."

Muhammad smiled and relaxed visibly, as the tension eased from his sloping shoulders. "I am pleased to hear it. You are fortunate to have wed the Sultan's daughter."

"I am blessed to call her my bride and the mother of my children."

"I have never met her."

"Likewise, I have never met your wife or children." Faraj sighed. "We can agree that the past is the past between us? It cannot be altered."

Muhammad nodded and Faraj continued. "The future, however, it is possible for us to change that. My wife is a very wise woman. She is also deeply devoted to her family in all respects. She has oft chided me that I have not restored relations with you since my departure to Malaka. We have not spoken for over fifteen years, Muhammad. It would please her greatly...it would honor me, if you would consent to visit us at our home, you and your family."

Muhammad drew back, but Faraj's hand closed on his meaty forearm. "Malaka was your home too, when we were children. I would like you to see it again, brother."

Muhammad did not answer for a long time. He only offered a stark gaze.

Then he said, "I shall consider it. First, we must both survive this."

He nodded toward Tarif's battlements, where Castillan warriors glared down at their company. Faraj followed his gaze. The rock he held now clattered against the other stones.

From the time of the Muslim conquest of the peninsula over five centuries ago, Tarif had been the gateway to Al-Andalus. Every invading army of the Muslims had landed at this strategic site. Tarif had also been the negotiating point of every monarch who vied for control of the Andalusi coast. Today would be no different.

Five thousand Marinid, Gharnati and Castillan warriors stood amassed for the recovery of Tarif. That he stood shoulder to shoulder with supporters of a rebel Castillan prince did not surprise Faraj. The taciturn nature of Gharnatah's politics never amazed him. He suspected his master, the Sultan, would one day be on the opposite side again and in favor of King Sancho of Castilla-Leon.

For now, Muslim imams and Christian priests strolled through the ranks, blessing the faithful. Faraj did not doubt priests behind the enemy walls performed the same actions. He only wondered whose prayers God would listen to today.

His gaze intent on the battlements, Faraj said, "Doñ Alonso Perez de Guzman is expecting our siege weapons again this morning. He must wonder why we are late. If we do not find a way to force the surrender of the citadel's defenders, I fear our cause shall be lost."

Muhammad replied, "I have never heard of this Doñ Alonso before this conflict. Yet Prince Juan said his brother the King once proclaimed the defender of Tarif to be the greatest strategist in Castillan history."

"He is wrong, brother. I have met their greatest strategist and killed him at the battle of Istija. In that battle, I fought beside our Maghribi brethren of the Faith. There is no warrior with more daring and cunning than the Marinid soldier. He uses tactics of attack and withdrawal. When you think you have him on the run, cavalry and mounted bowmen surround you. This Doñ Alonso Perez de Guzman shall discover what Marinid resolve can do against this citadel soon enough."

"You speak thusly of the Marinids, yet earlier you accused them of wavering and changing sides too often."

"I can only hope for better on this battlefield. In warfare, the enemy is the enemy and an ally is an ally, until fate alters all circumstances and exchanges friend for foe. In the long history of Castilla-Leon and Gharnatah, the boundaries between adversaries and allies have changed often. Today we meet them on opposing sides. Tomorrow, we may form an alliance with King Sancho and be at odds with the Marinids. That possibility does not alter my resolve today."

"It would seem you have no difficulty recognizing your allies among former adversaries."

When Muhammad offered him a lazy smile, Faraj inclined his head and returned the gesture. He was about to speak again, when a lone rider emerged from the midst of the encampment.

The Castillan Prince Juan wore the blackened iron mail and heraldry of a Christian knight over most of his body. His brilliant silk garments bore the red lion of Castilla-Leon on the tunic and mantle at the center in four yellow squares. His helmet, flat at the top, concealed most of his face except for the dark brown eyes, which stared resolutely ahead. He hefted a heavy mace in one hand and held aloft a spear affixed with a white flag in the other. His steed, caparisoned in the same colors that he wore, snorted as Prince Juan's silver spurs dug into his sides.

The horse clopped across the white sand and bore him steadily toward the citadel. Faraj shook his head at the Castillan prince's vain ornamentation of the animal. Surely, such rich finery would only encumber a horse in the coming battle.

Muhammad sputtered in confusion, "I don't understand how this is possible. Here comes Prince Juan, but why is he carrying the white flag of peace tied to his spear?"

His voice trailed off as Faraj pointed. "Look behind him. Look at the boy."

"Bah! A boy, likely his page..." before Muhammad's voice faltered.

Faraj's gaze narrowed, trained on the figure behind the prince's mount.

A small child stumbled across the sand. The warhorse's momentum dragged him forward. Someone had tied the boy's hands with rope and attached the length of it around the horse's neck. With his long arms stretched before him and waves of yellow hair clinging to his brow, the child kept pace. Even the distance could not obscure the wetness clinging to his cheeks or the ugly slice across his face encrusted with congealed blood.

Faraj clutched his throat at the sight of him. The boy could hardly be older than his second son was, a child who bore his grandfather the Sultan's cherished name.

Faraj cuffed Muhammad's arm. "What man do you know ties his own page to his horse?"

Prince Juan halted at the midpoint between the encampment and the citadel. He thrust his spear through the thick air. The white flag fluttered on a crisp breeze.

Movement and shouts echoed from the battlements. Soon, a dark-haired figure appeared on the wall in a cuirass of leather scales. His leathery, sunburned complexion drained of all emotion and color. The veins underneath his skin stood out in livid ridges. Bands of perspiration glistened on his forehead. Deep wrinkles gouged lines across his brow beneath a fringe of black hair, which almost covered his eyes.

Then a woman appeared beside him. She laid her slim fingers on his shoulder. Her companion covered her hand with his own. Wind whipped the folds of her sky blue mantle, ripping thick tresses like molten gold from the confines of her hood. She stared in stark silence before she fainted. The man caught her up in his arms and glanced over the wall, before he disappeared.

A prickling sensation crept up Faraj's spine. The couple had recognized the little boy. The woman and the child shared the same hair color. What relationship did the child bear her that caused the woman such fright?

The black-haired man reappeared on the rampart. In a voice that Faraj could not overhear at such lengths, he issued instructions. Footmen dispersed along the wall and stood shoulder to shoulder.

The dark-haired man shouted across the distance in his native Castillan tongue. "Traitorous dog! What cruelty is this that you should bring my son before me in such a state?"

Faraj sagged, as his worst suspicions became reality. He looked at the pitiable boy. The child's head drooped and his shadow cast a dark blot across the shimmering sand.

Prince Juan answered, "Indeed, Doñ Alonso, I am pleased you recognize your firstborn, Fernan Alonso. If you wish to see him leave this battlefield alive, surrender Tarifa to the forces before you. Otherwise, I shall kill Fernan. I give you until midday to send word that you mean to withdraw. If you give up the citadel, I shall return your son unharmed."

Faraj's gaze remained on the child and he shook his head at the cruelty of the Castillan prince. Prince Juan relied on the same brutal tactic he had once employed against Zamora. Many years ago, he forced the capitulation of that fortress by similar means. He had promised death to the young son of the woman who held the castle in her husband's stead. Clearly, he expected a similar result at Tarif.

"My son was a page at court where he nobly served your brother, the rightful King of Castilla-Leon, Sancho." Doñ Alonso's strident voice held no warmth or spark of life. "By what treacherous means have you brought him here?"

Yet when Doñ Alonso looked over the wall to his young son, his darkened face betrayed the agony within him. Faraj's heart wrung with pity, as he cast aside all he had said earlier to Muhammad regarding the defeat of an enemy.

This was no longer a contest between equals, not when the Castillan prince intended to force the capitulation of his adversary by foul means. Faraj thought of his own two sons, whom he would do anything to protect. He knew and understood the love of a father for his children. Had he been in the Castillan commander's position, his choice would have been clear. No fortress, not even his beloved home at Malaka, would be worth the life of either of his sons. Yet, he was not Doñ Alonso.

The little boy raised his hands as if in supplication. Doñ Alonso shook his head. The boy sank on his knees. He covered his face with his hands.

Prince Juan shouted, "Until midday, Doñ Alonso. Do not delay or the consequences shall prove deadly, for your son especially."

As he jerked the reins and the momentum of his horse forced the boy through the campsite, a din of conversation buzzed among various pockets of the Marinid soldiers. Those who understood the Castillan language, as Faraj did, spoke of the scene that had transpired. News of it spread through the encampment like wildfire.

Each man, from Marinid warrior to Castillan cavalryman offered his opinion on what had just happened. Some felt the Marinids forces should withdraw. Prince Juan could not gain the victory by unfair and dishonorable means. Others, especially the mounted horsemen supporting Prince Juan, believed Doñ Alonso should surrender and reclaim his son, though they were in the minority of opinions.

Faraj watched the walls of the citadel. The woman reappeared at Doñ Alonso's side, her eyes red-rimmed. Her gaze held the same stark fear as that of the man next to her. Yet, Faraj also recognized strengthening resolve in the firm line of her mouth and her unwavering stare, which followed the child's progress.

Although they could not have been more different, her bravery reminded him of Fatima's strength. He did not doubt what his own wife would have done if one of their sons faced such danger. She was a lioness where their children were concerned. He knew she would sacrifice everything for their lives and safety. Their sons and daughters had nothing to fear, safe behind the stout walls of Malaka, not like the son of Doñ Alonso.

The woman cupped Doñ Alonso's cheek. He turned and met her gaze. He bent slightly and pressed his forehead against her pale brow. Then she kissed his lips tenderly and withdrew.

"We cannot allow this, my prince."

Faraj turned at the voice of *al-Shaykh Khassa* Khalid of al-Hakam and witnessed his grim expression.

Five years after Faraj had claimed the governorship of Malaka, a band of bedraggled refugees appeared on the shore. They had fled the siege and bombardment of Mayurqa by Christian forces. Among them were Fatima's younger sister Alimah with her family, which included her brother by marriage, Khalid. Now, he served as commander of the garrison at Malaka's citadel.

A younger and much more solemn man than his elder brother Abu Umar, who had been prince of the pirates at Mayurqa, Khalid stood tall and thin with a scar that bisected his face. A deep furrow gouged a reddened streak from his forehead, across his nose and into his pale cheek, a reminder of his narrow escape from the long sword of a Castillan mercenary.

Faraj inhaled deeply, drawing the smell of saltwater into his nostrils. "What would you have me do?"

Khalid thrust his scimitar in the direction of the citadel. Sunlight caught and traipsed along the sharpened edge of the blade. "You are a father. Can you countenance this action? Would you stand by and allow your own sons to be used in such ways by a coward?"

Faraj glanced at Muhammad, who shook his head. "If you abandon this campaign, brother, you risk our master's anger. You may be the husband of his daughter, but if you disgraced him on this battlefield, the Sultan would never spare your life. He is determined to occupy Tarif again. He knows he cannot do it without the Marinids. Do not stir his wrath."

Faraj clapped a hand on Khalid's lean-muscled shoulder. "You should have married, my friend. Then you would have had a wife and children, someone who longed for your return home."

"Even with my ugly scar?"

"It does not frighten the women of Malaka, who favor bold warriors. I have seen how they regard you, scar and all. Even my children's governess, Amoda favored you."

Khalid said, "Amoda favors me still."

His stone-faced visage relaxed in the semblance of a smile that showed his even white teeth. Then he sobered and his brow furrowed deeply, the edges of the puckered skin around his scar slightly raised.

"If I had married, my wife would have wanted children. What right do I have to such happiness? I have slaughtered too many of the sons of others to deserve my own."

Faraj shared his grim expression. "I may call upon your sword soon."

Khalid bowed his head. "You shall always have it."

Muhammad cautioned, "Faraj, let us wait until noon. The Castillan commander may still make the right decision. What else can he do, when faced with such a burden?"

Faraj forced a chuckle. "Castilla-Leon has had the good fortune to produce worthy and admirable men, who also make excellent opponents. I suspect Doñ Alonso shall do what he must."

Khalid said, "Gharnatah has no shortage of men of the same ability. I am grateful to serve a prince such as you."

Faraj nodded in silent thanks.

His gaze strayed to the south again. The migrating birds flying across the Straits of Jabal Tarik were a speck on the horizon. "If only our escape could happen so easily."

At midday, Prince Juan and his beleaguered captive returned to just below the ramparts of the citadel. Although the Muslim call to prayer sounded across the shoreline, no one observed it. Faraj stood with Muhammad and Khalid at either side of him again. The sun blazed across the sky, beating down upon their heads mercilessly. He longed for the evening when the sky in its myriad colors ranged above. However, today he felt hollow and suspected the view would not provide the same enjoyment as it had in the past.

An abrupt silence descended. Even the wind had calmed, leaving the air brittle. Doñ Alonso returned to the battlements. He strode toward the wall with his men at-arms following him. Faraj's gaze swayed to the tower window to the right. Guzman's woman stood there. Her sharp nails gripped the ledge. She stared down at the child and waited to hear his fate.

Suddenly, a fierce coastal breeze reared up again, whipping about Doñ Alonso's short, red cloak. His gaze resolute on the boy below him, he withdrew a dagger from his belt, its handle covered with spinel and bloodstone. Christians believed gemstones carried certain properties that aided the bearer. Spinel improved character. Bloodstone, a form of jasper, strengthened the will. The cutting edge of Doñ Alonso's dagger caught the sun's rays. Prisms of light danced across the blade.

Doñ Alonso began, "Fernan Alonso de Guzman y Coronel is my firstborn son. No parent ever felt so much pride as when my wife and I first beheld him. No father has ever felt the satisfaction in a son as I feel today. Now, Prince Juan would have me choose between the pride of my heart and the honor of my family. I did not father a son to be a pawn against the country I love and the land I call my own. I fathered a son who, in my stead, might have one day fought against the enemies of Castilla-Leon, be they Moorish or Christian.

"Prince Juan has by his actions, by his treason, made himself an enemy of Castilla-Leon. I shall never yield Tarifa or betray the mantle of trust that King Sancho has placed upon me, not even to save my own son. If this rebel prince, who is little more than a dog, should put my son to death, he shall affirm my honor as the loyal defender of his sovereign, King Sancho. He shall ensure my son's place in heaven as a martyr of the Christian faith, who died doing his duty before a faithless lord. He calls down eternal shame on himself in this world and the everlasting wrath of Christ Jesus after death. If Prince Juan wants to test my resolve, if he needs a weapon with which to murder my son, he may have my blade for his cruel purpose!"

Doñ Alonso flung his dagger over the wall. The weapon spiraled before it landed with a heavy thud, a short distance from where the Prince sat mounted. Doñ Alonso nodded to his weeping son, bowed his head and turned away.

His shoulders stiff, he strode across the battlements. His steps never faltered. As one, those who ringed the ramparts bowed their heads as he passed them.

Faraj did the same to honor the noble but tragic sacrifice the adversary of Gharnatah had chosen. His heart tore inside his breast for his enemy's sake.

Prince Juan leapt down from his horse and now brandished Doñ Alonso's dagger. He dragged the kicking and squealing child against him and forced his head back, exposing the boy's tender neck. With a snarl directed toward the battlements, he pressed the glittering blade against the pale flesh. Tears flooded the boy's face. In a swift motion, Prince Juan sliced a deep cut from ear to ear. Blood sprayed in a crimson arc across the glittering sand. Shouts of dismay and horror flowed from those assembled on the citadel walls.

As the thick redness gurgled and spilled down the dying child's throat, he sagged against his captor. Prince Juan pushed him forward into the sand. The mutilated child fell at the feet of the horse. The stallion nickered and sidestepped the body. A crimson line ran from the dead boy's wound and pooled on the sand beneath his nearly severed neck. The Castillan Prince tucked Doñ Alonso's dagger, still stained with blood, into the empty sheath fastened to his belt. He wheeled his horse around and dragged the lifeless body behind him.

No one within the Marinid encampment spoke. Some turned their faces away from Prince Juan, who stared straight ahead. Even the wind stilled.

Faraj sought out Doñ Alonso again. He had halted at a doorway, though he did not turn around. Someone gripped his arm and spoke with him. Doñ Alonso's shoulders slumped for a moment and he bowed his head. Then he nodded and re-entered the citadel. He never looked upon the grisly, ruby-red trail leading across the white sand.

Faraj whispered, "As a father of two sons whom I love dearly, I shall honor this sacrifice. I cannot taint this battlefield with the blood of our enemy now that his child's life has been stolen in such a way."

Beside him, Muhammad shook his head. "Then you are a fool."

His murky gaze met Faraj's own. His weighty hand grasped Faraj's lean arm. "If you return to Malaka, I pray you shall hold your sons close. Tell them how much you love them and what you have sacrificed for them."

"I shall. If I am ever to return home, I need your help. There is a commander among the Marinids, who holds great sway over their leaders and warriors. He would not trust me to negotiate a peaceable solution with him."

"Your old reputation still bedevils you?"

"It does. However, you have always possessed the repute of a fair man, less given to...underhanded means to achieve your ends. He might trust you instead of me."

"Who is this man?"

"He is Abdallah of Ashqilula, Fatima's uncle. He was an enemy of the Sultanate. He may still be. Yet, he is also my greatest hope for the future of Tarif."

# Chapter 2
# Old Wounds

## Prince Faraj

Tarif, Al-Andalus: Dhu al-Qa`da 693 AH (Tarifa, Andalusia: October AD 1294)

With a shrug, Faraj ignored Muhammad's open-mouthed gape. "Don't look so shocked. We have played this part with the Ashqilula before."

Muhammad scratched his balding pate. "Yes, but do you grasp the full meaning of what you're about to do? You would have an Ashqilula chieftain, the avowed enemy of our clan, abandon the Marinid cause and break with those who gave him a home when he had none."

Faraj raised an eyebrow. "You are well-informed of his circumstances."

Muhammad sputtered, "I am not so ignorant as you would believe, brother! Abdallah of Ashqilula is no sentimental fool. His kinship with your wife aside, why do you think he would undertake the risk?"

"He has done it before. He abandoned the unjust cause of his kinsmen before they surrendered to the Sultan of Gharnatah."

"Yet, he is cautious. Abdallah only revealed himself until after all the Ashqilula chieftains were dead."

Muhammad paused and drew closer. "Ibrahim of Ashqilula promised to hunt down and kill Abdallah for his betrayal, except the old man died suddenly. He did not survive a month in al-Maghrib el-Aska. A silent assassin took his life in the night. A clever man to have snuck past Ibrahim's cadre of guards and poisoned his evening tisane."

"Do the Marinids still offer a reward for the capture of that assassin?"

"I would not know. Ibrahim has been dead for fifteen years. No one shall ever discover his murderer now."

"I am certain of it." Faraj had known for several years that his wife's chief eunuch, Niranjan, bore the responsibility for Ibrahim's sudden death. There was no cause to reveal the truth to anyone now, not even Muhammad.

When Muhammad eyed him with an unwavering gaze, Faraj continued, "Ibrahim took many lives, including that of my wife's mother. He deserved his end. Speak no more of him. Instead, tell me how I avoid my own death at Abdallah's vengeful hands."

"Even if you succeeded in placating him long enough for him to listen, how would you convince him to withdraw his men?"

Faraj scowled at Muhammad. "You're supposed to help me find answers, not raise further questions."

Muhammad shrugged.

Faraj said, "Fatima has described her uncle. He is a man much like you, honorable and deserving of the devotion of his men. Send word to him. If you spoke on my behalf, he would believe my intentions."

"And, if he does not believe me?"

"He must." Faraj gripped the hilt of the sword at his side. "He must, for the sake of us all."

He risked his life in this gamble. The Ashqilula would surely remember him.

One year after Faraj had taken control of Malaka, the combined forces of King Sancho's father Alfonso X of Castilla-Leon and the Marinid Sultan united against Gharnatah. They came with the Ashqilula, an enemy Faraj had never thought to see again. Swift, two-pronged attacks occurred at the port cities of Tarif and al-Jazirah al-Khadra. Afterward, the Marinid galleys sailed for Malaka.

The combined Ashqilula and Marinid forces had tried an incursion on the beach the first night. Faraj readied his men for them. Surprised in their turn by the defenders, none among the invaders lived. Faraj took no prisoners and offered no terms for ransom. Everyone died by his order. He held his city until the Sultan's reinforcements arrived from the capital. By then, Marinid naval forces had surrounded the port.

A second wave of Ashqilula landed on the same beach and found the bodies of their clan members rotting on the sand. As before, Faraj's men ensured they filled the air with the screams of dying men and painted the sand copper with the blood of his enemies.

Later, the victorious warriors of Malaka gathered the severed heads of their attackers into sacks and flung them into the White Sea. Faraj left the rest of their mutilated and bloated carcasses as a fine feast for the sea birds.

Now, he stroked the length of his beard. Yes, the Ashqilula would remember him well.

Faraj rowed a small boat with Khalid, Muhammad and one of Muhammad's guardsmen across the White Sea. A star-filled sky illuminated the late evening. Crackling sparks from cooking fires in the Marinid encampment glittered across the landscape.

The craft bumped against the black-caulked side of a sleek, low-lying Marinid galley. Dark eyes peered through the holes that held the oars. Faraj averted his gaze. Still he could not help but wonder about the cruelty of life in service on a galley.

He nodded to Muhammad, who groaned and muttered, "I remain uncertain about the wisdom of this plan. So, Abdallah agreed to meet with me. He does not know you are coming, too. He is still the enemy. He might try to kill us both."

Faraj rolled his eyes heavenward. "Either you intend to help me persuade him or not. Why else would I have asked you to come? You don't have to talk to him. Keep your tongue behind your teeth if you have only foolish words to offer."

Despite the shadows of evening, Muhammad's dark brown gaze narrowed visibly, before he grumbled, "I'm nervous. I cannot help it. This is dangerous."

A deep baritone voice rumbled over their heads. "Yes, very dangerous, especially with you two talking so much."

Faraj looked up the side of the ship, making out the image of a tall man who leaned over the railing. Another stood beside him holding a brass lantern. The taller one shook the length of a rope ladder and lowered it down. When Faraj tugged it toward his chest, it offered little resistance. He hoped they had secured the rope. Could he trust Abdallah not to cut the fibers while he scaled the ladder?

With Khalid's aid, Faraj climbed and leapt over the side and on to the deck. Behind him, it seemed Muhammad had a little more difficulty, as Khalid strained and groaned below. Again rolling his eyes, Faraj leaned over and heaved Muhammad into the galley. His brother drew deep gulps of air into his lungs after his harsh exertion. Faraj shook his head and aided Khalid. Muhammad's man remained in the boat, as it bobbed on the shallow waves.

A wizened Abdallah of Ashqilula looked them over with large, nearly opaque eyes. Then he scratched a thin, graying beard. Pockmarks had gouged holes in his olive-brown cheeks. Thin hanks of graying hair covered his rounded head. Faraj eyed him steadily, wondering when the man would note his resemblance to the Sultans of Gharnatah. He supposed it would not take long. He mused that the placid expression on Abdallah's face was hardly one of welcome, only curiosity.

Abdallah set his large fists, dotted with brown age spots, on his hips. He stood with narrow, sandaled feet spread apart. The rest of his form disappeared under a black *jubba* and a voluminous Maghribi cloak, the *burnus*.

He asked, "Which one of you is Prince Muhammad ibn Ismail of the Nasrids?"

Muhammad swallowed loudly and trembled beside Faraj, who cuffed him lightly between the shoulder blades. With Muhammad glaring at him, Faraj pointed and answered. "He is."

Abdallah offered them a rueful grin. "Then you must be his equally foolish brother, Prince Faraj ibn Ismail, yes?"

Faraj's jaw tightened. "If you knew me, why did you inquire?"

"I wanted to be certain which of you would prove to be a greater cause for concern. I wanted to determine which of you fools married my niece Fatima. I have judged correctly that it was not the fat one."

Faraj gasped unwittingly and Muhammad flushed the color of a pomegranate. Abdallah's thinned lips relaxed in the semblance of a smile.

"You must have guessed that I would speak with you for Fatima's sake. You knew I would remember the child of my sister. When I received your missive, Prince Faraj...ah, yes, I know it was your request and not that of your brother, I suspected you were the most imprudent man I would ever meet. Or, the most bold. A man would have to be courageous to hold the heart of a princess of the Nasrids. Understand that Fatima is the only reason you shall leave this ship alive. The enmity between our families has cut too deeply. For her sake, I dare not open that old wound or carve new ones into your conniving hide."

His owlish gaze swiveled to Muhammad. "Wait below in the boat. You have no part in the conversation to follow."

Muhammad's deep sigh betrayed his turbulent emotions. "I would stay, if only to ensure Faraj's safety."

Faraj cocked his head and looked askance at Muhammad, who shrugged.

Abdallah said, "I do not invite you to remain with us. I have given my word. You and your brother shall leave this ship alive. Do not test me. Disembark."

Faraj placed a hand on Muhammad's shoulder. "I thank you for your loyalty. I have done little in life to deserve it."

Muhammad nodded. "No, you have not deserved it."

With a grunt and some effort, he heaved himself over the side of the ship. A yelp and an ominous splash followed. Faraj rushed toward the railing. Abdallah's hand on his chest stayed him.

Abdallah glanced over the side, his man behind him holding the lantern aloft. From below, Muhammad's groans and sputters filled the air.

"I have you, my prince, come. The water is cold tonight."

Muhammad cursed his guardsman. "I know, you wretched son of a wild ass! I'm the one who fell in it!"

Abdallah straightened and leaned against the railing. He looked beyond Faraj to where Khalid stood.

Faraj nodded to his captain. "Go help my brother into the boat. Await me below."

Khalid saluted Faraj and scrambled over the side of the galley.

Abdallah crossed his arms over his barrel chest. His persistent stare held Faraj's own. "Why did you risk stirring the embers of hatred between our two clans with this nighttime visitation?"

"Neither of us can change the past. What concerns me is the present. Why are you here, Abdallah, serving alongside a Castillan prince who would dishonor himself with the murder of a child just to win this conflict?"

Abdallah grunted and raised one eyebrow in a questioning slant. "Are we not allied in this campaign, Prince Faraj? You and your men have not abandoned it. Is that why you have come, to sway me in your stead? Why should I care for the dead child of a Moor who has betrayed his people and their blood?"

Faraj shook his head. "You cannot mean Doñ Alonso? Prince Juan told us that he was born in Leon. He and his father before him have served the Castillans all their lives."

"He is a Moor by blood, even if not by faith. His grandfather was born in Al-Andalus. Yet, he holds to the beliefs of the Christians. Why should I care for his suffering?"

"You understand the nature of war and just dealings. What happened here was not fair recompense for Guzman's rejection of his heritage. It was not a test of one army's mettle against another. Murder and deceit flowed upon the sands of Tarif today."

Abdallah's gaze shifted to the encampment on the shore. "Speak your terms."

Faraj followed his stare. "Leave, retire from the field of this dishonorable battle. I saw the banners of your men unfurled among the mounted archer and cavalry divisions. How many warriors do you command?"

"Two thousand," Abdallah muttered, still looking at the beachhead.

Faraj nodded. Two thousand archers and riders amounted to less than half of their combined forces. That left another two thousand Marinids, in addition to fifteen hundred Gharnati warriors and less than three Castillan and Portuguese hundred and fifty mercenaries whom

Prince Juan had bribed into his service. Perhaps less than a thousand Christians protected the citadel at Tarif. If the defenses held, if King Sancho sent reinforcements south across the White Sea, he might lift the siege in time.

Although Faraj's head warred with his heart, warning him against such treasonous thoughts, he continued, "Take your men and go."

Abdallah pinned him with a ferocious glare. "Where should I go? Al-Maghrib el-Aska has been my refuge these last seven years. You do not know what it is to be hunted, to be without a home."

Faraj's belly soured. Bile rose up in his throat. He tamped down the fear and buried it beneath his resignation. Even before he spoke the words, he knew this action could only lead to his death. Before he surrendered to his fate, he would return to Malaka one last time, to his beloved.

He said, "I shall soon learn, after I have left this battlefield."

Abdallah turned his back on him, his shoulders rigid.

Faraj approached, heart hammering in his chest, his footfalls light and cautious. The galley swayed beneath his feet.

"The Castillan commander cannot surrender now. He has paid the price of delay and inaction with his son's life. His honor is at stake. Prince Juan's treachery has sullied whatever you and your men might do here from this day forth. Leave this place with your honor intact. A man such as you would be welcomed in any other land."

Abdallah's stark stare returned. His mouth tightened in a stubborn line. "Except the land of my birth, Al-Andalus. You cannot offer me protection here, not when your Sultan has vowed to take the heads of any among the Ashqilula who ever dared return. Where should we go, my two thousand warriors and I? Would you have me and my men abandon the Marinids, so they can call us cowards?"

Faraj shook his head. "Let others call you men of honor, who did not gain from the grief of another. There is no dignity in defeating a commander already broken by the death of his son."

Abdallah's lips pursed in barely suppressed fury.

Faraj added, "You have the power to change the course of these events. Men have always flocked to your banners and aided you, because they know you believe in justice and truth. If you are rightly guided, then you know what you must do. The Marinids cannot win without you. Could they strike at you in al-Maghrib el-Aska?"

Abdallah shook his head. "My wives and children remain safe in Jumhuriyat Misr, the land of the pyramids. It is where my wives were born, where our children have always lived. They have never desired to leave it and I have never forced them."

"Then it has been seven years since you last saw them?"

"Seven long years."

"Do you have sons, Abdallah?"

"Yes, I have five strong sons."

"Fatima and I also have sons, two beloved boys whom I treasure. A father's love for his children knows no limits. To lose a son, to lose any child must pain a father. Still, we can only imagine the pain Doñ Alonso must be feeling. Prince Juan has not buried Guzman's son. He has left the body to rot like carrion at the edge of camp. Would you let someone murder and defile your sons without seeking vengeance? If you would not, think of what you can do here."

Abdallah made no reply.

Faraj groaned and rubbed the back of his neck.

At length, Abdallah turned to him. "You speak with deep emotion for your children."

"It is second only to the devotion I bear their mother."

"Do you love my sister's child so much?"

"She is my heart, my life, my very breath."

Abdallah chuckled. "You could have simply said 'yes' and I would have understood."

"No, for you could not know the measure of my feelings for her in such a simple answer. The love I bear her is as unfathomable as the depths of the White Sea, even to me."

Abdallah grunted and looked across the blue-black water. The crescent moon's reflection glittered in its depths.

"If you disobey your Sultan, you condemn Fatima to an unfortunate widowhood."

"She shall know I met my death with conviction in my mind and everlasting love for her in my heart."

"Don't you think she has suffered enough losses?" Abdallah relaxed against the railing. "I mourn for her mother still. I shall mourn Aisha until my end."

Faraj heaved a sigh. The conversation had turned dangerous. He could not stop now, not when he sensed Abdallah's amenability to his suggestion.

"Fatima had told me that relations with her mother were strained in her childhood."

"Aisha loved her child. Surely, your wife must know that."

"She does. Each day I see her love for our children and her unending devotion to them. Fatima said she had made a promise to her mother before she died, to love our children always. My wife has become the woman, the mother she is today because of your sister."

"I have said before, Fatima is a child of my sister's spirit. I am glad to know Aisha lives on in her daughter."

"There is something else you must know, about the day your sister died. Fatima has long desired that you should know. If she were here, she would have wanted me to tell you. I know you must believe that the old Sultan had the princess Aisha killed...."

"I do not. I know it was Ibrahim of Ashqilula." Abdallah's gaze found the coast again. "I have known for fifteen years, just before I left Al-Andalus."

Faraj edged closer to him. "How?"

"My former slave Ulayyah finally told me. I had found her after Ibrahim dallied with her, as was his custom. She cursed me for giving her to a murderer, the man who had taken my sister's life. For so long, Ulayyah had kept the secret from me. Her betrayal was more than I could bear, as was Ibrahim's own.

"Ibrahim had surrounded himself with loyal men. I could not harm him personally. I took my vengeance in the only way that I could, in the manner that would hurt him the most. I abandoned the Ashqilula cause and took my fifteen hundred warriors into Jumhuriyat Misr, where I found a new life far from such treachery."

Faraj nodded, comprehending at last why Abdallah had fled Al-Andalus so unexpectedly. His sudden departure had paved the way for the eventual defeat of the Ashqilula.

"You should have taken the slave Ulayyah with you. She met her death at Ibrahim's hands. He strangled her."

When Abdallah whirled toward him, open-mouthed, Faraj rushed on. "Her children are safe. The boy Faisal serves as a eunuch in the Sultan's harem. His two elder sisters are the servants of the Sultana Shams ed-Duna, my master's queen. The younger twins, Basma and Haniya, serve my Fatima at Malaka."

Abdallah gripped the railing and bowed his head. The wood groaned beneath the pressure of his hands. "I could not forgive Ulayyah. Perhaps she could not forgive herself."

Faraj remained silent for a time and then cleared his throat. "Fifteen years ago, you did what was right. Without your support, the Ashqilula fell. Now, you have a chance to do the same again, here."

With a stiff bow, Faraj gripped the sinewy rope, vaulted over the side of the galley and clambered back into the waiting boat below.

The stars framed Abdallah's head. Even in the gloom and with the torchlight behind him, tears glistened on his cheeks. Faraj took a last look at him and then rowed with his counterparts back to shore.

When they reached the coast, he stepped on the shifting sand with Muhammad, while their men pulled the boat inland. From the center of the encampment, loud shouts echoed a warning of some vicious argument.

Faraj dismissed Khalid, waved Muhammad off and sank down. Then Faraj drew up his knees, clasped his hands together and rested his chin on them. His gaze contemplated the black hulks crowding the midnight blue waters of the White Sea.

At dawn the next morning, horns resounded throughout the encampment. In silence, Faraj and Khalid rolled up their prayer rugs. Neither man had slept. Both donned hooded, chainmail tunics and brass helmets. Faraj slid his sword into its scabbard, his *khanjar* in its sheath and fastened the sword belt around his waist. Khalid handed him a tasseled shield, bearing the crescent moon of the Faith at its rounded center.

Marinid catapults hit the citadel's defenses, as they usually did each morning. They concentrated on the battered length of the wall near the eastern gate, which Doñ Alonso's men had valiantly attempted to reinforce each night. Now it gave way, in a deep roar of crumbling rock. The screams of men vied with falling debris. The impact reverberated through the surrounding rock face. Shards of dust sprayed the air. When the thick clouds cleared, the jagged edges of what remained on either side of the breach looked as though the Hand of God had ripped away the masonry.

Heavy boulders whizzed overhead, pummeling the shattered remnants of the wall. Castillan common knights, distinguishable from their noble counterparts by their round shields of Moorish design, poured out of the rift.

Marinid light horse cavalry, with camel units in support, surged to meet them. The more powerful Castillan knights with kite-shaped shields and long swords fought for Prince Juan. He hung back in their midst.

The Ashqilula banners billowed in the midst of the other forces. Faraj spat in the sand and turned to Khalid, who stared stone-faced at the fighting near the wall. The edges of his scar were nearly white.

Faraj asked, "Nervous?"

"No," his captain said, his voice barely rising above a whisper. "If you tell me to fight, I shall fight. I value my life more than that of the enemy. I have no scruples about killing any man who raises his sword against me."

The Ashqilula under Abdallah's command drew up in a solid, unbreakable formation, bowmen hemmed in on either side by cavalry. They seemed prepared to ride out in support of the Marinid cavalry. Faraj shook his head.

Suddenly, the Ashqilula changed direction. They veered to the left and down to the coastline, toward the galleys bobbing along the shore. They cut a clear path between the Marinids at Tarif's wall and the rest of the invasion forces.

Faraj's heart thudded so loudly that it vied with the shouts of confusion and cheers from some in the Marinid encampment. Khalid grinned and clapped him on the back. "We make our move, yes?"

"Yes."

Chaos descended now. The Marinid cavalry fell back from the breach in the wall, while those at the rear engaged the Ashqilula warriors fleeing the battle. Metal clashed and clanged. Prince Juan cursed and whipped his horse, urging his men into the fray. Archers on the walls fired into the melee.

The Marinid forces scattered in disarray. Half their formations pursued the Ashqilula, vainglory or suicide their possible motives. Many of them died as Abdallah's crossbowmen protected the riders at the forefront. The other Marinid troops ran headlong toward the breach near Tarif's gate. They risked death under the mounts of more Castillan knights emerging from behind the walls. Doñ Alonso's archers also found easy targets. Volley after volley flew from Tarif's ramparts, piercing armor and flesh, man and beast. Screams echoed across the shoreline. Gharnatah's troops, caught up in the uncertainty, looked to their commanders for clear direction and found none.

Faraj said, "Those who believe and submit to the Will of God accept their destiny. *Qadar,* as Allah, the Compassionate, the Merciful, has written for every soul, speaks of all that has happened and all that shall happen." He turned and looked at Khalid. "Today, we make our own destiny. Come, we return to Malaka. Then, on to Gharnatah."

# Chapter 3
# Sacrifices

## Princess Fatima

Malaka, Al-Andalus: Dhu al-Qa`da 693 AH (Malaga, Andalusia: October AD 1294)

Waves washed ashore at Malaka on an otherwise quiet late morning. Fatima's gray Andalusi mare shied away whenever the tide surged. As sea spray billowed, the horse snorted loudly. With a steady hand, Fatima held the mare's reins and soothed her mount.

Her peripheral gaze lingered on the sinewy young man who sat his black stallion with comfortable ease. Whenever she looked at her eldest child, Ismail, she saw her father. After fifteen years, a wiry frame had replaced her son's tendency toward plumpness.

The autumn wind picked up along the shore, rippling through strands of his once-auburn hair, now the dark, russet-tipped color of her father's own. His keen eyes and placid, intelligent expression evoked her father's image. The same hawkish nose sniffed at the sea. A smile and drawn-out sigh eased the composure of his angular features.

"Whenever you stare at me, *Ummi*, especially when you think I do not notice, I often wonder whether you are seeing me or someone else."

Ismail's lowered tone, more a man's than that of a boy, startled her. Her mare shifted on the sand. She tugged the reins and calmed the horse. When her gaze returned to Ismail, he offered her a sly grin.

He possessed the same innate understanding and curiosity she had shown as a child. However, she suspected the pride and instincts that ruled his father dominated him, too. He held himself ramrod straight in the saddle, pride emanating in his elegant, though rigid bearing.

He always observed in silent prudence like her, studying people and situations, perceiving their nature with his keen glance. Yet, he reminded her of the men in their family, with his predatory instincts, always cutting to the heart of a matter and finding the underlying vulnerabilities. She did not doubt he would become a formidable governor of Malaka someday. Yet, she hoped that would not occur for many years to come.

She swallowed against a sudden lump in her throat, thwarting speech for a moment. "Who else would I see except my fine son?"

He flashed a knowing smile. "Your father, perhaps. Certainly not mine."

His gaze tracked the course of the undulating coastline and her stare followed his. Even at a vast distance, the rocky promontory at Jabal Tarik dominated the southwestern view. Beyond it, the craggy landscape of Tarif rose. Her husband camped along its shore, ready to bring death to her father's Castillan enemies. Did he yet live?

When she clutched at her chest at the painful thought, Ismail's stare flitted back to hers with hawk-eyed precision. She rubbed at some imaginary ache above her breast with two fingers. Beneath her, the mare danced on the sand again, signaling the return of the tide.

"Does he live, *Ummi*?"

She nodded. "I would feel it if he did not. Your father lives."

He did not question her certainty. His gaze alighted on the coastline again. A sigh of relief rippled through her. She sagged in the leather saddle.

Worry had plagued her for weeks after Faraj's departure. Yet, her words to her son comforted her now. She sighed and palmed her rounded belly beneath the loose folds of her tunic.

"I understand why Grandfather required Father's help at Tarif, but he should not have left us now, *Ummi*."

"You shall inherit your father's responsibilities someday. This land is yours and you shall defend it, as your father has done. When your Sultan calls upon your sword, you must answer. Do not blame your father for doing his duty now, or my father for demanding it. Blame King Sancho of Castilla-Leon instead."

Ismail snorted. "The Brave! His people should call him the Oath-breaker instead!"

Fatima nodded. "You see him as you should, my son. When King Sancho took Tarif two years ago, my father had every reason to expect the city would return to Gharnatah's control. King Sancho lied to my father and broke the terms of our last treaty."

"Now, the Sultan must rely upon the Marinids, who have been his enemies."

"Yes and upon your father, who has ever served him loyally."

"Is that why you haven't written to Father about the child you carry?"

She glared at Ismail. "A mother is allowed some secrets, is she not? You forget yourself at times, my son. Or, perhaps I have indulged you too much."

His lazy smile faded and he inclined his head, his gaze falling away. "Forgive me."

His outward sign of contrition did not fool her. A little smile teased at the corners of his mouth, though he strove against it.

"I have not told Faraj of this child because he would return home, when my father needs him at Tarif."

Ismail protested, "You need him, too! The Sultan would agree, if you only asked him."

She shook her head and reached for his shoulder. "The governor of Malaka must be loyal to the Sultan's cause, even above the wishes of his own heart and his family. Your father may return in due time. The siege cannot last forever."

His lips pressed in a thin line, he made no reply. She chuckled at his stubbornness and clutched his hand, pulling it to her abdomen. "Here, see if you can feel the first stirrings of your brother or sister."

His hand settled on her stomach too briefly, before he pulled it back and stared at his fingers with something akin to awe. "How did the baby get inside you? Is it the same way as when the stallions cover the mares in heat?"

She laughed, throwing her head back. A billowing wind carried the sound out to sea. “Not quite, my Ismail. You shall understand in time. You are yet young.”

She chose to ignore the fact that her husband had been thirteen, a year younger than Ismail, when he received the gift of three concubines from her grandfather.

“Why can’t you tell me now? I shall have my own harem someday.”

“A child should be sired in a loving union between a man and woman. The bond between us differentiates us from the animals. If you wish to know how a man feels about the act of love, ask your father when he returns.”

“I intend to.”

She did not doubt him. “Come, my son, let us return.”

Ismail followed, as she nudged her mare up the sandy steep incline from the beach below their home. They rode in silence along the worn track and entered through the southwestern gate, watched by guardsmen who patrolled the battlements. The effects of the sea had weathered the gray walls, which had protected Malaka for many centuries. The men averted their eyes as Fatima rode past. After she and Ismail crested the hill, their horses turned eastward and cantered toward the stables.

He dismounted first before he helped her. “I shall rub down the horses and feed them.”

“We have grooms for that.”

“I know. I like to work with my hands.”

Ismail loved horses as much as she loved hunting birds. He had learned to ride on his own at six years of age, despite Fatima’s useless protests to Faraj. Since her husband’s departure, she had taken to riding with Ismail. If she could not stop him, at least she could be with him.

Her hand rested against his cool cheek. Beneath her palm, the prickly beginnings of facial hair that would soon cover his angular cheeks scraped her delicate flesh. “Do not tarry for long. I am always at my happiest when you are beside me.”

Ismail beamed. He had not lost the childhood dimples. “I thought you only felt that way about Father.”

She caressed his cheek and returned his generous smile. He bowed before her and attended both horses. She lingered before turning from the stables and their pungent scent. She rounded the outlying buildings that bordered the familial residence. The red-roofed arsenal dominated on the left, its polished marble walls echoing with the sounds of the workers inside. One of the men stepped out and upon seeing her, immediately turned to the wall with his head bowed. Laughter bubbled up inside of her. She pulled the folds of her *hijab* closer around her face.

Heat and smoke from the firing chambers of the kilns escaped directly into the open air. The workers paid her progress no heed, their attention devoted to glazed and gilded ceramics. In the previous year, a Persian fleeing the onslaught of the Mongols in the east had sought refuge at Malaka. He worked a fine technique of luster faience for the benefit of her household.

Fatima drifted beyond the confines of the industrial quarter into the orchards. A light breeze rustled the bare tops of pomegranate, almond and fig trees. Malaka produced the best figs in all Al-Andalus. Earlier in the year, merchants had exported them as far as Baghdad and Damascus.

Columns graced the entryway to the governor's castle. As Fatima crossed the threshold of her home, rows of decorative tin objects gleamed on shelves fitted on either side of an elongated chamber. Some glistened in a turquoise color, with the addition of cobalt oxide from the Persian's skillful hand.

The room led to an inner garden courtyard, where the sounds of a child at play beckoned. Fatima leaned against a column and watched.

Six-year-old Mumina scrambled up the steps to an alabaster-colored woman. "Look, Aunt Baraka, I have more star thistles for my crown."

The concubine attended the little princess, tousling the dark hair tumbling down her back in thick curls. A slight smile curved Baraka's lips while she strung flowers together into a diadem.

She placed the delicate circlet on Mumina's head. "There now, you look like a proper princess."

"I am a proper princess!" Mumina insisted, stamping her tiny feet in that imperious nature she had developed of late.

"Yes," Baraka replied, "and a pretty one at that."

Mumina spied Fatima beside the column. "*Ummi*!"

She skipped toward her, her silken tunic bunched around her knobby knees. "Look, Aunt Baraka made me a crown."

Fatima picked her up and kissed her soundly on both cheeks. "You are very beautiful, my sweetness."

"I know." Mumina fingered the green jasper brooch that held Fatima's tunic closed at the neck.

When Fatima set her down, she scrambled back to Baraka, kissed her cheek and then played among the rows of flowers. At the opposite end of the garden, her governess Amoda sat feeding the youngest child of the family, baby Saliha, who was in her second year. Amoda inclined her head and offered a smile, which Fatima returned.

Then she greeted the concubine. Baraka clasped her hands together and returned the acknowledgment. Now in her forty-sixth year, Baraka and her counterparts Samara and Hayfa had been Faraj's companions from his youth, although he never visited them now. Fatima rarely saw Samara and Hayfa outside of the harem's walls. Only Baraka did not hide herself away.

Since the family had lived at Malaka, Fatima witnessed Baraka's increasing care and devotion to Faraj's children without comment. While the concubine did not interact often with the boys Ismail and Muhammad, she seemed to delight in the seven girls Fatima had borne. She had often kissed bruised knees and fingers, or mediated the little quarrels that often sprang up between the children.

In truth, Baraka's attentions had privately unnerved Fatima. She worried for her children's safety in the company of a woman who reviled their mother. Yet, she soon saw how her daughters responded to Baraka's kind gestures. They referred to her as their aunt, with an affection they reserved for no one else, even Fatima's sister Alimah who resided with them.

Mumina squealed with delight and Baraka's gaze sought her under hooded eyelids. Silent yearning flushed her face and glittered in the depths of her eyes. Then she glared at Fatima.

"I did not mean for you to find me here, Sultana. I thought you would still be out riding with Prince Ismail until midday."

"You are a part of this family, Baraka. My girls adore you. You do not need my permission to be with them."

"I did not ask for it!"

Baraka's emerald gaze pinned Fatima for a moment before her stare fell away. "Still, I thank you for allowing me to be of use to them."

A cool wind encircled the women and Fatima rubbed at her arms beneath the silken tunic. "I see the ache in your eyes when you are with my daughters. You once wanted children of your own."

"Your husband did not wish it. He wanted to sire heirs only with you. I would not have been so foolish as to give him sons to rival your own."

"Why do you say that?"

"Do you think I would allow any child of mine to be at the mercy of your offspring in the succession? No. It is better this way."

Vehemence embittered her tone.

Fatima sighed. "Baraka, my sons would never hurt any child of their father's blood. I had hoped you also understood that I would never do such a thing. Faraj may not love you, but he...."

"Is it not enough that you have the master's love?" The concubine's voice descended to a husky murmur. "The great Sultana must take every opportunity to remind me."

"Baraka, I did not mean....wait! Baraka, come back!"

Fatima's words floated on the empty silence in the place where Baraka had stood. The concubine's sobs echoed as she fled inside the house.

"My Sultana!"

Dual calls echoed from the opposite ends of the house. Amoda's twin sister Leeta came from the family quarters while Fatima's loyal eunuch, Niranjan, the twins' brother, entered from the narrow chamber that preceded the garden courtyard. Both bowed as they approached.

Leeta whipped her graying braid over a thin shoulder. "My Sultana, I believe the silk merchant has arrived at the market this morning. I shall go to him."

Niranjan suggested, "Perhaps the Sultana would wish to see the merchant's wares for herself?"

Fatima's gaze flitted from Leeta to Niranjan, who nodded. His dark eyes gleamed above crinkles in his leathery, sun-bronzed skin. She sensed hidden purpose behind his words.

Behind her, Leeta looked over Fatima's shoulder at him. "Brother, it has long been custom that I oversee the purchases of silk for this household."

"I am not suggesting someone should usurp your authority, my sister. Surely, the Sultana can judge the quality of the merchant's silk for herself."

Fatima turned to Leeta and stroked her arm. "How does Marzuq fare this morning?"

Leeta stopped glaring at Niranjan long enough to answer. "His fever has abated. He is still abed. I can summon him if you...."

Fatima's hold tightened. "Summon my sick steward from his pallet? Leeta, you must think me heartless. Tend to your husband this morning. I shall see the silk merchant."

Leeta inhaled sharply and shot a dark look toward her brother, before she sighed and bowed. "As the Sultana wishes."

Fatima chuckled. "Is Marzuq still such a trial when he is ailing?"

Leeta rolled her eyes heavenward. "You could not understand." Her shoulders sagged. She disappeared into the family quarters again, where she and Marzuq shared a room.

Niranjan gestured toward the entrance. "Come, my Sultana."

Fatima led the way and he followed. A groom held the reins of two horses, already saddled. Niranjan rounded Fatima and cupped his hands, offering her aid as she mounted. She grabbed the reins.

"My beloved has returned, hasn't he? That is why you wanted me to visit the marketplace instead of Leeta. Why hasn't Faraj come to us? Is he hurt, Niranjan?"

The eunuch avoided her gaze. "I cannot say."

She frowned at him. More likely, he would not say for some obscure reason only he understood.

Why did Faraj's return require such secrecy? If he had come home, surely it meant the defeat of the Castillans and the recapture of Tarif. Then Faraj should have arrived in triumph, not entered his own city in secrecy.

Concern and confusion preoccupied Fatima, as she left the grounds with Niranjan by way of the bridge between her home and *Al-Jabal Faro*. Guardsmen at the citadel averted their gaze while she and her eunuch rode past in a flurry of dust, which obscured the rectangular towers and massive walls. She and Niranjan took a steep hill at daring speeds, whitewashed and red-roofed houses all a blur on either side of the cobblestones. They entered the bustling precincts of the silk market. Each section of Malaka's marketplace, allotted to a special area of commerce, reminded Fatima of the crowded *Qaysariyya* at Gharnatah.

Behind a horseshoe archway, expensive garments of every variety and color beckoned buyers' eager hands brimming with gold *dinars*. A long string of camels, each beast held in the croup of its leader, blocked the entrance to an inn. Fatima pulled her *hijab* over her nose and quelled the stench of the animals. She dismounted without Niranjan's aid. He led the way up a staircase to the second landing. Loud curses echoed from within. When Niranjan pushed the door open, three merchants rained down violent epithets on each other's heads.

"Cheaters! Deceivers! I piss on both of you and your wretched silks!"

"I piss on your mother, you filthy dog! You're the cheat. Your *dinars* line the pockets of the market inspector. God confound you and your lies! Wait until Governor Faraj returns to the city!"

"You dare call anyone else a liar? You miserable son of a donkey and a whore!"

Niranjan pushed past them and grasped Fatima's hand, pulling her along behind him. They dashed down the narrow hall. Niranjan scratched at the olive wood door at the end. "Master."

The portal creaked on its hinges. Fatima rushed inside.

Faraj rose from his crouch on the wooden floor, his eyes widening. Fatima swallowed at the sight of him as he unwound the turban that hid the lower half of his face.

His sun-burnished cheeks glistened like copper. He wore a simple tunic, trousers and leather slippers, not the armor she had last seen him don nearly four months ago. She rushed toward him, but he grasped and held her at arms' length. Behind her, the door snapped shut and consigned them to the gloom of the windowless chamber.

He whispered, "I have the stink of the siege and a hard day's ride upon me, beloved."

"I don't care!" She struggled against him. "Faraj, why won't you kiss or hold me? Why are you here at this inn? Why haven't you come home to us?"

"I cannot, Fatima. I need you to listen."

She shook her head, her fingers itching for the coarseness of his beard, the planes of his cheek. "What has happened? Did the Marinids overcome the Castillans?"

"I do not know. I abandoned the siege."

Her hands fell away. Tears stung her eyes. She drew back from him. "The Sultan has ever been good to you. How could you do this to my father?"

Faraj raked long fingers over his face. Creases she had not noticed before now encircled his red-rimmed eyes. "Woman, be silent and let me tell you! The siege has continued for more than three months. The Castillans would not surrender. Then the rebel Prince Juan, the brother of King Sancho, brought out the son of the defender of Tarif. The boy had served as a page at King Sancho's court, entrusted to the King's family. You should have seen him, Fatima. He could not have been older than our little Muhammad. Prince Juan threatened to cut his throat if his father did not surrender. When the commander refused, Prince Juan killed the boy."

He lapsed into silence.

Fatima stared at him, her fingers tightened into fists. Her nails dug into her palms.

A scowl knitted and darkened his features. "Well? Have you nothing to say about this monstrous act?"

"Once, when you defended our home against the Marinids and the Ashqilula, you told me the enemy is the enemy. What difference does this conflict make? You once swore your sword for my father's benefit, for the pursuit of his will. Why have you betrayed him?"

"Would you have had me raise my weapon on a field dishonored by the blood of a child? By the Prophet's beard, Fatima, if you think I would sacrifice my principles for your father's sake, you cannot know me at all!"

She turned from him, shaking. Her hand crept to her belly, where the child inside stirred. She closed her eyes and let the tears fall, her shoulders quaking. She carried a babe who might never know his father.

"Bah! Not your tears, I shall not be unmanned by your tears, woman."

Even as he railed at her, his hands closed on her arms, his earlier hesitancy long forgotten. She struggled against his hold, but he pulled her close. She leaned into the warmth of his chest. His heart thrummed in a steady rhythm against her back. His lips skimmed the delicate flesh her nape. Sweat and smoke filled her nostrils. Still, she did not recoil from him.

"Always, these tears of yours. You use them against me, I think."

She swiped at her cheeks. "Never mind my tears. You cannot remain here. You must leave Al-Andalus."

His grip loosened and she turned to him. She cupped his face in her hands. Although her heart tore inside her, she rushed on. "The Sultan shall kill you. I cannot allow it. Flee to al-Maghrib el-Aska or al-Tunisiyah, wherever you can go."

"To live in exile like a coward? Truly, you do not know me at all, wife."

"I wonder if those who have loved even as we have can ever know each other. We have always understood each other well, I think. I have honored my father far longer than I have ever loved you. Still, when I seek comfort and the home of my heart, it is in you that I find these things."

She withdrew her touch while he searched her face. He could not hold her gaze. His lips tightened in a firm line and their color faded. The pain etched in his crestfallen features hurt her almost as much as his betrayal of her father.

"Faraj, we are so different from when we first married, those days in which we were uncertain and mistrustful of each other. Now, your heart is mine and mine is yours. Yet I must see now, even the hope that our love held sway over all else in our lives was a vain, foolish one. I was wrong to expect that both of us had altered in every way.

"I remain my father's daughter, as devoted to him as when I was a girl. Your nature is still the same. You do what you must for your own sake. Now, you would abandon our children and me, as you left Tarif. All for your ideals. Principles and conviction mean more to you than the love of your children. More than my love?"

He jerked her toward him, his eyes ablaze. She looked into their centers, unflinching. "Even if you would risk your death, beloved, I cannot allow it. Let me preserve our children's memories of you as a loyal warrior for the Sultanate. Better that they should believe you fell at Tarif than under the executioner's blade."

His fingers bunched in the delicate sleeves of her tunic. "I am no coward." He ground out every word and pushed her away from him.

She stumbled before righting herself. By the time she straightened, he had hidden his features beneath the folds of his turban again. Her belly soured at the thought of their angry parting and with regret that he would never know of the child she carried. She ignored an impetuous urge to tell him. She would spare him the pain he had not hesitated to inflict upon her.

"It is not too late for you, husband. You can change the course of the events to follow."

When he chuckled, her stomach knotted. "You make sport of my fears in what may be our last moments together. You do not know me either, Faraj, even after all these years."

"I laughed because I told someone else at Tarif that he could also change the future. We are more alike than you think, Fatima."

"In this moment, we are not. I would value my love for you more than my principles. I have done so before."

His gaze narrowed, hinting that he understood the reference, but she pressed on. "You lied to my father once. You defied his will and killed an Ashqilula governor under the Sultan's protection. You let me plead for your life before my father, knowing your guilt. He forgave you, as I did."

He avoided her harsh stare. "I shall always be grateful for his mercy and yours. I have repaid the favor to you at Tarif. I spoke to one of the Marinid commanders, who led a third of their forces and convinced him to abandon the siege, too. Your mother's brother, Abdallah of Ashqilula."

Fatima clutched the prayer beads beneath her neckline. "He was at Tarif? How does he fare? Did he ask about me?"

"He did and more. I discovered he knew the circumstances of your mother's death, had known since his defection to Jumhuriyat Misr fifteen years ago. He understood then and now, as I do, the utter cruelty of those whom he once supported." Faraj chuckled again. "In that moment as I spoke with him, I thought only of you, beloved. I was not so selfish then."

She stepped toward him, her hands outstretched, tears stinging her eyes. He shook his head, opened the door and bypassed Niranjan.

Fatima stifled a sob behind her hands and whirled away.

Behind her, Niranjan asked, "Shall I follow him?"

She swallowed past the lump in her throat and looked to him. "He would expect it. Who remains trustworthy among my father's servants in Gharnatah? Someone who would know of the dealings at court?"

"Ulayyah's son, Faisal. He exchanges letters at least once a month with his sisters Basma and Haniya. He can be trusted."

Niranjan ducked his head. Still, she noted the heightened color of his cheeks.

"You are fond of this boy?"

"He is a man now. Yes, I am fond of him."

Fatima swallowed and blinked rapidly. Her mind raced with questions she did not voice, for now was not the time. She nodded to Niranjan.

"Then warn him of Faraj's intent. Tomorrow, we shall follow. I won't let my husband sacrifice himself."

"And if we are too late to stop him?"

"We cannot be! Do as I command."

"It shall be done." Niranjan bowed at the waist.

# Chapter 4
# Treachery and Blood

## Princess Fatima

Malaka, Al-Andalus: Dhu al-Qa`da 693 AH (Malaga, Andalusia: October AD 1294)

The next morning in the courtyard outside the governor's castle, Fatima gathered her children together. Niranjan and her trusted maidservants, the twins Basma and Haniya hovered behind her.

Fatima's eldest daughter Leila presented herself first. At thirteen years old, she was the quiet beauty among her sisters with the dark red hair of her namesake, Faraj's mother. She hugged her mother and buried her narrow face in the folds of Fatima's tunic.

"I shall miss you, *Ummi*, now that both you and Father are gone. When is he going to come home?"

Fatima kissed the crown of Leila's head. "Do not fear for him, I'm sure he shall return to us soon." She pulled back and looked down at her daughter's bare feet. "Dearest, I do wish you might wear shoes sometimes."

Leila frowned at her. "It's not raining today. You know I only wear shoes when it rains."

Fatima shook her head at her daughter's odd penchant. As Leila drew back, Fatima embraced her twins Aisha and Faridah. Both kissed her cheeks in turn.

"You're taking too long!" Mumina insisted, stamping her foot and scattering her crown of flowers from the previous day to the ground.

The eleven-year-old twins turned in the circle of their mother's arms. Faridah stuck her tongue out at her little sister. Mumina would have delivered a kick to her sister's calves, if her elder brother and sister, who waited patiently beside Mumina, had not held her back.

A scant year separated Fatima's next child, Qamar, from the twins Aisha and Faridah, and from her younger brother, Muhammad. The boy and girl shared the same birth date and behaved in the same manner. They held each other's hands and bowed before their mother. A lock of Muhammad's black hair fell over his eyes. When he stood, Fatima smoothed his curls, which he promptly tousled again with a smirk.

After Fatima knelt, hugged and kissed Mumina, she also admonished the little tyrant to behave herself. Amoda brought the younger children, Qabiha and Saliha. Although four years of age, Qabiha barely spoke and her stare seemed vacant, as though she was not aware of the world around her. Fatima worried for her silent, wide-eyed child and lingered over her embraces with Qabiha, before she kissed Saliha's cheek.

Amoda said, "I shall take good care of them, my Sultana."

Fatima nodded. "Where is my Ismail?"

"I am here, *Ummi*."

He led two horses and one pack animal from the stables.

"I don't understand why we can't go with you." Mumina pouted. "We haven't seen Grandfather since Qabiha was born."

Fatima looked over her daughter's head to Amoda, who said, "Come, children, do not pester your mother. Allow her to take her leave."

Groans filled the air, but several pairs of feet shuffled into the house. Amoda set Qabiha and Saliha at her feet, squeezed Fatima's hand in her own and raised it to her lips briefly. "God go with you, my Sultana."

Fatima grasped her eldest son's narrow shoulders. "I pray our God guide you always, Ismail. You have charge of the household in the absence of your parents. You shall, I trust, defer to the wisdom of Marzuq, Leeta and Amoda. Watch over your brother and sisters."

"Yes, *Ummi*," Ismail replied.

Fatima kissed both his cheeks and hugged him against her. He groaned for respite and wriggled from her grasp. He smoothed the wrinkles in his sleeves and bowed, before he followed his chattering siblings into the castle.

Fatima had told only one person the purpose of her hasty departure to Gharnatah with Niranjan, but almost everyone suspected the cause related to Faraj, whom they assumed still fought at Tarif. Only her younger sister Alimah knew the truth.

The widowed Sultana stood in silence beside a column. The wind battered Alimah's body and billowed her blue-black veils behind her back. Years after the death of her husband, she still wore mourning colors.

Fatima held out her hand to Alimah. After a moment, her sister's slim fingers clasped hers. In silence, they stood together, foreheads touching. Fatima squeezed Alimah's hand.

"I wish you would change your mind and come with me to Gharnatah."

"I promised myself I would never return while the Sultan lived. Why should I go now?"

The pain of betrayal embittered Alimah's unforgiving tone. Fatima believed the feelings were justified, but she despaired at her sister's lingering hatred. "Dearest, he is still our father...."

Alimah pulled away and hugged her body against the descending chill. "He is the Sultan of Gharnatah first, a father second. It has always been this way."

"That's not fair!" Fatima knew Alimah spoke the truth, but she could not allow anyone to besmirch her father's reputation, even a beloved sister.

"When you see him at Gharnatah and he has condemned your Faraj, you shall understand. You see everyone so clearly, Fatima, except him. Love for him has always blinded you. I am truly sorry for your husband's fate. I remain grateful to him, for the sanctuary he has offered since my husband's death at Mayurqa. You cannot expect me to forgive the Sultan. I can never forget that my son and daughters are orphans because of him. His inaction killed my husband. Abu Umar would be alive if Father had helped us, if he had protected the people of Mayurqa. If your husband had not offered dowries for my girls, they might never have married. Their children shall never know Abu Umar. All this and more I lay at the Sultan's feet."

"He suffers regrets of the past."

Alimah's brown eyes, which had once glittered with vitality, met Fatima's own. Naked pain reflected deep within Alimah's watery gaze. "The Sultan has yet to know the meaning of suffering. I pray by God that he shall learn it before the end of his days."

Her words chilled Fatima more than the blustery breeze.

"You should forgive him someday, Alimah."

"You must learn to see the Sultan for what he is. He let my husband die. He may condemn yours without mercy. His own first wife, our mother, could not love him. Have you never wondered why? Have you never asked him?"

Fatima had often considered the pain-filled end of her parents' marriage, having understood from her own union that bonds could fray at the slightest disagreement. Yet each time memories of her mother's unhappiness plagued her, she dismissed them. To consider such thoughts would be a betrayal of her father. She loved him too much to condemn him for hurting her own mother.

Her stubborn refusal to accept her father's faults affected her relationships with everyone, even the bond with her beloved husband. She had argued so ardently against Faraj's actions because of the duty she still owed to her father. Fatima shook her head. Her loyalty to the Sultan vied with her care for Faraj. How could she hope to reconcile the interests of the two men she loved most in life?

Alimah turned away from Fatima, her last words carried on the wind. "If the Sultan wants forgiveness, let him seek it from God. I have none to give."

Three days later, Fatima, Niranjan and her maidservants had joined a camel caravan headed for Gharnatah. They traveled without guards from Malaka. The merchants did not ask questions regarding their haste, thanks to the full purse of *dinars* Niranjan had pressed into the eager hands of the caravan leader.

Fatima felt certain Faraj must have reached the capital by now. Would she arrive in time to find his head mounted on a spike atop the *Bab Ilbira*? Her heart, shredded into bloody, bitter pieces, rejected the inevitable. Her head cautioned that Faraj was still alive. She accepted this understanding without question. He lived and if only she might reach him in time, he might escape the Sultan's wrath.

When they sighted the burnished redbrick walls of Gharnatah in the distance, frigid air from the mountains descended without mercy. Heavy gray clouds clung to the peaks and nearly obscured their jagged heights. Fatima pulled her mantle tighter about her and ducked her head against the cold, urging her horse onward.

She and Niranjan parted with the caravan at the main gate. A sigh of relief rippled through her, as her gaze scoured the walls and found no grisly display atop the main city gate. The streets emptied, as the call of prayer at midday echoed throughout the bustling city.

Grateful for the diminished crowd, Fatima rode up the steep incline of the *Sabika* hill perched high above the valley below. The guards patrolling the palace precincts gave her and Niranjan entry at *Al-Quasaba.*

As they moved beyond the citadel's double walls, where her father's soldiers patrolled the stone parapet walkways, she whispered, "Please, dear God, don't let it be too late."

## Prince Faraj

Gharnatah, Al-Andalus: Dhu al-Qa`da 693 AH (Granada, Andalusia: October AD 1294)

Faraj lingered in the shadowy recesses of the council chamber, pacing the stonework floor. The call to prayer reverberated through the thick masonry of the walls. It was the second time he had heard it since his arrival in Gharnatah during the early morning. He had observed his ablutions and the rituals of *Salat al-Fajr* with a reverence and calmness he had never felt before. Was this how it felt for all who faced their ending? Did the same peace wash over them? He pondered this and his parting with Fatima.

He had forced himself from her side at Malaka, when his mind screamed a warning that he should listen to her pleas. She had never led him astray before, his most dutiful and loyal companion. Yet, he knew he could not forsake his convictions, even if it meant losing her forever. His sole regret was the bitter accusation simmering in her expression. She had fought for him before, accepted his lies. No one had ever recognized his frailties and loved him despite them.

Jumbled thoughts vied with each other. She was right. There was still time. He could return to her and their children, even if only for a brief moment. They might even escape together.

Still, he clenched his fists at his side, his feet rooted to the floor. Where could they go that the Sultan would not find them? How could he condemn his beloved and their children to a life of exile?

His determination wavered as time wore on. How long would the Sultan keep him waiting?

Only Khalid stayed at his side, leaning against one of four slender columns in the room. The faint golden glow of a central lantern at the apex of the columns provided the barest light, enough to illuminate Khalid's ever-present scowl. The rest of Faraj's men waited at *Al-Quasaba*. He had dismissed them at Malaka, determined that they would not share in his folly. For the first time, they had disobeyed his orders.

A door at the northern end of the *mashwar* creaked. Khalid stood at attention and his hand flew to the pommel of his sword. Faraj shook his head and the captain's fingers relaxed.

Muhammad II, Sultan of Gharnatah strode into the room, a row of his personal bodyguards on either side of him. Musk and ambergris wafted through the air with each footfall. Reverent admiration filled Faraj, coupled with the sensation of dread prickling along his spine. His resolve crumbled before the majesty of his father in-law.

The Sultan neared his fifty-ninth birthday, but he moved with a confident and purposeful stride that belied alterations brought on by age. Gray streaks lined the length of the Sultan's once dark hair, now curling at the nape. Small, dark blotches marked his sallow skin. Like Faraj, he also dyed his full beard with henna. Richly embroidered *tiraz* bands decorated the billowing sleeves of his green *jubba*. The sleeves nearly hid hands glittering with several gold rings. A silken cord trimmed at the ends with gold braid belted the *jubba* neatly at his trim waist.

Faraj fell on both knees, as did his captain. Both bent double until their heads touched the floor.

An interminable time passed while Faraj waited, in which the Sultan's raspy breathing filled the room. Faraj did not dare look up until his master acknowledged him. Then silken robes shuffled across the stonework before a shadow fell over him.

"You dare...." A hoarse wheeze escaped the Sultan. "You dare come before me, traitor. Did you forsake the campaign at Tarif? Has your treachery cost me that city? Look me full in the face and tell me you have not betrayed me. Stand up and answer, man!"

Faraj's heart pitched inside his chest, but he stood and met the Sultan's hawk-eyed stare. Cold rage glittered in his master's eyes.

"You do not even try?"

The Sultan's hand swung in a wide arc. Faraj stumbled and nearly fell from the force of the backhanded blow. He staggered before righting himself. All the arguments and pleas he had prepared on the swift journey to Gharnatah melted before his master's hot fury.

How was it possible? How could the Sultan already know what had transpired at Tarif? A heavy weight like stones settled in Faraj's stomach. Someone had divulged his intent. His heart rebelled against the likelihood of it, for there was only one person with motive and opportunity who could have betrayed him. It would seem he had been a fool, after all.

The Sultan turned to his guards. "Arrest the *Raïs* of Malaka. Bind his companion and take their weapons."

Six men, a third of the Sultan's bodyguards, surged forward and surrounded Faraj. One drew manacles and tugged Faraj's hands behind his back. He removed Faraj's sword and dagger from their sheaths. The other guardsmen glowered at him, their daggers in hand, prepared for his resistance. Faraj offered none, even though Khalid's furious gaze burned into his. Yet like Faraj, he stood still while the Sultan's men removed his weapons.

Then, Faraj's brother Muhammad stepped out from behind the Sultan's guards and waddled toward him. As he bowed at their master's side, Faraj clamped his jaw tight and swallowed back the bile filling his gorge.

Muhammad eyed him. "I was right about you, Faraj. You have never deserved my loyalty. For years, I have watched you prosper from the generosity of others. Our father named you his heir though scant days separated the dates of our births. I was his son too, but you were his beloved heir. After his murder, when we came to Gharnatah, you ingratiated yourself with the old Sultan. Your reward was his trust, his granddaughter and Malaka, which was my home, too. I have languished in your shadow, but no more. I have learned the lessons you taught, brother. I shall use them to gain as you have."

Faraj collapsed into raucous laughter, though as he bent, the movement strained the sinews along his arms. The Sultan's guards forced him upright again.

"You think the Sultan shall give you Malaka now? You forget I have sired a son who shall soon achieve his manhood. He has claim, not you."

Muhammad glanced at the Sultan, who turned his dark glower on him. "Is that why you came here in all haste with news of your brother's betrayal? You thought I would give the governorship to you, instead of allowing Ismail to inherit it?"

Muhammad blanched. Perspiration dotted his brow. "I...but, he is just a boy and his father is a traitor!"

"Ismail is my grandson. Malaka is his birthright." The icy precision of the Sultan's voice matched his frigid stare.

Muhammad sputtered and waved his hand at Faraj, "My Sultan, I have told you everything he did at Tarif, how he counseled the abandonment of the siege. He met with the Ashqilula, your enemies. He let them escape again. You cannot do this...."

When the Sultan's face colored a reddened mask of ferocity, Muhammad pleaded, "I have risked everything to bring you this news. I deserve a reward."

The Sultan clasped his hands together. "You shall have it. Not Malaka."

Faraj chuckled. "You took too long to learn those lessons, Muhammad. Mark me, for I shall see you again in the hellfire of *Jahannam*. We shall wear the garments of fire and be bound in boiling water for eternity, together."

"You shall meet your end there first!" Muhammad's guttural scream preceded his lurch toward Faraj.

"Stop him!" The Sultan's order rang through the chamber.

Two of his bodyguards turned. Their curved daggers plunged into Muhammad's stomach.

Faraj's own belly twisted as the Damascene steel sank beneath silk and flesh. Muhammad gurgled and his eyes widened. A froth of spittle and blood bubbled at the corner of his fleshy mouth. He sagged on his knees and toppled sideways.

His stare remained fixed on Faraj's face. "I curse you and all your lineage, forever."

The Sultan knelt beside him. His bodyguards panted at his side and stared at each other red-faced, almost catatonic. The Sultan retrieved their daggers, each time drawing a sharp cry from Muhammad. The men took their bloodied weapons.

Muhammad croaked in a harsh whisper, "I call down the wrath of Allah, the Compassionate, the Merciful upon you, Faraj. May God hear my prayer."

He groaned and his head lolled on the stone floor. "There is no God but God, and Muhammad, may peace be upon him-"

"-is His messenger," Faraj murmured, finishing the words of the *Shahadah*, the Profession of the Faith, as his brother breathed his last.

Faraj sighed at the loss of a final opportunity to reconcile their differences. He had truly hoped, as expressed at Tarif, to bring them together. It was a fool's hope. Their lives had always run divergent courses. Yet, he would see Muhammad soon enough, united in death.

The Sultan rose. "A waste of a life. He chased another's dream instead of his own."

Faraj met his stare again. "Send my brother back to Malaka. It is what he would have wanted. I beg only this indulgcncc, though I have no right to ask it."

"You are correct. You have no right to ask. The rivalry between you and Muhammad led him to this end. You bear responsibility for his death, too. His body goes to his family at Qumarich."

Faraj hung his head. "Whatever you may think of me now, know that I have always served you loyally."

"Except at Tarif. You thought only of your honor and in doing so, you have determined your fate. Just as your brother's actions sealed his."

The Sultan joined the remainder of his guards and left the room, saying as he went, "Take the *Raïs* of Malaka and all of his men beneath the *madina*, along the tunnels to *Al-Quasaba*, until I decree a time for the governor's execution. Summon slaves to cleanse the room of this morning's treachery and blood."

## Princess Fatima

Fatima sprinted across the crowded cobblestone street from *Al-Quasaba*, pushing her way among courtiers who cursed at her. She had found one of Faraj's men waiting in the shade of the barracks. He warned her that the Sultan had summoned her husband to the *mashwar* an hour after *Salat al-Fajr*.

"Faraj? Faraj! Where are you?"

"My Sultana, your skirts! I can see your ankles." Niranjan panted behind her.

What did she care for modesty when her husband's life was in danger? She regretted her harsh words to him in days past. He had to live, or she would die.

She entered the first courtyard of her father's palace and spied the Sultan crossing its northern border, shadowed by his guardsmen. She waved a hand for Niranjan and her maidservants to remain behind her.

Before her father disappeared into the cavernous throne room, she called out, "No, please wait!"

The Sultan turned at the echo of her voice, the skirts of his silk robe swirling around his feet. Fatima reached him and embraced him fervently, forgetting all the propriety that demanded she should have abased herself. Her eyes watered with tears of fear, joy, and heartbreak united. She had not seen her father for four years, since she had brought Qabiha to Gharnatah for her grandfather's blessing.

Now, the Sultan clung to her before he drew back and framed her face in his large hands. "Why did you come here?"

"I had to."

His fervent grip slackened and fell away. "You are here because of your husband."

"Noble father, you have seen him?"

"I have done so."

Fatima studied his pale face for clues.

He offered none. Instead, the fine lines etched in his complexion deepened. "Then you also know what he has done and why he came to Gharnatah. It would have been better for him, for both of you, if he had fled Al-Andalus."

Fatima grasped his fingers. "You know him, as I do. His honor would never have permitted it. Father, your anger must be terrible. Your wrath is blameless. I wept when Faraj came to me from Tarif and told me what he had done. We quarreled and I accused him of abandoning your cause, when you have always been merciful to him. I knew you could never forgive him for this. Yet I ask." She paused and knelt before him and clasped her hands together, "No, I beg for his life. Would you kill the beloved father of your own grandchildren? Would you leave me a widow?"

He shook his head. "Faraj has betrayed me again. I forgave him once before, but I cannot do so now."

"What do you mean, Father?"

"Do you think me a fool, Fatima? I have always known of Faraj's guilt in the death of the last Ashqilula governor of Malaka."

When she gasped, he turned from her, his voice low. "No one else would have dared kill Abu Muhammad of Ashqilula. No other possessed a more damning reason for his death. Faraj let you plead for his life, when he knew his own guilt. I accepted the lie for your sake. I freed him and restored his family's heritage. I did it for love of you. I could not bear your pain."

The memory of her same accusations against Faraj only days before weighed upon Fatima now. She sagged on her knees and buried her face in her hands.

Her father grunted and pried her fingers away. He knelt with her on the grass. "Do not cry for him, daughter. He cared nothing for my feelings or your own. He is unworthy of your sorrow or my forgiveness."

Fatima smiled through her tears. "I love him, Father, as my life. He is my life. My heart can bear the pain of his disloyalty. It cannot bear the loss of him. I must see him. Does he still live?"

When he did not immediately answer, she looked past him to where his guards stood. Two of them brandished curved daggers, splattered with blood.

Fatima rose and dashed past them, ignoring her father's voice. "Wait!"

She turned in the direction she had seen his men come from, toward the *mashwar*. She pushed the door before her. It flew back against the stucco wall and rattled on its hinges.

She froze, a scream trapped inside her throat. A pool of blood drained from a crumpled corpse in the middle of the floor. Her father's hand closed on her arm. She jerked away, startled by his touch. For a moment, she had forgotten him in the painful glare of death.

"Calm yourself, daughter. Your husband's brother Muhammad came to Gharnatah last night. He warned me of Faraj's treachery. He hoped I would reward him with Malaka. When I refused, he tried to attack Faraj. My guards killed him.."

Fatima turned from the sight. He gathered her in his arms.

She whispered, "Where have you taken my husband?"

"Faraj is in a cell at *Al-Quasaba*." When she drew back and looked at him, he continued, "He has committed treason. Not even you can save him. I am the Lawgiver. You shall accept my decree."

"If you kill him, Father, I shall die."

He kissed her brow and released her. "You think you cannot endure the pain. When the tragedy has faded, when you look to your children, you shall survive it. I know. I bore the treachery of your Ashqilula mother and her death. I accepted it. You shall discover the same courage within as I found it, after Aisha forsook me."

He turned from her and walked to the throne room.

"You never loved her as I love him!" Fatima's voice echoed.

Her father halted, glanced over his shoulder once and then continued without looking back.

# Chapter 5
# The Sultan

## Princess Fatima

Gharnatah, Al-Andalus: Dhu al-Qa`da 693 AH (Granada, Andalusia: October AD 1294)

Later in the evening, Fatima sobbed into her hands. She sat on a turquoise cushion in the apartments of her father's queen, the Sultana Shams ed-Duna. The heat of a metal brazier in the corner of the room did not cast aside the chill that pinched Fatima's shoulders.

Shams ed-Duna patted her arm. "You must cease these tears. They cannot secure your husband's release nor sway my husband."

"Shams! How can you tell her that? It is cruel." Nur al-Sabah, the Sultan's favorite, hugged Fatima and kissed her hair.

Shams rolled her eyes. "Nur, you cannot deny that Prince Faraj was a fool and coward to do such a thing. He has betrayed our master, and the love and trust Fatima showed her husband. Where was Faraj's love and concern for her feelings when he decided upon this foolish course?"

"Shams, hush! You are only making things worse." Nur pried Fatima's fingers away. "Look at me, please."

As her blurred vision cleared, Fatima managed a weak smile for her father's lover. She touched Nur's golden curls, tumbling free from a gossamer purple veil. Tiny amethysts and diamonds glittered at the fringe of the material. Nur's ice-blue eyes were perhaps as red-rimmed as Fatima's own might be.

Fatima sighed. "Don't be mad at Shams ed-Duna, Nur. She speaks the truth."

"You see! Even she must admit it!" Shams slapped the low olivewood table at which they sat. Her dark eyes, the color of obsidian, glowed with a spark of fury at their centers.

"How could he do this to us and to our children?" Fatima shook her head. "How am I to tell them they may never see their father again?"

Nur sat back on her heels. "I shall speak to the Sultan and beg for your husband's life. It is the only kindness I can offer you."

Fatima grasped the concubine's slender hand and raised it to her lips. "You offer so much more. You have been my friend of many years. To think, I once reviled you for claiming Father's heart."

Nur hugged her again. "That is long past, all forgiven. I have found three great treasures in my life in Al-Andalus. The love of your father. The friendship I have shared with you and Shams. The blessings of my children."

The *kadin* looked to the corner where her long awaited son, a golden-haired little boy of only seven years played with a wooden sword. He whacked it against the stucco wall beside him, fighting some imaginary adversary. The Sultan had named him Nasr. Like all Nur's children, Nasr had his mother's coloring.

Nur called to him. "Nasr, it is soon time for prayers. Go to your nurse, Sabela, for your bath."

"I don't like prayers! I don't like baths." Her son took out his spite on the wall.

As Nur gave an exasperated sigh and shrugged, Fatima said, "If you do as your mother commands, I promise to teach you how to use a bow and arrow tomorrow."

He pushed back the golden curls falling over his cherubic face and glared at her, every bit the prideful Nasrid prince like his elder brothers.

He muttered, "You don't know how to fight. You're a woman. Father says women should not fight."

"They should not, little brother, but sometimes they must. When I was young, perhaps twice your age or a little older, our brother the Crown Prince Muhammad taught me to use the bow."

Nasr's pale blue eyes widened. He approached her. His wooden sword dangled between his chubby fingers. "Truly?"

His mother chuckled and reached for him. "A Sultana's word speaks only truth. Little princes shouldn't question it."

He wriggled away from her embrace, his gaze still on Fatima. "*Ummi* says you're my sister."

"I am, Nasr. Your father is my father."

"Why don't you live here at *al-Qal'at Al-Hamra*?"

"I live with my husband and children at Malaka. I have a little son, Muhammad, who is two years older than you."

He frowned at her. "I'm not little!" He stamped away toward the corner, before he stopped and turned around.

"Would your son want to play with me? I have only sisters and slaves. No one fights me. My sisters don't know how and the slaves are afraid of me."

Fatima chuckled, despite the lingering sadness in her heart. "The slaves should be afraid of you, since you are the Sultan's son and a fine Nasrid prince."

She could have sworn he puffed up his chest a little when she spoke.

"The next time I come to Gharnatah, Nasr, I shall bring my son Muhammad. You can practice lessons in the bow together."

"Would you really teach me?"

"I have said so. Don't you want to learn?"

He rocked back and forth on his bare heels, looking from her to his mother, with her indulgent smile. Fatima had missed his birth and much of the early years. This visit, even under such trying circumstances, might give her some time for her newest little brother.

Nasr said, "Well, yes, if Father lets me. *Ummi*, can I ask him?"

Nur shook her head. "Not until after you've completed your bath and said your prayers."

He scampered from the room, his cries echoing throughout the harem. "Sabela! Sabela! It's time for my bath."

Nur giggled and kissed Fatima's cheek. "I've never been able to coax him into the *hammam* with such ease. Thank you."

Beside them, Shams said, "If only our husband could be persuaded so easily."

Fatima sobered and nodded.

Shams added, "You may try, Nur, but you know the Sultan as well as I do. He cannot go back on his word. He has promised death to Prince Faraj. Nothing can sway him, not even the love he bears you."

Nur reached across the table and laced her fingers with Shams' darker ones. "I have to try. It may be the only hope Fatima has left. I shall speak with him, after we have dined. Can you join us, Fatima?"

Fatima shook her head. "I cannot eat at my father's table and pretend to be happy in his presence, while my husband rots in his cell at *Al-Quasaba*. Father's decree has broken my heart. I shall never forgive him if he murders my husband."

Her sister Alimah had warned her that she might feel this way about their father. She had refused to listen then, but she could not escape the reality of Faraj's circumstances now.

Shams sighed and caressed her shoulder. "You gain nothing by further defiance. Dine with us and show your father the duty and loyalty he deserves as Sultan, as the sole parent who raised you in the days after your mother's passing. That alone must still command some respect and love from you. Submit to his power and perhaps, you may yet win your husband's freedom. Allah, the Compassionate, the Merciful, demands the submission of all. Would you defy even the Will of God for your husband's sake?"

Within the hour after prayers, Fatima shared the evening meal with her father, Nur al-Sabah and Shams ed-Duna. The women sat on either side of her father, while Fatima took her place across the table from him. She shared in their food and conversation. Whenever her father glanced in her direction, she kept her face impassive. Yet every swallow of the roasted kid almost choked her.

As she reached for the bowl of warm flatbread and spooned the eggplant dip over a slice, she studied the rapport between him and his women. They were always kind and generous to each other. The Sultan's wife and his favorite shared an easy companionship.

Yet, there was no great love between her father and his queen. There might never be, despite the son and three daughters she had given him. Only his passion for his *kadin* endured. Nur al-Sabah was the mother of eight of his children, Prince Nasr and his seven sisters.

Fatima shook her head. Her father should have married his favorite. Strange to think that in the past, she might have hated him for doing so. Now, Nur was her best friend, like Shams. As the women laughed at something her father told them, Fatima thanked God that her father's house knew such peace.

The Sultan spooned some of the tart yogurt on a thick slice of cucumber and offered it to Nur al-Sabah, who caught it between her teeth. For all her forty-two years and eight children, her beauty remained, with the aid of pulp from the cucumber, or so she believed. Her eyes glistened with mirth while she kissed the Sultan's fingertips. She held him enthralled as she had always done.

"Do you truly intend to build us a summer palace, my Sultan?" she asked. "Our Nasr's imagination and wishes aside, I think it's a wonderful idea, though I would not wish it built because of a child's demands."

He said, "Telling our son bedtime stories from the Persian poet Ziyad may have inspired the idea, but it is a good one, even if motivated by a seven-year-old. My summer palace shall be our escape. I have already spoken with the master mason about the project."

He glanced at Fatima. "After public audience tomorrow morning, I shall show you the plans. I want to build living quarters, kitchens, stables, a mosque, and *hammam*."

She nodded. "It would please me to know more, honored Father." In truth, she could have cared less.

Beneath the table, Shams reached for her hand and squeezed it in appreciation. Nur al-Sabah winked at her. Fatima concentrated on the last remaining chunks of tender meat on her silver plate.

Shams said, "Don't forget our Rabiah's garden. Some place where she and the other children can play."

The Sultan tilted his head to her. "You're sweet to remind me of our daughter's wish, wife." He took her hand. "When we have finished our meal, I wish you to remain with me tonight."

Shams' gaze widened and she spared a doe-eyed look for Nur al-Sabah. "I would, my Sultan, but this night is already promised to the *kadin*. Surely, you have not forgotten?"

"I am not an old fool, wife." The Sultan reached for Nur's fingers too and kissed them. "I wish Nur al-Sabah to stay as well."

Fatima gasped. It was not like her father to share his bed with his queen and favorite at the same time. A long established custom gave two nights a week in the Sultan's bed to each woman. Her father could also choose among them or any concubine for his pleasure on the other three nights. When had he changed the practice?

While she mulled her concerns, Shams beckoned her personal slave, Faisal, who had stood silent and unobtrusive in a corner. The black chief eunuch shuffled forward with his shaved head bowed. He knelt beside his mistress, who said, "Bring me the *habba souda*."

Fatima stared long after Faisal had left. He was the elder brother of her servants, Basma and Haniya. Their mother had been Ulayyah, a slave within the household of the Sultan's old enemies, the Ashqilula.

Fatima ducked her head and ate her food. Remorse still filled her. If she had never conspired with Ulayyah in the betrayal of her Ashqilula masters, Faisal and his sisters would not be orphans. She had stolen their mother away.

The eunuch soon returned, bearing a glass vial with a wooden stopper. He had his mother's coloring, but his height and dark eyes were traits of his father, the chieftain Ibrahim, who had murdered Fatima's mother.

Faisal raised his gaze and met hers in a bold, blunt stare. His stark features revealed nothing, as he uncorked the vial. An aromatic, pepper flavor drifted from the bottle.

After the Sultan took it from him, Faisal withdrew to his solitary corner. His stare returned to Fatima for a brief moment, until he dipped his head again.

Fatima asked, "Father, what is that?"

He dipped a spoon into a bowl of honey on the table and then mixed some of the tiny, black granules from the vial with it. He swallowed the spoonful before replying, "Seeds of blessing."

"It's black seed, Fatima," Nur explained, the blush still on her cheeks. "It's good for many things, coughs and pains in the abdomen among them."

Fatima asked, "Are you in pain, Father?"

He said, "My doctor says it is helpful for digestion."

Shams ed-Duna's fingertips alighted on the silken sleeve of his *jubba*. "That is rumor, husband. My eunuch procures it upon your orders, but we cannot know the true properties of the *habba souda*."

He shrugged off her hold. "How can you know? Are you a doctor, Shams? When I eat the black seed after a meal, my stomach feels better."

He spooned more of the seeds mixed with honey into his mouth.

Fatima said, "Everyone knows chamomile tea is best for digestion and relaxation, Father." She beckoned the eunuch. "Bring your master a cup."

"No, I don't want it," the Sultan said. His gaze narrowed. He seemed so quick to anger these days. Faraj's betrayal must have cut deep, beyond measure.

"Daughter, if I wanted chamomile tea, I would have asked for it!"

"There's no need to be so angry, Father."

The Sultan pounded his fist on the cedar wood table. "Do not tell me how to feel! If I am angry, it is because you are making me so. You forget that I am the parent and you are the child. You dare not disrespect me at my own table."

Shams ed-Duna shook her head and returned her attention to the meal. Fatima left the remainder of her flatbread untouched, no longer having an appetite for it.

The Sultan took another spoonful of the black seed and honey mix. Fatima stared at the vial. She needed to know more about the properties of the seeds. Her father's reliance on such aid bothered her. He had never required them before. Perhaps, she might have dismissed his need as part of aging, but her father was not so old. The men of her family had always lived for long years, seeing multiple generations come after them..

A knock sounded at the door and by the Sultan's command, a messenger entered. He bowed at his master's side and gave him a message on rolled parchment, tied with a red string.

Fatima's father read the letter in silence before saying, "The siege of Tarif is over. Our warriors are coming home."

He glanced at her. "It would seem the Marinids have no heart for warfare, now that your husband has persuaded half of the forces to withdraw. He should die for what he has done."

Fatima's heart thumped so loud, she thought everyone in the room heard the sound. She gripped the table, as fearful anticipation dissipated in sadness.

"Please...."

A spasm of irritation crossed the Sultan's face. "No, no more, damn you! I should have had him killed this morning, along with his greedy brother. You should not have married him."

"I did! I love him, Father! Please, I beg of you, do not take him from me."

Shams ed-Duna put her hand on her husband's arm. "Do not blame the withdrawal of my people on Prince Faraj alone. They could have stayed on and fought. Yet, the Marinids also understand the duties of honor and sacrifice. My brother, Sultan Abu Ya'qub Yusuf, is an honorable man."

Her husband turned to her, his face flushed. "He promised to recapture Tarif on my behalf. What do I care for his honor? What of his damned promises to me? How does my alliance with him or my relations with you serve me, if Abu Ya'qub Yusuf cannot even take one coastal city without his honor impeding him? You should have written to your brother and demanded he secure that city in my name!"

Shams' stare widened with astonishment before her eyes watered. She looked away, blinking hard.

Fatima shook her head. She could not believe her father would say something so unjust to her stepmother.

"Father, the Sultana has no control over Abu Ya'qub Yusuf. She severed ties with the Marinids years ago, when her father betrayed you and put his troops on Andalusi soil at the behest of the Ashqilula. Shams has ever been your most loyal companion in life."

His gaze swung to her. "What good is she if she cannot influence her damned brother? I did not marry for love! I made an alliance! I have yet to see the benefit of this union…."

"Father, stop! You're being cruel, without cause."

The Sultan's face became a dark mask. "Get out and take her with you. Your presence tires me."

Fatima flung her napkin on the table in disgust. She jerked to her feet and extended a hand to Shams.

Her father's wife ignored her and glanced at the Sultan. A plea shone in her eyes. "Forgive me, husband. If you wish it, I shall write to the Marinid Sultan this night."

"Are you foolish? The Marinids would have begun their withdrawal already. Go far from me! You are useless!"

Nur clasped her hands together. "My Sultan, please do not say so, for the sake of your queen and the children she has borne you!"

Shams clutched at his arm. "Do not send me from your sight in anger, my Sultan."

"I said, get away from me!"

The Sultan shoved her aside, pushing with such force that Shams flung backward, striking her head hard against the stucco wall behind her.

Fatima rushed to her side and cradled her stepmother. Blood seeped through the veil covering Shams' thin braids.

Openmouthed, Fatima glowered at her father. His jaw dropped as he stared in silence, perhaps as incredulous at what he had done.

Shams moaned in pain. Fatima beckoned for Faisal, who observed the scene without a word or altered expression. "Help me with your mistress."

The Sultan began. "I did not mean to…Shams ed-Duna, I would not…."

Fatima shut out the rest of whatever he might have said. She supported her stepmother's weight beneath her right shoulder, with Faisal assisting her on the left. They helped Shams at each step down the stairs.

Niranjan waited at the bottom of the landing. With a nod to Faisal, he took Shams ed-Duna in his arms. Instead of returning Shams to her rooms at the opposite end of the harem courtyard, Fatima escorted her eastward to the wing she occupied. They entered her chamber and went into the bedroom. Fatima's slave Basma had just turned down the damask coverlet.

Niranjan placed Shams on the bed. Soft shudders coursed through her body. She rolled on her left side. Tears squeezed beneath her thick lashes.

Fatima spoke to Basma. "Fetch warm water in a basin, a clean cloth and herbs for a poultice."

The servant asked, "Why, are you hurt?"

"Don't ask foolish questions! Can't you see the Sultana is in pain? Now, are you going to stand there staring all night, or can you do what I have asked?"

Basma's jaw tightened for a moment, but she complied.

Fatima shook her head, and nodded to Niranjan and Faisal. "You may leave us. I shall summon you both if you are needed."

Niranjan clasped Faisal's shoulder and waved him toward the door. The younger eunuch glanced at his mistress, before he bowed at Fatima's side and left the room, guided by Niranjan.

"I never thought Father could hurt you." Fatima sat beside her stepmother. "I didn't expect many of the things that have occurred."

Shams sniffled. "It was only his anger at your husband and Abu Ya'qub Yusuf. My brother is not the warrior our father was in life. Fatima, do not blame your father. It was an accident. I forgive him and you must, too."

Fatima's hands tightened into tiny fists. "Shams, what he did is unforgivable. No man should raise his hand to his wife. By the Prophet's beard, why is Basma taking so long?"

She went out into the antechamber, calling for her servant. Basma re-entered the apartment with everything she needed. "Why is the Sultana Shams ed-Duna hurt? What happened?"

Fatima yanked the cloths, herbs and basin of water from her grasp. "I shall clean her wound. You may go."

"Are you certain?" Basma peered around her into the larger chamber.

Fatima's gaze narrowed on her. "I don't like repeating myself, especially to someone who serves me. In the future, if I have to do so again, you shall regret it. I shall tend to Shams. You may go. Speak to no one of what you have seen."

"I would never...."

Fatima cut her off with a wave of her hand and returned to Shams ed-Duna's side. She staunched the bleeding with one of the cloths and cleaned the cut. She winced with her stepmother at every furtive touch. The poultice of dried herbs would prevent swelling, or so Fatima hoped. She bandaged Shams' head and tossed the bloodied cloths into the basin.

"Do not hate him," Shams pleaded.

Fatima sat beside her again. "Oh Shams, I wish I was more like you. You are too good, always willing to forgive even the worst in people. Do you not see that something is happening with my father? He is different. The man who raised my siblings and me with such tenderness would never have struck out at any woman. Even my mother, who reviled him all her days, was never a victim of his anger. At least, I never saw it, but perhaps I was a fool to think him incapable of such actions. He has changed, Shams. He is cruel now. The Sultan is not the father I knew, or the husband you married."

# Chapter 6
# The Crown Prince

## Princess Fatima

Gharnatah, Al-Andalus: Dhu al-Hijja 693 AH (Granada, Andalusia: November AD 1294)

Cold descended from the mountains in the month of Hajj. Fatima hugged her arms as she hurried from a visit in al-Bayazin with her old tutor, the former *Hajib* Ibn Ali, who lingered on his deathbed. She rushed past familiar buildings that had stood before her childhood, cursive script etched into the weathered marble. Niranjan followed her, his familiar footfalls scraping the cobblestone streets.

In the courtyard opposing *Al-Quasaba*, her little brother Nasr stood in a circle of young men, including their elder brother, Crown Prince Muhammad. Fatima had avoided him since her arrival in Gharnatah weeks ago. The sight of him now stirred the usual rancor in her heart, but for more than one reason.

Muhammad had grabbed the little boy, swung him up by his legs and dangled him over a cistern in the courtyard. His companions laughed at Nasr's squeals.

Fatima pushed her way through the men. She grabbed Nasr under his arms and tugged him from their brother's grasp. The little boy buried his face in her neck. His hot tears coursed along her flesh. She cradled him close and stared in horror at their brother, unable to speak.

Muhammad was exactly a year older than she was. At thirty-nine years of age, nothing in his physical appearance had changed since she had last seen him. He stood tall, the image of their father, with the same deep-set eyes, hooked nose and a fleshy mouth, almost obscured by a dark beard and moustache. However, it seemed his inclination toward cruelty had only increased.

His casual grin in the aftermath, as if he had done nothing wrong, alarmed her more than his carelessness with Nasr. "Why Fatima, I did not know you were here...."

"You wretched monster! How dare you frighten a child so, our own brother. You could have killed him!"

Muhammad laughed and clapped one of his friend's shoulders. The petty courtier made a hollow chuckle.

Fatima's brother shook his head. "Our father has another son. Besides, this one's the spawn of a slave."

"A beloved slave who holds our father's heart. What do you think the Sultan would do to you if Nasr had died?"

Muhammad crossed his arms over his barrel chest. "Nothing. I am his heir, after all."

Fatima set Nasr down and kissed his brow. She waved Niranjan over. He had stood at a respectful distance. His hand lingered on the fold in his robe, beneath which he always kept a dagger concealed, ready to strike on Fatima's behalf. As she summoned him, he drew back his hand.

"Take this boy back to his mother in the harem."

Niranjan bowed and took Nasr's hand. The little boy wrenched his fingers from the eunuch's grasp. He looked at Fatima with his chubby, moon-shaped face still red, his watery, blue gaze reflecting gratitude. Then he scuttled off to the palace, as Niranjan kept pace with him.

At the garden entrance to the Sultan's palace, Niranjan glanced over his shoulder. Fatima shook her head and he followed Nasr.

"Do you coddle your own sons in such a manner? You must be a tiresome mother to have about, Fatima. You've ruined my sport."

Muhammad rolled his eyes at her. She could not bear his thoughtlessness. Her hand came up of its own volition and she delivered a stinging slap across his cheek.

He reeled and clutched the side of his face. A thin trickle of blood seeped between his fingers, where her ring had cut him.

"You bitch! You'll be sorry for that."

"I already regret much concerning you, especially the fact that I must call you my brother."

"Wait until Father sees what you have done. You're mad!"

"Remember, Father has sons other than you. You might die before you can take the throne. Since you still have no children of your own, you cannot rely upon a legacy and heirs to follow our father."

When his face contorted in a fiery mask of fury at the reminder of his failure, she sneered and turned away from Muhammad and returned to the palace. She went to the harem, intent on Nur al-Sabah's private bedchamber.

Niranjan awaited her at the doorway to the *kadin*'s rooms, his hand on the concealed weapon at his waist. His lips had thinned in a grimace. He bowed low with his eyes averted.

She paused and clasped his shoulder. "Allah, the Compassionate, the Merciful, shall determine an appropriate fate for my brother."

He ground his teeth together and straightened. He still avoided her gaze. "If you prefer to wait on God, then so be it. Only remember that there are other moments when we must seek our own justice. It is not always the Will of God that decides men's fates."

"Muhammad is still my brother. He is no less deserving of compassion and just dealing than any other man."

"You cannot hold fair expectations of him after all these years. By the Prophet's beard, he tried to poison you! A secret you have long withheld from your husband and your father. How can you remain silent and keep Muhammad's cruelties from your father? Your brother is a dangerous animal, one who could harm those whom you love. You know him as you know yourself. Yet foolish attachment and fears impede you."

She gasped at his audacity, or perhaps, because she shared the same sentiment. To give it voice would mean she had accepted her brother Muhammad was beyond redemption. A small glimmer of hope flourished inside her that he could be the person she once knew. Even if it was a fool's hope, she could not risk harm to him. His loss would kill their father before his due time.

"Niranjan, do not gainsay me in this! He is my father's son. If I had told Father that Muhammad had tried to kill me all those years ago, Father would have condemned him. I hid the truth to spare my father such guilt. No matter what a child has done, no parent should kill his own child. How can I place such a burden upon my father? Whatever my brother's faults, his crimes, I must consider the consequences for us all, especially the Sultan."

Niranjan raised his gaze to hers. "You have always been too kind and mindful of the feelings of others. I pray you do not live to regret your generosity to Muhammad."

She bypassed him and stumbled into the antechamber. She swiped quick tears from the corners of her eyes and hurried to Nur's side. The *kadin*'s son nestled in her lap and she crooned softly to him. Shams sat beside the Sultan's favorite.

Nur placed Nasr on his pallet. He closed his eyes, his meaty hands nestled in the folds of a blanket.

The *kadin* rose, crossed the room and embraced Fatima. "Your servant told me what happened. I can only thank God you were there."

Fatima beckoned her and the queen into the antechamber, between the sleeping quarters and the receiving room.

She cautioned them, "You have to be careful with Nasr, Nur. Perhaps even you with your son, Shams ed-Duna. Muhammad is a foul, loathsome dog. He is not above hurting anyone."

Shams cupped her hand over her mouth for a moment. "I have never heard you speak so vehemently of him. This sentiment, it cannot come solely from a desire to protect Nasr or my son. What has happened between you and Muhammad in the past?"

Fatima sighed and sagged against the wall behind her. "I know how dangerous my brother is because he once tried to kill me. Promise me that you shall never reveal what I would tell you now, even to the Sultan. The knowledge would destroy him and our family."

She had not spoken of her secret in years. Yet, the words tumbled forth as though Muhammad's treachery had happened yesterday instead of fifteen years before. In the weeks before Ismail's birth, he had poisoned a slave with food that he had also offered Fatima.

Shams pecked at Fatima's tunic sleeve. "If he would risk such a move against his own sister, he is dangerous."

Fatima muttered. "I should have told Father."

"Perhaps the Sultan might have believed you then, but there was always the possibility he would not have done so. You shielded him, as you have protected Nur's son."

Nur al-Sabah shook her head, pale golden locks in disarray, as she paced the floor.

"But my son is no threat to the Crown Prince. Nasr, all of my children are the offspring of a slave. The Crown Prince is the future master of Gharnatah. He could not have meant to hurt my son, not my Nasr. They are brothers."

Fatima frowned. "I share Muhammad's blood. His mother was mine. Yet, he did not hesitate to strike against me and the son I carried in my womb. I still don't know why he did it, but I do not doubt he intended my death. I warn both of you, keep your sons away from him. I cannot hide my brother's treachery from Father any longer. He must learn of it now, of this incident with Nasr and the harm Muhammad poses to the boy."

A spasm crossed Nur al-Sabah's face and she stopped pacing. Her hands trembled, as she clasped them together like a supplicant.

"Fatima, no! Please do not say anything to your father, I pray. You saved Nasr from any possible harm. I do not know what would have happened had you not been there. Yet, you were and I am grateful. Now, please, leave it be."

Fatima gawked in disbelief. "What? You cannot mean that! If Muhammad had eased his grip upon Nasr, he would have died. Why would you hide such a thing from my father?"

The *kadin*'s eyes watered. "Fatima, it is over. We have been friends for some years now. I have never asked anything of you before, but I make this request now. Please, forget this day."

She fled into her bedchamber. Muffled sobs drifted from the room.

Fatima stared in her wake, incredulous. Then she turned to Shams ed-Duna. "I cannot keep such secrets from my father. If I had told him of my suspicions before, perhaps he would have dealt with my brother long ago. When I tell Father about Nasr now, Nur shall have nothing to fear."

Shams ed-Duna looked at her askance. "Why shouldn't Nur be afraid of your revelation to the Sultan? Muhammad is the Crown Prince of Gharnatah. Nur al-Sabah is a slave. For now, she shares your father's confidences and his bed. What shall befall her, when the Sultan breathes his last and your brother succeeds him? Forget Muhammad's behavior and be grateful that Allah, the Compassionate, the Merciful, sent you to intervene before Nasr died."

"Then, you believe Muhammad would have dropped Nasr into that cistern, as I do?"

Shams pursed her lips and crossed her arms over her chest. "Of course, I do. In my time as your father's wife, I have come to know his family, his children very well. I do not doubt Muhammad would have hurt Nasr if he believed he might escape justice for his crimes."

"Then, why do you agree with Nur al-Sabah?"

"You invite more harm to your little brother and the *kadin* by speaking out. Muhammad witnessed Nasr's return to the palace followed by your own. He knows you must have now warned Nur al-Sabah about him. Your brother is no fool. If you speak to the Sultan, he shall punish Muhammad. The Crown Prince may not rebel against his father, but he shall surely retaliate against Nasr and his mother. Do not endanger them both. The truth would only destroy your father now. Forget the past. Preserve the future."

On the next morning, Fatima stood alone in the second floor apartments of her father, awaiting his arrival. In winter, everyone in Gharnatah retreated to apartments on the second floor. She gripped his bejeweled *khanjar*. Lapis lazuli and gold filigree covered the leather sheath in ornate, swirling designs.

She removed the weapon from its encasing. It had been her grandfather's dagger. Her father kept it in his quarters, among the possessions he prized for display. The metal felt cold, but light against her palm. How many people had her grandfather killed with it?

"Are you contemplating murder, daughter?"

Her father's sudden appearance startled her. Fatima's fingers closed on the blade and it sliced into her palm. He rushed to her side. She opened her hand and revealed a long, bloody gash.

Her father took the dagger, while she dipped her hand in the ornate fountain at the corner of the room. Afterward, she accepted a clean cloth from him and bound the wound.

"No more playing with weapons for you," he said. "At least, not until I'm around to save you."

She mimicked his animated smile, but her mood did not allow for levity. His expression smoothed. He must have sensed the tension roiling inside her.

"Your note was delivered to me just after the council meeting. What could be so urgent, Fatima? Has something happened to one of my grandchildren?"

"No, I have had no news from Malaka since my arrival. Amoda knows well enough to write if something is wrong with the children. They miss you and long to see you again."

He turned toward the fountain. "Fatima, you know my grandchildren are welcome at any time in Gharnatah."

"Even after your executioner has murdered their father?"

Her shaking hand, wrapped in linen, closed on his shoulder. He stiffened at her touch. Despite it, she willed courage into her voice.

"Father, this cannot continue. How long shall you imprison my husband?"

He scowled into the depths of the fountain. The ripples of water made the reflection of his face appear blurred and older than his fifty-eight years.

"Fatima, do not speak of matters that do not concern you. When I am ready, I shall decide Faraj's fate. You cannot sway my decision. It's useless to try."

She shook her head. "Would you have me forsake him? You are my father and Faraj is my husband. Both of you are the two men I love most in this world."

"His actions have shamed me before the Marinids. I cannot ask you to choose between your father and your husband. You must decide."

He shuffled toward his writing desk and sank down on the cushioned stool with a grunt. She eyed him through vision blurred by unshed tears.

His anger rose swiftly these days. The years had changed him. The incident with Shams ed-Duna nearly two weeks before proved it. Although he apologized later to his queen with a gift of a turquoise and gold filigree necklace, Fatima had never seen her stepmother so withdrawn and submissive in her father's presence. Perhaps, Shams feared he had become a tyrant, like her former second husband.

Over his shoulder, the Sultan asked, "Did you come only to plead for forgiveness for your husband?"

She stared at his rigid back. "No. There is something else. Father, I have always trusted your judgment...."

He turned to her and raised a dismissive hand. "Then, trust me in matters concerning your husband. Consider him lucky that he lives in the security of my jail for now. If he were any other man, I would have executed him upon his arrival. It is my right."

Fatima nodded and bowed before him, though her heart pounded a tattoo behind her chest.

He gestured toward a carved cedar stool beside his seat. She settled next to him, gathering the silken folds of her *jubba* around her. Her stomach knotted and she drew a deep breath before speaking.

"Father, I must talk with you about the Crown Prince."

He raised one dark, russet-colored eyebrow in a questioning slant. "Your brother? What mischief has Muhammad done now?"

"He has not done anything wrong."

She had kept her word with Nur and Shams ed-Duna. She would not reveal the incident between Muhammad and Nasr. How her heart lurched and tore at the lie, but Muhammad's petty actions the day before paled in enormity to the risk he posed to the Sultanate.

She nibbled at her lower lip and glanced at her father, who waited in silence. Did she dare reveal secrets of the past?

What would he say if she told him how Muhammad had tried to kill her years ago? Would he believe her? The enormity of her quandary threatened to tear her heart in two. He could dismiss her words as fanciful or cruel imaginings, without any evidence. She could not bear his mistrust any more than she might have withstood his furious anger if he believed her. Muhammad's treachery would be a bitter blow for her father. If he condemned her brother, she would be responsible for her father's guilt over Muhammad.

The truth damned her as did further secrecy. Muhammad's impulsive and cruel nature signaled a dire future for more than just her family. A man like him, who could consider the murder of a once beloved sister, was capable of anything. If he ascended the throne, he would become a tyrant.

There had to be some other way to warn her father about his heir, something that would not result in the Sultan ordering his own son's execution. She would spare her father that burden at any cost, even if it meant she must conceal painful truths from him forever.

"Father, you know I would not speak ill against my own brother without just cause. I am concerned for Muhammad and the throne he shall inherit."

She stood and paced for a time. Her father's watchful gaze followed her. "Fatima, speak plainly."

She gathered strength from his plain interest. If he did not care about her opinions, he would have dismissed her without entertaining further discussion.

"Muhammad should be dearer to me than the sons of Shams ed-Duna and Nur al-Sabah, because he is the only son of my mother." She paused and gauged his reaction.

When he gave her a look of uneasy puzzlement, she rushed on. "Still, I have long suspected that his reckless nature as a child would make him a dangerous man. He cannot follow you on the throne of Gharnatah."

Her father stood. "You want me to deny my eldest son the succession? Do you forget the traditions my late father established, that it is the eldest son who should rule?"

Although his tone was even, the words belied his expression. His brow knitted, the veins in his neck stood out in livid ridges, while his gaze raked over her face.

She said, "My grandfather chose you as his heir because you are a wise and good man. He could have chosen from among my uncles or his own brothers. Grandfather saw the strength in you. He did not act simply because you were his eldest son. You have always held the conviction to do what is right. The humility to admit when you are wrong. My brother does not have these qualities. He is not fit to rule."

He slumped on his seat again and shook his head. "You have requested an audience only to tell me who should sit on my throne? You dare much, my daughter."

"Father, I meant no disrespect."

His gaze narrowed. "Yet you show me much the same, as your own husband has done! His ill-mannered ways have tainted you."

Mistrust darkened his expression. She had seen that look before, directed at other people, never toward her.

"Do you deny that my brother is unpredictable?"

"He is my son, as you are my daughter! Have you no loyalty even to him? Is your only duty to your husband?"

"Father, this matter we speak of has naught to do with the conflict between you and Faraj. The future of your country is at stake. Would you see your son destroy your legacy of learning and just laws because of some misplaced sentiment toward him?"

"Misplaced sentiment!" His voice thundered through the room. "You dare call my love for him 'misplaced sentiment' and expect me to listen. I thought you knew my heart and the honor with which I still revere his mother...."

"She is gone, Father. Gone! Do you think Aisha would know a mother's love and pride in Muhammad?"

"She never loved him! She never loved any of you! She abandoned you for the sake of the Ashqilula. Or, do you forget that, too?"

She turned away, as memories flooded her mind. Now that she was a mother, she understood the complexity of a parent's emotions. If anything, her experiences in the last day of her mother's life had taught her to show each of her children her devotion, so that they might always be certain of her love.

"It is the past, Father, it cannot be undone. Aisha's son does not honor you. Muhammad squanders the privileges you have given him. If he succeeds you, he shall make a mockery of every achievement you have attained."

She knelt before him and grasped his hand. He pulled it away, but she reached for him again. "I do not submit these claims with an easy heart or take pleasure in my warnings. Muhammad can never become Sultan of Gharnatah. If you love your people, if you love this land of your children's birth, do not allow pride and emotion to sway you. Your great father taught you that the future of Gharnatah is all that matters. If you would see the prosperity of this state continue, do not let Muhammad inherit. Do not leave such a legacy to your people."

He closed his eyes and blotted out the sight of her. She willed him to open them again, but he did not.

"Father, please think upon all I have said."

"You have said quite enough, Fatima. Leave me now, before I forget that you are the daughter I have loved and treasured above all your sisters. Just as you have forgotten I am your honored father and the duty you have always owed to me."

She raised the hem of his *jubba* to her lips and forehead. He opened his eyes then, but stared straight at the alabaster wall, his face like a statue carved of stone. She rose and left him. The door closed with a resounding thud at her back.

Deep in her heart, she knew she would regret hiding the extent of Muhammad's cruelty from her father for the rest of her life.

# Chapter 7
# Exile

## Princess Fatima

Gharnatah, Al-Andalus: Muharram 694 AH (Granada, Andalusia: December AD 1294)

Fatima wallowed in unending misery. For two months, her father had held Faraj at *Al-Quasaba*, with no apparent intention of releasing him. Her husband's travail had taken its toll on her. It also claimed more than just his brother's life.

She reclined on a pallet in the room she had occupied as a child, a marble alcove that connected with three others and rose to the height of a domed ceiling. The gold filigree and lapis-lazuli, which had once decorated the dome, was gone. White patches coated chips and cracks in the walls. The wind had swept leaves into each abandoned alcove. Stillness reigned in her former chamber, silent as a tomb.

It seemed so long ago that she had lain here with her sisters, each dreaming of their futures. Now, all of her sisters were long gone from this place, wed with children of their own. Only Alimah still resided within the Sultanate.

Soft voices drifted from beyond the alcoves, from the courtyard lined with myrtles and slender columns. Fatima squeezed her eyes shut, as if in doing so, she might shut out the murmurs of concern. A tear crept beneath her lashes and lingered on her cheek, before she swiped it away. Tears would change nothing, not even her losses.

"...Shall be well?" That was Niranjan's warble, pitched low.

She turned her face to the wall, hating the pity that softened his voice.

"...must take precautions....No more children...."

Fatima clapped her hands over her ears, something she had not done since her girlhood, when thunder and lightning frightened her. She did not want to hear anything else the Jewish midwife had to say.

Niranjan's gentle, common touch on her arm stirred her. When she opened her eyes, she found him crouched beside her, a gentle smile fixed on his lips. Somehow, it did not reach his eyes, which were wide and watering. She turned her face to the wall again. She could deal with her own hurt, but not his sorrow for her.

"The Sultana Shams ed-Duna has gone to the Sultan with assurances of your health. The *kadin* is escorting the midwife out of the harem. Your father's women have promised to return, when you are prepared to receive visitors."

"I wish they would leave me be!"

Fatima palmed her empty belly, where only yesterday, the child she had nurtured for months nestled inside of her. Tears coursed down her cheeks, unchecked this time.

Niranjan sighed and stood. He pressed his back against the wall next to the pallet and stood beside her with his head bowed.

Fatima kept to her room and saw no one, except for Niranjan, Basma and Haniya. If her rejection hurt Shams or Nur, she did not concern herself with the possibility. Each day, they came to inquire after her welfare and always, Niranjan turned them away with assurances that she was well.

Yet, she was not. Regret tormented her and disturbed her sleep. She dreaded nightfall, for it signaled the return to the bloody nightmares that haunted her. Faraj had never known about their child and now, he never would. She had to convince her father to release him.

One week afterward, Niranjan came to her alcove. "The Sultan summons you. He has sent a litter with bearers for your comfort."

Fatima looked around the dimly lit room. The stub of a beeswax candle flickered on a low table near the sole window, providing scant illumination. The cedar shutters covering the lattice window kept the hour a secret.

She rubbed at her sore, swollen eyes before she pushed back the damask coverlet and rose from the pallet. Her feet sank into a multicolored rug.

She mumbled, "What hour is it?"

"Just before dawn," Haniya answered from across the room. She held a candle aloft, lighting the brass lanterns affixed to the stucco wall.

"Where's your sister?" Fatima asked. "She should be helping you with that."

Haniya shrugged. "I have not seen Basma this morning. She slept on the floor beside me. When I awoke, she was gone."

Fatima shook her head and cleared her muddled thoughts. "Father wants to see me now? Is he ill, Niranjan?" Then she covered her mouth, even as a terrified shriek escaped her. "He intends to execute my husband today! It can be the only reason he would call for me at such an hour!"

When she swayed, Niranjan grasped her arm and held her steady. "You cannot know, my Sultana."

He reached for her woolen mantle on a peg and she slipped into its warmth. She shoved her bare feet into red leather boots. Niranjan folded the ermine trim over the band.

The gray morning of Gharnatah awaited her just beyond the entrance to the chamber, as did six bearers burdened by a litter on their shoulders. They lowered it to the ground. She stepped in and sagged against the silken pillows inside. The myrtle trees appeared like aloof sentinels braving the cold. She closed her eyes and shut out the bleak and colorless world around her. Even the bushes and borders, which had still blossomed with flowers at her return, were naked now.

The litter bearers carried her the short distance between the eastern and western wing of her father's harem. When they set her down, she groped for Niranjan's familiar hand. He helped her stand outside her father's door.

Sentries lined the wall, their teeth chattering, gazes fixed on the marble tiles at her feet. Torches flickered over their heads, their profiles cast in long shadows against the cold, dank walls. Two of the guards opened the massive, olive wood doors.

Niranjan released her and stood with his head bowed beside the litter. She clasped his shoulder in gratitude. He was always at her side when she needed him.

"My loyal one. Stay here until I return."

He offered her a curt nod.

Fatima found her father at his writing desk. His hand, dotted with brown age spots, hovered over a roll of parchment. He put down his quill and faced her.

A pungent scent like burnt hemp assailed her nostrils. She snorted in disgust at the odor and sought out the source. A metal brazier emitted vapors in the corner. She bowed before the Sultan and plodded toward him, with her eyes downcast.

Light shimmered in the chamber and she blinked against its harsh gaze. Of late, no matter the time of day, her father demanded several torches and lanterns lit in his rooms. Perhaps his eyesight was failing as he aged.

She remembered the days before his rule, when he was Crown Prince and she, his beloved daughter. The child whom he had taught chess and poetry, who shared his love of learning and brought him great joy at each of her accomplishments. Now, there were no more pleasant interludes between them. Now, she was the wife of a man her father no longer trusted. The moments where he was not the Sultan of Gharnatah, just her father, no longer existed. Perhaps, they never had since she was a child.

She bowed low at his feet and brought the hem of his *jubba* to her lips. As she stood, breath hitched inside her chest at the redness in his eyes, dark shadows beneath them. Had he slept fitfully or not at all? His pupils loomed large and glittered like the new moon.

She said nothing and waited for him. Their last exchange in this chamber still pained her, yet her regret at having caused him anguish would not give way to her fierce instincts. He was wrong about Faraj and he was wrong about Muhammad also.

It had never occurred to her, in all her years of devotion to her father that he could ever fall short of her esteem. Age had hardened his natural inclination toward bitter hatred of those who thwarted him, yet imbued him with love for a son who did not deserve his trust.

Sudden tears gathered in his hawk-eyed gaze. The sight of them tore at her heart. Before they could fall, she embraced him.

He slumped against her. Instead of staggering, she supported his weight with ease. He seemed so frail in her arms. How had the change in his statute and size gone unnoticed?

"Can you forgive me, daughter?"

His voice quavered against her hair, but she heard the question clearly. A lump swelled in her throat. "Oh, Father, what have you done that requires my forgiveness? Please, do not say that you have...."

He drew back, tears coursing along the lines of his leathery complexion. "No, first, you must do this for me. You must promise you shall forgive me. I am so sorry for what I said about your feelings toward your brother."

The breath caught in her throat. She wanted to rail against him. Her concern did not linger on her damnable brother Muhammad. What of Faraj's fate?

Yet, she forced herself to cup her father's cheek and meet his watery gaze. He smiled despite the tears, his eyes crinkling at the corners.

"You must know, I forgive you too, Fatima."

She blinked hard and gaped at him. "You forgive me?"

"Well, of course I do," he said, still bearing his cheerful expression. "You did not intend to hurt me with those words you said. I know that now. Your concerns for your brother are unfounded. He takes care of me and of you, too. You just don't realize it, because you have not lived with us for many years. You don't understand Muhammad. You shall see his goodness now."

She shook her head and withdrew from his familiar comfort. He did not believe the truth about her brother. Otherwise, he could not believe such things. She rubbed her arms again, despite the warmth of the room. Whatever had caused his sudden good mood, it had been a fool's hope to think he would deny Muhammad the throne. She looked heavenward with a long sigh. What would it take to make him listen?

She swiped at the tears of frustration in her eyes. "I cannot go on this way, Father. Please, tell me you have decided my husband's fate."

"Of course I have. Muhammad helped me see the truth. He has swayed my heart with his sound reasoning." He rubbed his hands together with a chuckle. "Faraj must live, you see, he must live to support Muhammad in the succession. My son shall need strong aides at his side to help him rule well. Your brother reminded me of that fact. He made me promise I wouldn't do anything to Prince Faraj. I won't. See, look here, I have already signed the decree which orders your husband's release."

Fatima could have fainted with the shock at his rambling answer. He tugged her toward the writing desk and gestured, with a childlike grin, at the parchment. She read the words, written in the Sultan's style of cursive *Naksh* calligraphy.

"This decree bans my husband from court unless the Sultan summons him."

Her father nodded vigorously. "Yes, yes, see, he is welcome at any time in which I or my son may summon him. He can never come to Gharnatah again as he is done, or he shall die. He must obey me, you understand, you must make him obey me."

He paced and continued rubbing his hands together. "I could have had him executed. I intended to, but your brother has made me see that I could not do this. No, no, I could not. Faraj has to live, but he has to obey. He has to. He has to...."

She sank down on his stool while he repeated the words. She did not know what to make of anything he said. Confusion tainted her joy, as his mutterings grew feverish. His frenetic steps matched the fervor of his words. He spoke words she could understand, just an incoherent babble as he whirled back and forth. She stood and grabbed his shoulders. While she held him steady, his gaze raked over her face and he blinked rapidly, as though unsure if he was seeing her.

"Father, you are not well."

He stared in silence. She leaned toward him.

"Father, can you understand what I'm telling you?"

A dark scowl marred his face and he wrenched himself from her grasp.

"Of course, I can! I am not deaf or foolish, Fatima, no matter that you seem to think I am. I have done what you wanted. I freed your husband. Still, you harangue me, just as your mother did. Perhaps, you are more like her than I realized. Yes, she was just the same, like you. She didn't want you to marry Faraj, you know, told me so many times...."

His voice trailed off and he covered his face with his fingers. Soft sobs echoed through the quiet room, before he lowered his hands again. His frigid stare sent shards of ice through her, as bitter as the chill outside.

"You shouldn't do that all the time, make me think of her whenever I see you. You know I loved her. I loved her too much. I hated her also. She was never good to me, or you, your brother and sisters. You shouldn't remind me of her."

His hands tightened into fists. She drew back, as his features hardened. For the first time in her life, she feared he might strike her. Something he had never done.

He shook his head. "I know you cannot help it. You have her nature. I know that. I have always known it, always...."

As he fell into disjointed rambling again, she gazed at him, incredulous.

"Father, truly, you are unwell. I think you should go to your bed."

His voice convulsed in bubbly laughter. His actions startled her more than the slap she had anticipated. He drew back, holding his belly as he bent over. A snort escaped him before a wheezing chuckle followed.

He wiped the corners of his eyes with gnarled fingers and then shook his head at her. "I am in excellent health or so my physician said when I summoned him earlier."

Fatima wondered whether the same doctor from many years ago remained at the Sultan's side. He must be an old man by now. Why would her father have him shuffling about in the cold at such an early hour?

"It is not even daybreak, yet you have called for your personal physician already?"

"He sees me twice a day, once early in the morning and then in the evening, before I enjoy my meals."

"Twice a day? Why would that be necessary if you were not ill?"

"It was Muhammad's idea. He recommended the man after my old doctor died in his sleep."

Confusion muddied her thoughts. She could no longer bear to look at him. The man who stood before her was no longer the loving, learned father she remembered. Something had affected these sudden shifts in his mood. How else could she explain his giddy euphoria as he spoke of releasing Faraj, followed by his tears, scorn and laughter, which then devolved into mere tolerance? Such a tempestuous emotional display was too abrupt to be normal.

He shuffled to her side and took her hands in his. "Fatima, look at me."

She feared what she would see. Yet, when she turned to him, his face no longer bore the animated expression of just a moment ago.

He pulled her close in a familiar hug. "Don't be afraid. Your brother takes care of me. He is dutiful toward his father."

She sighed against his shoulder. "Still, I remain concerned."

A soft chuckle rumbled through his chest. "I know you do. All daughters worry for their aged fathers. Be assured, I have my health and strength."

She drew back in the circle of his arms and looked up at him. How she wanted to believe him.

He traced a finger across her brow. "I shall release your husband today. When you are well, when you have healed from your travail, you may join him at Malaka."

When she nodded, he kissed her brow and hugged her again. She held him closer this time, still fighting against tears that fell anyway. They should have been tears of happiness, but they were not.

Only one person knew her father as intimately as Fatima did. Nur al-Sabah could help her understand some of the changes in him. Fatima left his quarter and went across the harem to the *kadin*'s apartments, opposite her stepmother's own at the end of the hall. Niranjan trailed a discreet distance behind her. His familiar footfalls could not quell the fear and uncertainty crowding her heart.

She knocked at the door twice, before Nur al-Sabah's Galician body slave, Sabela, opened the door. Sabela's eyes widened. She glanced over her shoulder, before her thinned lips softened into an insipid grin.

Fatima asked. "Is the lady Nur still asleep? I know the hour is yet early."

Dim light filtered through the silk curtains draped over the archway behind her. Sabela hesitated before she spoke. "No, my Sultana, but…."

Fatima slipped past her. "Then, I must see her."

"Wait, the *kadin* is busy!"

Fatima pushed the curtains aside. Nur sat with her back to the entrance, hunched over a low table. She shouted over her shoulder.

"Sabela, what are you doing? Come quickly, you must take this to the Sultan. See that he is alone when you bring it to him. No one must see him swallow it."

Fatima rounded the table and stared down at the *kadin*.

Nur gaped at her with a face flushed pink. "Fatima! You startled me. You should be resting."

On the table, a small silver cup held a thick mixture with small bits of yellowed pulp floating inside.

"What is that you're giving my father?"

Nur took the goblet in her hand. Fatima's gaze froze on the drinking vessel, which Nur held with such care.

Her heart hammered deep inside her chest, ready to burst forth. She closed her eyes for a moment and then scrutinized Nur. The pink hue that colored her face now deepened.

Fatima knocked the cup out of her hand, spilling the viscous liquid all over the table. Nur stood and drew back, gasping at the stains on her trousers.

"Have you lost your senses?"

Fatima's hands curled into tight fists. "Oh, no, I assure you. What poison were you concocting?"

The *kadin*'s eyes widened. "Poison? Fatima, I would never…you think I would dare poison the Sultan?"

"Then tell me what you were doing! What were you preparing to give him?"

Her failure to answer stirred a fury in Fatima. She lunged at her. Her nails pressed against the large vein at the side of her throat. She drove her backward. Nur hit the wall behind her with a strangled cry. Her screams vied with her servant's own.

"Tell me, you viper!"

"It's nothing!"

"Liar! Why were you telling your slave to be so secretive, if you did not want to harm my father? You shall tell me, or I swear I'll choke the very breath from you!"

Strong hands grabbed Fatima's shoulders and pulled her away from the *kadin*. "My Sultana, what are you doing?"

She struggled against Niranjan's hold. "Let me go! She is as a snake in my father's house! He loves her." She stabbed a finger at Nur. "He gave you a home, children, jewels, slaves to obey your every whim. Yet, you have betrayed him. You betrayed me! You had my trust and spat on it, when you tried to hurt my father!"

Nur clutched at her throat, at the red marks where Fatima's nails had scored her pale flesh.

Fatima lunged for her again, but Niranjan's grip tightened. "My Sultana, please stop! You do not know what you are saying."

She railed at him. "Do not protect her! You don't know she's trying to poison Father."

"No, my Sultana," Niranjan said. "I know what the *kadin* was doing. I helped her."

She pulled free from his hold, shrank away and staggered to the opposite wall. She curled at its base. They were deceived, both she and her father, by those whom they trusted. When Niranjan advanced on her, she warded him off with her hands. "Get away from me!"

He knelt at her side. She closed her eyes and blotted out the sight of him. She would have never believed it possible, but he had shattered the trust between them, a bond born out of her mother's cruel murder.

"My Sultana, please listen to me. It was no poison. It was the juice from mandrakes. It could never harm anyone. The Sultan desired it to increase his virility. The *kadin* knew my understanding of the nature of plants. She asked me to secure the mandrakes, knowing that I could render them harmless."

Fatima cupped her forehead and chuckled.

"By the Prophet's beard, Niranjan! The Sultan has fathered nineteen children! Yet, you would have me believe he needs something to maintain his potency."

"My Sultana, your father has sired three sons and sixteen daughters in his lifetime, but he has also aged. He is not the man of youth and vitality from your girlhood. The last child born in this harem was the lady Nur's Nasr. That was seven years ago. For a man of your father's potency, it is perhaps difficult to acknowledge that he may no longer be capable of siring children. The *kadin* only sought a way to restore his vigor. She never intended to harm him. I would never have allowed it, if I thought the juice of the mandrake could hurt him."

When Niranjan stood and clasped his hands together, Fatima looked up at him.

He said, "The lady Nur remembered that in her village, the Christians said that mandrake made men and women fertile and restored their desires. Nur al-Sabah and I discussed its properties with the Sultan. He believed it would help. I procured it and the *kadin* gives it to the Sultan in private. How do you think he would feel if anyone else knew he needed something to maintain his stamina? Your father has his pride, my Sultana, as all men do. He would feel great shame. That is why Sabela visits him when he is alone."

"But mandrake is poisonous! Everyone knows that."

"No, my Sultana, only when the fruit is not ripe. Otherwise, it cannot harm. You were wrong to accuse the lady Nur. The *kadin* loves your father. She could never hurt him."

A little sob hiccupped in the room. Fatima's brother Nasr stood at the archway, partially hidden behind the curtain. Tears streamed down his face. He must have witnessed the entire exchange.

Fatima stood and stretched out her hand. "Nasr, come."

He fled into his mother's bedchamber with a long wail. Sabela followed him.

A heavy weight settled in Fatima's stomach. She glanced at Nur. "I didn't know. I'm so sorry, I didn't know."

Nur shook her head. Her soft tresses cascaded around her shoulders, but could not hide the reddened marks covering her neck.

"I have to comfort Nasr. Please leave, Fatima."

She followed in the wake of Sabela and her son.

Niranjan stared at Fatima, his gaze soft and filled with compassion. She could not meet his stare. When she left the chamber, he followed in silence.

Later in the morning, Fatima told Shams what had happened. Her stepmother faced the window. The morning breeze stirred her thick braids and the damask wall hangings.

"I am less certain about the effects of mandrake than Nur. It was enough that your father believed, Fatima."

"Why didn't anyone tell me?"

Shams turned to her with an upraised eyebrow. "You ask after all you have suffered? I thought you had enough burdens to bear. Besides, there was no need for you to know of my husband's failings. Such matters are the concerns of a wife and a *kadin*, not his children."

Fatima sobbed into her hands. Shams came to her and stroked her arm.

"Nur loves your father. I adore the Sultan and cherish him for the children and the respect he has given me as his wife. Nur and I, we would never do anything to harm him. We value your friendship too much. You have hurt Nur al-Sabah badly, beyond those marks I saw on her neck. Yes, I spoke with her before you and I met. That you could think her capable of such deceit...I think you have wounded her to her very soul."

Haniya begged entry at Shams ed-Duna's door. She gave Fatima a letter, before she departed.

As Fatima read, a deep sigh escaped her. Would everything go wrong at this moment?

"What troubles you?"

"It's a letter from Malaka. My baby Saliha is very ill. The pox has descended on the city. The other children have all endured it, but for fear of their safety, my sister Alimah believes they should abandon Malaka. Amoda writes that my sister has taken the entire family to an estate in the mountains of al-Bajara, which Faraj gave to Alimah's son, so that he might have a home of his own. I must return. Father said he would release Faraj today."

"Fatima, you are in no condition to travel. The midwife cautioned you to let your body heal. You cannot risk it. Your Amoda shall care for Saliha. You cannot tend to your daughter in such a weakened state. You must stay here."

"What sort of mother am I? I have abandoned my children to sickness and death for their father's sake. Shall my heart always be torn in two?"

Shams ed-Duna sighed and returned to the window that overlooked the garden courtyard. "You are a loving mother and wife. Trust in Allah, the Compassionate, the Merciful that all shall be well with your daughter. She shall have her father again. It must be enough for now."

## *Prince Faraj*

The light blinded Faraj, as he staggered out of the dank cold at *Al-Quasaba* into the full light of midday. The sentry behind him shoved him up the last of the stone-carved steps and into the open courtyard. He glanced around him at the stone-built barracks of the Sultan's warriors, many of whom lingered in their doorways and eyed him.

He stumbled on a sharp, red stone. It cut into the bare soles of his feet. The jailor had taken his shoes and weapons and consigned him to darkness, with only the rats and the echo of Khalid's voice in the adjoining cell for company. Even now, his captain supported him with a hand on his elbow. He nodded to Khalid, grateful.

While six guardsmen surrounded them, the jailor removed the manacles encircling his wrists and ankles. Beneath, the metal had rubbed the flesh raw and red. He winced as crisp air touched the broken skin for the first time in many weeks. How long had he been mired in that place? After the third week, he had stopped counting the days while he awaited his execution.

Now the moment had come. At least, the jailor had released him from the brutal shackles. His clothing stank. Little, black insects crawled on his arms and through his hair. Yet, he vowed to meet God with conviction in his heart that he had done the right thing. If only it did not mean leaving Fatima behind.

He closed his heavy-lidded, stinging eyes. When the Sultan's guard had taken him to *Al-Quasaba*, at one point, he had imagined Fatima's voice ringing through the complex. Yet how could that have been? She was safe at home, in Malaka with their dear children. One day, they would see each other in Paradise again. Perhaps then, she would greet him with tears of joy, rather than the heartbreak she had shown at their last moment together.

He whispered, "But, not too soon, my beloved. I shall wait for you, always."

"What's that you're saying?" Khalid asked at his shoulder.

"Nothing." Faraj opened his eyes and nodded to his captain. "At least, I shall have a companion in death."

Khalid's grim smile did not soften his features. "If that is our fate. I don't see the executioner."

"Are you so eager to die?"

"At each day, we are a moment closer to death. I do not fear it. I would have liked to have said farewell to Amoda and kissed her just once. I shall always regret that I never did."

He fell silent and gazed in the direction of the gateway. Faraj followed his stare.

The Sultan shuffled as he shaded his eyes from the glare of sunlight. Fierce winds whipped through the alleys and along the ramparts of *Al-Quasaba*. The Sultan's robes billowed around his legs. His bodyguards protected him on three sides. His red-rimmed eyes revealed a lack of sleep.

Faraj scratched at an itch in his beard, before he frowned. The men who had followed him from Tarif marched behind the Sultan's guards. Had they remained in Gharnatah all this time? He had thought the Sultan ordered their deaths beforehand.

At his back, Khalid said, "The Sultan must intend to execute all of us at the same time. We have lived at your side and we shall meet you in death, my prince."

When the Sultan halted, everyone fell on their knees and their foreheads touched the ground. Faraj waited until his master's footfalls resumed and then stopped beside him. He did not dare raise his head.

Without preamble, the Sultan said, "I release you and those of your house. Go from my sight, from my city and return to Malaka at once, where you shall remain until I summon you. Do not return to Gharnatah except at the command of your Sultan. Do it and you shall die. I swear it.

"Upon your return, you shall summon the household of your brother, Muhammad. They shall live with you at Malaka, where you must raise them as my father raised you. Your eldest daughter shall marry your brother's son. The union shall seal the breach between you and your brother. You are as much to blame for his death, as his own avarice. Therefore, you should bear the burdens of his household. It is just that you should repay their loss."

He turned on his heels, the hem of his silken *jubba* trailing behind him. Faraj raised his head and caught sight of him, before he rounded a corner and disappeared through the gate.

With Khalid's help, Faraj stood and raked a hand over his face. His men surrounded him, tooth-filled grins and cheers breaking their formerly stoic facades.

Khalid slapped him on the back. "Another time, my prince."

Faraj nodded. "Yes, another time. Let us return home."

He shook his head in wonderment as his men escorted him through the gate. The horses they had ridden from Malaka awaited them.

A plump woman in white veils and a green mantle trimmed with ermine stood beside his mount, a black eunuch at her back. Her long, dark fingers patted the forelock of his stallion.

He gestured for his men to stop and closed the distance between him and the woman. He sank on his knees before her. "My Sultana."

Shams ed-Duna asked, "You recognized me?"

"There is only one woman with your queenly bearing. Forgive me, for I am an affront to your tender eyes in my wretched state."

She mused, "You are, but not for the reasons you would assume."

She rounded him, her black eyes hard as obsidian between the slits of her veils. "I must ask if you love Fatima."

His jaw tightened. "You do not need to ask."

"It seems I must, for how else can I explain how you have tormented her these last two months?"

Had such time truly passed in which he sat in squalor, apart from his beloved and their children?

Shams ed-Duna continued. "You men and your stupid, selfish honor and pride! It means more to you than the love of your women, than the sake of your children. The Sultan and Fatima have told me of your foolishness. Did you think of her when you risked your life? Did you ever consider how your children might feel?"

He hung his head. Fatima had tormented him with the same queries, yet he did not heed them. He had risked everything for his principles. If given another chance, would he make the same choice, to stand and fight for his beliefs despite the consequences? Would love and duty sway his heart?

"My prince, you cannot know how they have suffered in your absence, how Fatima has endured this trial."

"I shall never burden her so again. I make this vow to you and, upon my return home, to her. I shall hold her close to me and kiss the heads of our children."

"Fatima is not at Malaka. She has been here since your arrival." At his gasp, she added, "Did you truly believe she would have remained there, awaiting the news of your fate?"

"Is she the reason her father released me?"

Shams ed-Duna placed her hands on her hips. "My husband's judgment remains sound. He can think for himself, without his children's or anyone else's aid! You live because he determined it would be better to keep you at Malaka. Do not mistake his kindness for sentiment. You deserve none!"

Faraj stood and swiped at his knees. Thick grime coated his fingers. "I would never dare think it."

The Sultana sneered at the sight of him. "Then go from this place as my husband has commanded."

"No, I should wait for Fatima. I cannot leave her behind."

"Yet, you did at Malaka."

"It is different now. Please, would you let me see her?"

"She would wish to leave with you, as well, but she cannot. Your family awaits you in al-Bajara. Your daughter Saliha has the pox."

"All the more reason Fatima must come home with me!"

"She is too weak. I told you, she has suffered cruelly. She lost your babe."

He staggered. "She was with child?"

"She was."

"She never said anything, not before I left for Tarif, not even afterward when I saw her at Malaka. Was the child alive?"

"No, it was a stillbirth. The babe had fully formed, but he would never have lived outside the womb."

Her words stabbed his heart. "He? It was a boy?"

"Afterward, Fatima confided in me that she had always wanted to give you another son. She has lived for thirty-eight years, now thirty of them as your wife. In nearly seventeen years since Prince Ismail's birth, she has given you eight other children. Now, the midwife believes there should be no more babies.

"Surely, you must remember your concubines. Yet, you neglect them, according to your wife. Do you fear she shall think you do not hold her in your heart if you summon them? What other purpose do such women serve than to ease a husband's lusts and lessen the possibility of numerous pregnancies? If you love Fatima, if you would see her survive, you must not father another child upon her. A woman's body can bear only so much."

"Why didn't she tell me about the child at Malaka?"

The Sultana shook her head. "Perhaps she did not wish to burden you. If only you had been so kind to her."

Shams ed-Duna gave him a curt nod in farewell and swept from the courtyard. Her eunuch followed.

# Chapter 8
# In Shadows

## Princess Fatima

Gharnatah, Al-Andalus: Safar 694 AH (Granada, Andalusia: January AD 1295)

Fatima sat at a cedar writing desk on a high stool, beside the window on the second story of her childhood home. The mid-afternoon sun glinted through the unfurled lattice. She looked into the courtyard of myrtles below, as movement caught her eye.

She grimaced at the sight of her brother Muhammad, his dark hair slick with a sheen of oil. He walked in the direction of the Sultan's rooms, beside a man dressed in the attire of a Castillan knight. The stranger wore chainmail and heraldic symbols decorated the four squares of his yellow mantle. It was the red lion of Castilla-Leon.

"Who is that?" she asked over her shoulder.

From behind her, Niranjan peeked through the window. "Faisal warned me of him. He is Prince Juan of Castilla-Leon."

"The same rebel prince at Tarif?"

"The man is here at your father's invitation. The Sultan offers him shelter against the Castillan King."

Haniya entered and announced Shams ed-Duna's arrival. The scent of ambergris preceded Fatima's stepmother, as it wafted through the curtains. Blue-black silk fluttered around Shams. Gold gleamed on her limbs and around her neck. There were even flecks of it in the gossamer veil covering her black braids.

"My husband has asked me to dine with him, as he entertains the wretched Castillan Prince Juan. Shall the Sultan approve of me?"

"Father would be foolish if he did not."

"You are to join us. The Sultan commanded it."

The quill shook in Fatima's hand as she scribbled, nearly stabbing the parchment in a pique.

Shams loomed at her side, her shadow splayed across the letter. "You are writing to your husband again, begging him to understand your delay. He has urged your return for two weeks. You should go home, Fatima."

She snapped. "Don't you think I know that? My daughter needs me, but so does Father!"

The thin reed broke between her fingers. Niranjan went for another quill.

Shams came around the desk and took Fatima's hands in her slim, dark ones. "Your father shall be well."

"He is not himself! I am determined to find out why! I cannot leave Gharnatah until I know for certain."

Fatima pulled her fingers out of her stepmother's grasp and finished her letter.

Before she rose from the stool, she asked, "Is Nur al-Sabah joining us, too?"

"When she and I ate with the Sultan this morning, he invited her. She has declined."

When Fatima shook her head, her stepmother's voice fell to a whisper. "I'm sure she has no interest in the meeting with the Castillan Prince. Nur does not think about her past. She is content in her life here."

"Shams, do not dissemble. We both know the reason why Nur al-Sabah refused the invitation. She knows I shall be there and she is still avoiding me. I cannot blame her for it."

"That's not true! Fatima, after some time has passed, you and Nur shall renew your friendship."

Fatima made no reply, while she folded the letter and affixed the wax seal.

She had seen the *kadin* only once after their last encounter, at dinner with her father. Nur remained cordial throughout the evening, but nothing more. The formality of the *kadin*'s address and her avoidance of Fatima's gaze still pained her to the depths of her heart.

Shams ed-Duna's hand on her shoulder drew her from recriminations. "Let time pass. Nur shall forgive."

Fatima wished she shared her stepmother's optimism.

Within the hour, she suffered through the meal with her father, his wife, her brother and their Christian guest. Fatima missed the presence of Nur al-Sabah, but was also grateful that she did not have to endure the Castillan Prince Juan. He looked at Fatima in bold appraisal, each time she raised the fold of her veil slightly during dinner. She hated the indignity of his eyes upon her. Why had her father permitted this stranger into the sanctity of his harem?

After the meal, Muhammad handed the Sultan a water pipe. Fatima glared at her brother.

The Sultan excused his guest, escorted out by Muhammad. Fatima joined Shams at her prayer niche, while the Sultan performed his ablutions alone.

The evening cast long shadows by the time *Salat al-Maghrib* finished. Fatima had intended to return to her chamber and put this tiresome day behind her, but instead, she found herself at her father's door again. At her curt nod, the guards permitted her entry.

She went up to the second floor and found him already abed, with his eyes closed. Next to his bed, he had set the water pipe. A haze of vapor escaped the green glass and saturated the room.

She glanced at her father again. He was sound asleep, rumbling snores betraying his deep slumber. She touched the warm hose on the water pipe. When had he begun to smoke? She felt as though she did not know him anymore.

Tears threatened, but she swiped them away. A pungent scent coated her fingertips. She recognized the smell as one she had thought came from the brazier in the Sultan's rooms. She did not recognize it, but she knew someone else who might.

Niranjan drew heavy smoke from the water pipe and inhaled. With a cough, he nodded to her. "It's hashish. Are you aware of it? Do you know what this plant does to people?"

She clapped a hand to her chest. "Who in the world has not heard of hashish and the *Hashishin* of Persia? The drug made them crazed killers. It controls people, makes them act unlike themselves...."

Her voice trailed off. "This is what my father...this is what makes him behave the way he does."

She recalled his wide, reddened eyes and large pupils throughout the meal. His uncontrollable laughter accompanied by bizarre movements and thoughts on the morning she had learned of Faraj's release.

"How would your father gain access to this?" Niranjan asked. "The cannabis plant does not grow in Al-Andalus."

She rubbed her arms, despite the warmth of the room. "My brother brought it to him."

Niranjan's gasp echoed around the chamber.

She sank down on a red silk cushion against the wall. "He's poisoning my father with this drug. He's making him do things he would not otherwise do."

"You cannot be certain your father's actions result from the hashish alone."

"What do you mean?"

"You mentioned the Sultan also ingests seeds of blessing. They're corn cockle. Eat enough of them and even you would go mad. I remember the hashish eaters who stalked the streets of my birthplace. The drug creates a powerful need. If the Sultan is an addict, he may be beyond cure already."

She frowned at Niranjan. "What do you expect me to do? Relinquish all hope and let this thing take over his mind and body? I tell you, I shall not! I cannot let him fall into darkness. Don't you see? If my father is addicted to hashish, all his edicts are suspect. With Muhammad controlling him, the Sultan could agree to anything. Worse, if the *Diwan* learns the Sultan has lost control of his own mind, the ministers may decide he is unfit to rule and remove him."

"Then your brother would rule in his stead."

"Yes. I cannot allow it. I must stop Muhammad before he destroys our father and the Sultanate. Find out how my brother is supplying Father with hashish."

Niranjan bowed his head. "It shall be done."

Out into the moonless night and through murky, underground shadows, Fatima followed Niranjan westward beneath the palace complex. Her grandfather, the first Sultan Muhammad, had built most of the royal residences on the *Sabika* hill with subterranean walkways that aided an easy escape. No guards patrolled such hidden places. Only two persons controlled the keys that unlocked every portal, the Sultan and his Sultana's trusted servant, the slave Faisal. The eunuch's relations with Niranjan ensured Fatima would have access to the underground corridors and much-needed privacy for the task that awaited her.

She hugged the dank wall. Above them, sentries patrolled the grounds. Niranjan pulled her down a stone-covered path and to a doorway concealed behind dense shrubbery. He pulled her behind him into an underground chamber where a fetid pool gathered beneath an unused cistern.

Beside the murky water, a man knelt on the cold tile, blindfolded and gagged, with his hands tied in front of him. A boy at his side, a youth of perhaps no more than fifteen years old, wept at the sight of them. He could have been her Ismail, despite his ragged appearance, with his dark hair and large eyes. His hands were behind his back and tied via a short rope to the bonds that held his ankles together.

She circled the captives. The man angled his neck toward the sound of her shoes scraping the stone and mumbled something behind the gag. She removed her veils and untied the knot in his blindfold. The man struggled against her unfamiliar touch.

"If you relax, this can go very easily for you."

His balding pate swiveled in her direction. His entire body stiffened. Tiny lines marred his forehead, beaded with perspiration. He had not expected a woman.

Still, he nodded. She came around him again. A bloodied gash cut deep under his right eye and the left one was nearly swollen shut, with blue-black marks surrounding it. When he met her stare, his black eyebrows flared.

Then his gaze swiveled to Niranjan near the exit. He wriggled against his bonds.

Fatima gripped his chin, her nails sinking into the flesh with enough force to make him wince behind the gag. "Look at me."

He did as she commanded. Dark eyes bulged from their sockets and the muscles beneath his cheek twitched.

"He shall not hurt you again, unless I command it. If you make any sudden moves or cry out when I remove your gag, I'll stab you between the ribs. Do you understand?"

His head bobbed vigorously. She released him and took Niranjan's dagger from the leather sheath. She cut away the strip of cloth forced between his teeth.

"Please don't kill me! I beg you." The man's voice was shrill, near hysterical.

Fatima kicked the man square in his mouth. Her boot heel smashed into his teeth. He reeled and slumped on his side. Blood and spittle oozed between his lips.

"Silence. You do not speak unless I demand it."

She glanced at Niranjan. "Who is he?"

"Musa ibn Qaysi. The boy is his son, Ali."

Fatima brought the dagger to the corner of Musa's mouth. Bands of perspiration matted the remaining thin strands of his hair.

"You know who I am, don't you?"

He shook his head. She swiped a slice of red from his lip to his chin. He squealed in shock and pain.

"You recognized me. You had recovered from the shock at finding yourself held captive on a woman's orders. Then, you observed my face and noted the features. You have seen them before, in the face of Muhammad, Crown Prince of Gharnatah. I am his sister, Fatima, daughter of the Sultan Muhammad *Al-Fakih*. You, Musa ibn Qaysi, shall tell me everything you have done to aid my brother against our father."

His voice issued in a strangled cry. "I am a loyal citizen of Gharnatah. I honor the Sultan. I swear to you, I know nothing about the Sultan, nothing about the Crown Prince...."

"Hashish sellers have no honor!" She slashed another cut across his cheek, deeper than the first. His words ended on a maniacal scream. Crimson rivulets trailed down his face.

Niranjan stepped forward. "Please, my Sultana, someone may hear him, if you continue this. There are other ways to make him talk."

He jerked his head toward the man's son.

Fatima nodded. "So that we are clear as to what can happen to you, Musa, if you don't tell me what I wish to know…Niranjan, hold the boy."

The hashish seller yelped, as Niranjan seized his son by the nape. "Please don't hurt him! He's my only son. I have daughters, but he is the only one left to bear my name when I am gone. He helps me in my trade. He is harmless to anyone, blameless. I swear to you. I'll do anything, everything that you ask. Don't do it. Please make him withdraw, my Sultana. Tell him to let my son go! Surely, you have children of your own. You could not hurt an innocent boy. Don't kill my son."

Fatima waved Niranjan away. She clasped her hands together. "I promise you, Musa, I won't kill your son if you tell me what I want to know. I give you my word as a Sultan's daughter."

The hashish seller sagged on his knees, tears flowing uncontrollably across his sunburned cheeks.

She said, "Now, let us begin again. Do you know my brother, the Crown Prince of Gharnatah?"

Musa sobbed, "Yes."

"Why do you know him?"

"He buys my hashish at the *Qaysariyya.*"

"How long have you been selling hashish to Crown Prince Muhammad?"

"For six years now."

Her heart thudded. Had her father endured the throes of his addiction for so long?

Myriad emotions coiled in her gut. She recognized the rage that roiled inside her and the fervent desire for vengeance that threatened to consume her. She could slice the man and boy's throats without thinking twice. They deserved death after working with Muhammad to destroy the Sultan.

She had never murdered someone. She had considered it in the aftermath of her mother's murder. A child's foolish whim when the killer would have crushed her. Now she was a woman, stronger and wiser than in her youth, embittered by her brother's betrayal of their father.

Could she take a life for her father's sake? What would it feel like if she gave in to the impulse now? Niranjan had killed on her behalf, but never with such brutal tactics. In the aftermath of such acts, he seemed unaffected. Would it be the same for her?

She tapped Niranjan's dagger against her thigh. He caught her eye and shook his head. "Your brother's madness has already destroyed him. Keep the darkness at bay or surrender to his fate."

Her jaw tightened, but she released a pent-up breath and returned her attention to Musa. "Did my brother tell you why he wanted the hashish?"

"No, at first I thought it was for him. Then I knew better."

"Why?"

"He is not addicted. I know the actions of someone who smokes hashish. In six years, I have never seen him behave as one possessed by the drug."

Fatima rubbed her fists at her throbbing temples. The wretched monster! Her brother had robbed their father of his life with something Muhammad was too clever to take himself.

She glared at the hashish seller. "I could kill you for what you have done."

As Musa gulped air furiously, Niranjan said, "He is more help to us alive, my Sultana."

From the folds of his robe, Niranjan withdrew a small cloth. With care, he untied the bundle and revealed tiny green leaves. He pinched a few and held them out in the center of his palm.

Fatima touched the dried leaves. One clung to her fingers. She brought it to her nose and inhaled the aromatic smell. "What is this?"

Niranjan replied, "It is a perennial herb, native to the land of the Genoese sailors who trade with our coastal cities. They call it oregano, which means 'joy of the mountains' in their language. In its dried state, oregano leaves can be mistaken for the greenish-black leaves of the cannabis plant."

Niranjan looked down at the man, who trembled, before his potent gaze returned to hers. "Musa can mix the oregano in with the cannabis leaves and its flowers when he makes the hashish resin. It can dull the potency of the drug, if the right amount is added."

"I want my father to stop! If we let this fool live...."

"If Musa dies, the Crown Prince shall find another supplier. Do you want him to do that? Do you want him concerned by the sudden disappearance of this man? Or would you rather he maintained the services of someone he believes is supplying him with the most potent form of hashish he can buy?"

She turned away, but Niranjan continued. "If we control Musa, we control the amount of the drug your father ingests. If the Sultan stops smoking now, after possibly years of an addiction, he shall rage in the throes of madness, as you have never seen. We may not be able to stop your brother, but we can slow the effects of what he is doing. Musa ibn Qaysi must live."

She glared at him, before her shoulders slumped in defeat. "Very well, I shall not kill him, after all. We must ensure he does as commanded."

Fatima reached for the boy, whose head hung limp. With a light caress across his chin, she tipped his narrow face up for her inspection.

"He could be my son, for all his dirt and grime."

She smoothed a forelock of his dark hair away from his grit-covered face, smearing a black smudge across his brow. His large eyes blinked and watered. He shuddered softly. Tears coursed down his hairless cheek.

She glanced at the hashish seller. "Do you love your son?"

His eyes watered. "Yes! A father always loves his children!"

Fatima looked at Niranjan. "Restore his gag."

While he attended to the hashish seller, who struggled against Niranjan until cuffed on the head, Fatima's hand drifted down the tender column of his son's throat. Beneath her fingers, life pulsed at the base.

Niranjan returned to her and stood just behind the boy.

Fatima asked, "Child, do you love your father?"

The boy nodded. His tear-stained face sunk, but she raised it again and met his swollen stare. She asked, "And you would do anything for the love of your father, wouldn't you? No sacrifice would be too great?"

The hashish seller's muffled screams behind his gag filled the tiny chamber. His son nodded again.

Fatima smiled and caressed his chin. "All children should love their fathers. I love mine. I would do anything for him."

She circled the boy and Niranjan drew back. She touched the boy's hands bound at his back. "These are the fingers that helped your father destroy mine."

She nodded to her servant. "Cut off the child's thumbs."

The boy and his father yelped at the same time. The child struggled against Niranjan, whose iron grip shoved the boy forward. With his right knee planted in the middle of the child's back, Niranjan grabbed the tender limbs at the tiny wrists.

Fatima's gaze did not waver as tears and whimpers shuddered through the child. Niranjan grabbed the boy's left hand and sliced through the bone. A spray of blood arced and sprinkled Fatima's cheek. She touched and smeared the warm wetness against her skin. An agonized scream from the boy echoed in the darkened, musty chamber.

When Niranjan cut off the other thumb, it landed at the boy's feet. The hashish seller's son crumpled. His blood coated the grime-covered stone. His father also collapsed, his sobs disturbing the deathly quiet.

Fatima strolled toward him and knelt at his side. He had closed his eyes. Tears trickled beneath the lashes.

She whispered, "As I promised, Musa, I have not killed you or your son. Know that when I give an oath, you may rely upon its fulfillment. Your son has not suffered in vain. Nor do I permit his death. My servant shall see to his wounds and he shall live. Still, remember that your boy's mutilation is the only warning you shall ever have from me.

"If you do not do as I have asked, if you betray me to the Crown Prince, my eunuch shall find you again. He shall kill your entire family, starting with your son. Your daughters shall die also, before you join them. My servant shall cut your children into such tiny pieces that none may recognize them beyond a heap of flesh and bones. Do not test the sincerity of my vow. You would not live with the regret for long."

# Chapter 9
# Bittersweet

## Prince Faraj

Malaka, Al-Andalus: Safar 694 AH (Malaga, Andalusia: January AD 1295)

The winds whispered in a mournful lament, shrouding the shores of Malaka in an icy grip. Faraj stood with his head bowed at the site of the small grave, newly dug in the past week. The diadem of star thistles, which his daughter Mumina had set on the burial place yesterday, shifted in the breeze. Soon, flowers littered the mound. He picked one and twirled the green stem with its yellow petals. Then the wind snatched and carried it away.

Behind him, Khalid cleared his throat. Faraj stared at him, wordless. His captain gazed at the grave, with the same wounded look he had borne every day since the funeral.

"What is it, captain?"

"My prince," he began, pausing at a sudden hitch in his voice. "You asked me to inform you when your wife's caravan approached the citadel."

Faraj clutched the blue-black mourning beads draped around his neck. "Thank you."

Khalid looked at the burial mound again, now stripped bare of the flowers. "The Sultana shall blame herself for not having arrived sooner. This shall be very hard for her to accept."

"Fatima shall survive this. She is strong, perhaps even stronger than I ever understood."

Faraj clasped his hands behind his back. The scars at his wrists itched as they scraped against each other.

He left the small *rawda*, passing under the long shadows of pine and eucalyptus trees at the periphery. They remained stoic sentinels, stiff in the late afternoon breeze. There were several other graves in this small cemetery. His mother and father's resting places were at the northern fringe. Now, another member of his family had joined them.

Khalid fell into step beside him, but Faraj shook his head. "You may retire. I shall speak with my wife alone."

The captain nodded, as he shuffled the dirt with his boot.

Faraj rested a hand on his shoulder. "There are long, sad days ahead, in which we may comfort each other."

As Khalid returned to the gravesite, Faraj continued to the house alone. He bypassed walls covered with ivy. Rows of bougainvillea and wisteria hung from boughs draped over the masonry. The stone path between the hanging flowers led to a terraced courtyard, ringed with slender columns that supported horseshoe arches. He trailed his fingers through the fountain, which marked the entrance to the house. Water spilled over into fish-shaped basins extending around the base and flowed along the channels.

A horse snorted and he looked up. The beast's breath billowed from flaring nostrils. Its rider dismounted and stood beside the gray-colored mount. A crimson colored mantle billowed, caught in the sinuous motion of the wind. It stripped away the hood that covered her face.

He moved and grasped Fatima's icy fingers in his hand. She tugged her slim hands from his grasp. Her thumb trailed over the blue-black beads nestled against the silken fabric of his *jubba.*

"You're wearing mourning colors. Why?"

He shook his head and reached for her fingers again.

Her lips trembled. "Merciful God, oh, please do not say I have stayed away for too long!"

"Fatima, dearest heart, let me explain."

"Do not say it! Do not tell me our daughter, our little Saliha, is dead. I cannot bear it."

He gripped and held her in a firm embrace, although she struggled against him.

"She is not dead, Fatima. Our daughter lives. She bears the scars of the pox on her arms and legs, but she lives."

Fatima drew back, the mute appeal in her gaze now replaced with confusion.

He leaned toward her and rested his brow against hers. "Saliha survived. Amoda did not."

She said nothing, so he continued. "I went first to al-Bajara and ensured our children were safe. When I arrived here, Saliha had endured the worst of it. Amoda would not leave our daughter's side. There were blisters all over the governess' skin, some in great masses. I sent Saliha to *al--Jabal Faro* in Khalid's care. It was too late for Amoda. My physician believes that although she had nursed each of our children through earlier episodes, the strain of caring for Saliha on her own was too much. We buried her in the *rawda* three days ago."

Fatima remained silent. He framed her face, now etched in grief, between his hands. "I am so sorry. I know she was very dear to you."

"Take me to her."

He led Fatima through the grounds to the cemetery. She stepped along the worn path to the new grave, where Khalid still stood. She knelt beside the captain.

The trio remained silent in each other's company, before Khalid sketched a stiff bow and turned to leave.

Over her shoulder, Fatima said to him, "She loved you. From the first day she ever saw you, Amoda wanted nothing more than to be at the side of Khalid of Al-Hakam."

The captain stopped in his tracks. The dark shadows around his haunted eyes betrayed the pain he had endured since Amoda's death.

"I shall honor her always, my Sultana. I shall never love another."

She shook her head and hugged her arms. "Cold comfort, good captain, for the dead and the living. None of us should go through this life alone, never having felt the warmth of those whom we love. Mourn Amoda if you must, Khalid, but never deny yourself a chance at happiness again. Amoda would not wish it. She would wish you to live and love."

Wetness shimmered beneath his hooded eyelids. He turned on his heels and walked away.

For Fatima, it was a bittersweet homecoming. The unexpected loss of Amoda, who had been her faith servant for thirty years, vied with her joy at the prospect of a reunion with her entire family. Yet, as before, her heart remained torn in two. Her love for her husband and children vied with lingering concerns for her father in faraway Gharnatah.

Within the week, the children returned from the mountain stronghold at al-Bajara. Only the Sultana Alimah did not return. She and her son preferred the site. Faraj marveled at the power of Fatima's love for their children, as she embraced each of them. The way she held Saliha, he thought she might never let her go again.

Later, when the children were in bed, Faraj and Fatima stood side by side on the belvedere under a moonless night. They looked out on to the dark waters. Ships with shimmering lanterns sought safe harbor from the White Sea.

He sighed. "It is too long since we stood in this place together."

"Yes, it has been over six months since you first left for Tarif. So much has happened in that time."

Under torchlight, he scrutinized her features for clues of her resentment. She raised a curved eyebrow in a questioning slant.

He asked, "Can you ever forgive me?"

She turned and wrapped her arms around his neck. "You are my heart. I am yours. That shall never change."

She relaxed and laid her head on his chest. He rubbed her upper arms and inhaled the familiar scent of jasmine in her hair.

"Yet, you have kept secrets from me." His fingers drifted lower and palmed her belly. "You should have told me of the child."

She gazed at him, her eyes limpid in the light. "If you had known, would you have chosen a different path?"

When the response died in his throat, she sighed and leaned into him again. "Shams ed-Duna should not have taken such liberties. It was my news to impart, never hers. She should not have burdened you with it. You had suffered enough with the loss of your brother. Despite his betrayal, I am sorry you were never reconciled with him."

He nuzzled her forehead. "His children shall arrive soon. You understand the duty before me."

She nodded. "And the burden upon Leila. I had hoped we would choose a husband for our eldest daughter. Now, she must marry according to the Sultan's will."

"She is his granddaughter. He has the right to decide her fate."

Fatima's sigh betrayed her true feelings. "All of us, bound to the decrees of one man. My grandfather wanted us to marry and so, we did. Now, Leila's grandfather wishes her to wed her cousin. So, she shall."

She found his gaze again. Her eyes glowed like the embers of a fire at night. "But, I also know love can bloom from such matches. May it be so for our daughter. Love demanded that I defy you and go to Gharnatah. It would not allow me to part from you."

He wanted to know more about her father's decision, but Basma stepped out on to the belvedere, her gaze averted. "The children are prepared for bed. They refuse to sleep until the Sultana bids them good night."

Faraj nodded and Fatima waved Basma away, before she rested her head on Faraj's shoulder. The dark-skinned girl bowed, her wavy locks tumbling from beneath her veil. As she turned to go, her features hardened with a spasm of irritation. Faraj frowned at the sight and put aside further inquiry about the Sultan's actions.

"Has something happened between you and Basma, beloved?"

Fatima murmured, "Why do you ask?"

"It's not like you to conceal petty concerns."

She shook her head. "I spoke harshly to her in Gharnatah. I'm afraid she has not forgiven me."

"You are her mistress. You do not need her understanding."

"You are wrong. I need more than that."

Even as they drew apart, he linked his fingers with hers. "How long shall you let this guilt over Basma's mother plague your heart?"

"How can you ask me that? I am responsible for the death of her mother. Except for my meddling, Ulayyah would still be alive and with her children."

"Fatima, she knew the risks in spying on our enemies."

"She did so at my behest. When I look at Basma and Haniya sometimes, the deepest fear takes hold of me. I worry for what would happen, if they remembered my role in their mother's fate."

"They shall never know. Only their brother Faisal was of an age where he might recall it."

When she nodded, he pressed her further. "Is this the only matter between you and Basma?"

"No. She has requested that I appoint her as governess of our children. I refused. I had already asked Baraka earlier. She has accepted."

At his gasp, Fatima said, "She is devoted to our daughters. Do you give your consent?"

"If you wish it, I agree."

He sensed there were other matters that occurred at Gharnatah. When he would have asked, she nestled against him again with a sigh. "We have to tell Leila of the fate that awaits her."

"After the boy arrives. Let her remain our little girl for now. Children deserve the enjoyment of youth. They should not be manipulated and used like that boy was at Tarif."

"Promise me, we shall never allow our children to become pawns."

He stroked the dark curls down the length of her back. "Beloved, they are royal children. Ismail is the Sultan's grandson. He shall inherit this great province at my death. It is a rival to Gharnatah's wealth. I have accepted that I shall also have little say in his future, in the choice of his wives and alliances. For as long as there is a Sultan, be it your father or brother, we must bend to his will."

"Still, we have a duty to protect our children," she pressed him, "from all who would seek to control them. It is the destiny of our eldest son to claim the governorship. I pray it may not be too soon. I want you safe in my arms at the end, not lying dead on some distant battlefield."

She tugged his lips to hers. He groaned and pulled her against him. Yearning for her settled and radiated sudden warmth through his belly.

Still, he pulled back and whispered against her lips, "You are my heart's true desire. Believe in my love."

Her eyes glistened, as she called out, "Niranjan?"

The eunuch stepped into the light, from just around the corner of the doorway. As usual, he was never far from Fatima.

She swallowed loudly and nodded. “Summon the concubine Hayfa to my husband’s chamber. She shall await his pleasure there.”

## Princess Fatima

In the same month, the fatherless children of Muhammad ibn Ismail arrived at Malaka. When they alighted from their horses, Fatima and Faraj welcomed them and their mother, Princess Soraya, a black-haired, pale-faced beauty.

Ismail and his cousin were equal in height and coloring. Whereas Fatima’s son had inherited the features of the Sultan, his cousin clearly descended from the line of his grandfather, Ismail, whose name he also shared.

Fatima’s eldest son asked his cousin, “Do you like horseback riding?”

“Very much, but my mother does not let me ride alone.”

Ismail smiled and winked at Fatima. “We shall take the horses along the beachhead later, if you would like.”

“Only if your mother permits, my son,” Princess Soraya interjected.

Fatima shared a look and nod with her. Perhaps Faraj’s sister by marriage would prove a strong counterpart.

The boys led the way into the house, followed by the other children, Fatima’s own and Princess Soraya’s three young daughters. Fatima linked arms with Soraya, who patted her forearm. The women preceded Faraj, the household servants and the rest of Soraya’s retinue.

They entered the dining hall, where a feast awaited. Dishes of lukewarm rosewater and a towel were at each table setting. Everyone sat down to a meal of freshly baked flatbread accompanied by hummus. The eggplant dip tasted of *tahini*, olive oil and lemon juice. There was lentil soup and a salad of burghul, mint and cucumber. There was chicken in mustard sauce and roasted lamb topped with greens. Fatima's cooks had flavored the rice with garlic and onions. Fruits, both raw and cooked and desserts covered the table.

Later, Fatima and Soraya retired to the belvedere overlooking the sea. The younger children remained in the hall under the attentive gaze of their new governess, Baraka. Since Soraya had acquiesced, her son went with Ismail and Leila down to the shore on horseback.

Soraya removed her gossamer veil and revealed thick locks. "My husband often spoke of this place. He coveted it."

Fatima leaned on the balustrade beside her. "Malaka is your home now and that of your children, for as long as they would wish."

"Your daughters are so beautiful, Sultana Fatima."

"As are yours."

"My girls are fortunate to have each other. I was the only sister among seven brothers. I am glad my daughters shall know the joy of sisterhood."

"You have seven brothers? I have only three."

Soraya whispered, "All, but one of mine is dead. My father is sorry that he has lived so long, only to see the last days of his own sons. He keeps the youngest at home to protect him. But then, we cannot always protect our children."

Fatima looked to where their sons had dismounted. Now, they were throwing pebbles into the sea. "No, but we can try."

Soraya said no more. Fatima watched the interaction of their children. When Soraya's son seemed tired of throwing stones with Ismail, he picked a few seashells from the shore. Among the rocks, he found a larger one and held it up to his ear. He laughed and ran to Leila, who sat with her knees drawn up under her robe. He offered her the shell. She tucked her hair behind her ear and brought the seashell up to listen. She laughed and smiled shyly at her cousin. Fatima smiled, too.

# Chapter 10
# Union

## Princess Fatima

Malaka, Al-Andalus: Rajab 701 AH (Malaga, Andalusia: March AD 1302)

Fatima parted the damask curtain of her bedchamber with a hennaed hand. Gold thread shimmered within emerald green silk. A sea breeze drifted through the opened lattice window, bringing with it the familiar smells of Malaka. However, this was no ordinary morning. Leila's wedding day had arrived.

The procession of the groom and his family moved at a steady pace up the hill. Musicians at the forefront banged their drums and trumpets resounded.

"*Ummi*, why is it taking them so long?"

Fatima turned at the tone of anticipation in the soft, sweet voice behind her. As she did so, swirls of white silk and silver brocade rustled around her feet. Leila peered through the lattice with a gleam of delightful anticipation shining in her gaze.

Among all her daughters, Leila reminded Fatima the most of herself. She was outwardly quiet but inquisitive, shy yet certain of herself. Now, more than twenty years after her birth, Fatima still recognized the child in the apple-round dimples of her daughter's cheeks, in the sparkle of Leila's dark-brown eyes. A woman now stood beside her, soon to become a wife.

With wide-flung arms, Fatima hugged Leila and sighed against the gossamer, red-gold cloth covering her hair. Leila's four attendants looked on with smiles.

Leila's clothing was a palette of crimson, white and gold. A white cotton *qamis* peeked out from under her robes, as did the ankle-length *sarawil* that covered her legs. Her *jubba* shimmered in waves of blood-red silk. Over it, her attendants had draped another garment, a gold brocaded *khil'a*.

Fatima traced the motif of the Nasrid family embroidered on the hem of the ceremonial robe and smoothed the soft ermine trim at the neckline. Servants had sewn a red silk lining inside the *khil'a*. As a final touch, Fatima had personally embroidered the narrow, gold *tiraz* bands with a line from *Al-Qur'an*. She read the words of the delicate *Naksh* calligraphy, though she knew them by heart.

"Another of His signs is that He created spouses from among yourselves for you to live with in tranquility. He ordained love and kindness between you."

When she looked at her daughter again, tears brimmed, but she could not forgo an earlier promise to Leila that she would keep the crying at bay until after the ceremony.

"You are beautiful, my child."

Leila spread the skirt of the ceremonial robe wide, revealing her usual bare feet. "Do you think my betrothed shall approve?"

"Your cousin has been in love with you for seven years. He cannot help his natural inclination to approve. Only promise me that you shall wear some shoes on the journey to al-Jazirah al-Khadra."

Leila nodded and sighed. "If I have to." She tugged at her lower lip with her upper teeth. "He does love me, doesn't he?"

Fatima clasped her thin shoulder. "How could he not? You have been fortunate to know him for several years before your marriage. Do you doubt his love for you?"

Leila did not answer. Instead, she looked out of the window again.

Her betrothed rode on a black horse at the forefront with his high steward flanking him. The bridegroom was handsome in his clothes in black, silver and white colors. Leila's sharp intake of breath at the sight of him made Fatima smile.

"*Ummi*, you didn't always love Father, did you?"

"I did not. Your great-grandfather arranged our union to thwart his enemies. Yet, out of such necessity, I grew to love your father deeply. Ours is a bond that does not fade with time. It grows stronger, deeper and richer with each day. I want the same for you. The future is uncertain for all of us, but while we are here, we live and we love."

When Leila glanced at her, Fatima recalled the breadth of emotions that had once run through her on her own wedding day, when she did not have the maturity or wisdom her daughter possessed.

"You are fortunate, my lamb, like your namesake. Your father's mother wed at the command of a Sultan, too. She also married for love, in this very place."

"I feel the spirit of that union within me today. I was not fortunate to know her or your mother. I have always felt that those women watch over me."

"Let me tell you something now, which my mother told me after I had married." Fatima cupped Leila's face between her hands. Their eyes met. "You have the beauty of the females of our family, Leila, but never forget: beauty fades. What shall never fade is the wonder and intelligence of your mind. It remains your greatest asset. Your husband may rule your body and heart, but your mind is and always must be yours, where none but you rule. Promise me you shall live by these words, as I have."

Leila nodded and hugged her tightly. "I'll never forget them, *Ummi.*"

When they drew apart, the door opened and Faraj stepped into the room. Fatima understood her daughter's approval of her future husband, for she shared the same sentiment about her own.

Time had not dulled her response to him, even after thirty-seven years of marriage. He remained a handsome man, especially so today in his black and gold *khil'a*, embroidered with two rows of *tiraz* bands. The gray that had begun threading through his hair three years before had overtaken all vestiges of the former color since last spring. He thought it made him look older than his fifty-five years, but Fatima did not agree.

Faraj held his hand out to Leila. "I must greet the new governor of al-Jazirah al-Khadra and our guests soon."

She kissed his fingers and bowed before him, pressing her forehead to the cedar floor. Afterward, Faraj helped her stand. He set his hands on her shoulders and pressed his lips to her brow.

"The blessings of our God be with you, my sweet Leila. Since your birth, you have been the jewel of my house. May you be the glory of your husband's own."

With a soft sob, she threw her arms around him. As he held her close, Fatima struggled with the tears again.

When Faraj leaned back, he also swiped at his eyes. "Make your final preparations while I speak with your mother in private."

Leila nodded and glanced at Fatima again, who waved her on. Leila lifted the hem of her ceremonial robe and her attendants took its trailing edge. They followed her through the door.

Faraj strode toward Fatima. She looked at him, conscious of the strands of gray peeking beneath the veil at her temple. Somehow, on a forty-five year-old woman, they seemed less appealing than for a man ten years her senior.

"Was I ever so young and beautiful as she, husband?"

Faraj cupped her chin in his hand and kissed her. "You still are, beloved."

His brownish gray moustache tickled her and she drew back. "I fear for them, your nephew and our daughter, in this move to al-Jazirah al-Khadra. The Marinids and Christians still covet it."

"Al-Jazirah al-Khadra is one of the strongest defensive bastions along the coast of Al-Andalus. My nephew is strong, he shall hold it." He pulled her to him again. "Our daughter has your courage and wisdom. She is his match in every way. Do not fear the future, Fatima. Whatever may come, Leila shall have our support. We shall always have each other."

He ducked his head and kissed her again. She leaned into him and savored the familiar caress of his lips against hers. When his hands slid down her back along her spine, the same thrill rippled through her as from his first touch, ages ago. Still, she wriggled in the circle of his arms.

"Lest you forget, you sought me out with a purpose."

"You are good to remind me. I am becoming forgetful in my old age. Or, is it that your lips remain a distraction?" Faraj mused, before stealing another kiss. "Your father has come to Malaka. The chief eunuch of Gharnatah has sent word that the Sultana Shams ed-Duna, his *kadin* and their children shall be our guests also."

Fatima's heart fluttered. "They have all come for Leila's marriage? I never dreamed Father would accept the invitation. Nur, too? Are you certain?"

When Faraj nodded, she shook her head. "But Shams wrote to expect only her arrival with her daughters. In truth, I did not think Father would come because of...."

Her voice trailed off. Faraj continued, "...the discord between us."

She held his hands in her own. "You have not seen the Sultan since your banishment from court. Are you ready?"

"We shall welcome him as a proud grandfather, here to witness our first daughter's marriage."

"As my grandfather witnessed our own." She smiled at hazy memories of her wedding day.

Their fingers intertwined, Faraj and Fatima left her room and soon emerged in the garden courtyard. Faraj's concubines Hayfa and Samara bowed before they darted off to the harem. Leeta, her husband Marzuq and Baraka stood nearby, dressed in their finery. Faraj spoke with the steward and Leeta, who served as his treasurer. Fatima moved to the exit where Baraka waited.

"Walk with me," Fatima commanded.

Green fire glittered in Baraka's hard gaze, but she complied.

Fatima said, "I ask you to accompany me and escort Leila to the *nikah*. You shall sit with us to bless my daughter. It is only right, as you have been her governess in these last years."

Baraka halted. "You demand too much. Besides, I am a slave in your husband's house."

"You have been the governess of my children for seven years. You served them well for years before. My daughters admire and respect you. It is my command and Princess Leila's wish."

"If it is my princess's wish, then I accept."

Faraj's hand settled on Fatima's shoulder. As she turned to him, he wore his frown of concern, looking between her and his old lover.

"Are you ready, Fatima?"

When she nodded, Baraka bowed and left them, preceding Leeta and Marzuq.

Faraj asked, "What happened with Baraka?"

Fatima nuzzled his beard. "You're always so concerned when I am with her. You have no cause. Come, the Sultan shall be here soon."

At the entrance of the house, they emerged in the full glare of midmorning's light. Fatima shielded her eyes as the guests and her children thronged the bridegroom, cheering him. They stood so close together that he could not alight from his horse.

Ismail shoved his way through the crowd and upon reaching his cousin, pulled him down from his mount. "Don't keep my sister waiting any longer! She's dreamed of this day."

As the pair laughed and shared a hearty embrace, Fatima clasped Faraj's arm. "The breach between you and your brother is sealed at last, with each of your sons and this union with Leila."

"It would seem so."

She glanced at him. "You doubt it? You just told me not to fear the future."

"I don't fear it, but I'm not a fool either. I wish Ismail were more cautious in his attachments. People can turn on you when you least expect it. I know it firsthand."

"But your heir and his cousin are more like brothers than cousins." Fatima tiptoed and kissed her husband's cheek. "You worry too much, my heart."

She sighed and admired her son, who was a man full-grown at the age of twenty-three. He possessed the same appearance and disposition of his grandfather in the Sultan's youthful days. Even now, he flashed the same roguish grin as he escorted his best friend, soon to be a brother by marriage, through the crowd and toward her.

He said, "Wait until you see Leila, cousin. She is even more beautiful."

Leila's betrothed laughed, throwing back his leonine head. "Impossible, for my bride is the loveliest of women. Except for your mother, of course."

Fatima embraced him and kissed both his cheeks. Then he bowed before Faraj. "Uncle, this is a blessed day."

"Be good to my daughter. Her mother has raised her well, but she is tender and requires a gentle hand."

"I shall love her until the end of my days."

Soraya's eyes glittered with tears as she hugged her son. They had not seen each other for two months, since the Sultan summoned him to Gharnatah and proclaimed him the new *Raïs* of al-Jazirah al-Khadra.

A hush settled over the excited crowd. Fatima turned to the eastern gate along with everyone else. The Sultan emerged under an ornate horseshoe archway, mounted on a black stallion festooned with gold and leather. His bodyguards followed on horses too, flanking a long row of camels bearing the royal household.

With some effort, the Sultan alighted from his horse. He looked every bit his sixty-eight years, sagging for a moment against the side of his mount. Fatima released Faraj and stepped forward. The crowd parted for her. Then the Sultan straightened and smoothed the folds of his white ceremonial robe. Everyone bowed as he walked toward her.

In the ensuing silence, they stared at each other. She had not seen him in seven years. Regular reports from Faisal to Niranjan ensured that she knew of her father's progress. Yet, the lingering enmity between her father, who still had not forgiven her husband, kept her from Gharnatah. In the intervening years, she and her father exchanged correspondence, but the formal tone lacked the familiar regard they had once shared.

No dark shadows or signs of redness lingered around his eyes. He was not free of his addiction, but it no longer ruled him. She moved to make her obeisance. He stopped her. His hands clasped on her arms. A smile broke the craggy lines of his face, unlike any she had seen in several years. She propelled herself against him and cried as his arms came around her in a tight, familiar embrace.

"Father, I'm so happy you could be with us to share in this day. You must be weary after your journey."

The Sultan lowered his hands and shook his head. "I am not. I have not ridden in some time. The exercise was good for me."

He looked beyond her to where Faraj waited. She stepped aside and her husband came forward. He knelt and pressed his forehead to the ground, before he brought the hem of the Sultan's *khil'a* to his lips and forehead. The deepest sign of respect one person could offer another.

The Sultan grunted as he leaned forward and placed his hand on Faraj's shoulder. "You may rise. All of you."

The Sultan's touch lingered, although his fingers trembled. "The peace of our God be with you and your house."

Faraj responded, "And with you, my Sultan. Your presence honors us."

The quaver in both of their voices brought tears to Fatima's eyes, but she brushed them away.

The Sultan said, "I would not have missed my first granddaughter's wedding day."

A gentle hand on Fatima's arm drew her attention. Shams ed-Duna's broad smile greeted her. As they embraced, she looked over Shams' shoulder. Nur al-Sabah waited with her son Nasr and her youngest daughters.

Many months after their grave misunderstanding, Fatima and Nur had renewed their friendship, but they did not share the same rapport as before. Fatima had not presumed she would have come to Malaka. Now, as they hugged, tears glittering in Nur's ice-blue eyes, it seemed the discord was at an end.

Fatima escorted all her close female relations to the harem, where Leila hugged and kissed them.

Then Fatima said to the wedding guests, "The ceremony must begin before the noon prayer. Please make your way to the garden courtyard."

Alone with her daughter again, she glanced around the partially bare room that Leila had shared with her sisters. Her daughter stood before a long, silver gilt mirror, smoothing her garments, before she slipped on her red leather boots. Praise be to Allah the Compassionate, the Merciful, she did not intend to enter her marriage with bare feet after all.

Fatima asked, "My dear, you do remember on the morning after you and your husband consummate your marriage, Soraya's midwife shall fetch the bridal bed sheet?"

Over her shoulder, Leila said, "Yes. I have come to my husband's bed as a pure bride. Anyone may see the proof of it. It won't embarrass me."

"Purity is required, but ignorance and feigned or relinquished pleasure is not. *Sharia* law prescribes sexual gratification in marriage. After I wedded your father, there were many years before we shared the marital bed. Then, I discovered true pleasure in knowing him and in my desire for him. He took the same joy in me. I want such happiness for you and your husband. He has concubines, so he is not inexperienced. Still, a pleasure slave is not a wife."

Leila came to her and grasped her hands. "Do not worry. I do not fear the virgin's pain. You promised it would hurt only once."

Fatima bowed her head and touched her brow to Leila's own. "If he is gentle. When you are first with him, remind him of the Hadith of the Prophet, peace be upon him. *'Do not come upon your wife like an animal. Let the kiss and sweet words be the emissary between she and you.'* May God bless your marriage bed always, daughter. I pray you shall write me soon after with word of your first child."

"*Insha'Allah*, as God wills it."

After they left the chamber, both found Baraka outside the door. She swiped at her cheek and bowed.

"My Sultana, my princess."

Leila embraced her. "You have always been at my side, since I was a little girl. Thank you, Aunt Baraka."

Then they drew apart and Leila said, "Come, both of you. My husband awaits me and I do not intend to make him wait any longer."

The garden courtyard where Fatima's children had played in their youth served as the place of the *nikah*, the first part of the marriage ceremony. Under the archway leading out on to the courtyard, the Sultan waited with Ismail. Leila waved at her elder brother and he grinned.

Fatima took her father's frail hand. "Did you wish to officiate? I am sure the imam would step aside."

The Sultan shook his head. "I am here as the proud grandfather, nothing more."

Leila bowed before him. Ismail gave him a small, silk pouch. The Sultan dipped his gnarled fingers inside it. He withdrew a glittering, gold filigree necklace, with an oval ruby pendant the size of a pomegranate.

He looked at Leila's astonished face. "When I first married, my wife, your grandmother Aisha wore this jewel. I regret that she did not live to know our grandchildren. I hope she might have been very proud to see you wear such an heirloom."

He slipped the priceless gift over her head. When she would have bowed low, he grasped her shoulders and kissed her cheeks in turn.

"May your union bring you only joy."

He and Ismail joined the male guests already assembled. Fatima and Leila stared after him in amazement, before Fatima cupped the pendant.

"This jewel belonged to my mother. I have nothing of hers."

Leila sputtered, her fingers already at her neck. "Then, you must have it. It's not fair that I...."

Fatima stilled her hands. "No. You must have it. This is her gift to you. She gave me mine before she died, the desire to cherish my children. Strange that I should have learned more of love in her sacrifice than anything else. I have taught you her greatest lesson. Never let it go."

An arched gallery shaded the garden courtyard. Two lengths of brocaded red and gold silk separated the male guests from the females. Fatima and Baraka led Leila beneath the portico. Faraj sat at the forefront beside the bridegroom. The imam of Malaka stood before them and on either side of him, the notaries waited to record the proceedings.

The imam recited the first chapter of *Al-Qur'an*. When he finished, one of the notaries produced the marriage contract, which Leila and her husband signed. Fatima had preserved the generous principles of her own marital contract in the one for her daughter. It stipulated that if Leila bore her husband children, yet he took another wife while she lived, she could divorce him and he would lose all claim to the dowry Faraj had paid. The bridegroom's fingers shook as he scribbled his name. He paid the document scant attention, his gaze fixed on Leila with adoration and pride.

Before Leila signed, her husband brought forth the *addahbia*, her bridal trousseau that contained all the gifts to remain hers after marriage. When the servants removed the generous favors of gold jewelry and gemstones, a leather-bound copy of *Al-Qur'an*, silks, spices and coins, Leila scrawled her name across the page. As the witnesses required by *Sharia* law, Faraj and Ismail also signed. The imam prayed over the new couple and pronounced them husband and wife.

# Chapter 11
# The Sultan's Legacy

## Princess Fatima

Malaka, Al-Andalus: Rajab 701 AH (Malaga, Andalusia: March AD 1302)

After prayers, the mid-afternoon sun beat down on the heads of guests at the *walima*, the marriage banquet. With her daughter Leila attentive to the guests, Fatima escaped the crowded, open-air hall for the belvedere by the sea. As she approached the exit, voices drifted from beyond the door.

Fatima ducked into a shadowy corner and peered around the wall. Faraj and her father rested their hands on the marble ledge.

The Sultan said, "You have prospered here. You have made my daughter happy. I had no cause to doubt you."

Faraj replied, "Fatima is very dear to me and not only because she is your daughter."

Fatima's father straightened and rubbed the spindly arms under his robe. "I should move the capital to the coast, where it is temperate all year round. I believe my *kadin* Nur would like it."

Faraj chuckled. "Fatima would be pleased also. She misses the company of your favorite Nur and her stepmother Shams ed-Duna."

Fatima leaned against the wall behind her with a sigh. Her father and husband spoke as friends of old, as if the nightmare of the past years had not happened. Then the men regarded each other.

Faraj said, "Forgive me for the errors of the past, my Sultan."

"Only if you would do the same for me," her father replied. "I let myself be misguided about you. I was wrong to do so. You are a good man, a loyal governor, a worthy husband to my daughter and a blessing for my grandchildren. I ask your forgiveness, too."

Tears pricked at Fatima's eyes. As she turned away, the sea breeze picked up again and caught the hem of her *jubba*. The white silk and silver brocaded folds of the robe lapped at the wall.

"Fatima?"

Her father's voice beckoned and she stepped into the light. "I did not mean to intrude upon you and my husband."

"You are always welcome," her father said, holding out his hand. She rushed to his side and laced her fingers with his. His gnarled hand shook in her hold.

"Are you well, Father?" She studied the fine lines etched in his forehead.

He nodded. "I am overcome by the joy of this occasion. If you have a moment before you return to your daughter's wedding guests, may we speak in private?"

"As you wish, Father."

She glanced at Faraj. He bowed at the waist and then grinned at the Sultan, who said, "You shall return with me to Gharnatah in a month's time. I need your counsel."

Faraj nodded. "I am yours to command, my Sultan."

He pressed a hand to Fatima's shoulder. She squeezed her beloved's lean fingers and smiled at him, before he left them.

She slid her arms around her father's waist and pressed her cheek against his barrel chest. "It's so good to have you here, for Leila's sake. You have honored my eldest daughter with your gift and your blessing."

"I should have done more when Leila was a child. Now, my granddaughter is a woman. One day, she shall have children of her own. I have not spent enough time with my grandchildren. I should have known them much better than I do."

"It is the burden of your power. You shall always be my father and the grandfather of my children. Foremost, you are Sultan of Gharnatah. You belong to your people, not to us. It has always been so. I knew how it would be from the moment you ascended the throne. It has never diminished the love in my heart or the honor with which I revere you, as my father and lord of my life."

He sighed. "I have not always deserved your love and respect. I feared I might not be welcome here today, after all the things I have said and done to your husband. To you."

"Father, that is all in the past. You and Faraj have forgiven each other. My heart is whole again, not torn between the love that I would bear a father and a husband, once at war with each other."

"I have made many mistakes in these long years. Things I must undo. It is part of why I came to you and Faraj, to seek your forgiveness."

"You have it. Oh Father, you shall always have it!"

Fatima hugged him again. His frailty shocked her, bones and sinew knitted together in a wiry frame that was half his normal size. How did he possess the strength to stand?

She drew back and searched his gaze. "Something more than this resolution between you and my husband, more than Leila's union has drawn you to Malaka. Father, what ails you?"

His long sigh confirmed the suspicions that had dogged her since his unexpected arrival.

Fatima maneuvered her father to the carved stone bench on the belvedere. When he settled on the seat with a groan, she sat and took his hand. He held her fingers in an unsteady grasp and looked out on the water. Sunlight shimmered in the depths of the White Sea. Birds whirled and circled against the blue backdrop and wisps of clouds.

"Fatima, have you ever slept for so long that when you awoke, it seemed you had been slumbering for years?"

When she shook her head, her father continued. "I have lingered in a haze of dreaming. I am awake now. My eyes are open. I see the world as it truly is. I see my heir for what he truly is."

Her heart thudded.

He reached into the fold of his leather boots and pulled out a slip of parchment.

He gave it to her. "Read it for yourself."

Her gaze darted across the page once, before she re-read.

"This is a letter to Sultan Abu Ya'qub Yusuf of the Marinids, Father, inviting him to another alliance with

Gharnatah. Why would you do this? Your last letter to me at the beginning of the year mentioned new negotiations with the Christian King of Castilla-Leon. Why would you risk siding with his enemy, Sultan Abu Ya'qub Yusuf?"

"I did not write this letter."

She stared at the dried ink on the parchment. "But it's in your style. It bears your great seal."

"Look at the date on the letter."

She did so. "It says it was transcribed in Rabi al-Thani…but I don't understand, that was four months ago. I had written to Shams with invitations for the wedding then. She replied that you remained at the Castillan court at the time. How can it be that this letter bears this date and your signature?"

"Because it is a forgery, a damnable lie meant to draw me in with the Marinids again!"

Her chest tightened. She fought for every breath. "You know who created this forgery?"

"Yes, as you do. It was your brother, the Crown Prince."

The Sultan stood and shuffled to the ledge. Even with his back to her, she could not miss how his hand brushed his face with a quick swipe. His knotted fingers rested on the marble.

"How did you come to realize the truth, Father?"

"Ridwan of the Bannigash clan, a *talib* of the *Diwan al-Insha*, saw the letter mixed among others I had signed before I left for negotiations with the Castillans. The date puzzled Ridwan and he brought it to my *Hajib* Ibn al-Hakim al-Rundi. The Prime Minister showed it to me. Fatima, I have been a fool for my son. No more."

She drew in a harsh breath. "You confronted my brother!"

The Sultan nodded, though it was not a question. "Muhammad denied it, of course, saying anyone could have done it. I know his handwriting. It is very similar to mine. There are subtle differences. For several months, he has counseled me against negotiations with our Christian neighbors to the north. I refused to destabilize my regime with another war, a new *jihad*. Muhammad said we would not lose if we had Marinid help."

She shook her head. If the letter had reached the Marinid capital at Fés el-Bali, her father would have had no knowledge of it. The Marinids would have produced the proof and deemed him an oath-breaker. Wars began in such ways. Gharnatah could not risk a conflict with the Marinids. The Sultanate would never survive it.

"Father, what do you intend to do when you return to Gharnatah? Is this why you asked Faraj to accompany you?"

The Sultan looked over his shoulder. "It is. I shall need your husband's support, with the changes to come. Shams ed-Duna's son shall need him as well."

As she pressed her fingers just above her heart, he returned to her side and cupped her chin with his hand.

"I want you to know, you were right to caution me in the past about your brother. I have indulged him too much. The fault is mine. If he is deceitful, it is because I have failed him as a father, as I have failed you."

"No, no, you have never failed me!"

"Fatima, hear me in this. I should have trusted in you and your instincts about your brother. You have never led me astray before. Now I pray Allah, the Compassionate, the Merciful, may bless you with the knowledge I did not possess. Have the courage to see your loved ones as they are, not as you would wish them to be. Be strong, my daughter, in the days of trial."

He sighed and smiled, but it was a sad, empty gesture. Then he pressed his forehead to hers. "It should have been you, my Fatima. You should have been my firstborn and a male. What a formidable Sultan you would have made! I charge you, my most precious and beloved child, with a sacred responsibility. It is yours until death. I bequeath the glory of our family name and require your defense of it. Guide and protect those whom we love. This is my last and best legacy, the duty to our family. Promise me you shall hold fast to it."

She blinked hard against her tears and embraced him once more. She buried her face in his familiar comfort.

"To the end and with my last breath, I shall honor you and our family always, blessed Father."

## *Prince Faraj*

After Leila left for her new home at al-Jazirah al-Khadra, the Sultan remained with her family at Malaka until the end of the following week. He spent much time in Faraj's company, as well as with his grandsons, Ismail in particular. As Fatima often reminded Faraj, their son had his father's ambitious spirit, but something of his grandfather's pride and temperament swelled inside of him, too.

On a cloudy day, Faraj left Malaka at the Sultan's side. He and Fatima shared a poignant embrace. She had been restless all week. He supposed it had something to do with the matter she and her father had discussed in private. Whenever Faraj inquired, she had brushed aside his concerns, but he knew her well enough to remain concerned.

Now, he kissed each of her hands and her brow. More tears streamed down her cheeks.

She whispered, "Protect my father in Gharnatah."

He chuckled and traced one of her tears. "You doubt the Sultan's bodyguards?"

"Please, you must safeguard my father. Promise me."

"Against whom does he need protection?"

When she shook her head, he sighed. "How do you expect me to do as you've asked if you keep the Sultan's secrets? Your father must have warned you of his troubles during the wedding. Is this why he commanded me to accompany him?"

"It is. You shall understand in time. I cannot tell you more."

"Very well. Then I shall do all I can for him. When I return, we must talk."

"Faraj, the duties of a daughter to her father…."

"Do not compete with or exceed the loyalty owed by a wife to her husband! You are my wife. I expect your candor at all times."

His gaze narrowed on her, as though he might penetrate the morass of her thoughts. Her watery gaze revealed turmoil, but nothing more. With a sigh, he commended her to Ismail's care and mounted his horse.

Fatima sobbed against their son's tunic. The Sultan and his women waved, but she could barely force a smile for them.

Faraj looked down at Khalid of al-Hakam. "Protect them until my return."

His captain bowed his head. "Always, my prince."

The journey to Gharnatah remained uneventful. Yet, concerns plagued Faraj's mind. The Sultan suffered the same restlessness and unease as had plagued Fatima. Faraj could not help but feel each step in the direction of the capital brought them all closer to danger.

The massive red brick walls of the capital rose in the distance one week later, spread across the center of a wide plain. The ramparts shimmered in vibrant reds and gold under the mid-morning sun. Faraj glanced at the Sultan, grim-faced and silent, as he studied the familiar panorama. He turned in the saddle and looked over his shoulder to the first camel, which bore his wife. Then he leaned toward Faraj.

He said, "We shall share a meal with my sons this afternoon. I do not believe you are well-acquainted with the son of Shams ed-Duna."

Faraj shook his head. "I am not. I know little of him, except that he bears my name."

"He is a man of twenty-six years with his own family. He is burdened by a noble, dual heritage, the legacy of our family and his mother's people."

"Leila's marriage was also the first occasion to formally meet your *kadin*'s son."

"Nasr is a bright boy. He must be."

"Indeed. After all, he is your son. Allah the Compassionate, the Merciful has blessed you, my Sultan."

"That remains to be seen. Now, come."

Faraj stared as the Sultan kicked his horse into a canter down the slope, then Faraj followed his father in-law. They entered the city to the usual cheers and acclaim that always greeted the Sultan's return.

Within *Al-Qal'at al-Hamra*, the courtyard of *Al-Quasaba* seemed quieter than usual. The soldiers on duty came to attention, as the royal bodyguards escorted the family.

The Sultan dismounted first and tossed his reins to a waiting groom.

"I shall meet with you an hour before prayers, Faraj. I shall remain in seclusion until then. I wish to see no one, not even the Sultana or my *kadin*."

Faraj bowed his head. "As you command."

The Sultan brushed his hands free of dust and proceeded into his palace. His shoulders sagged as though he bore the weight of the world upon them.

Before the noonday prayer, a veritable feast covered the low table of the Sultan's quarters. Hot, fresh flatbread, *'tharid* made with lamb in yogurt sauce. Lentils flavored with onion and garlic mingled with the scent of lemon chicken kebabs and rice with carrot and scallion. The young prince Nasr and his brother relished the meal, but Faraj ate without appreciation.

His mood matched the somber, graying visage of his master the Sultan, who had pushed his half-eaten meal away. Instead, he reached for one of the desserts, a honey cake. He sniffed at it and broke off a piece before popping the morsel into his mouth. He chewed it slowly and then gave a nod, as if of satisfaction.

The Sultan grumbled, "Where is Muhammad? He said he would be late, but it has been half an hour by the water clock."

Faraj wiped his mouth and swallowed before speaking. "Surely, he shall be here soon. Whatever keeps him must have been important."

Nasr asked, "Why can't you tell us why you wanted to dine with us now, Father? Who cares if the Crown Prince isn't here?"

Faraj chuckled at the impetuousness of the fifteen-year-old. He reminded him of his brother at that age, always eager for their father's approval, yet living in the shadow of the heir.

"Nasr, what I shall say to you affects everyone, including your brother the Crown Prince."

Faraj shook his head at the boy's scowl. Perhaps his father's rebuff rankled more so because of some enmity towards the Crown Prince. After all, he was the son of a slave, despite the feelings the Sultan bore his mother. Even Shams ed-Duna's son ranked above him in legitimacy.

The Sultan chewed his honey cake and offered Faraj one, which he declined. The Crown Prince had sent them by his servant, likely to soften his father's apparent anger over the delay. Given the Sultan's ill humor, a few desserts would not alter the outcome of the day.

Faraj sought to improve the poor mood. "Did you enjoy your time at Malaka during the wedding, Prince Nasr?"

Nasr grumbled, "I hated all the women and the crying afterward. I'll never marry."

His brother rustled the golden curls atop his head. "Our father may choose otherwise. It is his right. You only say so because you haven't had a woman yet."

Nasr swatted his hand away. "I don't want one! Leave me be!"

The Sultan chewed his second cake. "My sons, you know your mothers do not condone tussles at dinner."

"But you do, Father," Nasr said.

The Sultan grinned and tossed his napkin at him. He ducked just in time. He and his brother teased each other under their father's watchful gaze.

Then, the Sultan's belly gurgled and a rumble of gas escaped him, fouling the room. His sons looked at him from expressions glazed with shock, before Nasr burst out laughing.

Their father frowned at both of them. "I ask your pardon. Perhaps I have eaten too much."

The call to prayer sounded. Nasr groaned. "I haven't finished my food yet!"

His father scowled at him. "You behave as an impudent child. You are a prince of Gharnatah. Surely, your stomach can wait upon the demands of prayer. When we return, my slaves shall bring you fresh food."

The men washed their hands and went to the antechamber, where each turned his back on the other and performed his ablutions in modesty. Then the Sultan led Faraj and his sons to the royal mosque, next to his palace. The Sultan's bodyguards followed at a discreet distance. When he entered, those gathered within the mosque performed the customary bow and averted their eyes from him. The courtiers, soldiers, merchants and slaves filled the room.

The Sultan alone approached the central nave of the prayer hall, where the imam of Gharnatah already stood. The *mihrab*, a niche at the bottom of the wall, demarcated the *Qiblah*, the direction of prayer. Faraj stood beside his master's sons. All of the men faced the *Qiblah*. Faraj breathed in deeply and exhaled. His body relaxed and focused upon the ritual to come. A sense of calm and quiet pervaded the chamber. Light filtered through the mosque's latticed windows. A mild smell of incense drifted through the room. With the rest of the congregants, Faraj raised his hands to the level of his shoulders and bowed his head slightly. Within his mind, he recited the *niyyah*, declaring before God his intention to pray.

Since the age of seven, he had followed the prayer rituals his father and uncle had demonstrated. He knew them by heart, could have completed them with his eyes closed. As he spoke the words he had learned as a child, bowed and prostrated himself at intervals, the comfort of familiar sacraments washed over him.

Yet, the Sultan's movements often interrupted his observances. When Fatima's father completed the first *rak'ah* with an audible grunt, several of the men in the room eyed him. By the third, he staggered to his feet. At the fourth and last *rak'ah*, he mumbled the words, "Peace be upon you and God's blessing," as though he struggled with his speech. His guards surrounded him at the end of *Salat al-Asr* and escorted him back to his chamber in haste.

When the quartet re-entered, the Sultan cupped his brow and staggered into the recesses of the room.

Faraj eyed the perspiration dotting his brow and his flushed cheeks. "Shall I have a slave open the window, master?"

"What?" The Sultan shook his head, before he pressed a hand to his brow again. He tore off the *shashiya*, the hair beneath close-cropped to his skull.

"Yes, I am very hot. First, I must relieve myself."

He righted himself on wobbly legs for a moment, but then his feet gave out under him. He crashed and slumped on the floor beside the table where they had dined, amid the cushions strewn around him.

Faraj reached him first. "My Sultan, you're ill!"

His father in-law's head lolled back on his arm. His face reddened and he tore at his throat, as though it had tightened and rendered him unable to breath or incapable of speech. With a sudden spurt, he reached across the table.

"Father, what are you trying to do?"

His second son clasped his hand, but he pulled his fingers away. His hand touched the porcelain platter of honey cakes, the only dish that remained from the earlier meal. He pulled it to the table's edge, where it teetered for a moment. Then, the salver clattered on the cedar floor. The cakes spilled and honey smeared the floor and cushions.

An animalistic growl escaped the Sultan, before he clutched at the tunic of Faraj's collar. The Sultan's hand shook, but he dragged Faraj down and whispered in his ear.

"She was right! Tell her...she was...right...."

Faraj's heart threatened to burst from his chest. Fatima had warned him to protect her father. Had she meant against her brother?

His gaze lingered on the honey cakes before he pulled the Sultan close to him. He shouted for any slave who would hear him, "Help! Summon the Sultan's physician now!"

## *Princess Fatima*

In the late evening, Fatima sat in her husband's receiving room, on a silk cushion of yellow and blue stripes at a small table carved in the shape of a pomegranate. The scent of cedar wood permeated the chamber.

When footsteps sounded, she swiped at her wet eyes and looked up, just as Ismail leaned against the doorpost.

Her cheeks warmed under his scrutiny. "I know. Saliha and Qabiha refuse to sleep until I come in to kiss them good night."

He stepped into the room. A frown marred his handsome features. "You've been crying for days since Father and Grandfather left. It's been a week."

"I know. Leila left me, too."

Ismail rolled his eyes heavenward. "Yet, you have other children here, who still need you. You should be happy. Leila and our cousin love each other. They shall make each other very happy. Father is no longer in exile. Grandfather returned to Gharnatah with him."

She nodded. "The change in my father is remarkable. I never thought he and Faraj would reconcile."

"You've never told us why Grandfather had banished him, only that the outcome of the siege of Tarif displeased him. Why?"

She waved a dismissive hand. "It is unimportant now. The years of mistrust and anger between them have gone, as a winter's snow in spring."

His frown deepened before he shook his head. "The Sultan is weaker than I remember him. One day, he shall be gone."

She blinked back the tears again and avoided his gaze. She feared for her father more than ever, now that he had returned home to confront his son's treachery and alter Gharnatah's future. Muhammad's treason warranted death. No one was above execution as a traitor, not even a Sultan's son.

What would her father do? He could exile his son. Would the act ensure Muhammad never harmed anyone again? No, he could not be trusted. Her father was right. Her brother had declared himself his father's foe. An enemy left behind would only rise up again. Muhammad would have to die. Could her father put his own son to death?

She gasped at the possibility. Yet relief flooded her at such a thought. When had she become so callous? He was her brother, but she had not thought of him as such in a long time, not since the day she knew he had tried to kill her and little Ismail, nestled in her womb.

"Where are you now, *Ummi*?"

She looked up at the sound of Ismail's voice. She had forgotten he still stood there. His gaze assessing, he folded his arms across his chest.

She asked, "What do you mean, my dear?"

"Something troubles you. It has since Leila's wedding day. I saw you return to the feast with Grandfather. He was gone for some time, at first with Father, but then, you came back with him. Your eyes were red then, as they are now. What did you and the Sultan talk about?"

"Matters concerning the Sultanate, nothing more." She forced a smile she did not feel.

Undaunted, Ismail crouched beside her, like a lynx ready to spring on his prey. She met his penetrating stare and again thought of how much he resembled her father in his youth.

"Why do you keep secrets from your own family?"

"I don't like your query or your tone. Do not forget I am your mother. You have no right to question me."

"Don't you trust me?"

"With my life."

"But not with the secrets of the Sultanate?"

"If there were any, they are not mine to share." She blinked back tears and brushed at her cheek. "Now, do you trust me?"

"With my life also."

"Then trust that whatever happens in the Sultanate, your grandfather ensures the security of his realm and I support him. I have always shared a close bond with him. You know that. Why do you question it now?"

"I question any bond between you and someone else that leaves you burdened by tears. What are you hiding? Please, tell me the truth."

So much time had passed in which she had carried the burden of her family's secrets alone. Years of her father's struggles with an addiction to hashish, his every action questionable and the harem officials bribed to hide his condition. She did not fear that her husband or son would exploit the information. She had to protect her father's legacy.

How could she confess that for years her father had been an imbecile in the sway of a narcotic, unable to think clearly, much less rule Al-Andalus? Without the loyalty of the eunuch Faisal and a cadre of slaves, his ministers would have discovered her father's failings and removed him long ago. Her father was *Al-Fakih,* the lawgiver, the prince of justice for his people. She would not let anyone take the last vestige of his glorious reputation from him.

She stared hard at her son. "If I keep secrets for my father, they are mine to keep. I am your mother, but foremost, I am a Sultana of Gharnatah. My loyalty is to the Sultan. That is the only truth that exists."

He would never have understood anyway. All her life, she had lived by the lessons her father taught of loyalty to family. She could not forsake them, not even for a beloved son.

Ismail stood. He stared at her without blinking. It seemed her heart stopped beating for a moment. Still, she met his regard without flinching.

"Then I pray that the consequences of your 'truth' do not damn us all, *Ummi*."

He turned on his heels and left without another word.

A sharp ache stabbed through her belly, eliciting a scream from the base of her throat. Spasms of pain rippled through her side. She gasped for air. The room swirled around her. Then all became blackness.

"*Ummi*? *Ummi*, can you hear me?"

Ismail's voice stirred her from darkness. She opened her eyes. Her son hovered beside her, his olive-brown features full of concern. His sisters and brother surrounded him. She touched his cheek, the neat trim of his dark-brown beard prickling her fingers.

"What...happened to me?"

"We hoped you might tell us, *Ummi*. Ismail came back when he heard you cry out." Aisha's hand closed on hers and she squeezed it in return.

Ismail caressed Fatima's cheek. His familiar touch made her regret the earlier harsh words between them.

He said, "An hour has passed on the water clock. Why did you faint?"

She blinked rapidly against the brightness of the lamplight. She tried to clear the haze of confusion in her head. She had argued with Ismail, just before an agonizing feeling overcame her.

She screamed. "Gharnatah! We must go!"

Ismail shook his head. "What? Why?"

"My father....We have to get to Gharnatah."

Ismail looked at his siblings.

Fatima pleaded. "My son, you must come with me. If you have ever trusted me, then do so again now."

# Chapter 12
## Loss

### Princess Fatima

Gharnatah, Al-Andalus: Sha'ban 701 AH (Granada, Andalusia: April AD 1302)

For five rain-soaked days, Fatima and Ismail journeyed to Gharnatah. Torrents enshrouded the terrain in a thick mist. A light wind could not disperse the showers. Fatima's camel snorted and shook off the cold droplets. Ismail rode his stallion at Fatima's side, his features hidden beneath a hooded, leather cloak.

They traveled under the protection of Khalid of Al-Hakam and his thirty guardsmen. They stopped only for prayers and kept a steady pace otherwise, despite treacherous, rain-slicked rocks. For the first time, Niranjan did not accompany Fatima. She commanded him to follow in a day or so, bringing Haniya and Basma, along with the family's provisions on pack animals. Her haste would not allow them to wait for her servants.

Fatima looked out from under the *hawdaj*. The leather canopy with its wooden frames offered her some measure of comfort. Lightning arced in vivid flashes and thunder rumbled across a foreboding sky. The wind whipped across her face and splashed fat droplets on her forehead. The rain continued unrepentant, as if the very heavens wept.

In the early evening, Gharnatah's redbrick walls rose above the heavy haze. Ismail pushed back the hood of his cloak. Brilliant streaks pierced a gray sky and illuminated the hard angles of his face. Dark shadows encircled his eyes. He had eaten little and spoke less during the journey.

Fatima had sunk into the same deep melancholy as her son. Her tears had dried along the journey. Now, she worried for how the consequences would affect them all.

When her father had departed Malaka two weeks before, she knew the grave decision he faced. Whatever fate he had decided for her brother Muhammad, it meant Shams ed-Duna's son would rule Gharnatah. His mother had broken ties with her Marinid family years ago. She would be a strong, positive influence in the life of the new Sultan. Yet, Fatima wondered whether Shams ed-Duna's son could shoulder such an awesome responsibility in their father's place.

The great, brass bell high atop the watchtower at *al-Qal'at Al-Hamra* pealed a mournful tone.

"The Sultan is dead, Ismail," Fatima whispered. "Long may his son reign in his stead."

Beside her, Ismail's horse shied away. Her son nodded, but said nothing. She did not ask him how he already knew the truth, too. Clearly, she had passed the dreadful foreknowledge of things beyond her understanding to Ismail. Could he learn to bear it, as she had?

She fingered the cold blue-black beads around her neck and bowed her head. A silent prayer filled her mind. *'By the blessings of Allah the Compassionate, the Merciful. Father, with my last breath and all that I am, I shall honor you. I shall watch over our family and protect them, as you would have done. Wherever you are in Paradise, know that in me, your legacy shall survive. I'll never forget the lessons you have taught me. I shall hold to your memory all the days of my life. Rest now in peace, Father, your spirit is free from earthly burdens. Watch over your son, the Sultan. Guide his thoughts and deeds that he might be a blessing to your people, a Sultan worthy of your throne. Rahim Allah. Amin."*

She feared the knowledge of what awaited her in Gharnatah. Her father's passing had not been peaceable. The jarring stab of agony she had experienced warned her of his pain-filled end. Had her husband been with him when it happened? Surely, Faraj would know the truth.

Beside her, Ismail swiped at his cheeks before he met her gaze with bloodshot eyes. "It is not manly to cry."

She shook her head. "Your sadness honors your grandfather. Do not be ashamed of tears when sorrow is the only thing left to us. Come now, our family needs us."

They entered the city through the towering arches of the *Bab Ilbira*. The cobblestone streets were devoid of people. The canopied stalls of the *Qaysariyya* stood empty. At the base of the *Sabika* hill and through the trees, the ramparts of *Al-Quasaba* glittered under brilliant torchlight.

Fatima's thoughts returned to Shams ed-Duna's son, a man with two concubines who had each borne him a daughter. He had served among the *talibs* of the *Diwan al-Insha*. In time, he rose to the rank of *wazir*. Yet, the experience might not have been enough to prepare him for the sudden rule of Gharnatah.

Darkness hastened to cover *Al-jazirat Al-Andalus*, as the party entered the citadel's precincts. Across a narrow gorge, Fatima spied her youngest brother, Nasr. He crossed the footbridge southwest of the complex. When her camel slowed and she alighted, drawing back the folds of her veil, he stopped. Ismail dismounted, too.

Nasr strode toward them. "What are you doing here? Surely you cannot have heard the news so soon."

Although she knew the truth, her brother's words confirmed her deepest sorrow. As she sagged against Ismail, he cradled her. Tears glided down her cheeks. The slick mud beneath her feet swirled before her watery gaze.

"*Ummi* said we should come," Ismail said.

Nasr stared at her. "She did?"

Fatima reached for him blindly and hugged him close. His arms did not enfold her to him. When she released him, his hands were tight fists at his side, his face twisted with grief and some other indiscernible emotion.

"Where is my father?" Ismail asked.

"With the Sultan," Nasr muttered. He ducked his head, staring resolutely at the earth.

A niggling worry stirred in Fatima's breast, but before she could speak, Ismail questioned Nasr. "When was my grandfather's funeral?"

"On the third day of Sha'ban, in the morning. He died the evening before." Grief strained Nasr's voice. "The new Sultan only sent word to all his provinces beginning yesterday, after his coronation. Word could not have reached you so soon at Malaka."

He glared at Fatima for a moment. She met his cold fury with growing puzzlement.

"He has already had his coronation? Father did the same shortly after his father's death, but I thought our brother would have invited all the provincial governors to witness the proceedings. They shall be unprepared for his reign."

Ismail frowned, just as Nasr raised his gaze to hers. His lips trembled, as though he seethed inside, fighting against some violent emotion.

"What are you talking about? Father prepared him for years to take the throne. The *Diwan al-Insha* has proclaimed your brother Abu Abdallah Muhammad, the third of his line, as Sultan of Gharnatah."

Her heart hammered deep inside her chest, as though it might burst forth. A sickening wave of acidity welled up in her stomach. She stepped back and shook her head. "It cannot be! Muhammad cannot be Sultan!"

Ismail said, "*Ummi*, you know Grandfather had made my uncle Muhammad his heir."

"No, no! You don't understand. Where is our brother, Nasr, where is Shams ed-Duna's son?"

"He is dead."

She collapsed with a cry. Tears blurred her vision again. "What? How…I…."

Nasr crouched before her. His jaw tightened and his gaze narrowed. "You seem shocked."

"Well, of course I am! How can it be that our father and his son are both dead?"

"Our brother killed himself on the day after Father's death. He poisoned his household, too. Even the little girls. I thought you knew."

"Why would I know about that?"

He stared at her in silence before he rose to his full height, turned on his heels and left them without another word.

Ismail gripped her arm, none too gently, as he hauled her to her feet.

"Why did you think anyone other than my uncle Muhammad would have been Grandfather's heir?

Grandfather warned you of his intent to name another, didn't he, when he was last at Malaka? Is that the secret you've been hiding?"

She shook him off. "I have to see Shams ed-Duna. She can explain everything."

She skirted around him and fled for her father's palace. Ismail's urgent cries chased her through the pavilions and myrtle trees.

Atop the apartments where her father had resided, his sodden flag drooped in the unforgiving rain. For thirty-one years, the banner, which featured a red lion with one claw upraised on a white background, a black border and thirteen white dots had been the symbol of his reign. Now the sigil of another Sultan of Gharnatah would replace it. That Sultan should have been the only son of Shams ed-Duna.

Fatima stood outside the heavy oak doors of her father's chamber. The guardsmen averted their eyes. She dared not ask them to permit her entry. She could not go into the place where he had lived the greater part of his life. Not yet. It would be empty, alien without his majestic presence.

Instead, she dashed across the harem and scrambled up the stairs. "Shams? Where are you?"

Nur al-Sabah's body slave, Sabela, appeared in the hall. "My Sultana, you have come so soon! How is it possible?"

Fatima gripped her arms. "Where is the Sultana?"

"Here, in the apartments of my lady the *kadin*. Come, they shall be glad you are here."

Sabela ushered her inside Nur al-Sabah's chambers. Fatima pushed the damask green curtains aside. The scent of ambergris and musk wafted up from a brazier in the corner.

Nur and Shams sat at a low table. Both wore the blue-black colors of mourning. Fatima hesitated at the edge of the carpet. Nur's face, so stark and pale, startled Fatima. Shams sat with her eyes rimmed red.

Sabela urged Fatima forward. She entered the room and sat with her father's women. Nur's hand covered Shams ed-Duna's own. Now, she reached for Fatima's fingers, as did the *kadin*. The trio sat in a circle of silence and grief.

Then Shams swallowed loudly. "You must have dreamt of your father."

Fatima had told her years ago about her strange ability to know of things happening far away. Fatima's maternal grandmother once possessed the same gift. Now, she viewed it as a curse. Her unnatural knowledge always portended pain for those whom she loved.

"But I did not dream of your son, Shams. I am so sorry. How could this have happened?"

She bit back a sob. Nur squeezed her hand. Gray streaks lined the *kadin's* pale yellow hair. Fatima had never noticed them before, not even at Leila's recent marital ceremony.

Nur said, "Shams suffers cruelly. They say her son was a traitor."

A heavy weight settled in Fatima's stomach. Dread crept up her spine. "Who says that? He loved our father and the Sultanate. He would never have betrayed Gharnatah or our family."

Shams sniffled. "The *Diwan al-Insha* proclaimed his guilt. The new Sultan has a letter, written and signed in my son's own hand. Before he took his life and the lives of my granddaughters, he confessed to his treason."

"To what?"

"He had written to the Marinids, while my husband was at the court of the Castillans in the spring. He promised the Marinids a new alliance with Gharnatah. Your brother, Sultan Muhammad, discovered this and confronted him. My son admitted his guilt. Before the guards took him to *Al-Quasaba*, he forced my granddaughters and their mothers to drink poison. Then he killed himself, too. The new Sultan has ordered my exile from court. He won't allow the mother of a traitor to remain in Gharnatah. He has banished me back to al-Maghrib el-Aska. I must leave at the end of the month."

Fatima pulled away from them. Her throat tightened, so that she could hardly breathe or utter a sound.

Nur screamed. "Sabela! Water, quickly."

Nur and Shams rushed to Fatima's side. Sabela hurried with the goblet. Shams massaged Fatima's throat, while Nur urged her to drink.

Afterward, Nur said, "It is a great shock to us all, but he confessed."

Fatima shook her head. Great rivulets poured down her cheeks. She clutched at Shams' fingers with trembling hands. She forced the words from her aching throat. "No, no! It's a lie. It's all a horrible lie. Your son was no traitor. Muhammad is! He killed your son, just as surely as he killed my father."

"Fatima, what are you talking about? My son confessed."

"No! Muhammad forced him to sign something that was a falsehood, I know it."

"You were not here. How can you make such a claim?"

Fatima shared everything with them, her talk with her father during the *walima*. The forgery he had discovered, how he identified his heir as the culprit and confronted him.

Shams stared at her with a gaping mouth, but Fatima implored her to listen. "Father knew, you see, he knew the truth. He wasn't going to let Muhammad get away with it. He was going to name your son as his heir in Muhammad's place."

"The Sultan never told me," Shams whispered.

"He could not bring himself to speak of it to anyone except me. He trusted me and I believed in him. I knew the monster Muhammad was and I had experienced his cruelty firsthand. I did not doubt Father's resolve. He intended your son to rule in his stead."

"And what would he have done to Muhammad?"

"The penalty for treason is death, Shams."

Nur shook her head. "I cannot believe my Sultan would have murdered his own son. Nor do I believe Muhammad killed him. Your brother is many things, but to murder his own father…."

"He tried to poison me, Nur! A beloved sister. Don't you remember what I told you, when Nasr was a child?"

"How can you know what your father intended with such certainty, when he never confided in me, or his Sultana?"

"Shams ed-Duna's son was next in line to the throne! Oh Nur, can you not see? Father confronted Muhammad about his treason. My brother knew when Father returned from Malaka that his life would be in jeopardy. He had to act. He murdered my father and accused Shams ed-Duna's son of doing exactly what he had done. Somehow, he forced him to bear the burden! He knew everyone on the council would believe it. The *Diwan* would look at Shams' son and they would not see a child of the Nasrids. They would see the grandson of Sultan Abu Yusuf Ya'qub al-Marini. Of course, they would reason Shams' son had motive to betray Gharnatah. He is a descendant of the Marinids through his mother. He is nephew to the current ruler of al-Maghrib el-Aska. Muhammad has deceived everyone about him."

Shams slumped against the green silk cushion behind her, with her head bowed. "And my son suffered the consequences of that lie. Now he is dead. Oh, he is dead! My sweet boy, my Faraj!"

Nur comforted Shams, holding her while she wailed and repeated her son's name.

Fatima sank back on her heels. Her throat ached with each haggard breath. "Tell me what happened. How did my father die?"

Nur responded, "Only Nasr knows the full details. He has not spoken of it. Not even to me. He was there that evening with his father. He dined with him, along with Shams' son and your husband."

"I must go to Father's burial site. Does he rest beside Grandfather in the *rawda* on the *Sabika*?"

"No," Nur replied, as she rocked Shams. "The new Sultan buried your father in the gardens of his palace."

"What? Why? He should have rested with his own father, with his family."

Fatima stood and left them. She crossed the harem to her father's residence. The rain had stopped. An evening breeze carried aloft the vapor that had descended on Gharnatah.

She grasped one of the torches from its brackets along the wall and ordered the guardsmen to open the door.

Darkness covered the room. The lattice shutters kept out the moonlight. Her gaze did not linger for long on her father's worldly possessions. She moved to a table, where a leather sheath rested on brackets, covered with lapis lazuli and gold filigree in ornate, swirling designs. She gripped her grandfather's bejeweled *khanjar* in her hand, before she turned and closed the cedar door behind her forever.

She walked westward under the cover an avenue of cypresses offered. The face of the full moon marked her progress. Sentries patrolled the grounds in silence. In a cleared patch of woodland in the midst of the gardens, a fresh mound rose. Someone had covered it with bell-shaped, honeysuckle flowers.

She dropped the torch. It sputtered once before dying. She sank to the ground. Her shoulders shook. The tears fell without restraint and blinded her. She seized clumps of the earth in which her father's body would rest for eternity.

"It is too late for your tears, sister."

Nasr's voice penetrated her sadness. When she looked up, he hovered beside her. His boot mashed the trailing end of her veil into the dirt. He crouched beside her.

"These false tears of yours do not fool me. I know why you have come."

He lunged at her. His hands wrapped around her throat. He stifled the scream inside her.

"Yes, I knew you would come at the beckon of your murderous brother. I can't do anything to him. His bodyguards protect him too well. Yet here you sit all alone. Now, I shall ensure some justice for my father. Before I kill you, let me hear the truth from your lips. Tell me how you and your deceitful brother conspired to murder our father."

# Chapter 13
# Vows

## Princess Fatima

Gharnatah, Al-Andalus: Sha'ban 701 AH (Granada, Andalusia: April AD 1302)

Nasr's stone-carved face loomed above Fatima's own. He tightened his hold on her neck. She gasped for air and clawed blindly at his hands and arms. Even at his youthful age, his strength overwhelmed her. With heavy eyelids, she drifted toward oblivion. She wheezed and air rattled in her lungs. She was about to die at the hands of her own brother, but not the one she had long suspected of being a murderer.

Then, she remembered her grandfather's *khanjar*. A gleam of gold flashed beside Nasr's foot. She raked her nails across his cheek. She gouged thin lines that drew blood. He cursed and his hold slackened. She reached for the dagger and slashed. The blade caught his forearm. Nasr yelped and clutched the billowing sleeve of his robe. Blood seeped from a thin wound.

She scuttled back on the wet ground and held the dagger in front of her. Nasr watched her. An impenetrable mask hid his intent.

She rubbed her throat with one hand. "Stop, please. Let me explain."

Each breath or attempt to swallow squeezed her chest.

Nasr smiled lazily. "Do you think the blade can protect you?"

"Stay back!" A raspy throat pained her.

"You shall die here next to our father's grave. Instead of Paradise, you shall find the gates of *Jahannam* open to you. The final judgment awaits your brother, too."

"I did not help Muhammad! I loved our father…."

"So, you know that your brother killed Father? The truth emerges, even from your lies. Before you die tonight, I shall have the full story of your plot against Father."

He lunged for her again. He knocked the *khanjar* aside with one hand. She scrambled away, crawling in the muck. When he grasped her veil, the pins in it scraped her scalp. His fingers tangled in her hair and pulled from the roots. His boot came down hard on her ankle. Whatever cry of pain she might have made died, as his free hand encircled her throat. He dragged her back against his body.

"Speak the truth before you die, Fatima. God may forgive you. I never shall. I swear it! You shall suffer as our father suffered in his death throes."

"I didn't murder him!"

She clawed at his wounded forearm and struggled against his solid grip, like a wall of rock that encased her. She gouged at the torn flesh and shredded the skin around it. His hold tightened. Panic wedged itself against her throat and chest. The awful blackness returned, to consume her.

"No! Nasr...the truth...I'll tell it!"

"You are ready to confess?"

She nodded, instead of trying to speak again. When he released her, she collapsed on her hands and knees with a pained wheeze. He gripped their grandfather's dagger in one hand and tapped it against his thigh. "Speak now."

"A moment! Have mercy upon me!"

"Mercy? You dare ask for it. When you and your brother have shown our father none? I have no pity for you. Tell me how you planned my father's murder. Then you shall die."

"You have condemned...." She faltered and drew another ragged breath into her burning lungs. "You have condemned me without proof."

"You are wasting my time. I shall kill you now and...."

"No! Hear me and judge whether what I say is true. I came to Gharnatah, knowing of our father's death because I have the gift of foresight. It does not come to me always, this understanding of things beyond the comprehension of others, but my fears are never wrong."

He pulled away from her. "You're a witch? You practice the black arts. All the more reason to kill you."

"No! My maternal grandmother was the same way. It is not my fault. She gave me this gift, or curse. I know not what to call it. Only know that it alone guided me here."

Nasr knelt beside her again, a sneer on his lips that turned into a deep chuckle.

"So, I am to believe you are a seer, who perceived Father's death and so came in all haste to Gharnatah. If that is true, then tell me everything! Tell me of the manner of his death and I shall know whether you are a liar!"

"I cannot do that! My knowledge occurs in a sudden alteration of my feelings. Joy that gives way to sadness without warning. The pain that stabbed at me when Father died. I never know the details!" She sank on her side. "Nasr, I hate Muhammad! He is a monster. Don't you remember how he tried to hurt you when you were a child? I saved you from him! Why would I have cared, if I did not despise him? By the Prophet's beard, he tried to murder me and my unborn child before Ismail was born."

"What folly is this?"

"I speak the truth! Why would I conspire with a man who once sought my death? If you do not believe me, ask Niranjan."

"Your creature? He would lie for you!"

"Niranjan is my loyal servant. He has always been devoted to me because of my love for Father! He knows the truth. Years ago, I dined with Muhammad and one of his slaves, a girl who suffered the loss of his children several times. I thought Muhammad wanted to get rid of her, to punish her failures. Later, I realized he must have been jealous of me, angry that I could have children and he could not sire even one. His concubine, she was eating sweet cakes. Muhammad tried to make me eat some, but I did not want any...."

Her voice trailed off. The memory of Muhammad's cruelty intruded. How he had watched and gloated while his slave perspired and vomited. How he refused to send for a doctor until it was too late. Afterward, Fatima had defended him at first, believing him incapable of such malice toward anyone. Including her. She was a fool. With the murder of their father, Muhammad had proved he could do much more.

She whispered, "He has killed innocents before, his own cook and another slave girl to hide his guilt. He would have killed me with those honey cakes too, if I had not…."

"What did you say?"

Nasr grabbed her arm. She shrank back. He held her imprisoned in his firm grip.

His gaze bored into hers. "What did you say about honey cakes?"

"That was how he tried to poison me, how he killed his slave girl. He hid the poison in honey slathered on cakes."

"He murdered Father in the same way."

Nasr released her and sat back on his heels. He stabbed the dagger in the mud. She stared at him, wordless.

He clasped his hands together in his lap. "Before the night Father died, he summoned all of his sons to dine with him and your husband that afternoon. Muhammad made excuses, said he would be late. We never knew why. He sent a plate of honey cakes, to apologize for his delay. Father alone ate of the platter. Then we attended *Salat al-Asr*.

"Soon afterward, Father began to perspire, swaying in some sort of delirium. He collapsed and withdrew into unconsciousness. Your husband called for the Sultan's servants. Within two hours, Father awoke again. He vomited blood. Then he grew quiet, so silent his physician feared he had died. Afterward he began to tremble violently. Even the frame of his bed shook. It was over soon after that. He never spoke again during all that time."

She listened in silence while Nasr recounted her father's death and burial. She recalled the murder of the Muhammad's slave girl in the months before Ismail's birth. The girl had experienced the swift effects of the poison and died in short agony.

Muhammad must have known Fatima would remember the slave girl's sudden death and link it to her father's own. Had her brother allayed suspicion about the Sultan's death by giving their father a smaller dose of the poison?

If so, Fatima was the only person who knew the extent of her brother's violence. She remained the only threat against him. She would have to safeguard herself and those whom she loved.

Fatima trembled though the evening wind did not penetrate her garments. She did not feel the chilling effect of the breeze. She did not experience the sensation of anything. Soon, even her brother's voice faded.

"Fatima?" Nasr shook her roughly and drew her back to the moment. "Did you hear what I said? I think, at the end, Father knew who and what had killed him."

She licked away salty tears. "Why do you think that?"

Nasr rubbed at a tic along his temple. "He reached for the platter of honey cakes. He was desperate to get them. He knocked the salver over onto the floor. I understood the message. He tried to tell us about the instrument of his death and who had sent it. Later, I told my brother about my suspicions. He was going to confront Muhammad, but then...."

"...Muhammad devised the lie about his treason," she finished for him.

In a rush of words, she confessed her father's warning and intent, as he had revealed it, including the Sultan's discovery of Muhammad's treachery. How he was determined to resolve the matter upon his return to Gharnatah. Muhammad had acted too quickly, well-prepared for all eventualities. He must have had assistance. She would discover who had helped him, but first, she had to protect those whom she loved from further harm.

She reached for Nasr's hand. When he did not immediately resist her, her fingers closed on his and held them. They shook, as did the lips that trembled. His eyes glistened with unshed tears.

She whispered, "Now is not the time for crying. Muhammad killed our father and brother. He tried to murder me once. If he believes you know the truth, he would not hesitate to execute or assassinate you as he did our father. You must be brave *and* cautious, Nasr. The eyes give us away. They reveal our true feelings. Bury your emotions, as I must do with mine."

She wrenched the dagger from the moist earth. Rain pattered on the ground again. Droplets splattered on the blade and rolled down its curved edge.

Nasr stood and she raised her gaze to his. "Go, we shall talk in the morning."

He nodded, despite his watery stare. "I didn't know I could trust you. I thought you had helped him."

"Now, you know better."

He turned to go, but stopped in mid-stride. He looked at her, his face stricken. "Can you forgive me?"

She joined him and cupped his cheeks. He closed his eyes. She raised his face to hers. "Nasr, look at me."

When he did so, she whispered, "You are a worthy son of our father and my true brother, the only one I have left in this world. Of course, I forgive you. Go to Nur al-Sabah. Comfort her. I shall come to you both soon."

They hugged each other and drew apart.

He asked, "What happens now?"

She shook her head. "Do not worry. Go to your mother."

Evening shadows encroached. Fatima shuddered, but not because of the cold or drizzling rain.

There were no limits to Muhammad's depravity. Left unchecked, he would shatter her father's legacy, as he had destroyed the last years of an old man's life. She could not let him get away with his crimes against the Sultan.

She returned to the fresh mound of her father's gravesite. She wiped the *khanjar* on the folds of her mantle and removed the dirt the rain did not wash away.

She gripped the dagger in one hand. As she closed her palm on it, the *khanjar* sliced deep into her palm. A thick crimson streak welled up. Blood trickled along the contours and channels of her flesh. It beaded at her wrist, before dripping onto the grave, dotting the pale, wet honeysuckle.

Fat raindrops splashed her forehead and cheek. She closed her eyes.

"Blessed and beloved Father, I vow by this blade, by my blood, with my last breath and all that I possess, I shall avenge your death. Muhammad shall not hold the throne of Gharnatah for long. I swear it."

## *Prince Faraj*

In silence, Faraj remained bent double on the floor of the throne room before a square patchwork of tiles inscribed with the ninety-nine names of God. Although his neck and back stiffened in a subtle reminder of his age, he held the pose without complaint. The cedar wood chair before him creaked, yet he kept still.

"You may raise your head, *Raïs* of Malaka."

At the Sultan's command, he did so in perfect understanding that his master had not allowed him to raise his eyes to him in his presence. The new Sultan sat amidst his bodyguards. His hands caressed the flower motifs carved into the cedar wood.

How many times had he seen his late uncle and Fatima's father seated upon the same throne? He could not remember every instance. Now Fatima's brother occupied the same chair, far sooner than Faraj might have expected a month ago. Nor had he anticipated the mockery the new Sultan would make of the Sultanate at his own coronation.

Earlier in the week, the court poet, ibn al-Hajj, whom Faraj did not even like because of his eager interest in alliance with the Christian kingdoms, entertained the audience.

Ibn al-Hajj had said, "For whom are the banners being unfurled today? For whom are the soldiers parading under the standards?"

At that moment, Sultan Muhammad had belched and muttered, "For this imbecile whom you have in front of you."

No Sultan's reign had ever started in such an inauspicious manner.

Faraj's thoughts turned from his embarrassment on the Sultan's behalf to his wife. How had Fatima suffered? He did not doubt that she, in her uncanny way, had known of her father's death when it occurred. How else might he explain Ismail's sudden appearance in

Gharnatah, only days after Faraj had reached the capital with Fatima's father? They had not spoken, as he spent most of the morning in meetings with the Sultan and his *Diwan*. Yet, his son's abrupt arrival with Fatima could only mean that she knew the truth. His heart ached for her and longed to comfort her. They would both have to wait upon his master's demands.

The Sultan did not regard him. Instead, he gave all his attention to the ceiling, which his grandfather's artisans had constructed. Faraj followed his stare. The inlaid work in the shape of circles, crowns and stars glittered with hints of white, blue and gold.

The Sultan looked down from the dais, but not at him. Instead, he focused on the eunuch also bent double beside Faraj.

He ordered, "Faisal, you may raise your head now."

The eunuch groaned as he moved from the uncomfortable position. He sat back on his heels, with his eyes still averted from his master.

The Sultan leaned forward and gripped the arms of his throne tightly. "Slave, you shall remove all of my father's possessions from his old quarters tonight. I do not care what you do with them. Burn or sell them. It does not matter to me. The palace is mine. I expect everything gone by tomorrow morning. On the following day, my slaves shall furnish the Sultan's apartments to my taste. Do you understand my wishes?"

"Yes, my Sultan," the eunuch said.

"You shall also ensure the departure of the traitor's mother, Sultana Shams ed-Duna. I want that Maghribi woman out of Gharnatah and on a boat within the month. She takes only what she brought to Gharnatah. Her bridal trousseau is forfeit. It belongs to the state."

Faisal met his master's gaze for the first time. His brow furrowed and his fleshy woman's lips quivered. "Begging the pardon of my noble master, but the *addahbia* belongs to a woman all her life. These things are hers, the Sultana's gifts from your late, honored father...."

The Sultan stood and Faisal's voice trailed off. The Sultan strolled across the sacred square tiles and stood in their midst. Faraj put aside his shock at the sight of one so careless as to tread upon the name of God.

The Sultan said, "He is dead. I am your master now. Never forget it."

Faisal's gaze dropped. "As you wish, my Sultan."

"You say that very prettily. I know your mistress does not care for my new role. She wanted her son to usurp my birthright. She has always desired it. This is my destiny, what I was born to do."

He turned on his heels and returned to the throne, lifting the hem of his *jubba*. He sank down and clasped his hands together.

"I have other tasks for you. Arrange for the sale of my father's remaining women in the morning. Sell the virgins and younger ones at the *Qaysariyya*. However, the older women might make suitable gifts for those among my governors who prove loyal. Specifically, the *kadin* might do well for the governor of al-Mariyah. He is aged, but she has advanced years as well. What would an old man want with a spirited wife? Better an older woman, don't you agree, Prince Faraj?"

Faraj had barely recovered from his shock long enough to realize the Sultan now addressed him. "I do not mean to question your sovereign will, master, but did you say the *kadin*? Surely, you've made a mistake."

"I do not make mistakes! I meant the *kadin* Nur al-Sabah al-Muhammad, the mother of that whelp Nasr. Did my father have more than one favorite? Surely not."

"But, master, a Sultan's favorite is like a wife to him. Protocol demands that she never re-marry after his death. To do so is a grave dishonor to the memory...."

"...of a dead man! He is dead! I am ruler of Gharnatah, not my father. You forget that the Sultan devises the rules of the harem. I am master here. It is my right!"

He jerked his head at Faisal again. "I shall not forget your service to me. Now go."

Faraj frowned at Faisal as he stood and bowed, before scrambling backward. What service had he rendered the new Sultan? Was Faisal not the chief eunuch of the Sultana Shams ed-Duna?

The guards at the entrance to the throne room opened the heavy oak doors, inlaid with brass. Faisal disappeared into the drizzling rain trickling across the marble.

"Are you eager to return to your home at Malaka?"

Faraj returned his attention to the Sultan. “I shall see it soon enough. My son Muhammad has charge of the house in my absence.”

The Sultan raised a dark eyebrow. “Not Prince Ismail?”

Faraj answered, “My eldest is here, with his mother.”

His master jerked upright from the chair. “Fatima? So soon? Yes, she would have come.”

Faraj did not ask how he had arrived at his conclusion. “Yes, she and our son came to Gharnatah today. He sent word of their arrival while I sat among your council.”

The Sultan took his seat again. He leaned forward and propped his bearded chin on one hand. His owlish eyes glittered in the torchlight from brackets set at each corner of the room.

“Malaka is a rich province. You perform a remarkable duty in keeping it profitable. I reviewed the reports of your administration, while I served as my father’s *wazir*. Do you enjoy the post as its governor?”

“It was my birthright.”

“But do you prefer Malaka? Wouldn’t duties here in Gharnatah, perhaps as a *wazir*, have suited you just as well?”

“It should have, but the past and my heart bind me to the city of my birth. By my choice, I would not leave it.”

The Sultan smiled at him. The gesture did not warm Faraj. He rushed on. “You must understand the sentiment, my Sultan. You were born here, but your father and grandfather were born in Aryuna. Does not your heart lie in Gharnatah? You do not consider Aryuna as your ancestral home. I hope you shall trust in me to continue my rule at Malaka in the same steadfast manner as I served your father. I remain loyal.”

“Be at ease, Faraj. I did not question your loyalty, nor do I ask you such things because I considered removing you. After all, you are my sister’s husband. You shall keep your governorship.”

Faraj gritted his jaw and prayed he kept his face impassive. The Sultan’s chuckle warned he did not.

“Other men would have pleaded with me or humbly accepted it were I to dismiss them from their posts. You have a stout heart.”

“My wife says the same of me.”

"My sister is an excellent judge of a person's nature. I am sure she must have heard the news. It must be a terrible shock to her."

Faraj averted his eyes in the space it took to draw breath, before he returned the Sultan's assessing stare. "Her grief must be beyond bearing. In less than a few days, she has lost her father. A man whom she loved and worshipped all her life. I would not have you think she is weak. Her strength is remarkable. It is one of her constant traits and the best among her talents. I do not doubt she shall bear the pain."

"Yes, I am well aware of her capabilities. Her strength is something she inherited from our forbearers. Luckily, the same blood runs in my veins." The Sultan grinned, while Faraj wondered at his statement. "You have talents as well. You must have to maintain Fatima's approval. I remember my father admired your talent for circumspection best of all. You seemed to have lost it in recent years. Instead, passion guided you at Tarif."

"I was a fool. I risked more than the loss of my life. My actions could have jeopardized my heir's inheritance. I shall never make that mistake again. Loyalty to the Sultanate rules my heart now."

Faraj's fists tightened at his side. He meant every word. He would never make such a foolhardy choice again, as at Tarif. His convictions be damned. He had to safeguard the future for himself and his family.

"Ah, there's that mention of your loyalty again, Prince Faraj. Not too many in the Sultanate claim such devotion, or inspire my belief in the virtue of it, as you do."

"All men can be judged loyal to one course or another at any time. I believe there are those who need an opportunity to prove their faithfulness and those who demonstrate it always without question."

"Which kind would you deem yourself, Prince Faraj?"

"I thought I had made that plain, my Sultan."

"We shall see. I need men of loyalty to administer my provinces and enforce my laws. May I rely upon you to support me?"

Faraj sensed that a moment's hesitation would have gone against him and his entire family forever. He had sworn an oath of personal allegiance to the Sultan, no matter who that Sultan might be. He would never forsake his word now.

"You have my oath, freely given in your throne room."

"Then if I order you to permit Ismail to remain here and serve as a *wazir* of my *Diwan*, you would not refuse the pledge?"

Faraj bit his lower lip. "You want Ismail to serve on your council? He has no experience of political matters."

"He is your son, a prince of Gharnatah, destined to control Malaka. He must learn. I need your son here."

"Fatima would want to have a say in this decision."

"You are the young man's father. My sister shall accept your decision. She is a woman, after all. Do you refuse my request because of her?"

Faraj dipped his gaze to the floor, but he could not put off the Sultan. He sensed grave danger in thwarting the man.

"What is your answer?" The Sultan's voice, tinged with impatience, rang through the hall to the rafters.

Faraj glanced at him. "Ismail shall be a *wazir* of council, for as long as you would wish."

"Good. Send your son to me tonight. I shall speak with him about his duties while we dine together."

"So soon? I would have liked to inform his mother of this favorable news. Fatima is very devoted to our son."

"You may speak with her. Leave me."

The Sultan waved a hand and signaled his permission for Faraj to go. When he stood, his gaze narrowed and focused on a spot at the back of the room. He settled against the throne and stroked the chair's arms again.

"Fatima, my dear, you're wet through. Have you been outdoors all this time?"

Faraj looked over his shoulder. His jaw dropped. Indeed, her garments clung to her, outlining the curves of her slender body. He growled low in his throat, as the guards posted at the door stared at her without naked lust. None of the old Sultan's guards would have dared, but then, these were different men. What had happened to the bodyguards who once protected Fatima's father?

She advanced. Water trailed in her wake. She stopped before the tile square, beside Faraj. He frowned at the reddened marks around her throat and the tiny pinpricks that dotted her eyes. Blood trickled beneath the edge of her sleeve. What had she been doing?

"I have been at the gravesite of my most beloved father, Muhammad."

The Sultan gripped the throne until his knuckles whitened. The wood creaked beneath his hands.

"Then, sister, you know you must offer me homage. Indeed, it is disrespectful of you to stand while I sit. I know you have not been at court for many years, but surely, you have not forgotten your obeisance."

He picked at the hem of his robe. "Come now. Kiss it."

She did not move.

The Sultan chuckled. "By the Prophet's beard, you still have the pride of that bitch of a woman who bore us."

Faraj recoiled at the Sultan's discourteous reference to his own mother, before he glanced at Fatima. Her lips trembled, pressed tightly together as though she repressed the depths of her feelings.

The Sultan's smile faded. "I am waiting, sister."

She hesitated still. He stood. "Now, you're being insolent. Shall I order my guards to force you to kneel?"

Faraj reached for her. The Sultan's baleful glare turned on him. His hand fell away.

She walked around the tiles and sagged on her knees at her brother's feet. She bent her head low to the ground, then the rest of her torso.

Faraj could have sworn a slight moan eased in the Sultan's throat. He looked down at her from a sloe-eyed gaze. His lips slightly parted, a raspy breath escaped him. His cheeks flushed a deep pink of pleasure.

She reached for his *jubba*, but he snapped the silk away before the mud on her fingers soiled his robe.

He muttered, "You would only dirty it."

"As you wish," she whispered.

She rose and sat back on her heels. He sank down on the throne and sniffed.

"Why is your face so red, sister? What are those marks?" He asked the question that plagued Faraj.

"They are not cause for concern, Muhammad. Other matters distress me."

"What do you want?"

"I have come to plead for the Sultana Shams ed-Duna. She was ever loyal to our father, a good wife to him. She does not deserve exile."

"Her son was a traitor."

"But she had no hand in what you have accused her son of doing. Is it not enough for you that he is dead?"

"By his own hand!"

"I never suggested otherwise."

Yet, Faraj heard the insinuation in her tone. What game was his wife playing? How dare she jeopardize all of their futures with her reckless inquiries?

Her brother's gaze narrowed on her again. "It is what you do not say, Fatima. Your tone implies that I took pleasure in his death."

She remained silent for a time, before she responded, "When I last saw Father at Malaka, he did not have suspicions about my brother Faraj being a traitor. I was surprised when Shams ed-Duna told me you had found the letter implicating him."

"Did our father say he suspected anyone of treachery?"

"Why would he have told me? What could I do about it?"

Faraj's jaw tightened. Either his wife's skills at deception were beyond compare, or she spoke the truth. With her back to him, he could not discern it. Her eyes would have revealed her innermost thoughts.

Something had troubled her in the days after their first daughter married her beloved. Yet Fatima had never spoken of it until the morning she had begged Faraj to protect her father. He had failed her, but she kept secrets from him, too.

Fatima knew more about the traitor than Faraj did and the danger her father had faced because the Sultan confided in her at the wedding. Why would she have withheld the Sultan's suspicions or her own from her husband? He bristled at the thought. Fatima's secrets had placed her family in grave danger before. Had she done it again? He hated to lay blame for her father's demise on her shoulders. Yet if she had spoken the truth beforehand, it might have saved her father.

Her brother interrupted Faraj's musings. "Your answer surprises me, Fatima. Our father trusted you, more than he trusted most." The Sultan stood and looked down at her. "Still, if you say he told you nothing, I must believe it. You would have no reason to deceive me, would you?"

"None. I was never close to Shams ed-Duna's son."

"I am pleased to hear it. Now, the hour grows late and I have much to do."

"What of the Sultana Shams ed-Duna?"

"What of her, Fatima? I have made my decision. She shall leave Al-Andalus. She is a relic of the past. I am its future. I intend to occupy my palace soon and prepare for the arrival of the governors. Your husband has already submitted. I have shown great honor to him and his house that he shall not soon forget."

"What do you mean?" Fatima looked up at him before she glanced over her shoulder. "Faraj?"

The Sultan chuckled. "Your husband shall tell you."

He departed the throne room and his guards followed. Fatima stared in their direction long after he had left.

Faraj waited until they were alone, before he stood. He groaned and shuddered, as blood rushed to his legs.

Fatima whirled toward him, as if jerked from a trance. She met him halfway, her eyes wide and wild. Mud clung to almost every part of her clothing, even smears of it slashed across her cheeks. He barely recognized her.

"Husband, what have you done?"

# Chapter 14
# The Wazir and the Kadin

## Princess Fatima

Gharnatah, Al-Andalus: Sha'ban 701 AH (Granada, Andalusia: April AD 1302)

Fatima shuddered as Faraj wrapped his arms around her and encased her in his warmth. "By the Prophet's beard, you're soaked. We need to get you warm and out of these wet clothes."

He removed his woolen mantle and coiled it at her shoulders, while she stood passive under his ministrations.

"What have you done to yourself? You're so cold...."

"Never mind me." Her voice rasped. "What promises have you made to this usurper?"

He drew back and stared at her. "Usurper? Fatima, Muhammad was your father's heir. He has always been the successor. Your father proclaimed it so after he ascended the throne."

"He did not intend it!"

Faraj clasped her hands in his. "You don't know what you are saying. Grief has overcome you. My God, look at you! The marks around your throat. What were you doing beside your father's grave? Were you there all this time? By the heavens, what have you done to your hand?"

His fingers caressed her open palm. An ugly red line gouged her flesh. Blood and smeared dirt congealed across the wound.

"We must clean it. Come to the fountain."

She pulled her hand from his grasp. "Answer me! Have you betrayed my father, too? Have you pledged yourself to his murderer?"

"Fatima! Have you lost your senses? I was loyal to your father! No one murdered him, certainly not your brother. He wasn't even there when your father died!"

He frowned, deep lines seared into his brow. "Your brother is Sultan. I am sorry your father died. It was a great shock. You must accept it. We must both accept."

"Never! Muhammad is not the legitimate ruler of Gharnatah. He is a usurper and a murderer."

Faraj looked around the empty throne room. "I beg you not to repeat such accusations within the hearing of others. You speak treason against your own brother."

"He is not even that. He ceased to be my brother many years ago. Now, he is a monster."

He turned from her, but she pursued him. "It is you who has sworn loyalty to him, not me. He does not deserve it. He murdered my father and brother. He schemed to bring about their deaths...."

"Fatima, be silent! Think of what you are doing! Your brother is my sovereign. I hold the governorship of one of his territories. Our son's heritage. Would you jeopardize Ismail's inheritance with such wild accusations? Would you see me stripped of power? I know you are grieving. You have endured great losses in so little time...."

"You only care about your selfish interests in Malaka. You know nothing of my losses! How can you?"

His face turned red with fury and his voice exploded out of him. "Do you think you are the only person who has ever suffered? We have all lost, not just you. You lost a father. I lost the man who gave me my greatest gift in you. One who treated me more like a brother than a cousin, more like a true son, than his daughter's husband. Or is your pain so great that you have no compassion or understanding?"

Her cheeks warmed under his scrutiny. Then she turned her back on him. Tears pricked at the corners of her eyes. She refused to shed them. No more tears.

After some time passed, his hands settled on her shoulders. He rubbed her arms through the rough woolen mantle and the brocaded garments beneath it.

"Before your father died, he said to me 'Tell her she was right.' What did you know beforehand about your father's circumstances, Fatima? What were you and the Sultan hiding?"

The moment was lost forever, the last time when she should have unburdened herself to him before his departure to Gharnatah with her father. She could have revealed everything, including how Muhammad had drugged her father.

She shook her head. It would not have made a difference. Faraj's sentiments were clear. He cared about Malaka and his hold on the governorship. He would not risk it, not even for her. She could not rely on him now.

"Fatima, I need you to listen."

When she did not move, he turned her to face him and cupped her chin in both of his hands. "Please. Hear what I have to say. The Sultan has made a request of us, of me. He offers a great boon. In truth, it shall be an immense benefit to our son, as well."

A tingling sensation prickled along her spine. Her expectant gaze roamed over his face. "What are you saying?"

"Your brother has offered Ismail a post in the *Diwan al-Insha*. Our son is to be a *wazir*. It is an excellent opportunity. Ismail shall remain in Gharnatah, but I feel certain we shall see him....Fatima? Why are you looking at me in that way?"

For a moment, she experienced the strangest sensation she had ever known, of being semi-present, watching another woman's nightmare unfold. Then a chill ran up and down her spine. Her arms tingled with gooseflesh. She stumbled backward as though wounded with an arrow to the chest. Yet, she was not dead, because for the first time in several hours, she experienced pain again.

"Fatima? Merciful God, Fatima, speak to me."

Grief grew and swelled in her chest, as a canker in her breast that slowly spread. She stared at him, wordless.

He grasped her fingers again. "Please talk to me."

Her eyes watered and she blinked rapidly, as if she could shut him out forever.

"You gave our...you gave my son over to that monster?"

He released her abruptly. "I knew you would be displeased. For once, think of our son and not your own selfish desire to have him near!"

"I can't believe you. You didn't, you couldn't have done it."

"Fatima, I am his father...."

"You gave my child over to Muhammad!"

Her fists struck his chest and face. She rained down blows on him. He struggled against her and got hold of her hands. When she could not use them or rake her nails across his face, she kicked at him. He pushed her down on the cold marble and straddled her. He wrenched her hands above her head.

"Stop this now! You're hysterical."

She twisted beneath him and spat in his eye. He swung his hand wide twice. Two stinging slaps made her ears ring. He panted and stood, wiping at the blood from a small cut, smeared beneath his right eye.

She stared at him in disbelief. "How could you do it, betray me and our son? You gave him over to the very man who tried to kill him, when he was in my womb!"

Faraj snarled, "You're mad!"

Fatima flung the truth at him, the brutal past that she had concealed, to her bitterest regret. He staggered and flopped on his backside across from her, his eyes widening with each word.

She stabbed a finger at him. "Now, you have put him in the hands of the man who could have killed him and me. The man who poisoned our father in the same manner that he used to kill an innocent slave girl. Muhammad must have known I would suspect him in the sudden death of our father. He does not claim Ismail for his *wazir*. Our son is his hostage, to compel my silence."

Faraj gaped. "Why did you never tell me before now?"

She shook her head. "I shall never forgive you. Do you understand me? Never!"

"I didn't know! You hid the truth from me. How can you accuse me when you have never spoken of this in all our years together?"

She ignored him and struggled to stand. It did not matter how his words damned her. Her father was gone and Muhammad threatened to take her son away from her.

She moved toward the door.

"Where are you going?" Faraj called out.

She halted at the entrance, but did not turn back to him. "To find my son and save him."

She dashed out into the cold night. The sentries on the walls of Al-Quasaba sounded the hour.

"*Ummi*! *Ummi*, what has happened?"

Ismail stood beneath a gate, sheltered from the lingering moisture in the air. Khalid and some of Faraj's men stood at his back. Ismail raced across the open-air courtyard. She stumbled in her haste to reach him. She hit the cobblestone pavement. Pain throbbed through her knees. Her son aided her and she launched herself at him. She held his lean-muscled form in her arms, safe and secure where no one could touch him. She intended to keep it that way.

"You have to leave Gharnatah now! You must go away, far from here, where Muhammad cannot hurt you!"

He drew back in the circle of her embrace. "What do you mean? The Sultan would never harm me."

She shook her head. "You think he would not, but you must flee this place."

"Where would I go? Besides, I have no wish to leave, now that the Sultan has made his offer. I am not leaving."

She whispered, "Muhammad has spoken to you?"

"No. A servant of his summoned me to dine at his side within the hour. He also sent word that I am to be a *wazir* of the *Diwan*."

She caressed his cheek. "Oh, my precious life, you don't understand. You think you're safe here. This place offers no protection. Come with me now. I shall tell you everything on our return home, after we have left this evil place."

She grabbed his hand. Ismail did not move. His mouth tightened into a stubborn line. "I am not leaving Gharnatah. It would be treason to defy the Sultan's wishes. Besides, I am a man now. You cannot make me return to Malaka."

"Why must you choose this moment to assert your will against mine? What you wish is irrelevant! Your safety is all that matters to me. I am your mother. Heed my warning, Ismail."

"I cannot, though it pains me to say so. I want to stay in Gharnatah. I want to be the Sultan's *wazir*."

A low moan escaped her. She sagged against him.

Ismail wrapped his arms around her. "I don't know what's happened to you since our arrival. Has someone tried to harm you? You are dirty and wet."

"Her grief has maddened her, son."

She and Ismail looked up at Faraj's approach. Their son's gaze darted between them. Then he scowled.

"Did you and *Ummi* argue, Father? Are you responsible for these marks on her neck? There's blood on your cheek, too."

Faraj heaved a weary sigh. "I would never willingly harm your mother. You know I would not."

Ismail's scowl deepened. His dark glare stabbed at his father. Faraj did not shrink under his scrutiny.

Fatima touched her son's shoulder. "Please, listen to me. Your grandfather's death has left me in agony, but I promise you, it has not altered my mind. Your father does not understand many things about my brother. You have to go from this place. Don't you see that? I would do anything to protect you!"

Ismail sighed. "What are you protecting me from? No more secrets and half-truths. If you would ensure my safety, then tell me everything."

He gathered her against him and led her away from Faraj and the men of Malaka. They sat at a distance on a cold stone bench, beneath the fragrant nighttime shade of bougainvillea trees. Purple blossoms floated around them.

Fatima spoke in full candor with her son. She held nothing back of the past several years, including Muhammad's attempt on her life, her discovery of her father's addiction to hashish and Muhammad's role. Then, she spoke of Leila's marital ceremony, where the Sultan confronted the truth about Muhammad and resolved to punish him. Finally, she revealed Nasr's accusation of the poison used in her father's sudden death.

Spent, she leaned against Ismail for comfort. He had said nothing while she spoke. She touched his bearded cheek. His handsome visage in the moonlight made her miss her beloved father more than ever.

"You must not stay here, son. You would be nothing more than Muhammad's pawn to use against me. I cannot let him hurt you. I would kill him with my bare hands before I allowed it."

Ismail clutched her shoulders. "You have the spirit of a lioness protecting her cubs. Even she must acknowledge when her offspring are full-grown."

"You do not know the full measure of your uncle's depravity!"

"Yes, I do, for you have armed me with the knowledge. I shall use it to protect myself. I shall ensure your safety, too. If my uncle believes you are a threat to him, then it is best for me to remain here, to be your eyes and ears, to witness and anticipate his actions."

"No! You cannot take such a risk for me."

"Listen to reason! Where do you think I could go that my uncle would not find me? The Sultan has issued a command that none of us dares disobey. He needs me here to ensure your silencc and prevent anyone else from knowing how Grandfather died. He requires Father's continued loyalty. I am safe, don't you see? He would never harm me, not while you remain to speak against him. He still needs my father. Trust in me! I shall never draw my uncle's suspicion. He'll never move against me."

Tears stung her eyes. "Please, no."

Ismail took her hands in his. She looked down at them and saw the familiar strength of her own father's large olive-skinned hands mirrored in her son's grasp.

"We must separate for a time. Yet, you remain in my heart, *Ummi*."

She sobbed and buried her face in his tunic. "You shall always be in mine, my blessed son."

That night, Fatima stayed in Shams ed-Duna's quarters, while Faraj and his men found rooms at an inn within the *madina*'s confines. Fatima did not sleep. She peered out of the window all night for a sign of Ismail's return from her brother's rooms. Finally, Shams pleaded with her to rest because she would not see her son from her vantage point. The Sultan now maintained his quarters in the most prominent tower of *Al-Quasaba*, a good distance from the harem.

Fatima muttered, "Muhammad is a monster to force you from this place."

Shams took her hands in her slim, dark ones. Fatima raised her fingers to her lips and kissed them.

Shams said, "In truth, it would pain me too much if I stayed. The memories of my Sultan and of my son linger. My eldest daughter married a prince of al-Jaza'ir. Before your father died, he promised my two remaining daughters to governors of al-Tunisiyah. Those men may not hold to their bargains now that my children are fatherless. I have asked Faisal to arrange for us to go to my daughter in al-Jaza'ir. If her husband has pity on us, we shall remain with her."

"You shall write to me often."

"I shall do so. My heart is heavy. The girls know of their father's death, but I have concealed the circumstances surrounding their dear brother. When we leave this place, I shall comfort them and they shall do the same for me."

Fatima hugged her stepmother and buried her face in her neck. How would she bear the loss of her, especially at this time?

Whenever she drifted off throughout the night, the memory of Muhammad's insolent grin jarred her from sleep. How he had relished his position upon the throne with her at his feet. She had not needed to look at his face to verify it. His throaty intake of breath and the sigh of pleasure that washed over him revealed all.

Morning came too quickly, the dawning of another horrible day since her father's death. Prayer offered her little solace, but she observed the rituals of *Salat al-Fajr* at Shams' side with her younger sisters.

In the midst of the morning prayer, a scream echoed.

Shams raised her head and glanced at Fatima. "Nur."

She admonished her two girls to remain where they were, while she and Fatima crossed the hall in a flutter of blue-black silk.

The door to the *kadin*'s chamber swung on its hinges. The turquoise-colored damask curtains, embroidered at the hems with gold filigree floated on the breeze coming through the windows. Soft sobs came from the room beyond.

Fatima pushed aside another curtain draped over an archway. Nur al-Sabah lay on her pallet with her eyes closed. Nasr stood at the foot of the bed. His mother could have been sleeping. She wore mourning colors with a wispy veil covering her pale gold hair. A necklace of finely cut opals, jade and sapphires gleamed in gold around her neck. Fatima recognized it as the gift her father had given the *kadin,* when they celebrated the feast of Nur's first child, some thirty years in the past.

Nur's maidservant Sabela rocked back and forth on the floor. She keened, as she held Nur's lily-white hand in hers. A pewter cup rested on a table beside the pallet. Fatima took it and sniffed the contents. She did not recognize the sticky, sweet-smelling, yellow liquid at first. Then she dipped her finger into the cup and licked it. The taste of alcohol and bitter fruit juice tinged her tongue. She spat on the ground and rushed to Nur's side.

Shams buried her face in her hands and sobbed.

Fatima stared at Nasr. "What happened, brother?"

"Last night, the chief eunuch Faisal came to *Ummi.* He warned her that Sultan Muhammad intends to give her to the old governor of al-Mariyah. She drank mandrake juice, mixed with wine."

Nasr paused and pointed at his mother's body slave. "That creature Sabela procured it for her!"

"Do not, my son. She did as I bid her." Nur's voice barely rose above a whisper.

Fatima dashed to her side and took her free hand. Nur opened her eyes. They were wide, the pupils like large black orbs.

Fatima kissed her fingers. "Nur, how could you do this?"

The *kadin* smiled weakly. "I belong with him, with your father. I want to be with him. Only then can I be safe from your brother."

"No! No, I can keep you safe. You could have escaped to Malaka with me. Please. Oh Nur, please do not do this. Nasr needs you now, more than ever."

Nur's head lolled on her pillow. She dragged her hand from Sabela's grasp and beckoned Nasr.

Fatima's brother moved on wooden legs and sank down next to her. He scowled at Sabela, who shrank away. Her sobs vied with Shams ed-Duna's own.

Nur reached for Nasr's hand and placed it on her stomach. Her grip on Fatima's fingers tightened briefly, as she placed her hand over the young man's own. A tear trickled down her cheek.

"Protect him, Fatima. He is a prince of Gharnatah, but he is also the son of a slave. Protect him! I never could."

A spasm racked her body. Her hips lifted from the bed.

Fatima got to her feet and grabbed Sabela. "How do we stop this? I won't lose her, too. Do you understand me? How do we stop the mandrake poison from killing her?"

Sabela shook her head, her graying hair wild around her puffy, pale face. "I don't know how! I swear I don't."

Fatima shoved her away. "Shams, stop crying and help me! Give her water, anything to purge her belly. There must be something that can help us."

A servant brought word that Niranjan al-Kadim and Fatima's maidservants had arrived in Gharnatah just after dawn. Fatima found her eunuch in the courtyard. She hugged him, as she had not done since she was a little girl.

"Oh, how I have needed you at my side!"

"I am here now. How may I aid you?"

Fatima gestured for Basma and Haniya to remain with the pack animals. She dragged her eunuch to the *kadin's* chamber. Nur had started vomiting.

A sigh of relief spread in waves through Fatima's stomach. "Good, if she brings up the mandrake poison from her belly, she can still survive."

Beside her, Niranjan said nothing.

She looked at him. "This is a good sign, is it not?"

He did not reply. He supported Nur, sitting behind her and holding her upright. Her head lolled on his shoulder. She seemed focused on a spot on the ceiling, except for the space of several breaths, in which she did not blink.

Fatima lunged to her side and pressed a hand over her heart. It thrummed inside her breast still, but very faintly.

She looked at Niranjan. "Do something! Anything."

He shook his head. "I cannot, my Sultana."

Within moments, Nur slipped into a stupor. She never recovered. Fatima could not hear her heartbeat.

Niranjan moved aside and Fatima cradled Nur's body in her arms. She crooned in her ear softly. Sometimes, a brief spasm shuddered through the *kadin*. Then the tremors lessened. Her breathing became shallower. Fatima held her, even when her head rolled on Fatima's shoulder and a final rattling breath escaped her.

A woman started sobbing again. Fatima did not look up to be certain whether it was Shams or Sabela. She was beyond caring.

Niranjan moved to her side. "My Sultana, you must let her go. The lady Nur is at peace now."

She jerked away. "Leave her be. Do not touch her!"

"My Sultana, you can do nothing," Niranjan whispered through trembling lips. "Your brother cannot hurt the *kadin* now. She is safe. She is with your father."

Fatima rocked Nur's body. Rage welled inside her, but she was not angry with her brother.

"Why didn't he do it? Why didn't Father marry her? She could have been his wife. Then Muhammad could never have moved against her. Nur would still be alive if Father had wedded her."

Shams stood with her hands clasped. "Your father wanted to marry her. He asked her every year on her birthday. She always refused him."

While Fatima gaped in stunned silence, Shams continued, "He could have forced her. Yet, he wanted her to wed him willingly. Your own mother resented her marriage to him. An alliance with the Marinids dictated his union with me. He wanted someone who had chosen him, as he had chosen her. At first, Nur was afraid of what would happen if she married him. She dreaded your anger."

"She feared me?"

Shams blinked back tears. "She knew how much you loved your father. You did not accept her, at first."

"But that changed! She became one of my dearest friends, a true friend, like you."

"Yes, in time, you became that for her, as well. When she had your friendship and mine, she felt it no longer mattered if she was the Sultan's wife or his slave. She was the queen of his heart. She had my husband's heart and he had hers. It was enough for her."

# Chapter 15
# Shades of the Past

## Prince Faraj

Gharnatah, Al-Andalus: Ramadan 701 AH (Granada, Andalusia: May AD 1302)

Faraj sat across from his master in the Sultan's quarters at the top of the watchtower. Sunlight filtered through the slit windows on the first day of the fast. Muhammad set pieces on an ebony wood chessboard. Faraj recalled having played upon it with his late uncle, Fatima's grandfather.

"It remains in remarkable condition, my Sultan, even after fifty years. Do you know the story of it?"

The Sultan shook his head. "Only that my grandfather treasured it, as did my father."

"They did so because my father gave it to your grandfather. One of the last gifts he had sent to Gharnatah before his demise."

"My father held another prized possession too, my grandfather's *khanjar*. Those damned slaves of mine had better find it. I shall slice open another neck if the culprit doesn't admit it!"

A deep spasm ripped across Faraj's belly at his cousin's casual cruelty. His gaze strayed to the guardsman, who cowered, prostrate on the floor. He had held this position while the Sultan arranged the gaming pieces in a leisurely manner. Faraj suspected that the sovereign took great pleasure in keeping people waiting on him. A streak of cruelty ran through him that neither his grandfather nor father ever possessed. Had Faraj done the right thing in committing his son to serve such a man? Was there another choice?

The Sultan glanced at him and then followed his gaze. "I had forgotten this fool was here."

Faraj doubted that statement. The Sultan demanded, "Well, you have prostrated yourself long enough, so what have you to report?"

The guard raised his head. "My noble Sultan, you commanded me to visit *Al-Quasaba* and see the jailor."

"Yes, to stop those screams at night. They disturb my sleep."

Faraj settled against the chair at his back. "Who disturbs your rest?"

The Sultan eyed him. "My father's personal slaves and bodyguards."

"You have jailed all of them?"

"All that remain, but they have proved hardy. My father fed them too well. I suppose it is for the best if some among them are still alive." He nodded to the guard. "Bring one of them to me. Man or woman, I do not care. Someone shall tell me where my grandfather's *khanjar* lies hidden."

With a wave of his burly hand, he dismissed the sentry. Instead, the guard stood and lingered on the spot. The fool tempted the Sultan's anger.

The Sultan's gaze narrowed. The chair creaked beneath his solid frame, as he leaned forward. "Is there more you would tell me?"

"The jailor begs pity on the slaves. He said he could not bear the screams of the condemned. When I was there, he tossed them some scraps of bread through the iron bars of the trap door over their heads."

"What?!" The Sultan lunged at him and grabbed the man by the collar of his tunic. The frightened soldier stared at him with eyes that bulged wide.

"Say it again," the Sultan ordered him through gritted teeth.

The guardsman trembled and struggled to get the words out. When he did so, Muhammad shoved him backward.

"He pitied them! The fool pitied them! How dare Ahmad defy me?"

He clapped his fists against his temples and whirled toward Faraj, who clasped his hands together and averted his eyes. He kept still. Any sudden movement might draw the Sultan's anger toward him.

Ragged breaths escaped Muhammad. Then he rubbed his hands together and turned his back on Faraj. The guard remained on the floor. The Sultan advanced on him.

"You say the jailor threw them dry bread only? What, nothing to drink, too?"

The guard shook his head. Faraj folded his arms over his chest and waited.

The Sultan dismissed the hapless man and laughed. "That was not very thoughtful. He cannot give them dry bread with nothing else to ease their parched throats. They must have some drink to wash their meal down."

He turned toward Faraj. "Come with me."

Faraj followed the Sultan down three flights of stairs within the squat tower at *Al-Quasaba*, flanked by his bodyguards in a line going down the steps, including the one who had just left the Sultan's presence.

The men emerged from the square central chamber on the second floor. Daylight shimmered between the rows of whitewashed houses, including the largest that belonged to the jailor, lined either side of the cobblestone street. A drainage ditch in the middle of the road carried water down the slopes of the *Sabika*. Some of the officers idled in the doorway, while their children played between the rows of houses.

A trap door with an aperture and iron bars covered the subterranean dungeon. Whimpers and mutters echoed from the hole. The jailor, a crook-backed pale man named Ahmad, whose head seemed too big for his body, stood with his whip over the trap door.

The Sultan gestured toward the jailor. Two of his bodyguards rushed forward and seized Ahmad. They jerked his arms behind him. The man yelped in fright, as they kicked his legs out from under him and forced him to his knees. Muhammad strolled to the trap door and peered through its aperture into the yawning chasm of darkness. He smiled again.

Faraj glanced at the poor jailor, but returned his attention to the Sultan when he spoke.

"Wretched people, my jailor has been kind enough to offer you food. Now, I shall give you something to drink."

He untied the sash of his robe. Faraj gaped, thinking he meant to urinate over the heads of his prisoners.

Shame-faced, he looked away. Neither the Sultan's father nor grandfather would ever have been so cruel to prisoners.

Muhammad shouted into the hole. "Your jailor showed you mercy. So can I!"

Faraj stared, transfixed. Though he recoiled inwardly, he could no longer turn from the scene. The soldiers shoved Ahmad at the Sultan's feet. Muhammad gripped the thin, black strands of the jailor's hair. He jerked back the man's head, exposing the neck.

Faraj covered his hand with his mouth, realizing at last that the prisoners would not suffer the indignity of Muhammad's piss raining down upon them.

The Sultan drew a sword buckled at his side beneath the *jubba*. While his men stretched Ahmad's arms, he swung the blade wide. It sliced through the jailor's whippet-thin neck. Blood spurted and arced in a crimson spray from the stump of the headless body.

Muhammad laughed and held the head aloft. Fat red droplets cascaded on the prisoners below.

"Now, your thirst is appeased, is it not?"

Faraj swallowed the bile in his throat and gripped the wall beside him. A madman ruled the Sultanate, a tyrant to whom he had pledged his loyalty. Had Fatima's father known the extent of his son's cruelty? Was she right to claim that Muhammad had murdered the old Sultan? Is that what her father had meant, when he clutched Faraj's tunic and begged him to tell her she was right?

## *Princess Fatima*

Every morning for weeks after Nur al-Sabah's death and burial, Fatima lingered on a pallet in the *kadin*'s former quarters. She had claimed them to remain close to Shams ed-Duna in her final days. Although Sabela screamed and warned her that her mistress' uneasy spirit would haunt the place, Fatima was never afraid. Nur was her friend until death. She had no reason to fear an apparition.

Ismail remained the most sympathetic to her plight. Often, before he attended to his new duties as *wazir*, he sat with her just after *Salat al-Fajr* for an hour each morning and held her hand. They did not often speak, only sat together and comforted each other. Their quiet communion offered a rare moment of peace in Fatima's ever-changing world.

For the first time in several days, when she looked at her eldest son, a spark of vitality rekindled within her. His tender smile had greeted her upon first awaking. For a moment, she pretended that everything remained the same. She caressed his chin, the hairs of his neatly trimmed beard.

She whispered, "You were the first child I carried within me. I loved you without ever having seen your sweet face."

He clasped her hand in his and kissed it.

He had grown even more impossibly handsome than his father. While she loved all her children dearly, a special bond existed between Ismail and her, which no other relationship rivaled.

"You are pensive today, my son."

He murmured, "The governors of Qumarich, Wadi-Ash and Arsiduna have approached the Sultan with offers of their daughters."

Fatima squeezed his fingers. "You shall inherit a great estate and a rich province. You serve my brother. The offers shall always come from those who believe it is advantageous to ally with us through marriage."

Her voice rasped from disuse. Ismail poured a cup of water from a beaker. She swallowed the fluid greedily and cleared her throat.

"For many, you are the means to an end, my son. Such is the danger of being an heir of Malaka's governor and the first grandson of a Sultan."

She framed Ismail's angular face between her hands. The coarse hairs on his face scratched her palms. "I pray you do not marry too soon. I am not ready to lose your love to another woman. Is that selfish of me?"

Ismail shook his head. "My heart seeks something more than a wife."

Before she might question him about his desire, he said, "Father received a letter from Leila at al-Jazirah al-Khadra. She heard the news about Grandfather."

Fatima sighed. Ismail pressed his forehead to hers. "I miss him, too."

"I miss them all, my father, your uncle Faraj and Nur. They would not want to see me in this way, would they?"

"No, they would not."

He kissed her brow and left the room.

Haniya appeared with a basin of water. She bowed low and greeted Fatima, who shook her head.

"Please, attend me in the *hammam*, Haniya."

Her maidservant smiled. "As you wish."

Haniya gathered the bathing implements. Fatima followed her from the second floor, down a long corridor that led to the upper floor of the bathhouse. As they strolled beneath a carved stone archway, a soft sob echoed to the rafters. The echo rang from the chamber below, where most visitors undressed.

Fatima grabbed Haniya's shoulder, tugged her backward and placed a hand over her servant's mouth in a bid for silence. A latticed railway ringed the gallery on the second floor. Fatima peered over the railing and into the room below.

Columns ringed the space, with antechambers angling off the square-shaped central area. Sunlight filtered through carved apertures in the ceiling, the silhouettes of stars. A cascade of radiance reflected off a large, brass lamp suspended from an iron chain at the apex of the roof.

Muhammad's bodyguards stood beside each column, while he reclined on his stomach. Bared, he sighed and pressed against the heated, marble slab covered with a long thick cushion. A *hakkak* leaned forward and massaged his muscled back with trembling fingers. His hands trailed up her wiry calves.

The girl shuddered and tears trickled down her pale, olive-brown cheeks. She stood naked beside him, dark waves of curled hair falling to her waist. Ribs poked beneath the lean flesh. Palpable fear revealed itself in her shaking shoulders and the quaking knees that knocked against the stonework.

When she finished her ministrations, Muhammad grasped her hand and brought it to his cheek.

She pleaded, "Please, my Sultan, do not."

Dread soured the woman's plaintive voice. Fatima recoiled and withdrew into the shadows. Muhammad had slave girls whose sole duty was to give him pleasure. Yet, he forced himself on someone.

He sat up and dragged the slave against him. She cried out in a childish whimper.

"Be silent," he ordered.

He buried his face in her neck. The *hakkak*'s tiny hands pushed at his shoulders.

"Master, please do not do this! Not again."

"I said be quiet!"

He stood. His fingers grasped her waist. His other hand lifted her legs so that they encircled his hip. He pushed her up against the wall beside him.

Haniya whimpered behind Fatima's fingers. She glared at her maidservant until Haniya quieted. Muhammad's back was to Fatima, but now, she could see the slave's face more clearly. Fatima stifled her own gasp at the woman's familiar features.

Muhammad's hand traveled up to her throat, while the other toyed with a nipple. His cruel touch choked back the plea behind the weeping girl's lips.

He said, "But this is what you truly want."

The girl sobbed, as he pressed his mouth against the apex of her throat and shoulder. Then she screamed. When he raised his head, reddened teeth marks marred her pale olive skin.

"Tell me this is what you want. Admit it and I shall give you pleasure."

"No! I don't want this."

She writhed against him, her fists beating his back. He gripped her with one hand on her neck and the other on her hip. Then he pushed her on to the cushion atop the stone slab. His weight dwarfed her smaller frame. She slapped him and snarled something incoherent, twisting in his grasp. He laughed and pinned her wrists together with one hand. The girl screamed as he drove into her with a vicious thrust.

Haniya's silent tears trickled over Fatima's hand. Muhammad's cruel laughter echoed in the tiled chamber. His violent battering matched the rhythm of the girl's blows. He arched his neck, blue veins livid under his flesh as he keened his brutal pleasure.

Fatima sat on a low stool at a window overlooking the harem courtyard. A breeze rustled myrtles and rosemary bushes. She stared without truly seeing them.

A wave of terror brimmed inside her belly. The horrific memory of her brother, whose twisted mind took pleasure in rape, still assailed her. Etched into her mind now, she knew she would never forget the sight.

The girl's pleas of despair, her naked fear were not what had frightened Fatima. Rather, the similarities in the slave's coloring, her build and even her wavy dark hair - all reminiscent of Fatima's features. The thought of any resemblance between the slave and herself made Fatima bridle again. She swallowed the bile that almost choked her.

Until now, she had never suspected her brother harbored such unnatural desires for her. Yet, when she had stood there in the shadows of the *hammam*, a long forgotten memory sparked to life. After their mother's murder years ago, she and Muhammad argued in a cruel exchange. On the day they had reconciled, he arrived at her chamber just after she finished her ablutions and almost saw her naked through the thin folds of her robe. He had lingered in the doorway and later, sealed their renewed friendship with a kiss. Something about that kiss had disturbed her then, though she did not understand it at the time.

After living with her husband, she gained the full understanding of Muhammad's actions. He had kissed her full on the mouth, as a man would have embraced a beloved woman he wanted in his bed. That was almost thirty years ago. Had he desired her, even then?

A light touch on her shoulder drove a sharp spike of fear through her chest. She gasped and drew back from Haniya, who stared at her with wide, wet eyes.

"Do not! I pray, Haniya, do not touch me just yet. I cannot bear it."

The maidservant nodded and averted her gaze. "Forgive me. Niranjan has come. He has asked to speak with you."

Fatima shuddered and forced back a sob. She joined Niranjan. He stood in the center of the antechamber, ringed with red and gold striped cushions. Fatima shook her head. How could such delicate beauty exist in this place of horrors?

As he sank into a deep bow, she whispered. "None of that, my old friend."

He smiled, but it required some visible effort and in the end, the gesture lacked any genuine spark of emotion. His leathery-brown countenance never altered.

She asked, "You have completed the task?"

He nodded. "The hashish seller is dead. Musa ibn Qaysi cannot harm anyone. I doubt the Sultan shall be concerned by his disappearance."

"No. The man gave him what he wanted. What of his family, his children?"

"I have taken care of them as well." When he paused, she raised an eyebrow. He elaborated. "The caravan left for Runda just after dawn. I warned the boy and his sisters that they must never return to Gharnatah. They understand the limits of your mercy."

"Good. Thank you."

"The Sultana Shams ed-Duna is also leaving at midday."

"I know. I shall go to her soon. Niranjan, with all that has passed, I have not had the chance to thank you for your aid to my father in these last years. He maintained the façade of strength for his people and his advisors, with your help."

"I did it for you. Always, only for you."

The tension coursing through her body eased at his pronouncement. "Without you and Faisal, the court would have known all my father's secrets, too. I must thank the chief eunuch before he goes with Shams and his sisters to Al-Jaza'ir."

The eunuch sagged, despair etched on his face. "He is no longer in Gharnatah."

She frowned. "Faisal has left in advance of Shams ed-Duna? She did not tell me he would when we dined last night."

"Faisal is dead. Stabbed through the heart."

Niranjan bowed his head. Great, gulping sobs shook him to the core. Bewildered, she hugged him. He pulled from her embrace. His face twisted in agony, a dark mask of grief.

"He betrayed us all. Faisal was never the loyal servant of your father. He helped your brother Muhammad to destroy the Sultan. All those years, he lied to us, to me."

The breath caught in her throat before she could speak again.

"He served your brother. He confessed it all to me last night. I went to him, as is my custom. I begged him to allow me to buy his freedom. He said he would not remain one moment longer in this accursed land. He asked me to come with him, but I refused. He said I loved you more than I loved him. He cursed you, said you were just as deceitful as your brother the Sultan."

Her hands fell listless at her hips. A tremor rippled through her heart.

"Faisal told me he had helped your brother poison your father's mind, to bring down your family. He had found the hashish seller Musa ibn Qaysi and aided your father's belief that the *habba souda* would help him, when instead it and the hashish drove him mad. Surely, the Sultana Shams ed-Duna's heart would break if she knew her chief eunuch had a hand in the betrayal of her husband. Faisal used my knowledge to work his treachery. He wrote to me, you see, to understand the power of plants and poisons. I thought he admired and loved me. I am to blame for what happened, all of it. Without my understanding, he would never have succeeded."

When Niranjan said no more, Fatima placed a tentative, gentle touch on his shoulder. He shrank away. She pushed aside her own reticence and reached for him again. He was her Niranjan. He was a man. Still, he would never hurt her. She grasped his face in her hands and wiped at his wet cheeks with her thumbs.

"No, you are not to blame for anything. Muhammad planned too well to do away with Father. We can make it right again."

"Would that I could see your treacherous brother dead along with Faisal," Niranjan muttered. "After Faisal told me the truth, I beat him about the head, I railed at him. He begged my forgiveness, but I cursed him."

She forced his chin up. "Did you kill him also?"

"Never! When I left him last night, he was alive."

"Is there anyone who can verify that you were with him?"

"No. We have always been discreet."

She laid her forehead against Niranjan's own, bathed in perspiration. "Faisal cannot wound you or my father again."

"He did it to hurt you, because he knew the truth."

She sat back on her heels. "About his mother Ulayyah?"

As Niranjan nodded, Fatima's heart ached. Ulayyah's death haunted her. She lived daily with the fear that if her remaining daughters, including her servants Basma and Haniya knew of her role in Ulayyah's death, she could not hold their loyalty.

She asked, "Who else would have had motive to kill Faisal?"

Niranjan answered. "Only your brother. Faisal knew all of his secrets. Now he is gone and your brother believes his plots can never be discovered."

"Except by me. Are you certain Muhammad did not discern the full nature of your relations with Faisal? Could my brother use such knowledge to come after you?"

"*Al-Qur'an* forbids the love Faisal and I shared. He would not have informed your brother or anyone. It saddens me that I must tell Basma and Haniya of their brother's death. They should not learn of it from anyone else."

She shook her head and sighed. "Do not tell them yet. I do not know that my Haniya can bear much more today."

"What do you mean?"

"You are grieving for Faisal, even in your anger with him, but I must ask you to put such emotions aside. I need your help."

"As ever, I am yours to command."

She caressed his bronzed cheek. "My loyal one. You have always been at my side."

He cupped her hand against his skin. "I shall be with you until death."

"Then aid me now. There is a *hakkak* in the baths of *Al-Qal'at al-Hamra*. I want her found and taken from Gharnatah today, in secret."

"How shall I know the woman?"

"Her resemblance to me shall lead you to her. I do not know her name, but perhaps it is Fatima also. Muhammad raped her in the *hammam* today. I do not believe it was the first time. Haniya was with me. We witnessed him forcing the *hakkak*."

Niranjan stared at her in silence, before he said, "You cannot protect every slave girl from him. You have heard he cut off his own jailor's head. He is cruel and clever."

She returned his rapt gaze. "Then, I must be as he is. My father, my brother and Nur al-Sabah, all dead at his hand or because of him. Their spirits cry out for justice. Even poor Faisal."

"Your father, your brother and the *kadin* are at rest in Paradise, my Sultana. If you thwart Muhammad's ambition, it shall only end in sorrow."

"He shall be the one to know sorrow. He shall suffer for all he has done. I swear it upon the lives he has stolen and destroyed."

# Chapter 16
# Debts

## Princess Fatima

Gharnatah, Al-Andalus: Ramadan 701 AH (Granada, Andalusia: May AD 1302)

After a poignant farewell with Shams ed-Duna and her sisters, Fatima prepared for her departure from Gharnatah. Faraj would follow later. For now, he pursued negotiations of Muhammad's proposed treaty with the Castillans. Fatima could not remain any longer. She could not look upon her father's beloved city again, once a haven, until she had cleansed it of the filth of Muhammad's reign.

Yet, she could not leave those whom she loved defenseless against him. An hour after dawn, she paced Nur's old chamber. Niranjan rushed into the room.

She whirled and faced him. "What took you so long? The caravans bound for Malaka leave this afternoon!"

He sagged in a bow. "Forgive me, but after I returned from the *Qaysariyya*, I learned that your brother Muhammad returned for his ablutions. He could not use the facilities because the *hakkak* took her own life in the *hammam*. She cut her wrists and bled to death in the water."

With a sob, Fatima turned from him and gripped the stucco wall. Yet another innocent life lost, another needless death that resulted from Muhammad's cruelty.

Over her shoulder, Niranjan said, "Forgive me for failing you."

She made no reply. Her hands curled into fists at her side and shook with the rage she had buried deep down inside.

Niranjan laid a long, feminine finger on her shoulder. She stiffened at his touch. He removed his hand.

At last, she turned to him. "Come, we must not keep Nasr waiting."

Nur al-Sabah's son had taken a house in the southwest of the complex, among a row of small estates built for members of the royal family. Two juniper trees shaded the entryway of Nasr's new home.

When Fatima appeared on the step, Sabela opened the door. Her eyes widened before she bowed demurely and held the portal open.

Fatima stepped around her. "Where's your master? Tell him his sister Fatima has come."

The slave girl scurried away. Fatima and Niranjan waited with the men he had brought from the *Qaysariyya*. Fatima crossed her arms over her chest.

Nasr did not take long to arrive at the indoor courtyard. Dark shadows loomed beneath his eyes, but he spared her a smile. The golden visage of his mother Nur al-Sabah was in his large, iridescent eyes and in the curve of his full lips. Fatima missed her friend, taken too soon from her because of Muhammad's treachery.

"I am leaving Gharnatah, brother."

"I saw your husband yesterday in the evening. He told me."

"I must go. I cannot leave you without ensuring your safety."

She turned to Niranjan, who gestured to eight yellow-haired men behind him. In unison, they fell to their knees.

Nasr asked, "Who are these men?"

Niranjan replied, "They are Galicians, young master."

Nasr's mouth gaped. "My mother's people?"

Fatima said, "They shall serve you as your guards and protect you in my absence. The Galicians are Christian slaves. They do not speak Arabic. I know your mother taught you her childhood tongue and her religion."

Nasr ducked his head, as if ashamed, but Fatima nodded.

She said, "The secret remains between Nur al-Sabah and me. Niranjan would never speak of it to anyone. Nur knew our father would have disapproved. I am glad she had the good judgment to teach you her ways. Now, her wisdom shall protect you when I cannot. The Galician guards answer only to you. Command their loyalty. It is yours."

"Muhammad could still strike out at me at any time. He has rid the court of our father's most trusted servants. He has even begun to dismiss men of the *Diwan al-Insha*, those who served Father all their lives."

"Let us hope he does not murder them, too."

Nasr glanced at her. She bit her lip at her flippant tone. "Forgive me. I should not have spoken so carelessly, when so many lives remain in danger. You must become accustomed to assigning these men orders. Do so now."

When he faltered, she glared at him. "You are a prince of the Nasrids! A prince does not falter before his minions. No son of my father's blood would hesitate. Now command them, in *Galego*, as your mother taught you!"

His jaw tightened. He spoke in a somewhat nasally tone. The men dispersed to the fringes of the courtyard and stood in silence.

Fatima grasped Nasr's shoulders. He returned her fervent stare. "I thought I could come to Malaka with you."

She shook her head. "You must remain here. We must not arouse suspicion. Muhammad would worry if you were with me. He cannot suspect my plans."

"What do you intend to do?"

She frowned. "I should think it would be obvious. You must replace Muhammad on our father's throne."

Lines crisscrossed Nasr's youthful brow. "You want me to be Sultan in his stead?"

"Who else is there? Our father and our brother are dead. Muhammad ensured that. You are the last and best hope of our father's legacy."

"But I don't know how to rule! I don't even have a *wazir*'s post."

"That is why you must stay here and learn what you can of governance. You must cultivate friendships among the *Diwan al-Insha*. Learn where their loyalties lie. Muhammad cannot replace all of them. Some of the ministers were devoted to my father. We must see which of them shall be loyal to you."

"But my mother was a slave...."

"She was queen of my father's heart!" Fatima waved a dismissive hand through the air. "You are her beloved child, the last son of my father. Muhammad cannot hold the throne. You must take his place upon it."

"Even if I found supporters, a prince's stipend from the royal treasury is not enough to pay my bodyguards and buy the support of the army. Without the army, I could never rule."

"Gain loyalty first among the *Diwan*. That is coin you can spend to sway others. When you have the allegiance of the ministers, we shall turn to the military. My money shall secure their backing."

"Your husband's money, you mean."

"My bridal trousseau is worth a fortune. I shall sell every last piece of it if I must, only to secure your throne."

Nasr turned from her. "This is treason."

She grabbed his arm and jerked him around to face her again. "Muhammad's birth alone determined Father's choice! Our father was wrong to think his eldest son would remain faithful to him. You are Gharnatah's last hope! I cannot let Muhammad destroy our father's legacy. Now, are you going to stand here sniveling about treason, or can you do what our father's blood demands? You must rule and Muhammad must face justice for his crimes. Our father, our brother and his family, and your mother! Muhammad is responsible for their deaths. He cannot hold the throne. It belongs to you!"

When she loosened her hold, Nasr rubbed his arm.

She sighed. "I do not mean to be cruel. You must see this is the only way."

After some time, he nodded. "Yes. I must take the throne and Muhammad must die."

"No! If we kill him outright, we are no better than him. Killing him is not justice. It is what he would do. No, he must live with his crimes. A cell in *Al-Quasaba* must be enough for him. Promise me, Nasr, if we succeed and you secure the throne, you must not kill Muhammad. He deserves death, but we cannot do it. Swear it now. Swear that when you take your throne, you shall consign Muhammad to prison for the rest of his life. Nothing more."

Nasr muttered, "Very well. I swear it."

Later, Fatima said farewell to her family. Ismail stood between his father and his master Muhammad. She embraced her son. His response was just as fierce, but he also drew back first.

"Go with God, *Ummi.*"

"I pray the Hand of Allah the Compassionate, the Merciful, shall always guide you."

Faraj stepped forward and placed his hand on her shoulders. "Travel safely, Fatima. I shall see you soon again."

He pressed a light kiss on her brow. She said nothing in reply, not even afterward, when he frowned at her.

Instead, she stared at Muhammad. "My son relies upon your protection, as I do."

He smiled, more of a leer than a true sign of affection. "Ismail shall prosper in my care. He has nothing to fear while he is at my side."

"I shall hold you to that promise."

She knelt in the windswept dust. Soft gasps escaped Ismail and Faraj. She bowed her head low and raised the hem of Muhammad's robe to her lips. "Until we see each other again."

He helped her stand. She suppressed a flinch, as his fingers enveloped hers. The same hands that had restrained that poor, innocent girl in the baths.

He led her to the camel outfitted with a leather *hawdaj.* Niranjan sat on a mule, with Basma and Haniya mounted on mules on either side of him.

When she settled on the camel's back, she looked down at her brother. "Thank you."

Muhammad leaned toward her. "You are full of pleasantries today, but I am no fool." He pitched his voice low. "Tread carefully with me, Fatima."

She forced a smile. "Your caution is unnecessary."

A scowl darkened his visage. "I don't believe you. Each time you look at me, there is a silent accusation in your eyes."

"Why do you think so? Have you done something that you feel guilty about, brother?"

"Put such foolish fears aside. Don't try my patience, Fatima, or my capacity for forgiveness. Remember, I know you as I know myself."

"That is a truth neither of us can deny. Remember, I remain my father's daughter. His spirit lives within me."

The camel master gave the order to move out. The drivers urged the beasts, which lurched to their feet. The caravan began its weeklong trek to Malaka. Fatima leaned forward under the *hawdaj* and waved to Ismail one last time.

As he returned the gesture, Muhammad placed his hand on Ismail's shoulder and smiled. She locked eyes with her brother, until her camel snorted and dipped down the *Sabika* hill.

Malaka, Al-Andalus: Ramadan 701 AH (Malaga, Andalusia: May AD 1302)

After Fatima had returned to Malaka, two weeks later, Leeta burst out on to the belvedere where Fatima kept a solitary vigil. "The master! He has sent word that he is a few hours away."

Fatima leaned on the marble ledge and looked out across the White Sea. Had Shams ed-Duna reached the coast of al-Jaza'ir in safety? Fatima would not know for some time until a letter arrived.

"My Sultana?"

"I heard you, Leeta."

Why could no one just leave her alone? She wanted to ask the question. Instead, she inquired, "Have the silk shipments arrived?"

"Yes, we received them just after dawn. Marzuq has directed the bolts to the storerooms."

"Good. Thank you, Leeta."

The treasurer hovered at Fatima's back.

"Is there something else you would share, Leeta?"

"You cannot go on like this."

"What do you mean?"

"I understand pain, my Sultana, for I am bereft of a beloved sister. You have endured more than perhaps your fair share of loss in these last months. I cannot pretend to know your pain...."

"Then why do you speak of it?"

"You are my good mistress. It hurts me to see your sorrow. Even when we break the daily fast, you pick at your food and barely swallow more than three mouthfuls before you retreat to your room. Each night, I hear you crying before you go to bed. You do not let young Prince Muhammad or your daughters comfort you. We worry for you."

"You worry for naught, Leeta. I am grateful for your concern, but it is unnecessary. Now, leave me."

Before Leeta withdrew, Fatima added. "It is unfitting for you to gossip about me with anyone. You are a servant of this household. Do not overstep your bounds again."

"Forgive me."

Fatima waved her away and rubbed her shoulders. A brisk afternoon wind blew in from the White Sea. Yet, she remained on the belvedere for the rest of the day, lost in thought. She spoke to no one and kept her silence.

Faraj found her upon his arrival. His appearance startled her at first. She had almost forgotten Leeta's warning. He pulled her close and kissed her hair. "I have missed you."

"You traveled without incident?"

"Yes, under the protection of my guards and Khalid al-Hakam. Our son sends his felicitations."

"Ismail is safe?"

Faraj drew back. "Of course, he is safe. Fatima, you really must stop believing the Sultan intends to harm him. Our son is strong and wise. He has your cleverness."

When Faraj stood beside her at the ledge, she regarded him. The area where her nail had scratched, just under his eye, was still pink.

He covered her fingers with his. "We have to talk. We both said and did terrible things to each other before you left Gharnatah. I want you to know I regret them. I am sorry, Fatima. I never meant to hurt you."

She stared at him in silence. If she followed the path of vengeance, she did not doubt Faraj would oppose her. Could she speak the words that might doom her marriage forever?

Soon, lines marred Faraj's brow. "Have you nothing to say in return?"

"I'm sorry, too."

He smiled at this and looked ready to speak again, but she cut him off. "I am sorry my father placed such faith in you, only to be betrayed by your blind ambitions."

He moved his hand. "What do you mean by betrayal?"

She laughed at him, a hollow sound. "How easily you forget how much you owe him. The precious land that you cling to, which you would not risk for even my sake. My father gave you Malaka. Yet you care more about your power and control over this city than justice for him!"

Faraj shook his head. "Again with this? Woman, have you not the good sense God gave you? I know you are convinced that the Sultan killed your father. If your father had wanted another to succeed him, he should have named him! I owe him no debt. I owe it to my son to keep what is ours by right. Nothing you say can make me feel guilty about my devotion to this place. What would you have me do? Give it all up for you? I am not so foolish as the man who turned his back on all he held dear at Tarif. I shall hold Malaka until I am dead!"

"I thought I knew you. Now, you are a stranger to me."

She turned from him and looked out to the sea again.

"What are you planning, Fatima?"

She did not respond. Faraj grabbed her arm, his face a dark guise of enraged passion. She met his wild-eyed stare with quiet fury of her own.

"If you intend to hit me again, husband, do so. It shall not undo my sentiments about you, or your master in Gharnatah."

"I tell you, do nothing to jeopardize our children's future. If you harm my interests, I promise I shall strike at you in any way I can. Muhammad is Sultan and you shall accept it. Obey me! Never let me hear of your involvement in any intrigue against your brother. Do you understand me?"

He released her from his harsh grip without awaiting her answer and stalked away.

For a long time, she stared at the archway through which he had disappeared. Then, she looked down at the puckered slash across her palm. The vow she had offered at her father's gravesite echoed in her mind. It weighed upon her.

She whispered to the wind, "I can promise you this, husband, you shall never hear of it."

# Chapter 17
# The Spy

## Prince Faraj

Malaka, Al-Andalus: Shawwal 704 AH (Malaga, Andalusia: May AD 1305)

When the family finished the morning meal, Faraj dismissed his children and retired to the belvedere overlooking the sea. The summer sun burnished his forehead and warmed the marble ledge as he leaned against it.

At the base of the promontory, Fatima rode her dun-brown mare down to the shoreline. A gentle breeze tugged at the gossamer black veil over her face and revealed contours of her profile. She lingered and looked out across the expanse of the sea. Her horse shied away each time the surf rushed to the shore. She calmed the mare with a steady hand.

Faraj bridled with jealousy at the sight of her long finger on the beast's neck. How long had it been since she touched him with such familiarity?

How had it come to this? He and Fatima were strangers to each other. They had shared nothing more than polite words in the months after the death of her father. Almost three years later, they hardly conversed except when necessary. He did not understand her anymore.

He could not forgive or forget her angry words spoken upon their return to Malaka, in the wake of her brother's ascension. She had accused Faraj of betraying her father's memory. Until then, he never suspected that her words would have wounded him more keenly than a blade thrust to the heart.

Even after three years, Fatima held her brother responsible for their father's death. Faraj had seen the Sultan's depravity. He no longer denied Muhammad could have committed the deed. The Sultan had spilled too much blood to deny the title of murderer.

Yet, Faraj could not risk the governorship in an ill-starred attempt of rebellion against the Sultan or question his rule. Faraj had taken too many risks and endured too much to secure Malaka. The province belonged to his heir. Faraj held out the hope Fatima would do nothing to jeopardize his administration of Malaka. He could not lose his birthright, even if it meant going against her wishes.

She glanced in his direction. From between the narrow slit of her veils, her eyes found his. In previous years, he would have been lost in those liquid pools, seeing love, desire and admiration reflected in her tender gaze. Now her eyes revealed nothing. Her stare did not waver. Her expression remained impenetrable.

Still he offered a faint smile and waved, certain that even at a distance, she would see his gesture. She jerked the reins and wheeled the mare around. Her horse nickered. The mount swayed as it cantered along the shoreline, away from him.

Khalid appeared at his side. He stared at the lone horse riding across the sands. "The peace of God be with you, my prince. I see the Sultana enjoys her morning ride."

"Yes, in her usual fashion." Faraj stared at her until she disappeared from view behind a craggy rock.

He turned to Khalid. "Thank you for coming."

His captain nodded. "I am yours to command."

"I have never doubted it." Faraj crossed his arms over his chest and settled his backside on the ledge.

"How may I aid you?"

"I need your assistance with my wife. Fatima is very dear to me, but her behavior of the last few years is troublesome. She goes for long rides by herself, on the beach or through town. She is cold and silent, even with our children. She takes no pleasure in the things she used to love. Indeed, we have not enjoyed our marital bed in some time. The tension between us is a matter of great pain to me. Otherwise, I would not speak to you of such troubles. You understand?"

"Your confidence honors me. I would never speak of matters between you and the Sultana with anyone."

"It is a sign of my trust in you, captain, that I share my travail. I want you to help me. To help the Sultana."

"I shall do anything I can to aid you."

"I cannot allow anyone outside our home to question my authority or loyalty to the Sultan, least of all because of Fatima."

"I'm afraid I don't understand, master. Who would question your loyalties? What does that have to do with the Sultana?"

"Her grief for her father has made her do and say strange things. She thinks her brother poisoned their father. She despises Muhammad and cannot bear the thought of him on the throne. She is a danger to herself, Khalid. I want you to assign someone to watch over her whenever she leaves our estate. Someone who can be discreet."

Khalid exhaled sharply. "You want me to have someone spy on the Sultana?"

Faraj nodded. "I do it as much for her protection as my own. It must be someone she has never seen before. She knows most of the garrison at *Al-Jabal Faro* on sight, even if not by name."

The captain shuffled his stance and looked down at his feet. Faraj grasped his burly shoulder. "It is a heavy burden, I know, but I must ask you to bear it for a time. I would not risk such a venture if necessity did not demand it. I love my wife. I must protect her, even from herself. Do you trust me to do what is right by her?"

Khalid stared at him for a moment. "I trust you, master, in all things."

"Then do as I command."

Khalid nodded and sketched a stiff bow, before he departed. His heavy boots resounded on the marble floor. After his footfalls had faded, Faraj looked to the craggy rock behind which Fatima had vanished.

He whispered a fervent plea. "Allah, the Compassionate, the Merciful, please, show me my concern is for naught. Tell me I have nothing to fear. Let Fatima be guiltless. Let her forgive me for this thing I have done."

# *Princess Fatima*

Fatima returned from her solitary ride in the late afternoon. She dismounted just outside the stables and slapped the reins into the waiting hands of a groom. Niranjan approached, bowing stiffly.

She joined hands with him and squeezed with lingering affection. "You've returned at last. Your trip to the slave market at Madinah Antaqirah was a success?"

"As you knew it must be, my Sultana."

The gravity of his sullen tone made her extract her fingers from his hold. "You do not approve of my choice."

"I do not. Think of what your husband would say of your gift."

"He should thank me for a show of wifely devotion."

"Forgive my boldness, but I doubt that very much."

She raised an eyebrow at him. "You were ever bold, loyal one. You've never needed to ask forgiveness before."

They walked the pathway together, he in his customary position just at her back.

"There is another matter we must discuss, my Sultana. I have kept ties to the few servants of your father's household who remain in Gharnatah. Praise be to the one God that the Sultan has not murdered them all. A eunuch has informed me of the reason the Sultan cannot attend the marriage of your daughters."

Fatima slowed and turned to him. "Muhammad has refused Faraj's invitation? I do not know why my husband bothered to extend it. Why would Muhammad care about the unions of Aisha and Faridah?"

"Your husband knew it was the proper thing to invite the Sultan, of which the Sultana is also well aware."

Niranjan's gaze narrowed on her. For a moment, a spark of anger flared in her heart at his attempt to chide her. Then she recalled his lifelong devotion. For it, she could forgive him anything.

As she continued walking, his footsteps followed.

"Speak then. Why won't Muhammad come to Malaka?"

"One of his concubines has delivered a child. As the court astrologers have predicted, his long-awaited son has arrived."

Fatima stopped. "A boy?"

"An heir."

She grasped the blue-black prayer beads hanging from her belt. A pained breath wheezed between her lips.

She faced Niranjan. "Then we must do something about the child."

He halted at her side, his sheepish gaze downcast. He mumbled, "I do not see what we can do."

She shook her head. "Surely, you must."

A long, tense silence passed before Niranjan sighed. "I have done much to aid you against the Sultan. I have kept your secrets from your husband, even from my own sisters. You tread a dangerous path. You are advocating the murder of a woman and her child."

She sighed and pressed a hand to her temple. "A child that can ruin our plans forever!" She paced before him. "Don't you see? If Gharnatah already has an heir, if this child lives, no one shall dare support my brother Nasr's claim to the throne. I cannot allow that to happen! The blood of my father demands an end to Muhammad's cruel reign."

She paused and cast a glare at him. "You have aided me before against Muhammad. Why do you hesitate now?"

"The murder of the hashish seller was just. He deserved death after all he had done to your father. We have removed him and his poison from this world."

"Muhammad's son is an obstacle we must also remove."

Niranjan drew back with a sharp cry of disgust. She met his gaze, unflinching.

"Years ago, you chided me for my kindness to my brother. I let him live. He has murdered our father. I have paid a terrible price for my generosity. I have learned the error of sentiment, as you wished. Why do you recoil from me now when your caution has proved justified?"

"I marvel at how hard you have become. Where is the good and sweet lady I knew from her childhood? The kind mistress whom I have served and loved? The one who would never hurt an innocent babe?"

She turned away from him. In the privacy of her chamber at night, she had often wondered the same thing. Nothing gave her any pleasure. Not even the celebration of her daughters' marriage within a few weeks stirred her heart to joy. She lived only for vengeance now. It comforted her in the lonely dark of night and gave her the will to survive the Sultan's tyranny each day.

When Niranjan touched her arm hesitantly, she jerked away from him.

"Do not! I shall tell you where your kind and good mistress is." Her voice lapsed into a low whisper. "She lies dead and buried at Gharnatah, beside her murdered father."

She raised her chin a notch, eyeing him. "I made a sacred vow to avenge him. If you remain loyal to me and my cause, then get rid of the slave and her child."

"I would not be your dutiful servant, if I did not caution you against this move. If you have become so cold and ruthless, if you no longer care for the sanctity of life, then the Sultan has already won. He shall have turned you into a likeness of himself."

She shook her head. "You do not understand. To defeat him, I must be like him. I must be cruel. I must be without care. How else can I avenge the deaths of those he has taken from me?"

"This cannot bring your noble father, or the *kadin* Nur-al-Sabah or anyone else back from the grave. This slave girl and her son are blameless."

"Yes, yet more innocent lives that must suffer because of Muhammad! The woman and her son must die if Nasr is to take the throne."

Her chest tightened, rising and falling rapidly with each breath. When she resumed walking the pebble path, Niranjan fell into step beside her. They mounted the steps together.

He said, "I shall hasten to Gharnatah. I must first learn whether the slave nurses her child."

"Why is that important?"

"If she does, there are certain poisons which, if introduced into the mother's body would slowly weaken her, but shall certainly kill the child."

Fatima nodded. "I don't care how you do it, only be certain that it is done before you return to Malaka."

Niranjan stopped as they reached the portico of columns. "It shall be, but I go to my duty with a heavy heart full of sorrow for you."

She paused and eyed him over her shoulder. "Save your pity for Muhammad. He shall need it in the end."

Niranjan whispered, "It saddens me to see you this way. You risk everything to pursue this course, but it may cost you everyone you hold dear. Do you not fear the madness that lives inside your brother has tainted you?"

She laughed, throwing back her head, before she continued into the house. "I am not afraid. If I am mad like Muhammad, at least I can control it."

"Can you?" Niranjan's voice echoed on the breeze as she left him.

Late in the evening, Fatima bathed and retired to her chamber without dinner. She often preferred her meals in solitude. Except for the nightly ritual her younger children still insisted upon, she would have spent her days and nights alone. She preferred it.

At the unexpected knock on her door, she exhaled a pent-up sigh. Haniya set the hairbrush down on the windowsill. Fatima sat naked on a low cedar stool, covered by a gold silk cushion. The brazier near her feet emitted fragrant ambergris and warmed the room.

Haniya swung the portal open and Faraj entered. Fatima looked at his reflection in the silver gilt mirror she held in her hand. He stood in the doorway.

Her jaw tightened for moment, but she fixed a well-practiced smile on her face. "Husband, surely you have not finished dinner already?"

"I had no appetite. Baraka dines with our children tonight."

His gruff response rankled her. He still resented her absence at meals. Too bad.

He said, "I did not see you after your ride along the beach. There are matters regarding the wedding we should discuss. I hoped we might talk in private."

Haniya scurried through the entryway. She cast a frown over her shoulder, as she pulled the olive wood door in behind her. Fatima waved her off.

Faraj stood behind her. His warm hands pressed against her bare shoulders. She suppressed a flinch and held herself rigid.

"Shall I continue?"

At her nod, he picked up the brush and ran the bristles through her hair. "The children missed you at dinner. They always miss you these days."

How dare he appeal to her role as a mother? Was that part of his ploy to soften her heart toward him?

She thought of her poor silent Qabiha, a child who understood so little of the world around her. She often whimpered like a baby throughout the night after Fatima left the nursery, or so Baraka often reported. She responded to no one except little Saliha, the youngest of her siblings at the age of thirteen.

Fatima could not bear the sight of them. Her children would hate the woman she had become, if they knew her ways and means. How dare Faraj mention them?

"You wished to speak of Aisha and Faridah's wedding ceremony," she reminded him over her shoulder.

He swept her dark curls, streaked with gray, from her shoulder and neck. A harsh sigh escaped him. "Later."

"Now," she insisted.

"Fatima, I have missed you too much." He dropped a kiss on her shoulder.

A wave fluttered through her belly, a stirring she had not felt in years. She recognized faint desire, its pull coursing through her stomach.

His light kisses pressed along her shoulder and across her back, before the brush clanked on the cedar floor. Faraj came around and pulled her up into his arms. His harsh breathing filled the otherwise silent room. His hot gaze bored into hers.

He was no longer the young man who first made love to her years ago. Yet, the same passion inspired her husband's eager, questing touch. His fingers threaded through the mass of her hair. His other hand palmed her belly, no longer maiden flat after several episodes of childbirth, before his fingers swept along her fleshy hip.

"We have been apart for too long, wife. We must put the past behind us and start afresh. I'm willing to do this, Fatima, if you shall also try."

She stepped back from the circle of his embrace. Deep, even breaths slowed and steadied the rhythm of her fluttering heart. She had forgotten how his touch affected her.

"I am no true wife to you, Faraj. It is wrong of me to neglect your desires."

He reached for her again, but she warded him off. "Wait."

She went to the door and called for Niranjan. When he came, she informed him of her instructions. With a frown, he glared at her for a moment before he nodded.

Faraj chuckled. "What are you doing, my love?"

She looked over her shoulder. "Please, wait."

When Niranjan returned, Fatima swung the door open wide. She permitted the entry of the black-haired beauty, who strode past her and stood in the center of the room.

Fatima nodded to Faraj. "She is yours. Her name is Abeer." To the woman, she said, "Remove your clothes."

The slave worked the knot holding her robe closed. Unabashed, she let the silk garment slide to her feet. Her pale olive skin, small rounded breasts and generous hips would have tempted any man.

Her luminous eyes met Faraj's own. His mouth gaped.

A frown of confusion crisscrossed his brow. "Fatima, you want to bring another woman into our marriage bed?"

She shook her head. "I asked Niranjan to purchase her on his recent trip to Madinah Antaqirah. It has been wrong of me to neglect your desires as a husband, though I no longer have such needs. As you can see, she is fashioned for pleasure."

Faraj's face reddened. "You cannot mean this. I don't want her!"

Fatima looked the slave girl over. "There's nothing wrong with her. Your concubines have grown older. Surely, you wish for someone new."

Faraj crossed the chamber and snatched up the girl's robe. He shoved it at her. "Get out! Now!"

When she ran, he grabbed Fatima's arms and yanked her toward him. "How dare you!"

"How dare you! You would disdain my gifts. I don't know what you want from me any longer!"

"I want you to be the wife I married, the woman I love!"

He shoved her on to the bed. She lay there, panting.

"That woman is gone. You must accept it. I did this for you! I thought she would please you!"

He turned to the door, but before he left, his gleaming eyes raked over her. The fiery anger and maddened desire in his hot gaze burned into hers.

She grasped the damask coverlet and dragged it up her shoulders. Would he hurt her now, like Muhammad had done with that innocent girl in the baths?

"You are a fool, wife. As if anyone else could truly please me! I am twice the fool for loving you in spite of everything and hoping you still held room in your heart for me. You no longer have a heart."

# Chapter 18
# The Emissary

## Princess Fatima

Malaka, Al-Andalus: Dhu al-Hijja 704 AH (Malaga, Andalusia: June AD 1305)

On the day of Aisha and Faridah's joint marriage to the sons of the foremost *Qa'id* of Lawsa, chaos descended on Malaka. Forbidding clouds appeared on the horizon just before dawn and unleashed a torrent of rain. It forced wedding preparations indoors. In a frenzied jumble, servants scrambled for boughs of flowers draped around the columns. They crushed tender blossoms in their haste. By mid-morning, the downpour caused a mudslide in the east of the town. Many residents lost their homes or lives. Worse still, the mud blocked part of the main route of the wedding procession.

Fatima hoped that those trapped in the mud did not include her eldest son Ismail, who had come to Malaka.

When Faraj informed Faridah and Aisha of the delay, their third daughter sobbed. "It's so unfair! Why must this happen now? Everything's ruined!"

Fatima stood beside a window to the east. She peered through the lattice. The unrepentant rain stirred a heavy mist that blanketed the terrain. Nothing came into view beyond the boundary of their estate.

Beside her, Faraj tried in vain to comfort their daughter. "Faridah, do not upset yourself. All shall be well, you shall see, my love."

"Stop coddling her, she is hardly a child." Fatima turned to them. "Our people need your help, husband. You must send men to aid those who remain trapped. We do not know what is happening. Perhaps the bridegrooms and their guests and our son are also ensnared in the mud."

Instantly, she regretted her words as Aisha sobbed against her sister's quaking shoulders. "What if my betrothed is dead? He could be buried under that mud, too!"

Over their daughters' heads, Faraj glared at Fatima. She pursed her lips and met his cold stare.

He framed Faridah's puffy face in his hands and kissed her cheeks. "I'll return soon. Don't worry, you shall marry today."

Fatima kept a solitary vigil beside the window. Her daughters hugged each other and buried their mewling sobs in each other's marital robes.

Fatima closed the distance between them and yanked both of them up by their arms. Their yelps of surprise mercifully brought the crying to an end.

"What an embarrassment! Would both of you rail at God for sending the rain? He alone determines our fates. Now, compose yourselves. Would you have your new husbands meet you for the first time, with your bloated faces and red noses? You are princesses of the Nasrids, the daughters of a Sultana of Gharnatah and the governor of Malaka. You cannot crumble at the slightest hardship. Life brings many disappointments, daughters. I expect you both to meet them with the courage of your forbearers."

Fatima called for their attendants, who led the women away. When they had gone, she shook her head in their direction and returned to the window.

In the afternoon, sunlight peeked out from behind the pale, gray clouds for the first time that day. Faraj returned, his waterlogged clothing clinging to him. He sat ramrod straight on his stallion's back. The men who were soon to be his sons by marriage followed on horseback. Each tried to appear unflustered, but their sodden states and muddied shoes belied the attempt.

Behind them, several of the last guests rode. When Fatima caught sight of one of the men through the window, a little sob escaped her. She raced down two flights of stairs and out into the courtyard.

In the flurry of activity, with men dismounting and greeting each other, she had eyes for only one person. She dashed through the group and launched herself at him. “Ismail!”

His arms closed about her. In his warm embrace, something that resembled peace settled in her heart. Even if only for this moment, he was safe with her and far from Muhammad’s clutches.

Since Ismail’s sojourn in Gharnatah, they had traded letters every few weeks. Always, he invited her to visit, but she could not go back there. Not yet. Not while Muhammad ruled Gharnatah. Someday soon, she hoped the city would feel like home again.

She looked up at her darling son and touched the thick growth of his beard. Time had not changed him. He remained handsome, with thick dark hair and the piercing, hawk-eyed gaze of his grandfather. Her heart soared at the sight of him, tall and proud in his green silk *jubba*, trimmed with gold brocade at the hem.

“At last you are home. I’m so glad. How was your journey, was it well? Are you hungry? Come with me, I shall have the cooks....”

“Stop.” Even Ismail’s gravel tenor reminded her of her father. “It would be unseemly to eat before the other guests have the same opportunity.”

She studied him. When had he ever spoken with her in such a clipped, formal tone? Perhaps he was just tired after the journey. Besides, he was a man and did not need her to cosset him.

She relaxed and slid her hands down his chest, patting just above his heart. “You’re right, of course. Come into the house. Let us talk in private. I want to hear everything about your life.”

“I need to speak with Father first. I carry an urgent message from the Sultan.”

“What does he want?” When Ismail looked at her sharply, she bit her lower lip, hard-pressed to hide her natural abhorrence for Muhammad. “He could have sent a messenger to your father before now. You are here for the wedding of your sisters. Why should Muhammad have bothered you with such petty duties?”

“I am here as the Sultan’s emissary. Please let me speak with Father first. Then we can talk. We have time. I have much to share with you. I intend to remain at Malaka for a month."

"So long? That is wonderful news. I am truly pleased."

"I did not anticipate that the Sultan could spare me, but I am grateful. My uncle suffers cruelly. He has good reason to dismiss the courtiers around him."

Fatima shuddered with the effort to hold back her excitement. Her fingers curled into fists. The nails bit into her palm. She relished the pain. It kept her calm and focused. "Why does Muhammad have reason to sorrow?"

"Last week, he lost his long-awaited heir. No one knows how or why. I learned the extent of his fury when he ordered the child's mother drowned in the *Hadarro* for her carelessness."

She exhaled in a rush of relief and turned away from her son for a moment. Niranjan had done well. Was he on his way home?

Ismail touched her shoulder and she turned to him. "Yes, it is all very unfortunate."

He cocked his head. "I would have thought you might show a little sympathy. I know you revile my uncle with reason, but you also know what it is to lose a babe."

Her jaw tightened.

He shook his head. "Forgive me. It was unkind of me to remind you."

"You have never been cruel before. Is this some new talent your uncle has taught you?"

When he did not reply, she shook her head. "Please, I don't want to quarrel with you over Muhammad. We have been apart for so long. Tell me this, at least, before you go to your father. Are you happy in Gharnatah?"

"I am not unhappy."

For the first time since his arrival, a smile brightened his sober expression.

On tiptoe, she kissed his cheek. "I'll return to your sisters. Take as long as you like with your father. It's so good to have you home again."

"I am glad to be here."

During the wedding feast, Marzuq found Fatima and asked her to come to the belvedere.

Fatima left the female wedding guests. As she passed by the curtain that separated the men from the women, she searched the bustling, noisy room for Ismail. He stood deep in conversation with his younger brother Muhammad. Something Muhammad said made Ismail throw back his leonine head in raucous laughter.

When they were younger, Muhammad had always followed his elder brother's lead. Now they stood before each other as grown men. Fatima smiled with the knowledge that their easy rapport continued.

She followed Marzuq to the belvedere. Moisture hung heavy on the breeze. As he stepped aside, Faraj came into view. Marzuq bowed and left them. They were alone. Gooseflesh tingled along her arms. She shivered. They had not been alone in a month.

Faraj's gaze narrowed. "Have no fear. I don't intend to demand my husbandly due."

She hated how her heart pounded with unfathomable disgust. Yet, she could not look at him the same as before. His support of Muhammad's actions had tainted her view.

Emboldened, she raised her chin a notch and joined him. "You may demand whatever you want from me and I shall comply."

"We both know that has never been true, Fatima. You have always done as you wished. Yet you offer me your cold compliance now. What a dutiful wife you are! Why do you pretend when we both know the truth?"

She crossed her arms over her chest and stood next to him. "Did you want to talk or snarl at me all evening, husband?"

He offered her his profile and looked out to sea. "Perhaps I am still the fool, but I thought you might care about this."

He thrust a rolled parchment at her.

She stared down at it and then regarded him. "What is that? Is this what Ismail wanted to talk to you about?"

"Yes." Faraj pushed the missive into her hands.

As she read the words on the page, she shook her head in disbelief.

"Is Muhammad trying to kill you?"

"He is Sultan, he may command me. I wish you would accept that fact."

"But he demands that you lead a contingent of his army in his disastrous wars against Castilla-Leon! Faraj, you must refuse the order. Muhammad's double-dealings started this feud. He has isolated Gharnatah from everyone. Now, he looks to his governors to counter his misfortune. You are not in the flower of youth. You cannot do this."

Faraj glowered. He lunged at her and gripped her arms so tightly that pain shot through them. She refused to cry out and bit her tongue.

"Do you still care? Do you?"

"Yes! No matter what's happened between us, I've never stopped caring."

He shoved her away from him. "No, you care more for Gharnatah's fate than mine. You blame Muhammad for our misfortunes. What about us, Fatima? What about the mockery that this marriage has become? Is that of Muhammad's making as well or our own? You do not trust me anymore and I certainly no longer trust you."

She did not expect to feel the sharp pain that stabbed at her heart after he spoke, or the sting of tears in her eyes. When had she last cried over anything?

She turned her back on him and crumpled the parchment.

They stood together on the belvedere, but never more far apart, for long and tense moments of silence.

Then Faraj said, "Our son has told me that Nasr's name has been mentioned as the Sultan's rival in Gharnatah for months."

She rounded on him. "Nasr is no rival! He is loyal, although Muhammad denies him a position on the council of ministers. Nasr would never be so foolish as to usurp Muhammad's rule. Those who take such risks would die. Your master has shown how he deals with threats, real or imagined, swiftly and mercilessly. I wish you would not endorse such talk about Nasr. It is just as likely that Muhammad encourages such misinformation so that he can move against my brother without causing alarm."

His arms dropped to his side and he turned away sharply, looking at the closed door behind them. She followed his gaze, puzzled by the suddenness of his actions.

He said, "I acknowledge this is possible. Sometimes, I don't know what to think."

She swallowed back a sigh. How much longer would she have to lie to him, to hide her role in Nasr's ascendancy? She gritted her teeth, determined to keep to her course until Nasr sat on the throne of their father. If Faraj did not trust her, she would have to be more cautious and avert his suspicions.

He interrupted her reverie. "I cannot refuse the Sultan's order. I leave in a week's time." When she rushed to speak, he held up his hand. "Do not try to convince me otherwise. You know I have no other choice."

She shoved the parchment at him. He sighed and took Muhammad's order, tucking it into his belt. "There is another matter we should discuss. The Sultan has arranged Ismail's betrothal."

Her eyes watered. Why hadn't Ismail told her first? "When does he marry?"

"He shall marry a girl of the Hudayr clan in Qirbilyan in three years' time, when she is of an age to wed."

"Qirbilyan is just a border state buffering Gharnatah from Aragon. What do we gain by such a union?"

"I am uncertain. Ismail did not explain. Perhaps he does not know."

"Why did he tell you first and not me?"

Faraj scowled. "He is my son, too. I love him no less than you."

"I did not suggest otherwise. Why must you always...."

"Hush!" A deep frown marred his leathery complexion as he glared into the shadows by the door. She followed his gaze. He called out, "Ismail?"

The portal creaked on its hinges and Ismail came into view. He walked toward his parents.

Delight filled Fatima again. Faraj's displeasure soured his expression, his lips pressed firmly together.

"How long were you standing there?"

"I just went in search of both of you. Marzuq told me you were out here. I heard you and *Ummi* talking. I did not wish to interrupt, but the *qa'id* is about to offer his blessing upon his sons. I knew you would want to be present, Father."

Fatima embraced Ismail. "Your father told me the news of your betrothal. I am pleased, if you are also pleased."

Ismail nodded.

Faraj waved him away. "Return to our guests. I shall come in a moment."

His frown deepened and he continued staring in the direction Ismail had gone.

Fatima asked, "What is the matter?"

"Ismail has changed."

"He seems a bit taller, if that is possible."

"I don't mean that! You haven't been to Gharnatah, to see the rapport he shares with the Sultan."

"If they share commonalities, recall that I was against Ismail's appointment as a *wazir*. What would you have me do about it now?"

"You shouldn't let your love for our son make you careless. He was listening to us. I heard his distinctive footfalls earlier. He did not find us only now."

She drew back. "How dare you accuse our son of spying on us? Why would he ever do such a thing?"

Faraj only looked at her while her blood grew colder than the rain-filled breeze.

## *Prince Faraj*

Two weeks after Aisha and Faridah departed to Lawsa, Faraj stood under a red-gold sky next to Khalid on the belvedere. Ships returned to the harbor at sunset, laden with treasures from the sea and faraway ports, all to enrich Malaka's coffers. In his youth, Faraj had dreamt only of the wealth the governorship might offer. Now, he desired only peace and comfort in his home. Malaka no longer offered him sanctuary from his concerns.

He glanced at his captain. "I find it hard to understand how your man has uncovered none of my wife's activities in these years."

Khalid's rapt gaze lingered on the vessels coming ashore. "Perhaps because the Sultana Fatima is guiltless."

With a snort, Faraj rolled his eyes heavenward. “Or she is too clever for the Tuareg.”

Khalid gazed at him. “Master, have you considered that you might be wrong? Have you any reason to believe she is treacherous, other than your suspicions?”

For years, the same questions Khalid posed had plagued Faraj. Was he wrong? Was he a stupid, mistrustful fool who unjustly spied on his wife? What sort of man did such a thing to the woman he loved? Had he wronged Fatima instead, with the assumption that her desire to avenge her father’s death would override her good judgment?

It seemed he had no legitimate reason for concern. Fatima kept to herself whenever she went outdoors, or so the one assigned to watch her had said. She never met anyone on her long walks through town or while riding on the beach. On market day, she stopped at the usual stalls in the company of Marzuq and Leeta. She purchased everything their household needed. She never deviated from her usual route or strayed out of sight.

Faraj sighed. Why couldn’t he just accept her word that nothing was amiss?

“I shall seek God’s forgiveness in prayer tonight. I’ll decide tomorrow whether to remove the watchman.”

His captain’s sigh rent the crisp air. “As you wish, master.”

Faraj entered the house where their servants lit the torches in brackets. Leeta approached him, burdened with bound scrolls. A determined look etched fine lines into her face.

He put up his hands. She shook her head. “Forgive me, master, but I can’t continue without your approval of these expenditures. You have not reviewed them in weeks. I know the wedding has occupied your time. I wouldn’t be doing my duty as your treasurer if I did not insist you review household accounts, though I have no right to make demands.”

“Marzuq speaks the truth. He says you can be stubborn as an old mule.”

Leeta bristled and shook her gray- streaked tresses. “This old mule shall deal with that old ram later. Please, master, we must settle the accounts.”

Faraj sighed and chuckled. "Very well. Come to my receiving room."

Nearly two hours later, he and Leeta sat by candlelight still.

He scratched his head where the hair had begun thinning last winter. "I could not keep track of all these matters without your attention to detail. My wife was wise to suggest your appointment as treasurer years ago. You have accounted for every coin spent and all in my possession. We seem to be spending a great deal on silk though. What is Haniya sewing so often?"

Leeta smiled. "Not just her. In the absence of her daughters, your wife also takes some of the silk stock to sew gifts for your children. I believe she also sends garments to Prince Ismail and her brother."

Faraj's gaze lifted from the ledger. "To whom, Nasr?"

"Yes, I believe so." Leeta ducked her head. "I don't think my Sultana would send gifts to the Sultan. Forgive me for speaking plainly."

"No need to apologize. My wife has made her feelings about Muhammad very clear to everyone." He paused. "Did you say Fatima sews these garments herself?"

When Leeta nodded, he shook his head. "Why doesn't she let Haniya do them? I dearly love my wife, but sewing is not one of her superior talents. I don't recall ever having seen her express much enjoyment in the task...."

A chill swept up his spine and he stood abruptly.

Leeta stared at him. "Master, what's the matter?"

"Come with me."

He did not wait to determine if she followed. Quick strides took him to Fatima's door. He knocked. No one answered.

"Perhaps she's asleep."

He tried the door handle. When had Fatima started locking her room?

The seed of doubts planted in his mind now burgeoned. He pounded the door and demanded Fatima open it. From his position down the hall, Niranjan eyed him.

He glared at the eunuch. "Why is this door locked?"

Niranjan shrugged.

Just then, the portal swung open. Fatima stood in the doorway, dressed in her sleeping tunic. Her slim hand gripped the door. Ink besmirched her fingertips. "What's the meaning of this? Have you gone mad, husband?"

He strode past her, his gaze scouring the room.

She tapped his shoulder. "What are you searching for?"

"Where are they?"

"What? What are you doing?"

He shook his head. He desperately wanted to be wrong, but deep in his heart, he knew what he would find. "You cannot hide them from me forever. Even you do not possess such cunning."

He opened her clothing chests and rummaged through them.

Fatima grabbed his arm. "What's the matter with you?"

He pushed her aside and went through the next chest and the next. Still nothing. A throbbing pain centered on his forehead. Her loud curses made it worse.

"Damn you, look at what you're doing! Faraj! Have you lost your senses?

His hands fisted at his side. "Where are the silks you send to Nasr?"

"What? Why do you want to know?"

"Do you believe I'm a fool, Fatima?"

"Yes, at this moment I do believe that! If you wanted to see the robes, you could have just asked me!"

She went to a chest beside the smaller one where she kept her jewelry and handed him two bolts of silk. "They're nearly finished. Are you happy now?"

He laid the bolts in the chest again and straightened. He raked hands through his hair. "I should not have...that is...."

He could not continue, not with her eyes damning him for a wary fool. His head bowed, he turned to leave.

Then he noticed the gleam of something shiny under the far corner of the chest. He removed the silk again and realized the coffer was not made of solid cedar wood. Instead, a thin lattice framework, neatly constructed, secured the bottom. Metals gleamed in tiny dots reflected from underneath the frame.

He raised his foot and smashed it with his boot. Fatima screamed. Sparkling gems and pearls inlaid in gold and silver brimmed inside, as did one golden *dinar* atop the pile.

He snatched up the gold coin and frowned at it. "Why is this here? Why are you keeping jewels under a false bottom in this chest? You never keep *dinars*. I never do. Leeta always has our money."

"I keep my valuables in many places, husband. Would you like to ransack my room and find all of them? Leeta must have dropped the coin somehow. I found it."

Faraj looked at their treasurer, who dipped her gaze. "Forgive me, but that is impossible. I have just reviewed household finances with the master. Every coin in his possession or spent. All accounted for to the very last *dinar*. I have never missed a coin in all my years as treasurer."

Faraj raked his hand through the precious stones and more coins came into view. Startled, he looked up at Fatima. Then something coarse brushed against his finger. He gripped the parchment and withdrew it.

Fatima lunged for the letter. "You have no right to search my things!"

He stood and held her off with one hand, though she desperately snatched at the parchment. He read aloud the still wet *Naksh* calligraphy smeared across the letter.

"Greetings in the name of God. More gifts for those that aid us to overthrow the tyrant. Do not let your courage fail, when we are so close to our ambition. Soon you shall hold the prize. As ever your loving sister, Fatima."

He glared at her. "More secrets sewn in silk, hmm? You've returned to your old tricks?"

She stopped her struggles and crossed her hands over her chest. "Old tricks are the best ones."

His fist opened and his hand swung wide. He backhanded her so hard that she crumpled in a heap on the floor. He crushed the parchment between his fingers. Their eyes met. Hers glittered like the hardest jewel. Blood trickled from her nose.

Faraj stabbed a finger at Leeta, who stared at both of them in shock. "Wake our children. All of them! I want to see them in the banquet hall, now."

She ran from the room.

Faraj yanked Fatima to her feet and dragged her to the hall.

"Master, what are you doing?" Niranjan called out to him. "Where are you taking my Sultana?"

He whirled toward the eunuch. "Keep your wretched tongue behind your teeth. I know you helped her. She never makes a move without you! Her damned shadow indeed."

He pushed Fatima into the center of the room. She clattered on the floor and rubbed at her hip. She caught his glare and stopped. Her eyes still shimmered in defiance. He unfolded the creases from her message.

"Father, what's happening?" Ismail arrived at the head of his brother and remaining sisters.

"Be silent," Faraj insisted.

He spoke then and told their children of Fatima's hatred for the Sultan and her treason.

Muhammad asserted, "It cannot be true! You must be mistaken."

Faraj turned a furious frown on his second son. "Then read the truth of her betrayal, if you don't believe me!"

The parchment circulated the room in trembling hands, met with gasps of shock or stares. Leeta, whose husband had joined her, sobbed into her hands and refused to read it. Instead, she shoved the letter at Niranjan.

Faraj snatched the missive from the eunuch's hand lest he attempt to destroy it. "Now, you all know the truth. My wife collaborates with her brother Nasr to undermine the Sultanate. She risks the lives of everyone here. Her life! My life! Your lives! As of today, none of you shall see or speak to her, unless I allow it. She shall remain under guard in her room at all times. She shall perform her ablutions and prayers alone. She shall dine alone. Under no circumstances may she have a quill, ink, parchment or anything on which to write. Do not speak of this day to anyone. This is my judgment."

He stared hard at Niranjan. "Ismail, fetch my captain. Tell Khalid to consign this dog to the dungeon of *Al-Jabal Faro*. Niranjan al-Kadim can rot in a cell until the end of his days."

# Chapter 19
# A Gilded Prison

## Prince Faraj

Malaka, Al-Andalus: Dhu al-Hijja 707 AH (Malaga, Andalusia: June AD 1308)

The day before Faraj's departure for Gharnatah, there to witness Ismail's wedding, he sat at his writing desk. The glare of sunset intruded into the room. For two hours by the water clock, he had stared at the blank sheet of parchment until the evening stars glittered in the sky.

Yesterday, he had received word from Leila's husband at al-Jazirah al-Khadra. She died in childbirth after having delivered of her third son. Faraj's sweet, smiling Leila was gone. Only six years before, he had commended her to the care of a loving husband.

His grip tightened on the quill, just below the feathers. The wood snapped in his hand. He tossed it aside in disgust and buried his head in his hands. His chest heaved with silent sobs.

Someone rapped at the door. He dried his cheeks in the sleeve of his silken tunic. "Enter!"

Khalid opened the door. "My prince, Amud is here."

The captain stepped aside and the Tuareg eunuch entered. Khalid had recruited Amud and his brother Bazu to spy on Fatima years ago. The men remained in Faraj's employ.

"What does he wish, Khalid?"

Amud and Bazu spoke only the language of their mother's people. Khalid understood it as well as many of the Berber languages.

He translated for Amud. "The Sultana wishes to see you, my prince."

"Of course Fatima wants to see me. She hopes I shall release her in time for Ismail's wedding."

"Are you still going to Gharnatah on the morrow?"

"In truth, I do not have the heart after the news about Leila, but I must go. I must write to her husband. I do not know what to say to my nephew."

The eunuch began gesticulating, his hands in a flurry. Guttural sounds issued from his throat.

Khalid said, "Amud says your wife has been upset all day. You should tell her of your daughter."

Fatima's behavior did not surprise Faraj. She would have known, in her way, of Leila's passing. "Still, I refuse to see her. She shall soon tire of her antics. Leave me now."

"As you wish, master."

Faraj waved them away and the door shut with a heavy thud. He closed his eyes.

Years later, Fatima's betrayal still hurt. It did not matter the risk she took or that, in truth, he now believed the Sultan was capable of everything she had alleged. Muhammad was unstable. Did his wife also suffer from such madness?

Yet, he knew no woman who had been as deceitful as Fatima had, could have spoken her untruths from an addled mind. She had destroyed his trust in her, built after decades of marriage. How could the woman he adored for so long have betrayed him for the sake of her brother? How could he ever trust her?

The door creaked again.

"Khalid, I said I didn't want to be disturbed."

"Good evening, master." Baraka glided into the room.

He frowned at the sight of her hennaed hair dyed a garish orange. It did not hide the gray, not entirely. Her thin, twisted lips and emerald eyes remained the same, if impossibly harder. No warmth dwelled in her. He hardly fathomed how years ago, he had known pleasure in this viper's sinuous limbs.

"What do you want, woman? I am not inclined to listen to any of your foolishness. Have you come to tell me yet again how the slave Abeer discomforts my former concubines? They have not shared my bed for years. Why should they be jealous of this woman?"

Baraka's throaty laugh filled the room. "That one, we do not worry for her."

Something about her caustic tone and sloe-eyed glance made him look at her askance. "You haven't harmed Abeer, I trust?"

The Genoese slave smiled, a lazy gesture. Baraka settled herself on a cushion across from him. "We have not troubled her. She is nothing to anyone and shall learn this soon enough."

His jaw tightened. "What do you want, Baraka?"

"That brute, your captain, he says I must ask your permission if I want to see the Sultana. So, I ask."

"Don't call Khalid a brute. He is loyal and dutiful. He has traits you do not possess and could never understand. Why do you want to see Fatima? To gloat over her? I shall never allow you to do that."

"Master does care for the Sultana still? Pity you are too foolish to let her know."

He pounded the cedar wood table. "You dare insult me! I should have you whipped."

She laughed, threw back her head and exposed her slim, white throat. "What can you do to me that you have not already done?"

"I didn't know you cared so much to lose my favors. I never denied you the joy of our moments together."

"No, you denied me your heart! You gave this to the Sultana and more."

For a moment, she seemed contemplative, a withered former concubine reminiscing about the lost pleasures of youth. Yet when she looked at him, fire sparked deep within those hard green eyes.

"You are a fool and a tyrant, Faraj, who hurts the women who love you. You are selfish. You do not deserve the Sultana's love. I understand her pain, for you've broken my heart, too."

"You wish to commiserate with her? I doubt Fatima would welcome you."

"Not her choice, if you say otherwise."

"The eunuch Bazu is always with her. He may not speak Arabic, but he is watchful. I shall know what happens when you are with her, Baraka."

"Then, you are giving your permission?"

"I'll allow the visit. You may see her in the morning before I leave for Gharnatah."

He wrote on a strip of parchment instructing Bazu and Amud to allow Baraka into Fatima's room. The Genoese woman smiled and stood, taking the missive with her. At the door, she bowed low.

"Poor master, such a lonely bed tonight. Perhaps in the dark, he wishes for me to comfort him?"

"I have no use for such an old woman as you."

She laughed again. "One day soon, Faraj, you shall learn I still have my uses."

He stared in her wake long after she had left. Misgivings filled him. He dismissed the concerns that Baraka might be in league with Fatima. The former concubine would never put aside her petty hatred of his wife.

Weary, Faraj withdrew to his room without composing a response to Leila's husband. He found no rest in his chamber. Fatima's screams and pounding on her door filled the harem. With his room next to hers, he could not hope to sleep. He drew on a tunic over his nakedness and left the chamber. Torchlight set in a bracket illuminated Amud's face.

"Open my wife's door."

Amud did so and stepped aside.

Fatima whirled and faced Faraj, wild-eyed. He looked around the room, took in its disarray and beckoned Bazu.

The eunuch bowed and nodded. When Faraj waved him away, he closed the door behind him.

"So, like a child, you upset your room, Fatima. I thought you would have been more considerate of your Haniya."

Faraj gestured to the overturned bed, the silks and linens strewn on the floor. Broken glass littered one corner. Several pieces of jewelry spilled from Fatima's chest of ornaments.

The state of the room reflected his wife's condition. Her unruly hair and loose wrinkled robe, stained with the remnants of something she must have eaten, showed her lack of care. On closer examination, he realized blood dotted her garments. A crimson stain marked her palm. She had cut her hand.

He ripped a strip of linen from his tunic and grabbed her. She pulled away, but he bound the jagged cut.

She whispered. "I didn't think you still cared enough to help me."

He tied the material, perhaps tighter than he should have. Still, the little wince that escaped her gave him some satisfaction. At least, she could still feel pain.

"I never stopped caring, Fatima. You forgot your marital vows in favor of some ridiculous revenge plot. You disturb the peace of my house this night. Why?"

She dragged her hand from his grasp. "I had just finished my meal when the water goblet dropped from my hand. Something has happened. Please tell me."

He shook his head. As difficult as it had been to learn of Leila's fate, he could not blurt out the truth. He still cared for her, as he had said.

"I asked those Berbers savages," she muttered and pointed to the door, "to let me see you! They refused. They may not speak Arabic, but I am certain they understood my request. Ismail's wedding shall occur in a few days. Have you received word from Gharnatah? Has something happened to our son?"

"No, not to him."

Fatima's eyes widened. "Please, you must tell me."

He sighed and then did as she bid him. In a monotone voice, he relayed the news from al-Jazirah al-Khadra. She covered her mouth with her fingers and turned from him. Her shoulders shook.

He raised his hand, almost placed it on her arm, before his fingers fell useless at his side. He could not comfort her. He could not even find solace for himself.

"Now you know the truth. Our daughter's final resting place is at al-Jazirah al-Khadra. Her child lived, another grandson for us. His father named him Ali. After I attend Ismail's wedding, I shall go to Leila's children and see them."

She spun around, her cheeks wet. "You cannot leave me here. They need me. Ismail needs me."

"He's not a child. He is a man, soon to be married. Our grandchildren have their father and their governess. They don't need you."

"Would you have them suffer alone? They have lost their mother! Please Faraj, I know I have failed you, but in your anger, do not let me fail our family!"

"Ismail does not expect you at the wedding."

"You told him I would not attend? How could you?"

She shrank from him, her gaze stark before her eyes watered again.

"Bah! A curse on you and your damned tears! I cannot let them unman me. Do not dare look at me that way, after all the lies you have told. I should think you would understand. Your own deceit has brought you to this end."

"Every lie I told broke my heart! I only did it because I had no choice. Please do not punish me this way. I shall live in this confinement for the rest of my days if I must, but please don't keep me from our family, from our grandsons and our son!"

"Ismail serves the Sultan! Praise God he is loyal to his parents foremost. Had it been another man, we might not have kept your treachery from the Sultan. You think I would let you near Gharnatah now, to seek out your treacherous allies, to let you devise some new plan with Nasr. No, Fatima, I am wise to all your tricks. You'll remain here!"

He turned on his heel. Halfway to the door, her arms slid about his waist.

"No, I won't let you leave. You must listen to me."

He removed her hold. "Go to bed."

"No!" She launched herself at him again. Her limbs wound around his shoulders. "Please, let me go with you."

She pressed her trembling form against him. He reveled in the feel of her. His traitorous body would always respond to her touch.

Then her kisses alighted on his nape, soft as feathers. Little nips and caresses at his neck and jaw line followed.

He groaned. "Fatima, stop. This changes nothing."

Her tongue flicked over the curve of his ear. She nibbled at the fleshy lobe. He turned and found her mouth. He kissed her wildly, all thoughts of gentleness gone from his mind. He hauled her up against him. Her fingers delved between their bodies and tugged his tunic upward. Cool air danced across his belly, replaced by

Fatima's fingertips. She cupped the length of him, stroked from root to tip. He shuddered.

He wrenched the folds of her robe aside, touched and kissed her everywhere. She moaned. His fingers glided along her slender throat, her beautiful breasts with the nipples that hardened beneath his touch and her rounded belly.

Before he became lost forever, he whispered against her shoulder, "You would do anything, wouldn't you, to escape these rooms and see our family again?"

"Yes," she whispered. She grabbed his hips and wrapped her legs around them.

"Even make love with me?"

"Yes! It has been so long. Please."

He grabbed her throat and shoved her head against the wall with a satiating thud. She panicked and struggled for each breath.

"Who'd have thought you would become a great whore in your old age?"

He released her and she slid down the wall. He crossed the room and opened the door. It flew back on its hinges and banged against the stucco wall.

He yelled into the dim light for a servant. One peered around the corner. "Yes, master, what is your desire?"

He looked over his shoulder at Fatima. "Summon the slave Abeer to my room. I need her tonight."

## *Princess Fatima*

Bleary-eyed, Fatima still sat on the floor adjacent the wall on. Light filtered through the closed lattice window. The ugly eunuch Bazu stood beside it, his gaze fixed on her. She closed her eyes and blotted out the sight of him. The sounds of camels and men issuing orders drifted to her from outside. Faraj prepared to leave Malaka.

The door to her gilded prison opened. Baraka entered.

"Isn't it a splendid morning, my Sultana? The sun is shining, the sea birds circle overhead. The gardens smell of fragrant flowers and the sea spray…oh, but you wouldn't know about any of that in your confinement."

A smile fixed on Baraka's angular face. She closed the door and leaned against it. She twirled a flower stem between her fingers.

Pain knifed through Fatima at the sight of Baraka. Fatima closed her eyes. "Get out! Leave me be!"

"I think not. You shall suffer me as I have suffered you all these years. So proud, so beautiful, a Sultana of Gharnatah. Look at you now! No wonder the master called that cow Abeer to his bed last night. You're a disgrace."

"Baraka, if you don't shut your mouth, I'll forget that you have been a dutiful governess to my children!"

The harridan crossed the floor and hovered over her. "You'll do what? You don't even have the courage or the good sense to get up off the floor. Look at you, cowering here, mewling like a wounded kitten. You! I have nothing to fear from you. Now, the Sultana Fatima, the one who threatened me with death for stealing her necklace, she was once a woman to fear. What has become of her?"

Fatima buried her face in her hands. "Why can't you leave me alone?"

Baraka laughed and crouched in front of her. "I've waited a long time to see you brought low. Proud Sultana. You're a fool, you know."

Fatima raised her head and met the slave's regard. "Is that so?"

"Yes, a fool to throw away your husband's love, to risk it all by writing your treacherous plans on parchment, when you could have used a trusted messenger instead. I used to think your judgment was sound. Your husband is a fool, too. I told him so yesterday evening."

When she gasped, Baraka laughed again. Fatima hated her even more for taking such pleasure in her poor circumstances.

"There were other ways to trick your husband, I know them. After your husband chose you over his slaves, I vowed I would not be alone. I took a lover and kept him for all the years we lived at Gharnatah. There have been others since, here at Malaka."

"You've signed your own death warrant, Baraka." Fatima glanced at the eunuch, Bazu, who stared at them.

"He is no fool. Unlike everyone else, including my husband, I believe he and his brother understand Arabic perfectly well. They do not deign to speak it."

Baraka leaned forward and cast a sloe-eyed glance at the man. "I do not worry for him. He is a man. Do you know there are two ways to make a eunuch? Some just have their testicles removed, instead of the penis and sacs. This one can still perform as a man. I have watched him in the *hammam*. His scars do not frighten me. If I wished, I could make him sigh with delight. He would forget all he has heard today. If I commanded it, he would crawl across the room on his belly, just to lick the spot where I have sat."

The man swallowed and straightened his stance against the wall, confirming Fatima's suspicions.

Baraka ran her pink tongue over her lower lip. With her painted face, gleaming hair and the hint of still youthful curves under the billowy, light robe, Fatima did not doubt her conviction.

She muttered, "Too bad you could not hold my husband with such tricks."

The former concubine looked at her hennaed nails. "Love was the drug with which you took him from me. For a long time, I hated you. You gave him a life with purpose and children. You left me with nothing. You bewitched him."

"Now, you are here to take pleasure in my downfall?"

"No. I have come to bring you this." She extended her hand.

Fatima looked at the blossom she offered, with its white florets and the golden disc at its center. "Chamomile?"

"From your garden outside the kitchens."

Fatima raised an eyebrow. "Did you think I needed something to aid my sleep?"

"Why should I care how you sleep? Before I came to live with your husband, I had another master. A Turk who had stolen me away from my home, ages ago. I learned much from him. In the harems of the Turks, the women believe that flowers have symbolic meaning."

As Fatima took the flower and inhaled the aromatic smell, Baraka's gaze held hers. "If you would like, I could teach you this language of flowers. Since you have nothing better to do in this place, you can pass your time in such instruction."

"Why would you teach me the language of flowers?" Fatima asked, her peripheral gaze on the eunuch, who leaned forward. "Besides, who says Faraj shall permit you another visit?"

"Don't worry about whether I can persuade your husband. He is only a man. It delights me to torment him and you. I know how much you enjoy your gardens in bloom. You cannot see the flowers from this place."

Baraka got to her feet with the agility of a woman half her age. She looked at Bazu and licked her lips. He gasped and averted his eyes. Laughter escaped her in a throaty rumble.

She glanced at Fatima again. "Let me offer a measure of advice, if you would accept it. I doubt a Sultana of Gharnatah can bear sleeping on the floor for long nights. You would not want to risk ruining your delicate, pampered skin, would you?"

She rapped at the door. Amud threw it open. He stepped aside, but she leaned into him. His grip on the handle tightened. Baraka giggled at his reddened face.

Fatima called out, "Is there a meaning to the chamomile flower among the Turks?"

"Yes. It is for patience, my Sultana."

The door slammed shut on Baraka's back.

Fatima stood and waved her guard over to another corner. His lower lip jutted with resentment, but he moved.

She peered through the lattice window and held the flower up to her nose. She inhaled the scent again. For the first time in years, she knew some measure of comfort. If she remained patient, God would answer her prayers and bring peace and justice to Gharnatah.

She looked around the room, her prison. Once, it had been a place of joy and celebration of the love she and Faraj shared. She had squandered those memories in a quest for vengeance, a purpose that no longer needed her guidance. How could she ever regain the precious time she had lost, mired in cruelty and abandonment? How could her wounded heart ever heal?

# Chapter 20
# The Language of Flowers

## Prince Faraj

Malaka, Al-Andalus: Shawwal 708 AH (Malaga, Andalusia: March AD 1309)

During the last course of the evening meal, Faraj looked down the table at Baraka. "Almost each day for over nine months, you have visited Fatima and brought her flowers. Why?"

The spoon of yoghurt and sliced fig hovered just beyond her parted lips. "My visits cheer her, master."

She smiled at him and swallowed the morsel. Her spoon dipped into the bowl again and she continued eating.

He glared at her. "You'll understand if I find it hard to believe Fatima enjoys your visits."

"They do not displease her. You do not know many things about the Sultana. Shall I tell you?"

His fist thumped on the cedar wood and sent a blue faïence vessel tumbling. "Don't you dare think to inform me about my own wife!"

Pomegranate juice splashed the carpet. Saliha dragged Qabiha with her vacant stare back from the table. Saliha was always protective of her elder sister. She would leave the house with her in a year, when she married.

Faraj's second son muttered something through thinly pressed lips, before he set down his spoon.

His father demanded, "Do you have something to say, Muhammad?"

"I am not hungry. May I be excused, Father?"

"You shall remain and repeat whatever you mumbled before! If you have something to say to me, then say it."

Muhammad looked at Faraj with eyes like his mother's own. They pierced to his father's soul, as Fatima's own would have.

"Saliha cries every night, Father. She thinks no one hears her. I do. Now that you have arranged her marriage, she worries for the future. If the love you and *Ummi* shared can end so easily, what hope can there be for happiness in any union? The discord has shattered our lives. You have the power to change these circumstances, Father, yet you do nothing."

"It is your mother who has endangered all our lives with her lies."

"I don't care about that! You're hurting and she is in pain, too. What can she do, who can she harm now, locked up in her room for years? If Aunt Baraka comforts her now, at least, it's more than you've done."

Faraj looked around the room at the faces of his youngest, unmarried daughters, his steward and treasurer. Almost all averted their eyes from his stare. Still, he suspected they shared the same sentiments. Only Baraka dared meet his regard with a smile.

Silence pervaded the room. The smell of the sea breeze filtered into the open-air courtyard and preceded Khalid's appearance. His heavy black boots echoed on the marble.

"My prince, news from Gharnatah."

Faraj took the missive he offered, broke the wax seal and scanned the page's contents with widening eyes. He showed it to Khalid. "Can it be true?"

"It bears the seal of the *Diwan al-Insha*."

Muhammad asked, "What's happened, Father?"

"We'll discuss it later." At his son's scowl, he softened his tone. "I promise to tell you, but I must see your mother first. Captain, come with me."

Baraka's smile widened, but Faraj did not question it.

Khalid followed him to Fatima's chamber, where Amud stood beside the wall. At a gesture from Faraj, he opened the door and the men entered. When Faraj waved Amud's brother Bazu away, the Tuareg bowed and left the room.

Fatima stood before the window. The mid-afternoon sun swathed her in golden light that penetrated the lattice. She wore a red silk robe, her hair in lustrous waves tumbling down her back. Streaks of gray threaded through her curls.

When she turned to Faraj, she held a yellow poppy blossom. Her countenance revealed nothing, yet in it, he recognized a glimmer of the wife he had known and loved for long. Something had changed inside her.

"Good-day, Faraj. You also, Khalid of al-Hakam. The peace of God be with you."

"News has come from Gharnatah." Faraj waved the parchment in her face. "Do you want to know the contents of this letter?"

"If you wish to tell me, then I am glad to hear it."

He snorted at her demure tone. "The *Diwan al-Insha* summons all governors of the provinces to attend the coronation of the new Sultan of Gharnatah, Abu'l-Juyush Nasr, fourth of his line. According to this letter, the ministers have forced Sultan Muhammad the third to abdicate in favor of his younger brother. The Sultan has been ill for some time. The council believes his mind is affected. He has become an imbecile. He cannot rule. The council claims to have the support of the military. The new *Hajib*, Ali ibn al-Jayyab, signed this letter. I can only assume that Muhammad's prime minister, Ibn al-Hakim, has been removed or is dead."

An audible sigh escaped Fatima. "Then, it is over."

"Yes. Nasr's treachery is complete. Now tell me the truth, if you can still speak it. This news does not surprise you, does it? Before I came here, you knew what I would say."

"Yes, husband, I did."

Faraj dismissed Khalid and sank down on Fatima's bed. "I await your explanation."

Fatima sat beside him. "Baraka spoke to me this morning."

She glanced at him. Her lower lip trembled. Did she fear what he thought of her meetings with Baraka? Bazu had reported through Khalid that the Genoese woman had come earlier and, after a trifling discussion about the weather, gave Fatima a flower, presumably the one she held now. "You may continue."

She sniffed the petals. "Yellow poppy is the flower of victory and success among the Turks. Almost each day for a year, Baraka has brought me flowers with many meanings. Chamomile for patience. Blue violets for faithfulness and watchfulness. Even the rose leaf for hope. The flower always reflected the mood she hoped I might adopt. Her blossoms also served as warnings of danger or great tidings."

"How did she know of the *Diwan*'s actions before I did?"

"She has a...an old friend in Gharnatah among the council members."

"You mean one of her former lovers, of course."

Though he did not ask a question, she nodded. "They are not lovers now, I assure you. I believe the man may remember her with some fondness."

"My pride doesn't suffer because of her betrayal. Her lovers - yes, I have always known of them, but they never concerned me. I should whip and sell Baraka for her defiance now. I told everyone you were to remain ignorant of anything that transpired beyond the walls of our home. What am I to do with you?"

She bowed her head. "You may do whatever you wish to me. I shall submit. Please do not hurt Baraka. She has been kind to me."

He chuckled. "Perhaps it's a little too late for you to practice submission. It seems your understanding of kindness has also altered. You have accomplished what you and Nasr wished. I suppose you're proud."

She shook her head. "I am not. Many people have died because of Muhammad. His abdication means nothing compared to the loss of those lives. Yet, I recognize in it, there is a chance restless spirits may be at peace finally."

"The dead may have their peace. What is there of it for those of us who yet live?"

Fatima looked at him. "I don't understand."

He cupped his forehead in his hand and closed his eyes. He could not bear the sight of her.

"What you and Nasr have set in motion has greater consequences than justice for your loved ones. Gharnatah shall never be safe for another ruler, because the *Diwan* or some other faction shall presume they can remove a man from his throne whenever they see fit. No Sultan shall ever keep his throne without fear of an insurrection. A precedent has been set here, because of you and your traitorous brother. Muhammad may have destroyed those closest to him. You and Nasr have shattered the sanctity, which held the Sultanate of Gharnatah inviolate."

For a time, neither of them spoke.

Then Fatima's furtive touch alighted on his forearm. "What about us?"

"Us? There is no 'us', Fatima. There can never be, not in the way we were before."

Tears pooled in her eyes.

He sneered at her sorrow. "Don't concern yourself. I won't divorce you. No, I'm not so stupid as to divorce the sister of the next Sultan of Gharnatah."

Her fingers closed on his limb. "I mean more to you than that!"

"You'll remain my wife in name only. You'll have the freedom of this place, to do as you wish. The Tuareg brothers shall join the corps at *Al-Jabal Faro*. They shall never spy on you again. I must warn you, keep far from me. The sight of you wounds my soul. How can I look at you now and see anything, except your years of deceit?"

Her trembling hand remained on his arm. "I know I have hurt you. I can make it right."

He looked down at where they touched. "You are so quick to resolve matters between us, now that you and your brother have won. If only you had thought of the consequences of your actions before you ruined our marriage. You have jeopardized our lives. You want me to forgive. I'm afraid you ask for more than is possible."

"In time, you could forgive me, if you tried. Please Faraj, I have much to atone for. My heart...."

He jerked away from her. "Your heart! What of mine? If I have no heart with which to love you, the blame lies with you. You betrayed my trust. How could I ever give you my heart whole again?"

She dashed to the window. Her shoulders heaved. Once, those tears would have moved him, but no more.

"I'll summon Basma and Haniya for you. We leave for Gharnatah in the morning." When she raised her head, he added, "This is your brother's moment of triumph, what you have worked so hard to accomplish. Surely, you would not miss it?"

After four years of confinement, Fatima took her first steps to renewed freedom later that day. Her children's hugs and kisses were a joy, but they could not comfort her. Saliha, the youngest who remained unmarried, looked at her with eyes that shone with pleasure, but they also reflected uncertainty. Her second son Muhammad seemed more reserved than when she last spoke with him. Although she and Nasr had achieved their goal after eight years, she had paid the price with her children.

Basma and Haniya packed her garments for the journey to Gharnatah. Haniya was more pleasant than Basma, who did her duty in silence.

While they toiled, Leeta appeared in the doorway. "Forgive the intrusion, my Sultana."

"There's no need to seek forgiveness for anything you do." Fatima embraced her. She did not return the gesture.

"Your husband is leaving for Gharnatah now. He has said that you and the children may follow tomorrow."

Fatima swallowed. "I understand he is angry with me. I've disappointed you too, Leeta. I shall atone, if you'll let me."

The treasurer shook her head. "I have no right to cast judgment. I am, but a servant of this house, as you have reminded me in the past."

Fatima recalled the exchange, when she had shunned Leeta's kindness.

"Pray excuse me, my Sultana."

Fatima went to the window, took the yellow poppy from the sill and looked down into the courtyard.

Faraj emerged from the house with Khalid. Soldiers rode to the summit of the hill from the citadel. An aged man in dirty rags shuffled between them. Fatima covered her mouth as she recognized Niranjan.

She bit back a sob and she peered through the lattice. Faraj spoke with Niranjan, who abased himself. Remnants of stringy, whitened hair fell over his eyes. He was a shadow of his former self, all because of his devotion to her. She had to make amends to him, too.

Then Faraj mounted his horse, along with his captain. Her husband looked up, his gaze fixed on the spot where she stood. Deep lines scoured his face and his brows knitted together. Did he sense that she stood hidden behind the lattice?

She shrank alongside the wall and did not dare look again, until the sound of clattering hooves faded.

She shuddered at a light touch on her arm.

Haniya asked, "Are you well?"

"Yes. Thank you for your continued kindness."

Fatima touched the rounded belly jutting beneath her servant's tunic. "The child thrives within you?"

"Yes. It shall come soon, I believe next month."

"Who is the father?"

Haniya lowered her gaze. "Khalid of al-Hakam."

Fatima covered her mouth with a hand. "Khalid? I never knew you shared the captain's bed."

"He is still in love with Amoda. He is also a man of natural desires. The news of a child did not please him, but he has promised to acknowledge the babe as his own."

Fatima struggled with her shock. Haniya patted her shoulder. "Nothing stays the same forever."

# Chapter 21
# A Vow Fulfilled

## Princess Fatima

Gharnatah, Al-Andalus: Shawwal 708 AH (Granada, Andalusia: March AD 1309)

The next morning, Fatima and her children traveled with a camel caravan to Gharnatah. She left a weakened Niranjan in Malaka. His imprisonment had robbed him of his former strength. Sores and bruises covered him. He could not make the journey homeward. She missed him at her side.

On the outskirts of the capital after the sixth day, she studied the expanse of white clouds and azure sky over their heads. Did her father watch over her in Paradise?

"Now, there is justice for you. You can be at peace."

Beside her camel, mounted on his horse, Muhammad asked, "Were you speaking to me, *Ummi*?"

When she shook her head, he said, "Ismail shall be very happy to see you. You have not met his daughters. In his letters, my brother has often said they have your eyes."

Ismail's wife had died in childbirth a year before, leaving him a widower with two daughters, Fatimah, named for his mother and Leila, for his beloved sister. In time, Fatima hoped he might re-marry with a bride of his own choosing.

When she arrived in Gharnatah, the city markets thronged with residents. A buoyant mood, as under the days of her father, rose up under a mid-morning sun. They climbed the steep incline of the *Sabika* hill. Courtiers milled about, some haggling with vendors who offered their wares near the citadel gate.

Sadness tinged Fatima's return. Many things were different now. Muhammad had razed their grandfather's mosque and built his own to the south. The gardens where she had played as a child gave way to jumbled buildings juxtaposed against each other. Smooth stone supported terraces and columns, instead of marble walkways and porticos. A portion of a new palace covered the area where Faraj's old house once stood, where they had spent several happy years together.

Fatima's father had died more than seven years before, his beloved Nur al-Sabah gone to Paradise with him. His Sultana Shams ed-Duna lived across the White Sea. She had never returned to Gharnatah. His remaining children were scattered throughout Al-Andalus or to distant lands. For years, his power and love had bound their family. She recalled her promise to him before his death.

She closed her eyes and offered a silent prayer. *'Honorable father, oft remembered, grant me this one wish. Watch over us always. I shall guide our family until my last breath, Father, if you would do the same for me. Let your wisdom and strength flow through me, so I may protect those whom you love. In my care, let your legacy be fulfilled."*

Her second son's touch on her arm stirred her. "Look, here are Ismail and Father."

Faraj had aged. Even at sixty-two years, his mannerisms remained dignified and the actions of a younger man. She drew a sharp intake of breath at the sight of him. Nervousness coupled with fear. Her stomach fluttered.

Ismail helped her from the camel's back. They clasped each other's forearms and stood in silence. Then she caressed his bearded cheek and recalled her father in his youth looking down at her. Ismail returned her watery stare and smiled.

"It has been too long, my son." Fatima's voice wavered.

"I'm glad to see you again, *Ummi.* I've missed you."

"And I, you. Where are my granddaughters? Are they both well?"

"They thrive in the care of their nursemaid. You shall see them tonight. Your brother Nasr has granted us rooms in the new palace."

He gestured to the structure behind him. Though Fatima hated the thought of residing in any place

Muhammad had commissioned, she appreciated Nasr's thoughtfulness.

"May we see the Sultan today, my son?"

"No, he is in solitude before the coronation. His Galician guards have barred anyone from seeing him."

Ismail greeted his sisters. Fatima snuck a furtive glance at Faraj. He did not look at her, as he embraced their second son.

Soon, they strolled through the new palace, a gaudy tribute to the power Muhammad once held, with its slender, carved columns, silk cushions and bedding. Ornamentation fashioned in gold and inlaid with mother-of-pearl shimmered throughout the rooms. Fatima met her twin granddaughters, who did possess her eyes. She nuzzled their sweet, smiling faces and knew the simple pleasure of being with part of her family again.

The morning of the Sultan's coronation arrived. All the governors had converged at the capital at the request of the *Diwan al-Insha*. Fatima reunited with some of her family members. Her daughter Leila's three sons came to with their father. Her daughters Qamar and Mumina had also married provincial governors, while the husbands of Aisha and Faridah had risen to similar positions of power. With the addition of Ismail's daughters, twelve exuberant and loud grandchildren surrounded Fatima. Only one other thing could have completed her happiness.

Her husband, absorbed in the beauty of his grandchildren, embraced and spoke to them in loving murmurs. He had ignored her since her arrival. She sighed, understanding how he must have suffered through the years. What could she do to bring them back together?

Her domestic concerns would have to wait. Sunlight glittered among the courtyards and pavilions of *Al-Qal'at al-Hamra* as the large family followed Faraj to Nasr's coronation. Foremost among the governors, Faraj proceeded to the front of the throne room. As sister of the new Sultan, Fatima joined him. The rest of their family except one hugged the recesses of the chamber. Others congregated outside the square-shaped building, while those who could not enter peered through the oak and brass doors.

When Nasr strode into the room, Fatima marveled at his resemblance to his mother. From his blond curls swept back from his forehead to his robe of state, the traditional *khil'a* of red silk, he radiated the majesty of his office.

Ismail stood among a cadre of fellow ministers. He had begged Nasr's leave to resign his post as *wazir* and return to Malaka. Fatima did not question the timing of his withdrawal from the capital. It delighted her heart to know he would be at home again. She could spend as much time as she wished with her granddaughters.

The court herald, Ibn Safwan, stepped forward and with a nod from Nasr, he recited the Profession of Faith. Then the *Hajib*, Ali ibn al-Jayyab, stooped with age, now shuffled forward. His venerable state reminded Fatima of the first minister of the *Diwan*, her former tutor, dead for almost fourteen years. Ibn al-Jayyab held aloft the crown of state, which all of Nasr's predecessors had worn. He placed it on her brother's head. He listed the new Sultan's titles and praised him.

As one, every occupant of the room fell on their knees. Fatima pressed her forehead to the cool floor. A tear trickled from the corner of her eye.

Nasr commanded everyone to stand. At the age of twenty-one, he would be the youngest sovereign Gharnatah had ever known. He possessed his father's calm exterior despite his youthfulness. He stared straight ahead, while each of the provincial governors rounded the square patchwork of tiles before the throne and offered him homage.

Faraj followed suit. When he returned to Fatima's side, her furtive glance spied his lips set in a firm, thin line.

At the end of the ceremony, he stepped to the forefront. "My noble Sultan, I am your loyal governor. May I speak?"

Nasr smiled and beckoned him. "You are kin and a brother by marriage. Speak what is in your heart, Prince Faraj."

Fatima whispered to her husband. "What are you doing?"

He ignored her.

"I would ask a boon of you, my Sultan. It is a tradition, which your brother established, for the new master of

Gharnatah to favor one request from his courtiers upon his ascension to the throne."

The court filled with murmurs, some of assent and others like Fatima, who wondered why anyone dared mention the name of the old Sultan.

Fatima's stare darted to Nasr, who leaned forward on his chair.

"So it shall be with me. What would you have of me, Prince Faraj?"

Faraj glanced at Fatima before his gaze returned to Nasr. "The life of your brother, Sultan Muhammad the third."

Silence filled the room. Then grumbling followed. The governors closest to Faraj shied away. Fatima stared at his back, incredulous that he would make such a demand before the whole court.

He continued, "I would have your oath, my Sultan, that your brother Muhammad shall suffer no harm by your hand or order. If you swear it, your sacred vow cannot be broken."

Nasr stood, his brow furrowed. "I know what is required of an oath-taker!" He sank down on the throne again. "I shall swear that pledge now. I vow by the noble blood of my ancestors that my brother Muhammad, the former Sultan of Gharnatah, shall never suffer harm at my hand or by my order. He may live out the rest of his days in exile at Munakkab."

Fatima expelled the breath she did not know she held and moved beside her husband. "Are you mad, Faraj?"

He scowled at her. "A woman does not speak to a man in this court. It seems you have forgotten the ways of our forefathers."

Their gazes held, until she looked away. Nasr stared in their direction, his icy stare narrowing on Faraj. She glanced at her husband again, whose grim visage mirrored Nasr's own.

As the pair glared at each other, Fatima clutched at the sudden tightness in her chest. Her brother had little choice except to give his assent to Faraj's request, but he possessed the pride of the Nasrids. He would not soon forget how Faraj had compelled his oath, reminded all the courtiers that Nasr had stolen the throne, as Muhammad had also done. She feared the future, for herself, her husband, and brother.

When the *Hajib* stepped forward, Nasr's gaze softened and he waved Ibn al-Jayyab to his side. After a whispered exchange, the *Hajib* looked out onto the assembly.

"The Sultana Fatima bint Muhammad, daughter of our beloved master Muhammad *Al-Fakih* shall come forward. The Sultan commands it."

Faraj cast a sharp glower at Fatima. She returned his stare, bewildered. Other women milled around the court, but no one openly acknowledged their presence.

On unsteady legs, she moved toward Nasr with her gaze fixed on the ground. She offered her obeisance again. His light touch on her head commanded her. His wide smile greeted her.

She whispered, "My Sultan, you honor me with your attention."

Nasr shook his head. "I could not have achieved this moment without you, who always believed this day would come. By your wisdom, the son of a slave is master of this land."

His features blanched and his upper lip trembled. "I miss *Ummi*. I wish she were here."

When his voice wavered, she touched his chest, just above his heart. Shocked dismay erupted from the courtiers at her informality, but Nasr's hand closed over her own and pressed hers to him.

She smiled at him, despite her watery eyes. "Nur al-Sabah is here, my Sultan, always within your heart. She lives on in you."

In the afternoon, Fatima and the Sultan ambled arm in arm through the gardens just outside his palace. His workers repaired the older buildings.

She loosened her hold on him and stared at the red brick façade behind them. "You'll make no changes to the old palace, although Muhammad's presence tainted it?"

Nasr replied, "It was Father's palace before Muhammad claimed it. It was our home when we were both children."

He offered her his arm again and they resumed their promenade. Fatima turned again and regarded the guards who trailed at a distance.

"The Galicians proved loyal."

"Each day, I thank you for them. There were times I feared for my life, a prisoner in all, but name within Muhammad's domain. His men shadowed my movements. It is miraculous that we were able to plan as we did. When you stopped communicating years ago, I feared the worst. Until your husband came to see me."

She halted. "Faraj visited with you?"

"Yes, after Prince Ismail's betrothal. He warned me you would have no more to do with my dealings. I understood then why the messages had ceased. It was too late to turn from our plans. My friends in the council had the support of the military."

He sighed and patted her hand. "In the last year, Muhammad became even more unstable, cutting off heads at a whim. At midnight, lights from the palace were so brilliant everyone could see them from the surrounding areas. He rarely slept, roaming the complex at odd hours. When he did retire, terrible screams echoed from his chamber."

"Did a physician examine him?"

"He would allow none near him. He remained convinced someone was trying to poison him."

"Was there truth in this?"

When Nasr said nothing, she nodded. "It is also likely the demons of his past pursued him. Muhammad is evil, but he shares our blood. I have not thought of him as my brother in a long time, though we have the same mother. Where is he now?"

"At *Al-Quasaba.* My jailor says he keeps the citadel guards awake at night with his cries."

"By your consent, I would like to see him."

Nasr frowned. "I warn you not to trust him, even in shackles. He remains chained in his cell for good reasons."

"I thank you for the advice. I must see him. I must have answers from him."

"I'm not certain what he could tell you, but if you wish to visit him, I shall allow it. You may not enter his cell, for any reason. I forbid it."

"I understand."

"Do not visit him today, for this is a day of celebration."

"Yes, it is. Thank you, my Sultan."

The next morning, two of Nasr's Galicians escorted Fatima into the basement of the watchtower, with a second prison carved into its walls. They awaited her at street level.

The descent into the heat and fetid smells beneath *Al-Quasaba* left Fatima dizzy. The jailor carried a torch before him. When he halted, her eyes grew accustomed to her surroundings. She ignored the groans coming from adjoining cells and the squeaks and scurrying of furry rodents across the muddied floor. She followed the spindly man down a dank corridor. Beneath her veil, curls clung to her temples and neck. The jailor stopped at the last cell and shone the torchlight into it.

Fatima peered past the iron bars at the outline of a cadaverous shape, crouched on the floor, fettered to a rusting chain. The remnants of stale urine and vomit assailed her.

She scowled at the jailor. "Is this how you treat a member of the royal family?"

He avoided her persistent stare. "I bring him food daily and he spews it at me. He gouged out the eyes of one guard and bit off the finger of another last week. No one goes near him, my Sultana."

Disgusted, she tugged her black veil over her nose. "Muhammad?"

The jailor warned, "He speaks to no one."

"He shall speak with me! Muhammad, answer me. It's Fatima."

The wretched man scuttled backward and looked around the room with murky eyes, as if uncertain of what he heard.

She rattled the bars. "I'm here. Muhammad, look at me."

He shook his head wildly, matted dark hair falling over his eyes. She stared at the jailor again. He lowered his gaze.

"Open this cage."

The jailor drew back from her. The torchlight illuminated the stark etched on his face. "I dare not!"

"Nevertheless, you shall do as I say."

"The Sultan would have my head if your brother escaped!"

"I'll have your throat if you do not do as I have asked."

She withdrew her father's *khanjar* from a sheath buckled beneath the sleeve of her robe. The blade's edge gleamed. Nasr would not have approved of her disobedience, but the claims of justice for her father guided her now.

The jailor clutched his neck. "You would not do it. You're a woman!"

"Foremost, I am a determined one, foremost. I shall have my way. Now, open the door."

The key rattled in the lock and the door creaked. The jailor stepped back a few paces.

Fatima stood at the threshold of the cage. She studied the silent form of the grubby figure on the floor. Thoughts crowded her mind. She struggled with what she must say. She had waited too long for this moment to lose courage now. Muhammad could not defeat her, not in her triumph.

"You were my cherished brother. In my first memory, I was five years old and you were six. We were playing in the nursery. The Princess Aisha passed by, but she took no notice of us in her usual fashion. I followed her. You told me to come back. At the bottom of the stairs, I lost my footing. The Princess did not look behind her to see whether I had hurt myself. You helped me stand and you kissed my knee. You said, 'Don't cry, little sister, I'm here. I'll always be here for you.' I never thought I would shed so many tears, all because of you."

She moved two paces into the cell and halted a short distance from Muhammad.

"I loved you once, more than any other of our siblings, with an affection that rivaled my devotion to our father. For years, you manipulated him. You drugged him with infusions of hashish and corn cockle seed. You made him go mad. Later, you poisoned him with honey cakes. He died in the knowledge that his heir had betrayed and murdered him. Our brother Faraj suspected your treachery. You forced him to take his life and that of his children.

"You sent my father's wife from her loving home into exile. His beloved concubine killed herself to avoid the shameful fate you meted out for her. You raped a slave, simply because she resembled me. She committed suicide, rather than bear your cruel touch again. You poisoned a girl who wanted nothing more than to bear your children and killed two other innocent slaves to hide your misdeeds. You have tortured and slain countless others at whim. You are a liar and usurper, a rapist and a murderer. Yet, your blood is my blood. Why did you hurt the ones who loved you? Why did you destroy the lives of those who would have served you loyally?"

Muhammad rocked back and forth. His eyes bulged. They scoured the room and looked everywhere, except at her.

She sprang at him. Her nails dug into his sunken cheek and drooping chin. He did not cry out. She was not sure he felt anything now, even pain.

"You do not answer, but I know your crimes shall haunt you until the end of your days. Your soul shall never know peace. Mine shall, because you are here. You must live with the nightmares of all you have done. You'll stay in this dank hole forever, where you can never harm another person."

She wiped the grime from his face on her mantle and vowed to burn her clothes, upon her return to the palace.

"You took everything and everyone that ever mattered away from me. Almost. I won't let you destroy my spirit, as you have done to your own. It is too late for you to atone for your sins. I pray it is not too late for me."

She shook her head in dismay at him and turned away.

"You never loved me."

His voice quavered, whether hoarse with age or for some other reason, she could not tell.

She looked over her shoulder. "What did you just say?"

Muhammad stared at his empty palms, his hands shackled at the wrists. "You never cared about me. I was the firstborn. That didn't matter. Everyone loved her, even our father did. He wished she could have been his son, instead of me. She had it all, everything I wanted. A happy home, filled with children and love. Even from you, she had love."

"Who are you talking to, Muhammad?"

"I used to cry at night while she and my other sisters slept. I wondered what was wrong with me. Why couldn't you love me? Why did you look on your own son as a stranger? I never learned to love. You never taught me."

Tears left muddied tracks in dirt streaks across his cheeks.

She swallowed against the lump in her throat. In her youth, she had envied the bright boy of her childhood memories, who would be Sultan one day. His gender and birth order had guaranteed him every liberty, unlike her. She had done her duty, married as her father and grandfather determined. He always had the freedom she had wanted, yet he envied her.

From her childhood, she remembered the bitterness Muhammad had felt toward the Princess Aisha. How he had reviled Fatima after her passing. A lifetime of their mother's rejection had led him on the path of insanity and vengeance. Would his descent into madness claim her life?

Somehow, in the last few years, she had lost sight of her mother's warnings and her sacrifice. She had become the sort of wife her mother had been to her father, one who only showed her hatred and intolerance. Her children were bereft of their mother's love. In her burning desire for revenge, she had abandoned her duty to them, but never again. They would never wonder at her devotion and caring for them. Someday, Faraj would remember her love for him, too.

Muhammad had let their mother's abandonment destroy him. He had lashed out at everyone around him and killed those who loved him. She had to forsake his path, or she would end her days alone, like him.

She bent and cupped his cheek, gently this time. "I pity you, brother. Aisha may not have shown us love, but we learned of it from Father. Still, you betrayed him. He is dead because of you. You have destroyed the one person who loved you always, until the end of his days. Now, you have to live with the guilt for the rest of your life."

He made no response. She shook her head and turned from him forever.

His hand caught her ankle and jerked her back into the cell. She screamed at the suddenness of his actions. The jailor came inside and beat Muhammad's hand with the end of the torch. Flames licked dangerously close to the hem of Fatima's skirts. Her brother was strong and would not let go, no matter how she twisted in his resolute hold.

"*Ummi*, you won't leave me. You won't leave me again! I won't let you."

She slashed at his fingers with the dagger. She almost severed his thumb. Blood spurted in an arc from the wound. Muhammad cradled his injured hand and cried.

The jailor shoved her from the cell and closed it behind her with a heavy thud. Although he trembled, he locked the gate.

"I told you to stay out of there! Now I shall have to summon the doctor. The Sultan shall know I opened the cell. It is not my fault. I'll tell him, you made me do it!"

She sneered at him. "Your sniveling is unworthy of a man. I shall tell Nasr I forced you to do it myself. You have one task now. Ensure Muhammad's survival. Get a doctor for him."

She gripped the iron bars and rattled them. "You cannot die, not now. Nasr has vowed you shall live. You must!"

Muhammad looked at her for the first time. Recognition filled his reddened eyes, as they widened.

Then, he laughed. The blood-curdling, throaty cackle reverberated through the plastered walls. Even after she left him, his laughter chased her through the dank jail and followed her up the narrow, musty corridor into the daylight.

She stared at the steps to the basement for the last time and then closed her eyes. Tears seeped from beneath her lids, but she did not wipe them away.

"Farewell, brother. May Allah, the Compassionate, the Merciful grant your soul forgiveness."

# Chapter 22
# The Oath-Breaker

## Prince Faraj

Gharnatah, Al-Andalus: Rabi al-Thani 709 AH (Granada, Andalusia: October AD 1309)

When Faraj pushed aside the oaken doors of the throne room with their corroded brass handles, rusted hinges creaked and groaned as an old man stirred from slumber. Windswept leaves preceded him. They scattered and joined dried husks of dead foliage in the corners of the chamber. Cobwebs hung in tatters, draped across the lattice-covered windows. Even the air smelled musty and stale. A state of decay enshrouded the throne room, within six months of the Sultan's reign.

Nasr leaned back in the cushiony comfort of his throne. An entourage in brocaded robes sat at his feet. Faraj assumed they were the usual sycophants who sought his favor, until he drew closer at the Sultan's beckon. Nasr surrounded himself with boys, presumably the sons of those who sought the Sultan's esteem. The children gazed at him, as though held in the sway of a pagan god.

Nasr, with his turban askew and falling over one eye, and his wrinkled clothes did not have the appearance of a divine or even kingly presence. His robes were not traditional Moorish garments. His clothing mimicked the garments of the Castillan nobles. His loose-fitting robe fastened at the neckline, but revealed a white, embroidered tunic that fell just above his knees. Two long tubes of cloth encased his legs, which ended in ankle-high boots. His un-bearded chin rested on his hand, while a gold cup dandled between two fingers of the other. With his booted feet propped up on two silk cushions, the master of all Gharnatah seemed bored.

Faraj knelt and bowed his head. A flurry of movement followed. The Sultan commanded him to rise and come forward, in a somewhat slurred voice. Someone had righted his turban and taken away the cup, though a dark red stain tainted the cushion at his feet. Some of the thick liquid dribbled along the channels between the tiles.

The boys sat on the left and right of the throne. Faraj shook his head at the extravagant waste of fine silk and brocade worn by the children. The Galician guards stared straight ahead, lances and swords at their sides. They wore chainmail in the Castillan style. Faraj halted at the base of the dais.

The Sultan asked, "Leaving so soon, brother?"

The heady scent of alcohol warned of Nasr's drunkenness. Faraj looked away and concealed his disgust. The sot was not fit to rule Gharnatah.

Nasr tried to stand. One boot slipped on the liquid pooled at his feet. A boy wiped the wine with the hem of his garment. The Sultan scowled at him, despite his haste, before Nasr's heavy-lidded gaze met Faraj's own.

"You do not stay for the celebration?" Nasr swayed on his feet. Then he sank down on the throne again with a jarring thud.

"No, my Sultan. I believe it is best to return to Malaka."

"Yet, you are the hero of this day. You, who brokered this new peace between Gharnatah and al-Maghrib el-Aska...." He stopped in mid-sentence and glanced around him.

A boy appeared at his side, with the gold cup in his hand, brimming with dark scarlet liquid. Nasr reached for it. Some sloshed over the rim and speckled his white tunic. He frowned at the gathering stain, as though uncertain as to why it had appeared. Then he downed the cupful and belched.

His lopsided grin fell on Faraj. "Yes, because of you, the representatives of Sultan Abu al-Rabi Suleiman of the Marinids have signed the treaty. Now, I have peace at my borders."

If the Sultan thought of the subjugation of Gharnatah to Castilla-Leon, Aragon and al-Maghrib el-Aska as peace fairly won, Faraj would not contradict him.

He had brokered the humiliating terms through which Gharnatah acknowledged a state of vassalage in its relations with Castilla-Leon. In Rabi al-Awwal, just a month earlier, Fernando IV of Castilla-Leon had besieged the coast of Al-Andalus. He attacked first at al-Mariyah and Al-Jazirah al-Khadra, territories defended by men who had married Faraj's daughters. Aisha survived as did her children, but she lost her husband in the resistance at al-Mariyah.

Then, as hounds scenting blood in the air, the Marinids launched a naval blockade at Malaka. Faraj held his city. Despite his bravery, the brutal bombardment left *Al-Jabal Faro* a scarred relic of its former glory. The Sultan feared if the city's stout walls fell to this new menace of gunpowder artillery, the Marinids would sweep across the Sultanate.

He sent word to Faraj and ordered him into negotiations with the Marinid delegation at Gharnatah. The princes Abd al-Haqq and his cousin Prince Hammu led the Marinids in their talks. Nasr acknowledged, or rather his ministers warned him, he could not wage warfare on two fronts against three enemies. This time Castilla-Leon had proved stronger than in previous years, aided by its erstwhile ally, Aragon.

As a result, in addition to yearly payments of tribute to Castilla-Leon and losses of territory to Aragon, Gharnatah would also endure heavy tariffs on all its goods imported from al-Maghrib el-Aska. The Volunteers of the Faith would also return to Gharnatah and secure the interests of the Marinids in the peninsula.

The Sultan shifted on the throne. Faraj pushed aside his embittered memories and focused on the moment.

Nasr said, "I wish you would stay, but I cannot prevent you from going."

He whispered something to one of the boys, who disappeared behind the lattice *purdah*. Faraj stared hard at the space, certain no royal women lurked behind its confines. Nasr had refused all offers of marriage and alliance.

The boy returned with a large leather pouch.

The Sultan said, "Another extravagant gift from the King of Castilla-Leon. He also sent me plans for an almanac and the building of an astrolabe, which I am eager to try. In addition, he has provided casks of wine from his best vineyards. Who else should he favor with his gifts except me? I am his loyal vassal."

Faraj's jaw tightened. "The Prophet, may peace be upon him, deemed wine an intoxicating indulgence, best avoided."

"This is why I only drink it on special occasions, like this day. Surely our God shall forgive."

The boy offered the leather pouch to the Sultan, who snatched it from him and shoved the empty cup into his hands. "Enough for now."

The child scrambled back to the rest of the group, his face downcast.

Faraj asked, "Who are these children?"

The Sultan answered, "The youngest sons of my loyal nobles. Most make good pages."

"I thought all boys of the nobility trained in the service of the *Diwan*."

"Yes, those who are worthy, the heirs of governors and such, but minor nobles do not deserve the honor."

"May I ask, my Sultan, what of your brother Muhammad?"

Nasr wiped his mouth, his gaze suddenly intent and alert. "What about him?"

"Does he fare well in exile at Munakkab?"

"Of course. I made my oath to you to keep him alive, or have you forgotten? He lives...but, you make me very angry each time you question me about Muhammad."

"He is the Sultan's half-brother and bears the same blood as my wife."

"Fatima could care less about him!" Nasr snarled. "So should you. I am Sultan now. You should care more for my moods."

Faraj said, "Then I beg your forgiveness. I shall trouble you no more. By your gracious permission, I take my leave."

"Wait!" Nasr tossed him the leather pouch. "A gift for you. You may look at it."

Faraj bridled at the permission his master deemed necessary. From the pouch, he withdrew a weighty necklace of gold, studded with stones, including pearls and amber.

"An interesting piece, my Sultan."

"It is a gift from the King of Castilla-Leon. They call it a car...carca...I don't remember the name now."

"A *carkenet*, my Sultan."

"Ah, indeed. The King's emissary had told me. I forgot the name. I'm sure you shall wear it with pride."

He looked around and bellowed for his empty cup. A petulant pout darkened his face. He twirled his hand through the air in a sorry attempt at dismissal.

Faraj bowed stiffly and retreated. Each footstep took him far from the indolent court of Sultan Nasr. Yet, his departure did not ease the burdens that crowded his heart.

Faraj waited on a groom who saddled his horse in the courtyard. Behind him, Khalid cleared his throat. Faraj looked aside and bit back a groan.

The powerful minister Ibn Safwan sidled toward him. He stood long and thin as a bowstring, with his elegant features drawn to a point, so that his nose and lips jutted. He did not walk so much as he glided across the cobblestones.

"The peace of God be with you, honored *Raïs* of Malaka."

Despite the pleasant greeting, a chill ran down Faraj's back, which had nothing to do with the cool breeze in the courtyard.

Ibn Safwan observed, "You do not come to the capital often."

"I prefer the comforts of home at Malaka."

Ibn Safwan leaned in. "Your voice is missed here."

"By whom?"

"Those who support the rightful ruler of Gharnatah, Sultan Muhammad."

The groom cleared his throat. Faraj waved him off and walked a short distance from his companions with Ibn Safwan.

"My wife's brother Nasr holds the throne of Gharnatah. It is the will of the *Diwan al-Insha*, which if memory serves, you are still a minister of the council. Sultan Muhammad is in exile at Munakkab. He has no further claim."

"Nasr's not fit to rule either, the drunkard! I voted with the minority. Others including the *Hajib* ibn al-Jayyab wanted to seize power. Nasr is weak! The ministers looked for a ruler they could control and they have found such a one. Say what you may of Sultan Muhammad, but for all his unpredictability and cruelty, he is the legitimate heir of his father. Who is this Nasr, but a child of a Christian slave? Muhammad must regain his throne!"

Faraj looked around them before he pitched his voice low. "I want no part of this intrigue. I wish to live in peace with my family. Nasr is Sultan. You stood before the entire court and acclaimed him ruler of us all. You must accept your decision."

Ibn Safwan drew back and sneered at him. "Whose voice speaks to me now? That of the *Raïs* of Malaka, who showed his lingering support for Sultan Muhammad at Nasr's coronation? Or do I hear the words of a certain Sultana of Gharnatah?"

"Leave my wife out of this!"

"Everyone is well aware of the Sultana Fatima's support for Nasr. I warn you, Faraj, if you are not with us, you shall not share the spoils when Muhammad returns."

The minister shuffled off and viewed the faience vessels and pottery displayed in the courtyard of *Al-Quasaba*.

After almost forty-five years in the service of the Sultans of Gharnatah, Faraj tired of these conspiracies. He cupped his forehead and closed his eyes, as though he could blot out the treasonous words Ibn Safwan had spoken.

## *Princess Fatima*

Malaka, Al-Andalus: Rabi al-Thani - Jumada al-Thani 709 AH (Malaga, Andalusia: October - December AD 1309)

Fatima sat on an olive wood stool before a full-length, silver gilt mirror. Haniya applied black *kohl* to her eyes, and stained her lips and cheeks a deep pink with iron oxide. Behind her, Baraka's crinkled features reflected in the mirror.

Fatima looked over her shoulder. "You disapprove?"

"I did not speak," Baraka replied. Her eyes fixed on some imaginary spot on the Persian rug. She twirled her smooth locks between nimble fingers.

"Yet, your expression betrays what you would not say," Fatima snapped at her.

While Baraka tittered behind her hand, Fatima sighed and nodded to Haniya.

"Please, a basin with some water. Let me wash these cosmetics off my face."

Baraka pulled another stool beside hers and patted her hand. "You do not need such enhancements. Your beauty remains."

Fatima scowled at her. "You're mocking me. I'm fifty-three years old, Baraka. My husband no longer sees the beautiful woman I once was."

She rose from her stool and left Baraka's side. She walked to the window of her bedchamber. A midday sea breeze drifted through the lattice. The wind stirred lavender damask curtains, sewn with gold thread.

"He'll return soon. I wanted to look my best for him, as if it would help."

Baraka moved beside her, a contemplative, far-off stare in her eyes for a moment. "I used to feel the same way." Then she met Fatima's gaze. "Your betrayal hurt him terribly. His anger, even after a year, is a sign of Faraj's love. If he did not love you, he would no longer care enough to be angry."

Fatima rolled her eyes. "I'm not so certain of his feelings. Still, I thank you for saying so, if only to comfort me."

"Why should I care how you feel?" Baraka sniffed and studied her hennaed nails.

Fatima smiled at her pretense at disdain. "Who would have thought in our old age we would become friends?"

Baraka threw her head back with a bark of a laugh. The skin on her throat did not sag as Fatima's did, even though she was ten years older.

"Friends? I do not even like you. As for me, I shall never grow old. If you wish to think so of yourself, you may."

Haniya returned with a basin of warm water. Fatima washed her face and dried it with a towel.

Baraka touched her hand, her look wistful. "I was Prince Faraj's companion for many years, before he took you to his bed. After he did so, I saw the change in him. I never thought the master would desire another more than he wanted me."

Fatima squeezed her fingers and Baraka continued.

"I tried hard to convince myself it was only the pleasure of someone new in his bed. As his devotion increased, I admitted the truth. He loved you, as a woman wants a man to love her. Such devotion can withstand all trials. One day, he shall forgive and you shall have his heart again."

Fatima swallowed against the tightness in her throat and forced a smile.

Haniya interrupted them. "The master has come. He nears *Al-Jabal Faro.*"

Baraka pinched Fatima's cheeks so hard that she glowered at her. "Damn you! Why did you do that?"

"For color. When your maidservant spoke, you looked pale. Now, come. You have desired his return for weeks."

She grabbed Fatima's hands and pulled her along. They left her chamber and went to the indoor courtyard, where Ismail stood.

The smile with which Fatima would have normally greeted her son faded. He hovered at the side of the concubine Abeer. His long fingers stroked the smooth skin of her rounded shoulder. The woman inclined her head to Fatima, who nodded to her son only and continued walking with Baraka beside her.

"Why do you dislike her, my Sultana? She's your son's concubine now. Besides, you brought her into this house."

"To my ensuing regret. It is shameful that my husband should have given his concubine to Ismail. Faraj bedded her first and now, he has cast her off on our son."

Baraka cackled. Her laugh echoed through elegant columns supporting horseshoe arches. "Don't tell me you believe your husband took her to his bed?"

Fatima sputtered, "I was there on the night he summoned her! You told me she crowed about the pleasure my husband gave her for the entire harem to hear."

Baraka shook her head. "Poor Sultana, you shall never understand the weapons a *jarya* must employ. Our lives are very different from those of a pampered princess. We must compete with our masters' wives and each other to hold his attention. Faraj has bedded you countless times. Has his passion ever left you with enough strength to praise him afterward? Or, were you so awash in pleasure, you could hardly stand the next day?"

Fatima paused and thought about the question.

Baraka shook her head and patted Fatima's arm. "Faraj never touched her. Abeer said those things only to make me, Samara and Hayfa jealous. Well, the other two. I'm too beautiful to be envious of the master's lovers!"

She bowed before Fatima at the entryway. "Remember what you would say to him. Greet him with a pleasing smile and welcome him home. Show that you have an interest in what he would say."

Fatima clutched her hand. "Stay with me!"

"No, though it gives me much joy to see him frown at my presence. You must face him. Have courage. You shall win his heart again."

Fatima waited alone. Her fingers bunched the folds of her silken *jubba*, before she released the garment. The clip-clop of Faraj's solitary mount struck the cobblestones. After a moment's silence, he entered the house.

His weathered complexion, under a full graying beard, stirred her heart to pounding. She feared another rebuff, but steeled herself against a quick retreat.

When he approached her, he averted his eyes and bowed. "I have returned, my Sultana."

"I trust your journey was a pleasant one. You have been gone too long."

"It was little less than a month."

"How does the Sultan fare?"

Faraj didn't even bother to hide his scowl. "Your brother enjoys his privileges, some more than others."

Fatima sensed some deeper meaning beneath his statement, but he strode past her into the house before she could inquire.

She called out, "We dine at the usual hour...."

Her voice faded on the sea breeze. He disappeared through the archway.

Eight weeks later, Fatima stared into the darkness of her chamber. A mournful wind howled outside her window. She had enjoyed the freedom of her house for eight months. Yet, she missed the comfort of Faraj's arms around her, his light snores lulling her to sleep and the warmth of his body. With every beat of her heart, every breath she took, she missed him.

With a shudder, she rolled on her side. Tears soaked her pillows as they had on most nights.

A door creaked on its hinges and distinctive footfalls scraped in the hall outside her door. He had just finished his bath. She held her breath, as she had done many nights in the past months. She hoped he would come. The footfalls continued past her chamber.

In the gloom, she listened to the water clock, as steady liquid drops marked the time. Raised voices drifted through her door. She pushed the coverlet aside and smoothed her tunic. When she stepped out into the hallway, Marzuq brandished a torch over the heads of Ismail and Faraj bent together, as they studied a parchment in silence.

She whispered, "What is happening?"

Marzuq nodded in her direction, but he did not reply.

In the glow of the light, Faraj's visage hardened like a stone carving, severe and unyielding. He raised his head and glared at her.

"Nasr has broken his word. He has blinded Muhammad."

Fatima clutched the doorpost. "Why? What did Muhammad do to provoke him? Nasr made a sacred promise before the whole court at his coronation. Muhammad must have done something."

"Sultan Nasr fell ill last week, *Ummi*," Ismail began. "He suffered a fit of apoplexy. There were those who attempted to regain the throne for Muhammad's sake. He arrived from his exile at the city of Munakkab on the next morning. By then, Nasr had recovered. The conspirators failed. Nasr ordered them jailed and dispatched his Galicians with the command to hold Muhammad and prevent his retreat. When they found him, he denied knowledge of the conspiracy. He said he had only returned to Gharnatah out of concern for Nasr."

"You can't believe that, my son!"

Faraj growled at her. "It doesn't matter! Later, by the Sultan's decree, the Galicians blinded Muhammad."

Fatima covered her mouth with her hand for a moment. "Muhammad's eyesight has been poor for years anyway." When Faraj's face reddened, she rushed on, "Nasr had to do it. Muhammad gave him no choice. He came to Gharnatah to steal back the throne. Nasr only defended what is his."

Faraj sneered. "And you defend him always! Not even you can protect him now. He did not have to maim Muhammad. He did it because he knew the rebels would not rally behind a broken man. Nasr made a sacred vow, Fatima, to safeguard and ensure the life of Muhammad. Such a promise cannot be broken for any reason. Otherwise, what power would oaths have in this world, where a man's words and his willingness to uphold them comprise his honor?"

"You always supported my mad brother. You still do. What has Nasr ever done to you to earn your enmity?"

"He stole a throne that was never his to claim! He risked civil war. Now, he has broken his sacred oath. I warned you, Fatima, no Sultan would ever know security within his own realm after Nasr's reign. Nasr shall learn that lesson firsthand. I shall teach him!"

"What do you intend to do, husband?"

"A Sultan who breaks sacred pledges for the safety and well-being of those within his power cannot be trusted. Such a man would be a tyrant over his people. Nasr has given me no other choice in this, Fatima. He lied to the *Khassa* of Gharnatah, to his governors."

Even as she shook her head in denial, he turned to Marzuq.

"Wake the citadel and the servants at the armory. We march on Gharnatah at dawn."

# Chapter 23
# Allegiances

## Prince Faraj

Malaka, Al-Andalus: Shawwal 709 AH (Malaga, Andalusia: March AD 1310)

Blackened chainmail snagged at the shoulder of Faraj's *qamis*. The eunuch beside him adjusted the mail and prevented the links from ripping the cotton shirt. Faraj gestured for the quilted leather tunic. He slipped the garment over his head. A gasp came from his doorway.

Fatima stood there. He ignored her and took his sword belt from the eunuch. He girded it around his waist and tucked his *khanjar* into its sheath. Thc leather bonds encircling the dagger's hilt chaffed his fingers.

While he slipped the mail mittens on his hands and finished dressing, Fatima remained just outside his room. She did not utter a word. Nor did she have to say anything. He prepared to make war on her brother, whom she had supported in his bid for power. Faraj did not have to guess at her feelings.

Still, when he turned to her again, the tears that streamed down her cheeks took him aback. After years of icy mistrust between them, the sight moved him as nothing else had.

His jaw tightened. He grasped his helmet and approached her.

She stood aside and leaned against the doorpost. "I wish you would not go."

"Of course, that is your wish." He did not bypass her. "Your support of Nasr has brought us to this end. I warned you. Your actions against Muhammad have sealed Nasr's fate. Neither he nor any other Sultan in the future shall be secure on the throne of Gharnatah."

She swallowed a sob and raised her gaze to his. "That is not why I don't want you to go. He is my brother and you're my husband. If either of you should die, it would break my heart. Yet, it is you whom I shall pray for in this strife."

His hand itched and tightened into a fist, but he kept his fingers balled at his side. He had vowed after the last time, he would never stain his own honor further by hitting her ever again.

"Do you think because Nasr is young and I am old that I cannot prevail against him? Years of warfare have taught me the skills I require for survival."

"Promise me, if Nasr is amenable to peace, you shall not harm him."

He grunted. "What do you think shall happen at Gharnatah, Fatima? Do you believe your brother shall submit easily? He shall meet my challenge and if I must kill him, I shall not hesitate."

"I do not fear his death. I fear the loss of you." Her lips quivered. Her gaze never wavered. "I forsook the bonds of our marriage once because of my loyalty to a Sultan. I shall never value another life more than yours. You have my allegiance."

His heart ached, desperate to believe her. He had misplaced his trust in her before. "You cannot give it whole, when your heart is still torn between a brother and a husband. You cannot lose me, when you no longer call me your own."

He moved past her, but not before Fatima clutched his hand and cradled it against her cheek, seemingly uncaring as the mail mitten dug into her soft flesh. "Return to us."

Then she released her grip on his hand. His feet remained rooted to the floor. He stared at her, sinking into the depths her watery gaze held. The chainmail had left tiny indentations on her skin's surface.

Her eyes glittered. She whispered, "Go with God, husband. May He protect and guide you."

He left her then.

Their sons awaited him in the courtyard in the soft, pink glow of dawn. Muhammad wore his armor, but Ismail did not. Ismail offered Faraj his sword. Sunlight danced upon the fine edge of the Damascene steel. Ismail slipped the sword into its leather scabbard, wrought with gold.

Faraj clasped his eldest son by his shoulder. "Protect our family. If I should fall, hold Malaka in my stead."

Ismail scowled. "If you fall, the governorship shall be the least of my concerns. The Sultan's wrath would descend upon this place. Never fear, Father. I shall protect our family no matter the outcome."

With a curt nod to his heir, Faraj went to his horse and mounted. Muhammad rode beside him. Khalid awaited them at *Al-Jabal Faro.*

He inclined his head. "We are ready to serve you, master."

A detachment of the Marinid Volunteers of the Faith also sat on their mounts behind the soldiers of Malaka. Under the terms of the treaty Faraj had negotiated with the Marinids on Nasr's behalf, the Berber and Gharnati expatriates returned to occupy several of the coastal cities and Gharnatah, under the supreme command of their *Shaykh al-Ghuzat.*

The garrison commander urged his horse forward. Light delineated his pale, angular features, hollow cheeks and hooked nose.

"I am Uthman ibn Abi'l-Ula. We have heard of the troubles in Gharnatah this past night. Your reputation is as a strong leader of men, Prince Faraj. We shall support you in your bid for power against the Sultan."

Faraj scowled at him. "I seek to correct an injustice, not grab the throne. Whose voice do you speak with, your own or that of your master in al-Maghrib el-Aska?"

"Your move against Sultan Nasr is justified. He is too weak, the pawn of the Christians. I do not doubt that he is secretly a Christian himself. Surely, his mother taught him their ways. If my master were here, he would understand. Sultan Nasr is not fit to rule this land. You must take the throne of Gharnatah in his stead."

"Whoever believes I seek the Sultanate must be a fool and a liar!" Faraj stared the man down. "If that is what you expect of me, prepare yourself for disappointment. After Nasr has publicly acknowledged his crime, the *Diwan* can decide how to sanction him. I do not intend to stay in Gharnatah."

"You do not go to your capital if you wish to confront the Sultan," Uthman said. "He is at al-Atsha."

"How do you know the Sultan's movements?"

"The Princes Abd al-Haqq and his cousin Prince Hammu are with him. I remain watchful of their activities."

Faraj nodded, as he recalled the princes who had bargained for humiliating terms from Gharnatah.

"You do this at the behest of your master?"

"Princes Abd al-Haqq and his cousin Prince Hammu are rival princes, once contenders for the throne of al-Maghrib el-Aska. My Sultan trusts such men to do his bidding. I do not. For now, they serve him. How much longer shall they remain in his sway? Your Sultan is weak. He shall not last long on the throne. I would be at the side of the man who must replace him."

"I tell you, I do not seek the throne!"

Faraj's mare whickered and tossed her head at his tone, but he calmed her with a reassuring touch.

Uthman returned his stare and then shrugged. "We waste the hours here. We should ride now."

Faraj nodded. "If the Volunteers of the Faith are with us, then command your men to follow. If you have chosen the wrong side, you may find the Marinid princes are not weak. They'll see to it that your master strips you of your command, or worse."

The men left the citadel in a long column down the sloping hill. At its base, they rode the horses northward to the city gates. The sea breeze came onshore, as though it hastened their departure.

A few days later, the awestruck denizens of the large village of al-Atsha, which rose from the floodplain outside Gharnatah, watched Faraj's scouts from the southern ramparts. The villagers closed the gates against the approaching warriors.

Uthman cursed and slapped his thigh with his riding stick. "Do they mean for us to lay siege to this place?"

"No!" Faraj ordered. "I shall not fall upon my own people as a pack of ravenous wolves."

The sun reached its zenith. Someone in Faraj's company shouted, "Look to the northern hills!"

In a flurry of dust, riders and their mounts fled from the northeastern gates of the village, which straddled two sloping mounds. It could be none other than Sultan Nasr and the Marinid princes.

Faraj led the chase. A splinter group from the Sultan's warriors broke off from the others and wheeled their horses around. The Sultan's Galician guards led the way to the capital, discernible by their distinctive red capes billowing on the breeze. A small portion of cavalrymen charged Faraj's host, their swords held high, their lusty battle cries resounding in the crisp afternoon air.

Faraj yelled at Khalid, who rode beside him, "No time for this folly! We have to stop Nasr now or we'll never get to him. Follow me!"

Khalid spurred his horse on. The Gharnati cavalry engaged most of Faraj's forces and the Marinids. Shouts and the clash of steel filled the floodplain outside al-Atsha. The horses kicked up mud and obscured the orchard fields surrounding the village. Faraj could not view the battle, even if he had wished it.

He and his men came down a slope and sighted Gharnatah in the distance. The Sultan and his Galicians were at the outskirts, riding hard for the city's main entryway, the *Bab Ilbira.* A strong midday gust picked up and whipped the hood of Nasr's mantle from his yellow hair. Just outside the gate, Nasr's horse buckled. The beast went down hard, its legs jerking spastically. The fall sent its rider tumbling.

Faraj ducked his head and dug his heels into his mount's flank. Someone rode hard against him, determined to stop him. Sweat coated the sagging jowls beneath the man's helmet.

At the last moment, Faraj drew his sword and met the clash of Prince Hammu's scimitar against him. He lifted his foot from the stirrup and kicked out at the Marinid prince. Hammu evaded him and whirled again.

Faraj cursed under his breath, as he defended himself. Up ahead, one of the Galicians wheeled his mount around and returned to his master's side. Nasr did not move.

"No! Damn you. I won't let you escape, Nasr. Khalid, after him!" Faraj bellowed.

His warning came too late for his captain, who rode the Sultan's man down. The rest of the Galicians circled and protected their master. Nasr staggered to his feet. He shouted orders to his Galicians, who rode toward Khalid and Faraj, while he hobbled the short distance to the capital. When he breached the *Bab Ilbira* on foot, the Galician guard bolted for the city as well.

Prince Hammu broke off his attack and sped in the same direction. A lone rider followed him, likely his cousin. Khalid flung his dagger, but the blade glanced off Prince Hammu's shoulder. He ducked and entered the gate in a flurry of dirt, followed closely by the other man.

Gharnatah's soldiers lined the massive outer walls. Archers overlooked the plain from towers built up to the height of the city walk. Their bows at the ready, they aimed high. Faraj pulled back on the reins. At the foot of the walls, in a morass of wet earth, the Sultan's fallen mount whinnied in its death throes. A flurry of bolts descended from the battlements. Arrows struck the beast in its neck and forelegs. Its movements ceased.

With a wave to Khalid, Faraj wheeled his horse around. They sped across the plains, arrows whistling behind them.

## Princess Fatima

Malaka, Al-Andalus: Shawwal 709 AH – Sha`ban 710 AH (Malaga, Andalusia: March AD 1310 – January AD 1311)

For weeks unending, Fatima waited for word from Gharnatah of her husband's survival, of her brother's fate. She might lose Faraj or Nasr, or both men in the ensuing conflict. She had envisioned the possibility. She once thought the end of Muhammad's tyrannical reign would bring peace to her family and the Sultanate. Now, those who shared blood prepared to shed each other's again.

On the tenth morning after Faraj had gone, she stared at the ceiling above her bed, lost in thought, as she had been every day since his departure. Fear for his safety consumed her. Yet, the silent tears that streaked down her cheek and wet her pillow were not for him alone.

Thoughts of Muhammad's suffering pained her more than she had expected. He was a monstrous despot, but they were brother and sister. When he went into exile at Munakkab, she had silently questioned Nasr's wisdom in releasing him from the prison at *Al-Quasaba*. Deep inside, her heart recoiled at the thought of any family member, even a man as dangerous as Muhammad, consigned to the darkness of a dank, vermin-infested cell.

Now, questions tortured her. Were Nasr's violent actions any different from when their brother had plotted their father's death?

She swung her feet off the bed and buried her face in her hands. Arguments vied within her tormented mind. Nasr could have spared Muhammad and consigned him forever to the dungeon in *Al-Quasaba*. The conspirators had failed and they deserved what is due to all traitors. Their actions and Muhammad's response had left Nasr bereft of choices. Still, he had sworn a sacred oath. He had broken his word. No, the conspirators broke their word. They had sworn oaths of loyalty when Nasr ascended the throne. A throne he had stolen, with her help.

Her folly had led their family to this moment. Whatever madness ruled her brother Muhammad, she had not escaped its reach. Recriminations taunted her. She let the tears fall unchecked. What had she done in choosing Nasr as an instrument of her vengeance against Muhammad? Now he or her husband would die. Their blood, the shame of it would be upon her head.

She fell to her knees and bowed her head. Surely Allah, the Merciful, the Compassionate would hear her private prayer, even if she did not follow the rituals now.

"Merciful God, I have squandered my days in intrigue and revenge. I have forsaken duty and love, embraced strife and discord. Now I pray, let me live the rest of my life in peace. Protect and watch over those whom I love. Wherever they may be, let my husband and my brother know peace. If it is Your Will that I must lose one of them this day, let Your bidding be done. But if it must be one of them, please, I pray, let my husband live."

A knock came at the door. She wiped her cheeks and smoothed the folds of her garments, before she answered.

Two brown-haired girls swathed in gold silk launched themselves at her.

"Leila! Fatimah! What are you both doing up so early? It is not even dawn."

Leila's chubby hands patted her cheeks. "Why are you sad today?"

"Your grandmother could never be sad, Leila, not when you and your sister are here to gladden her heart." Baraka stood in the doorway and nodded to Fatima. "I thought a visit from the little princesses might cheer you, my Sultana."

Fatima said, "You were kind to bring them."

Baraka inclined her head and closed the door behind her.

Fatima spent the rest of the day with her granddaughters, delighting in their eager, precocious natures at just two years old. They were both the image of their father Ismail, but each one had her grandmother's eyes.

For them, for the security of all her descendants, Fatima vowed to set things right. She could not stop the confrontation between Faraj and Nasr. Now, she would do all she could to protect her heirs and strengthen the bonds between her family.

Hours later, when the children rested their dark heads on her shoulders and drifted to sleep, Fatima stood beside the window and looked to the north.

She whispered against Leila's tiny brow, "Let him come home to me."

Ten months later, Fatima stood on the battlements between *Al-Jabal Faro* and her residence. Her eyes scanned the horizon and the city below. A bitter wind stabbed at her flesh through folds of clothing. With a sigh, she bowed her head and clasped her hands together. Her lips offered an oft-repeated plea.

Familiar hands settled on her shoulders. She looked over her shoulder at Ismail. He rested his chin atop her head and studied the view in silence.

"Do not fear, my son. He lives, I can feel it."

"Then why has he not returned home? He has besieged Gharnatah with the aid of other governors. *Al-Qal'at al-Hamra* has not fallen to them. Nasr has sought the aid of the Castillans. What if they have arrived? My father could be dead."

She hushed him. "We must wait."

She and Ismail lingered on the walls until midday, when the call to prayer sounded. She turned and hugged him. She clasped his hands in hers.

"Go to the mosque. Say a prayer for your father and brother's safe return, for Gharnatah."

He looked beyond her. "I don't have to. They're home at last."

Fatima whirled and looked beyond the northeastern gate. A flurry of dust coated the plains. Hooves rumbled and pounded the dry earth. The gateway opened and admitted a large contingent of riders. Even from this distance, she made out the green and white banners of the Sultan unfurled over their heads. Beneath them, the standard of the governor of Malaka billowed.

Ismail started toward *Al-Jabal Faro* and down the citadel's steps along the sloping incline. Her feet stayed rooted to the spot. All coherent thought fled from her mind, as though scattered by the sea breeze. Cheers echoed, but the boisterous sound did not calm her fears.

Only the sight of Faraj riding beside their second son, with Ismail walking between the pair, restored her sensibilities. Her second son Muhammad slid down from his mount and rushed to her. He drew her into his burly embrace. She kissed both his cheeks and forehead, before she looked him over.

He grasped her shoulders. "I'm well, *Ummi*, not a scratch."

He and Ismail clasped each other's forearms and continued along the walkway.

In the glare of sunlight, which formed a halo around his grizzled head, Faraj stared at Fatima.

She bowed at his side. "It pleases my heart to see that you have returned, husband."

He dismounted with a grunt. "Nasr lives. Have no fear."

"I knew you both lived. I would have felt it if you did not. All my concern was for you."

"It should have been for your brother, Muhammad. The Galicians drowned him in the courtyard pool of your father's palace, within a week of the siege. I learned of his death a month later."

Fatima's hand covered the place where her heart thumped against her chest. She whispered a silent prayer for Muhammad. She had not felt the moment of his passing. Still, she regretted his demise at Nasr's hands.

Faraj urged his mount onward at a trot. She fell into step beside him. She reveled in the nearness of him. God had answered her prayers. He would allow her the chance to renew her commitment to Faraj and their marriage. She would never squander His blessings again.

"Don't you want to know what happened, Fatima?"

"If you wish to tell me. I had thought you would refresh yourself before revealing the news to our family."

Faraj shook his head. "We besieged Nasr at Gharnatah. After a month, we learned of your brother Muhammad's final fate. Nasr managed to send word to King Fernando of Castilla-Leon. His emissaries arrived seven months later, but they did not do as Nasr intended. Instead of defending him against the siege, the Castillans demanded that we come into the city under a flag of truce. A small contingent of us, including the sons of our daughters who had joined me, entered Gharnatah. I spoke for us, laid bare our grievance before the remaining members of the *Diwan al-Insha* and the Sultan regarding the solemn vow, which the Sultan had broken by killing his brother.

"At first, they would hear none of it. The new *Hajib* Ibn al-Hajj, whom I believe is a secret Christian, proclaimed the Sultan was the only power in Al-Andalus and could do as he willed. However, the rest of the *Diwan* defied the prime minister and said Nasr should have held to his oath. His actions had plunged the Sultanate into civil war. Nasr could not deny his crime in killing Muhammad and breaking his oath. We could do nothing about it, since Muhammad was already dead. Ibn al-Hajj wanted everyone jailed, including me. Nasr bowed to the wishes of his Castillan master, who dictated an accord. I have renewed the oath of loyalty to Nasr. I remained at Gharnatah for another six weeks until he permitted me to leave."

"So there is peace again?"

"I did not say that. You and Nasr share the blood of your brother, Sultan Muhammad. Lest you forget, vengeance begets vengeance. Nasr has reconciled with me for now, but I doubt he shall forget this uprising."

# Chapter 24
# The Assassin's Blade

## Prince Faraj

Malaka, Al-Andalus: Shawwal 711 AH (Malaga, Andalusia: March AD 1312)

The overzealous guardsman, who led Faraj and his company through the narrow, torturous streets of the marketplace, earned the irate stares of those whom he shoved aside. "Make way for the *Raïs* of Malaka! Move, fool or you'll feel Damascus steel in your gullet!"

His eagerness did not impress Faraj either. He looked askance at his captain, who strolled beside him.

Khalid shrugged. "We'll never clear a path through the vendors, if we are polite and patient."

At his father's right, Ismail nodded. "If we must reach the market inspector's house before he attends to his duties, we'll never get there in this crowd without dispersing them."

The guard sent a fruit vendor sprawling across the cobblestone street. Clusters of figs, plump oranges and ruby-colored pomegranates spilled from sacks. Grasping hands from voluminous cloaks pilfered the fruit. Dim light peeked around the awnings of each building and made it difficult to tell where the thieves had gone. In his haste and carelessness, the guardsman mashed bits of fruit to pulp beneath his booted feet.

Khalid and Ismail helped the merchant as he regained his footing and gathered his goods, while Faraj grabbed the shoulder of the one who had shoved him. "This man has had his wares stolen. You shall remain and help him find the thieves...."

"But, my prince, I did not see them."

"Or, your wages shall compensate him for the value of what he has lost," Faraj continued, as though the guardsman had not interrupted him.

The man's jaw dropped and he stared at him wordless.

The vendor grabbed Faraj's ankles and kissed his feet. "Thank you, my prince! Truly, you are merciful and generous to your people."

"Get up man, no need for that."

Despite Faraj's protestation, the merchant would not leave off. His balding pate glistening as he bowed in supplication, his lips making loud smacking sounds on the rounded tips of Faraj's red leather boots. Exasperated, Faraj glared at Khalid and Ismail, who barely hid their bemused smirks behind their hands.

Ismail pulled the grateful vendor to his feet again. The man was unable to resist one parting acclamation. "You are the best among men who serve God. A prince fit to rule Gharnatah."

Faraj scowled at him. The man displayed his gap-toothed smile before haranguing the guardsman about his stolen fruit.

Ismail touched his father's arm. "He only says what the people are thinking."

"Anyone would be a fool to think it, my son, much less speak of it. More than a year has passed since I reconciled with Nasr at Gharnatah, yet people believe I want the throne."

Khalid said, "Despite all your denials, the rumors persist. Perhaps, you should consider their source."

Faraj ignored him. The cause remained the same, the malcontents who thought Nasr was a secret Christian, like his *Hajib*. In the intervening months, since Faraj's rebellion had ended, the stares, whispers and pointing, the deferential bowing wherever he went in Malaka still rankled him. He was not the Sultan. How long could he keep the rumors that he still wanted the throne from reaching Nasr at Gharnatah? Or, was it already too late?

Camels laden with bolts of precious fabric blocked the ground floor entrance to the market inspector's house.

Khalid bellowed for the caravan leader, who at length pushed his great bulk through the camels. He spied Faraj and bowed in deference.

"Great prince, your presence honors us today."

"Enough with your salutations, man. Just move these beasts out of the way. I must see the market inspector."

"Begging your pardon, great prince. The market inspector is gone. It's his daughter's wedding in Qumarich. I don't think he'll return before month's end. I follow in his wake, with gifts for the bride."

The caravan leader patted the lead camel. The beast snorted and urinated.

Faraj's hands clenched into tight fists. He cursed under his breath. He had informed the market inspector of his intent at the end of the previous week. Still, the fool went away without speaking to Faraj.

He grabbed the caravan leader by the folds of his robe. The man yelped in surprise as he dragged him closer.

"You tell that son of a donkey to see me when he returns. He shall explain why the eastern ports have rejected our shipments of figs for the past year. If he has not done his duty to ensure that the fruits are preserved for their transport, I'll have his head!"

The trembling caravan leader could only nod.

Faraj and his men returned the way they had come. They found the fruit vendor still yelling at the guardsman.

From an inn across the muck-filled street, cardamom-scented tisane wafted down from the upper floor through latticed windows. The carved door on the first floor opened and revealed a heavily veiled woman. She stepped out into the cobblestone thoroughfare, followed by two maidservants. She glanced at the men and bowed demurely, her dark eyes sparkling between the slits of her veils. Her fragrance, cassia and jasmine, filtered through the air.

It seemed so long since Faraj had smelled jasmine in Fatima's hair. His gaze followed the woman's form, hidden under billowing folds of silk, through the marketplace. Longing filled him, but not for her. He wanted the woman who smelled like her, who awaited him at home. He had not looked upon Fatima with any emotion untainted by anger in years. The sight of the woman reminded him of her.

For the first time in years, he admitted to himself that he missed Fatima at his side. He had buried his feelings deep. Now, he only wished to return to their home and hold her in his arms, recalling the days when they loved and trusted each other. Could they return to the past?

Ismail cleared his throat. "Shall I follow the woman you're staring at, Father?"

Faraj jerked his gaze away. "Of course not!"

He rubbed his hip, which had started aching every morning. A general stiffness in his bones accompanied the twinge. Often, he felt very much like the sixty-five year-old man he was.

His hand alighted on Khalid's shoulder. "Put a watch on the market inspector's house for the next month. Inform me the moment he returns."

A flurry of dust rose up and made the men cough. The Marinid commander Uthman emerged from the haze.

From atop his horse, he grinned at the men and exposed his overbite. "A fine morning."

Faraj had not liked Uthman from their first meeting. Whether in his cadaverous face with the sunken eye sockets or the pale skin that never seemed to darken even under the bright Malaka sun, Uthman unnerved Faraj. The man had the cunning of a fox.

After Faraj's reconciliation with Nasr, Uthman had been quick to ingratiate himself again with the Marinid princes Abd al-Haqq and Hammu, who supported Nasr still. Faraj did not know how Uthman managed to retain command of the garrison, but he doubted Uthman accomplished his methods through fair means.

Uthman said, "I have heard the Sultan's troubles continue, Prince Faraj. Now the *khassa* of Gharnatah have kicked his tax collectors from their doorsteps. The nobles claim the Sultan has unduly burdened them."

Nasr had bought peace with Castilla-Leon, Aragon and the Marinids at cost to his own people.

Faraj responded, "It is interesting how you are always aware of events in the capital, commander."

"I have a keen interest in the politics of Al-Andalus, my prince."

"I do not doubt it."

He strolled past Uthman, who jerked the reins of his horse and wheeled his mount around. "You have nothing more to say than that?"

Faraj halted. He did not face Uthman. "Do you think I await the downfall of Nasr in Gharnatah? Did you believe I would rejoice in the end of his regime, in watching the birth of anarchy and strife destroy my beloved land?"

"There are those who believe the days of your Sultan on the throne cannot last for much longer. They wait for you to lead them."

"Then they wait in vain...."

"My prince!" Khalid shoved Faraj aside, but not before a sharp pain stabbed into his chest. Faraj staggered and looked down. The hilt of a dagger protruded from his breast. A crimson stain spread slowly across the yellow tunic. He gaped at the sight and fell.

A heavily garbed figure ran toward him. A sword gleamed in his hand. Uthman's horse whickered, the stallion's hooves striking the ground. Then there was the clash of steel. A gurgling cry followed.

"Khalid!" Ismail's voice echoed through the haze of Faraj's pain.

Faraj gripped the hilt of the dagger. Warm, sticky wetness coated his fingertips. Darkness threatened to overwhelm him, though he fought against it. He struggled in vain.

## *Princess Fatima*

Fatima swung the lattice window open and welcomed the mid-morning rays. She leaned against the windowsill and inhaled the draft of sea breeze gusting over the shore. Behind her, Niranjan's raspy chuckle dissolved into a cough.

"You reminded me just then, my Sultana, of the little girl leaning out of the camel caravan."

The memory of the child rescued by the boy who would become her lifelong friend made her turn and smile at him, but it was a sad gesture. For months, she recognized the symptoms of decline in Niranjan. He had never been the same after his imprisonment at *Al-Jabal Faro*.

His claw-like fingers reached for a cup of peppermint tea on the floor, beside his pallet. With trembling hands, he raised the hot drink to his lips before setting it down again. She brushed away moisture from the corner of her eye.

"Do you shed such lovely tears for me? You should not."

She sat beside him and took his gnarled hand in hers.

He squeezed her fingers in his dry, rough hold. "My sole regret is that I cannot always be at your side now, when you have found peace again. You are the good, gentle mistress I have ever known. My heart is glad. I can die a happy man one day."

She sighed. "Who shall I be without you, Niranjan? You have always stood by me, at my best and worst. What shall there be for me of comfort in this world, when you are gone from it?"

"You shall live for your family and the future. Then one day, you shall die also, an old woman in your bed, surrounded by those whom you love."

She raised his hand and held it against her cheek.

A terrifying wail rang through the hallway outside. The tranquility of the moment ended. A furious knocking came at the door and without waiting for permission, Haniya burst into the room. Her red-rimmed gaze flew to Fatima's face.

"The master, I think he's dead! An assassin attacked him. You must come to his room."

Fatima stared at her, as though uncertain of what she had said. Niranjan cupped her cheek. "Go, now."

She dashed to the room, where their servants had placed a body stiff and unmoving on the bed. She could not believe it was her husband, whom she had seen an hour before he went to the marketplace. Faraj lay on his back, the hilt of a dagger embedded in his chest in the area above his heart. His tunic clung to him, mired in the blood.

She scrambled to his side and looked down at his pallid expression. No sound issued from between his pale lips.

"My Sultana, let me see to him." Niranjan shuffled into the chamber, using the walking stick he now required.

Her lips trembled. She could not move from the spot.

Niranjan touched her shoulder. "Please let me help your husband."

She drew back, though not far from the bed. Haniya rested her chin on Fatima's shoulder. Soft sobs wracked the maidservant's body.

Niranjan knelt beside the bed. He peeled away the matted cloth around the wound, then placed his hand on Faraj's chest, over the heart. Niranjan pressed his ear to Faraj's mouth and listened.

Niranjan raised his head and nodded. "He is not dead. The master's heart beats with life still. It is very faint. Haniya, send for the physician."

Fatima stayed with Faraj, even after the physician arrived and suggested, then ordered her to leave. Her gaze never wavered, no matter how the wound bled or stained the bedclothes. When he withdrew the weapon with care, breath rattled in Faraj's chest. Fatima covered her mouth and stifled her sobs.

After the doctor's assistant closed and bound the savage cut, she offered the pair payment and sent them away, with the command that they should not leave Malaka in case Faraj worsened.

Niranjan said, "Prince Faraj has lost a great deal of blood. This wound is dangerous. Still, it should not have caused this result. I want to examine the blade."

He grabbed the weapon the doctor had set aside. He sniffed the dagger and studied it. "Do you recognize the weapon, my Sultana?"

She shook her head, her gaze on Faraj's wan features.

Niranjan grasped her fingers and slid the golden hilt between them and her palm. Blood clung to the blade. "Look at the handle. Does it not seem familiar?"

Carved with an overlay of gold, the pommel was the shape of a goblet.

Niranjan said, "It is shaped like the Holy Grail, what Christians believe to be the cup of Jesus Christ before the crucifixion."

"I know of the Christian religion, but what does this have to do with an attempt on my husband's life? Are you saying someone among the Christian kingdoms has tried to kill him?"

"The flag of the Galician people bears the same symbol. The Galician guards of the Sultan's court carry such daggers as a symbol of their heritage. One of them has tried to kill your husband. This cannot have happened without the knowledge or sanction of the Sultan."

Ismail, who stood beside his mother, embraced her. "I still can't believe someone tried to kill Father, even though I was there to witness it."

"Tell me what happened."

After he described the events leading up to the assassination attempt, Fatima sighed. "The loss of Khalid of al-Hakam shall pain your father. Khalid must have fought bravely to defend your father until the last. He gave his life for Faraj's sake. He has left us too soon. Who was the assassin? Is he anyone from Malaka?"

"No one knows him. The man is dead. I killed the assassin, *Ummi*. He ran through the marketplace. He could not evade me."

Niranjan commented, "You and your father's men should have brought the man to the citadel for questioning."

Ismail scowled at him. "My apologies for my lack of forethought, but I thought only of avenging my father's death when I cornered the assassin."

"But your father did not die. You must have realized he was still alive. You said he was still breathing after the assassin felled him," Niranjan replied, his eyebrows upraised.

Tension enlivened his tone and he seemed revived. Ismail's frown deepened, as the eunuch held his regard without flinching.

Fatima nodded. "It matters little now. The one who tried to murder him is dead. We must be grateful he cannot harm my husband or anyone else."

She reached for Haniya's hand. "I am sorry your Asiya did not have more time in which to know Khalid. My husband lost his captain, but your daughter lost a loving and attentive father."

Haniya bowed her head. "My daughter is too young to understand the loss. When she is older, I shall tell her of Khalid's bravery."

Fatima said to her, “Please, pack some of my garments. I’m going to Gharnatah.”

“What?” Ismail sputtered.

Despite his outburst, Haniya bowed and went to Fatima’s chamber.

Fatima repeated Niranjan’s suspicions about Nasr’s involvement to her son.

Ismail shook his head. “What difference can it make if you go to Gharnatah? If the Sultan wants to rid himself of Father by treachery, I don’t see how you can persuade him otherwise.”

She patted his cheek. “Your uncle Nasr owes me a very large debt. It is time we settled it.”

# Chapter 25
# Old Debts Repaid

## Princess Fatima

Gharnatah, Al-Andalus: Shawwal 711 AH (Granada, Andalusia: March AD 1312)

On a bleak gray morning, the camel caravan slowed at the outskirts of Gharnatah. The endless, whispering wind rustled pebbles before the ground rumbled. Gritty dirt gusted and stung Fatima's eyes. Her camel snorted and scented the air. From beneath the black-and-green striped *hawdaj*, she leaned forward and patted the neck of the dark brown animal.

Up ahead, the caravan leader bellowed to make himself heard above his snorting animals. "I don't care how tired the beasts are! Get them into Gharnatah now!"

The earth hitched and trembled again. In the distance, dust hovered in a thick, swirling haze. The caravan descended the hillock that overlooked the floodplain outside the capital. Shepherds and goatherds drove their flocks by the hundreds, while merchants jostled each other for entry into the city first, cursing and hollering in their haste.

The sentries on the ramparts seemed more intent on keeping people out than defending Gharnatah from any possible threat. When the caravan halted again, Fatima leaned forward and called for the boy who guided her camel.

"What is the delay? What is happening?"

He looked toward the dust cloud, before his eyes widened. The youth scrambled back the route they had come. She yelped and grabbed the rope he had discarded.

Over the heads of others, the caravan leader hollered. "Make way, you fools! The Sultan's sister travels in my retinue."

Someone cursed and spat at him. "Liar! You just don't want to lose your silk stores to the Castillans. You'll wait your turn."

The ground quaked. Panicked screams sent the crowd surging forward and the caravan with them. On the way to Gharnatah, Fatima had learned from the caravan leader that the Castillans attacked the town of Martus three days before. The peace treaty of their King had ended and as before, they resumed hostilities at the border, perhaps sensing Nasr's weakened bargaining position.

Bolts groaned on their hinges and a loud creak followed. It sent a rush of joy through the waiting crowd. In waves, those who sought refuge within the city limits spilled through the *Bab Ilbira*. Through narrow roads teeming with onlookers and the labyrinthine streets of the *Qaysariyya*, still bustling with trade despite any threat Gharnatah might face, the caravan mounted the summit of the *Sabika*.

After she threatened them with the Sultan's wrath at the delay of his sister, the citadel guards cautiously allowed Fatima entry to the precincts of *Al-Qal'at al-Hamra*.

The patrol outside the palace proved less pliable, even with her promises of retribution. Their captain held to a solitary refrain despite anything Fatima said. "The Sultan is with his council. No one may disturb him."

"You'll be the first to hang when I tell my brother how you've kept me from him." She glowered at the man from atop the camel's back, but he remained unmoved.

After more than two hours, Nasr emerged from the council chamber with his ministers. Fatima demanded that the guards alert him to her presence. He came out of the palace and found her alone.

"Fatima! By the Prophet's beard, what are you doing here?"

"Forgive my haggard appearance, noble brother. I knew you would not fail to hear the entreaties of a most loyal and beloved sister. Your overzealous guardsmen would not allow it."

His face pinched tight, Nasr scowled in the direction of the soldiers in the courtyard. Then he took her hand on his arm and walked with her.

His Galician guards fell in on either side of them. Beneath lowered eyelids, she counted the seven men. There should have been eight. Her heart sank as if confirming Niranjan's suspicions.

"One of your bodyguards is missing, my Sultan."

Nasr halted beside her. "Why do you comment upon it?" The pitch of his tone rose higher than usual.

She halted and scrutinized his features for clues. He offered none.

"Are there not always eight Galicians in your company?"

A sheepish grin transformed his face to the boyish flush of his youth. "You always notice every change. My captain Adulfo has been ill, but I hope to have him at my side again."

He led her to his quarters, where luminous silk, glittering embroidery, and plush carpets covered almost every surface. The Sultan sent word to his chief eunuch to prepare a room for her and ordered a meal.

While he dined on roasted lamb chunks, flatbread, and lentils, Fatima ate little.

Nasr relaxed and swirled the contents of his cup.

She asked, "When did you start drinking wine, brother?"

He swallowed a mouthful. "Only on happy occasions such as this one, I promise."

The redness and enlarged veins in his puffy face belied Nasr's claim. Yet, she could not confront his falsehood about the alcohol consumption. Other untruths remained unresolved.

"How can you say this is a happy time, brother? The Castillan army marches on our capital. What do you intend to do about it?"

"The *Hajib* Ibn al-Hajj sees to the defense of the city. I have also sent messengers to my faithful governors, demanding their aid."

"Do you count my husband among those loyal men?"

A deepening hue flushed Nasr's face. His insipid grin had returned. He refilled his goblet.

"Of course I do. Why would I think otherwise? After our unfortunate disagreement, he has since renewed his oaths to me. Why do you ask me such a thing? Has some concern about your husband brought you to Gharnatah?"

She reached into her satchel at her feet. She placed the dagger Niranjan had retrieved on the table before him.

Giddy with drink, he asked, "You don't mean to murder me?"

He laughed again, seeming to think the idea very funny. She did not share his mirth.

"Someone tried to kill Faraj a few days ago, Nasr. By the Will of God, the assassin did not succeed."

She shared the details of the attempt on her husband's life, as Ismail had relayed them. Nasr recoiled in horror, his eyes blinking with incredulity. The breath seemed caught in his throat and he struggled with his speech. Perhaps he was a better liar than she had ever been.

"I am shocked, shocked and saddened, but glad that your son caught the man who did this."

"There is more, Nasr. The assassin stabbed him with this very blade. Look at the hilt!"

She pushed the dagger by the blade toward him. He flinched, but he would not reach for it. He stared at her, slack-jawed.

"Fatima, you don't mean to accuse one of my men? That is why you brought this here, why you asked about the Galician guards? No, no, no, none of them could have done this."

Tears pricked the corners of her eyes. How could he lie to her so easily, after all she had done for him?

"I have ever been loyal to you, my Sultan. When your mother, my dearest friend died, she commended you to my care. I have been faithful to you, Nasr, protected you …."

"Fatima, stop this."

"No, you must listen to me! I love you, flesh of my flesh and blood of my blood. I love Faraj equally well. He has my heart. I beg you, if you have ever loved me as a sister, do not take him from me. I would be lost without him. You owe me this, Nasr, for all the deeds and misdeeds I have committed on your behalf."

"Fatima, I swear to you, I had no hand in this!"

Nasr set down his cup and stood. He raked his hands through thinning blonde hair.

He muttered, "How can I prove myself to you?"

Then he pulled her to her feet. "You cannot lose faith in me now."

He dragged her out of his chamber and into the courtyard where the Galician guards protected the only entrance to the Sultan's residence. He had his men draw their daggers, same as the one she had shown him.

"You see, not a blade missing among them!"

She shook her head. "One of your men is not here. You don't have to pretend for my sake. I know Faraj has dared your ire in the past...."

He pulled her behind him again, beyond the confines of the palace. They entered the precincts of the royal *madina* where those who served the Sultan dwelled.

They entered a whitewashed house, suffused with the scent of camphor. A little girl in the first chamber yelped when she saw them and spilled water from a basin that brimmed in her hands. She darted beyond a linen curtain. Nasr followed, tugging Fatima after him.

On a bed in the center of the room, a pale man reclined against the comfort of a woman's lap. The child stood trembling in the corner.

The woman gasped. "My Sultan!"

"Be at ease, I know your husband is still racked with fever. I do not call him to his duty just yet. Where are the garments he wears in my service?"

The woman pointed to a chest in the corner. Atop the clothes, glittering in its curved leather sheath, a dagger rested.

Nasr gave it to Fatima for her brief examination.

Then he nodded to the woman. "Tell Adulfo I make prayers tonight for his improvement."

"I shall, my Sultan. Thank you for your kindness. I promise when Adulfo recovers, he shall be your worthy captain again."

"I don't doubt it."

Outside the house, Nasr clutched Fatima's fingers in his grasp. "Say you believe me. Castilla-Leon is at my gates and my own people want to see me destroyed. Don't turn from me, too."

The Castillans tested Nasr's resolve, as they held his city under siege. Fatima remained trapped for six months, unable to send word to her children in Malaka or receive news from them. She worried for their father and prayed each day that Faraj lived and his health improved.

Her doubts lingered, but not about Nasr. He could not have arranged the assassination of her husband. Yet, if he did not, who had done it?

Gharnatah, Al-Andalus: Jumada al-Ula 712 AH (Granada, Andalusia: September AD 1312)

A hot wind hastened Fatima's approach to the Sultan's residence under the watchful eyes of the Galician guards. Their captain Adulfo bowed reverently and averted his gaze, as he had every morning since his full recovery.

A brazier emitted its fragrant warmth. Nasr shivered underneath a woolen blanket, seated on a chair beside the window.

Fatima said, "The peace of God be with you, my Sultan. What news of the siege?"

"Fernando of Castilla-Leon is dead. The *Cortes* has recalled the army. It seems the ministers have no heart for fighting without their master. I hear the new ruler Alfonso, is a child."

"He is a babe in arms, born last summer with his uncle and cousin as regents. I remember his birth year because the Castillan merchants at Malaka traded heavily with us for extravagant gifts in his name. I am surprised the Castillan ministers accepted Prince Juan, the butcher of Tarif, as one of Alfonso's regents."

She reached for Nasr's icy hand beneath the coverlet. "Such developments do not concern us, except it seems Castilla-Leon is no longer a concern for you."

He trembled. "Now, you shall leave me again."

"I'll never leave you, dear brother, not truly. We are one flesh."

Her fingers smoothed the crinkles and dark circles that marred the skin beneath his eyes. A sigh escaped her.

Nasr grinned. "Do I look so terrible?"

Despite her help over the previous months, he struggled with his addiction to wine still. She prayed he might overcome it one day.

He cupped her hand in his against his cheek. "Think of me, sister."

She bent and kissed his brow. "I always do, my Sultan."

Fatima returned to Malaka a few days later. Workers had almost cleared the cotton fields. The sun rode high above their heads.

Leeta greeted her in the courtyard now lined with palms. Despite the years, tension remained between them. Leeta, like Faraj, could not forgive her betrayal.

"How does your master fare?" Fatima asked, as they walked together.

"He recovered in the months you have been away." Leeta paused. A frown marred her expression. "Prince Faraj is not the same as before. He grows tired easily and does not take his usual walks. It is by God's blessing alone that Prince Ismail has been here to undertake his father's duties. The physician has come often, to see him and Niranjan."

"Your brother lingers on."

When she nodded, Fatima halted beside her and touched her arm. "I am truly sorry, Leeta."

She flinched, but accepted the sympathy with a nod.

Fatima found Ismail's daughters playing under Baraka's attentive gaze. The women shared a smile. The girls remained intent on chasing each other through the indoor courtyard and did not notice their grandmother. There would be time for them later.

Fatima went to her husband's chamber. The door stood ajar, but he was nowhere in sight. Then she heard familiar snores emanating beyond the walls of her room, next to his. She pushed the door and stepped inside.

He rested comfortably in the bed they had not shared for over ten years. Her stomach contracted to a tight ball. On wooden legs, she sank down beside him on the cedar floor. She placed her hand above his heart, which pounded in a steady thrum. A soft sob escaped her, before she buried her tears in her hands.

Behind her, the door creaked. “Oh, my Sultana, you’ve returned.”

Haniya entered and bowed at her side.

“Just a moment ago. How do you fare?”

Haniya hesitated. “I am well. I see the master still sleeps.”

“Who can sleep…with my wife’s crying. Just like an old woman.”

Faraj’s voice filled the chamber, feeble and hoarse. Still Fatima thought it the sweetest sound she had heard in months.

His eyelids fluttered once and opened. “You were not here, when I first awoke.”

She did not know if he meant in the days after her departure for Gharnatah or earlier today, but it did not matter.

His hand reached for her. His thumb stroked her cheek. “Just as I said, like an old woman.”

He sighed. “My old woman.”

She remained with him, even after he drifted off again. She cupped his hand to her cheek, a healing balm for her wearied soul.

She never noticed when Haniya brought in a meal of flatbread and stewed lamb with chickpeas, except she asked later if Fatima was not hungry and gestured to the cold meal.

“Take it away. I have everything I desire at the side of my husband.”

“As you wish.” Haniya reached for the tray and then hesitated. “My Sultana, I need to tell you something.”

Whatever she might have said died with Ismail’s sudden, boisterous entry into the room. “*Ummi*! Why didn’t you tell us you had returned?”

Fatima rose from the floor for the first time in hours. “Good evening to you as well, my son.”

Behind him, Haniya darted out of the room.

Fatima spoke with him about the months spent in Gharnatah during the siege and of Nasr’s innocence.

“So you believed his claim?” Ismail sputtered. He paced the room and raked his hands through his dark hair. “How can you take the word of that usurper?”

"Son, Nasr is your uncle and the Sultan of Gharnatah. I trust his word and he showed me the proof of it."

"He's the son of a slave. He has no honor. I know she was your friend, *Ummi*, so don't frown at me that way. Gharnatah cannot bear his misrule for much longer."

She studied him. "You sound like your father. I didn't know you resented your uncle so much."

He stopped pacing. A frown marred his features. "I know you favor him, so I'll say no more. I bid you good evening. I promised the girls I would tell them a story before they fell asleep."

"Just as your father used to do with you and your siblings. Sleep well, my son."

He did not reply.

Haniya returned and prepared Fatima for bed. Faraj still slept peaceably.

Though the maidservant answered her inquiries about how she and her sister Basma fared in Fatima's absence, her voice shook. Her hands trembled at each of the fastenings on the tunic.

When Fatima clasped Haniya's wrists, she gasped.

"Do you know you've behaved like a chicken fearing the pot since you first saw me? What troubles you?"

Haniya shook her head. "Oh my Sultana, forgive me, I shouldn't have been spying as I was, but I know how the master hates that man."

"Haniya, please, speak as though I have no idea what you're talking about, because I truly do not."

"Yesterday, the Marinid commander Uthman came here. I listened in secret as he spoke of sending a letter from Prince Faraj to al-Maghrib el-Aska. Uthman said the Marinid Sultan would be pleased to receive it and promised the master would rule the richest port in al-Maghrib, at Chella."

"Haniya, I don't understand one word of what you're saying. Faraj has no interest in Chella, nor would he ever contact the Marinids."

"I know he didn't. Uthman was talking to Prince Ismail."

Fatima grabbed her chin hard. Her nails dug into Haniya's flesh. "Be careful what you say of my son! Why would we make an offer to the Marinids? Why would you spy on Ismail?"

"Oh, my Sultana, he's betrayed you both."

The horror of Haniya's suggestion robbed Fatima of her speech. Her hand fell away.

Haniya sank down on the carpet at her feet. "For days after you left for Gharnatah, none of us knew what would happen. The master would awaken and call your name. Some days, he never woke. He thrashed in his sleep. The doctor visited, but he could do nothing. He said it would be the Will of God if the master lived or died. When master was alert and he called for you, I begged Prince Ismail to come to his father. Once, he asked the master if he would wish him to assume his duties, since master was unwell."

Fatima reasoned Ismail had every right to perform the duties of his father. She waved Haniya on.

"Master consented, well, he only gesticulated. I think Prince Ismail understood his father's expectation. He toured the marketplace in his father's stead. He heard the people's grievances and promised them help. He appointed a new captain of the guard."

Fatima asked, "Whom did he choose?"

Haniya shook her head and the lines deepened across her furrowed brow. "Prince Ismail did not ask for one of the officers who served with Khalid. No, he summoned one of the Marinids, one of Uthman's men and named him captain."

The Marinids remained ambitious for a foothold in Gharnatah. The Volunteers of the Faith ensured their Marinid masters would have solid military backing in any enterprise. Yet, the Marinid rulers had long ago proved themselves unpredictable. Surely, Ismail understood of the danger which the *Ghuzat* posed in Al-Andalus. Why would he trust any among them?

Haniya continued. "Prince Ismail dined with the Marinid commander almost weekly and always in private. I never heard what they said to each other, but I grew suspicious. I have heard Prince Faraj speak of the commander Uthman many times and I knew he did not like him. What could endear the man to his son? I did not understand it.

"On the last night Uthman was here, on the eve of your arrival, I listened. I followed Uthman and Prince Ismail to the inner courtyard. It was very dark. I hid behind the rosemary bushes in the corner of the garden. Prince Ismail gave Uthman a roll of parchment. It bore the red wax seal of the *Raïs*. Prince Ismail asked if Uthman's servant prepared to sail. The Marinid commander said, he hoped for favorable winds in the morning, permitting his ship to leave for al-Maghrib el-Aska. A fierce storm came ashore on the next day, in which no ships left the harbor. Uthman's emissary must still be here. Uthman then said his master the Marinid Sultan would be pleased to receive Prince Faraj's letter. Prince Ismail laughed at this. Then Uthman promised him that master would soon rule Chella."

Chella was the northernmost port of al-Maghrib el-Aska. Even Fatima's late brother Muhammad had coveted it when he ruled Gharnatah.

"There is more. Prince Ismail said the letter had to reach the Marinid Sultan before your brother inquired about the taxes Prince Ismail has withheld."

"Ismail has withheld Malaka's taxes from Nasr's collectors? It is treason! Nasr would be within his rights to demand Faraj's head. Ismail would have to answer the Sultan's challenge. It would plunge the Sultanate into civil war again."

Fatima stifled a cry, as understanding dawned. The victor in a conflict between Nasr and Ismail would rule as Sultan. Could Ismail's ambitions extend beyond Malaka? Birthright and destiny would grant him the governorship. Did he want something more?

She sank down on the bed. Faraj stirred beside her, but he did not awaken. Her mind raced, as she revisited Ismail's story of the assassination attempt upon his father. Ismail had been with him when it happened. Just before it, they had met with Uthman. Had he and Ismail arranged the meeting?

Khalid fought against the attack and he died as a result. Had there been a plan to get rid of him? His unquestionable loyalty to Faraj would have made him a target. Ismail alone gave chase. He never brought the would-be assassin's body back to the citadel for identification. Had the attacker truly intended Faraj's death or did he plan only to incapacitate him? Faraj's wounds came close to his heart, but did not kill him. Had the attack been a ruse? Was its inevitable outcome a chance for Ismail to gain access to his father's power, for a greater purpose?

Haniya clutched Fatima's knee and drew her gaze again. "Your husband has written no letters. By your command, I have tended to him in your absence. I knew his every waking hour. He has hardly possessed the strength to leave his bed in the last months. Prince Ismail has undertaken all of his duties. He has used the opportunity to betray his father."

Fatima's hands balled into such tight fists, the knuckles turned white. Ismail's treachery dwarfed the travail she had experienced in the last ten years. His betrayal stabbed at her heart.

Haniya whispered, "I knew you would understand the full measure of these events and the consequences, for more than just Malaka. You must protect the Sultanate and the master."

Fatima clasped a hand over her mouth and bit back a sob. Protect her husband against his own son?

Ismail had always been dutiful and loving. Had she imagined it? She knew him intimately, had always admired the strength of his heart and the inner workings of his mind. His attitudes and ideals reflected the values his parents had taught him. When had he changed?

From somewhere in the depths of her mind, the memory of her last meeting with her brother Muhammad stirred. A maniacal cackle filled her ears, rising to a crescendo.

Dawn broke. Its glittering rays stirred Fatima from sleep. Faraj snored beside her, his hand on her hip. The sounds of birds and the scent of salted sea spray drifted through the lattice-covered windows. It seemed nothing had changed, but in truth, everything was different now.

Haniya sat on the floor still, her head cradled on her arm. Light snores escaped her. Fatima touched her dark hair tenderly.

She shifted Faraj's hand, careful not to wake him. She slid to the foot of the bed and stood. With a final glance at her husband and Haniya, she left the chamber.

Niranjan's quarters at the opposite end of the harem overlooked the White Sea. When she opened the door, the cleansing odor of incense engulfed her. Sparse furnishings that included a pallet, a cedar-carved stool and table, and two clothing chests suited Niranjan's asceticism.

His shriveled form lay on the pallet. Her heart wrung with pity at the sight of hollowed cheekbones gouged deep into his parchment-like skin.

She knelt beside him and he opened his eyes.

She whispered, "The peace of God be with you."

"And with you." Although a foul odor saturated his breath, she did not draw back from him. "I have what I want from God, but it would appear you are in need of His peace this day, my Sultana."

She clutched his hand and kissed it.

"You went to Gharnatah and saw the Sultan." Though he did not ask a question, she nodded. "Then you know he could not have ordered the murder of your husband."

Her gaze met his. "How did you know?"

A lopsided grin softened his haggard appearance. "I did not. You told me, or rather, the despair in your eyes did. Do you know you have the most expressive gaze? Your eyes, like the window to your soul. Anyone can look into them and see what you are feeling. Anyone who has known you for as long as I have. That is why I am sorry to leave you now, when you may need me the most. Darkness surrounds you."

"And you have always been my light, leading my way."

"Have I? I would be so again, if God would give me the strength. Tell me all that has happened."

Niranjan listened in silence. She shared the events that had transpired in Gharnatah and since her return. When she spoke of Ismail and Haniya's account of his betrayal, Niranjan's countenance did not alter. He expressed no astonishment at the revelation.

She said, "Your eyes give away as much as mine do. You have long suspected my son's hand in his father's attack. It was why you questioned his actions in the aftermath."

He nodded.

"What can I do, Niranjan? He is my son, my firstborn. Through him, I learned to be a mother. How can I bear this pain?"

"You shall bear it. You shall do as you have always done. You'll protect those whom you love from those who would hurt them."

# Chapter 26
# The Betrayed

## Princess Fatima

Malaka, Al-Andalus: Jumada al-Ula - Rajab 712 AH
(Malaga, Andalusia: September – October AD 1312)

Later, in the stillness of Niranjan's room, a knock at the door intruded. "Compose yourself, my Sultana," he whispered. He cleared his throat before speaking. "Enter."

Ismail stood in the doorway. His gaze flew from Niranjan to Fatima's face. She swiped at her cheeks and held his stare.

"*Ummi.* I went to your room to ask if you would join us for the morning meal. Father is awake. He's asking for you."

"Since he was resting when I left, I thought it a good time to visit with Niranjan." She forced steely resolve into her voice and stood without trembling. "I had not visited with my servant since returning to Malaka."

"You seem tired, *Ummi.* Let me help you to your room."

Ismail advanced and with each footfall, her heart heaved. She could hardly abide the sight of him, the bearing of his noble grandfather in his lengthy stride, his visage. Every part of him echoed the image of her father at his full strength. How could he have betrayed an honorable legacy in such a way?

His lean-muscled arms rose up and his hands clutched her shoulders. She shuddered with the exertion it took to keep herself steady, without falling at his feet in tears.

"Truly, you look overwrought. You should not be here. You need your rest, too." His tone almost accusatory, he glared at Niranjan.

"My son, I am hardly a child to be hastened to bed!"

Ismail's stare returned to her. She bit her lower lip, instantly regretting the harsh tone.

"Forgive me, Ismail. I'm perfectly capable of knowing when I need rest. I promise I'll only remain with Niranjan for a little while. Is it just you and your brother at the morning meal?"

"Baraka too, though I don't understand why she thinks she's part of this family."

"She is." Ismail's gaze widened and she continued in a rush of words. "She's always been. Never forget, she was governess to your younger siblings and she cares for your children, too. Where are the girls? I did not have the chance to speak with them yesterday."

"In the nursery, still asleep."

"I shall join you after I have finished here and seen your father. You should not keep the others waiting."

Ismail nodded and turned on his heel.

When he closed the door behind him, Fatima sagged against the adjacent stucco wall. After a moment, the echo of his footfalls down the marble walkway faded.

Niranjan whispered, "That was the first test of your strength."

"I can't bear much more!"

"You shall! You must!" He spoke with renewed, fervent strength. "If you love your family, you shall do all you must to protect them."

"But how? He conspires with others to destroy his father."

"Then we must stop him, or at least, thwart the plans of his allies."

"How can we? If there is a favorable wind, the Marinid ship may leave today. I cannot ask anyone to send a contingent of guards to the docks to stop all ships from sailing. Ismail would learn of it and know of my suspicions."

Niranjan nodded. "You must not give Prince Ismail any warning. We can still stop him. Fetch me a quill, ink and parchment, if you please."

Fatima went out into the hallway. Basma came out of a room with a pile of dirtied bed linens. Fatima beckoned her and asked for the things Niranjan requested.

The maidservant looked beyond her into the room for a moment. Fatima frowned. "You know I despise repeating myself for anyone."

Basma went away and returned quickly. Fatima took the writing implements and parchment. She closed the door on Basma's curious expression.

Niranjan dictated and Fatima wrote all he said on the parchment.

She asked, "How shall you send word to intercept Uthman's servant to al-Maghrib el-Aska?"

"Do you trust Haniya?"

"Without fail. It took great courage for her to speak of all she knew."

"Then send her with this message to the Jewish quarter of Malaka. Tell her to give it to the Sitt al-Tujjar."

"The Sitt al-Tujjar? She must be long dead!"

"The granddaughter of the woman you knew now supervises the mercantile business. There has always been a Sitt al-Tujjar, a mistress of the merchants, in their family line. I trust this one, as I have done her forbearers. If she follows the instructions to intercept Uthman's messenger, that treasonous letter shall never make it to the Marinid court."

One week afterward, Fatima visited Niranjan again, as she often did in the morning. She sensed the end neared for him. Death hovered over him, its shadows haunting his leathery, wizened complexion. The once copper-colored, ovoid eyes had dulled to a shade of burnished brass.

He begged her, as he had in the last few days, to leave Malaka. "If you do not go, Prince Ismail has already won. For as long as you remain here, he shall control his father."

Niranjan's warning resounded in her mind after she left him. On wooden legs, she ambled through the hall and slammed into her son Muhammad, as he turned a corner.

He steadied her and kissed her brow. "I'm sorry, I didn't see you there. I was just coming to find you to say farewell. I'm off with Ismail this morning."

"Where?"

Muhammad chuckled. "Don't you remember? Ismail mentioned it at dinner last night. He makes his tour of the province, just as Father did each year. We shall be gone for at least a month."

"Why are you going with him?"

"He may have found me a suitable wife in Naricha. Ismail believes it time that I married."

"And why should it be his decision? Your brother thinks too much of himself to choose a wife for you. It is your father's responsibility and he has not abdicated it!"

Muhammad's arms dropped at his sides at the vehemence of her tone.

"Father remains weakened." When she glared at him, he faltered. "Besides, Ismail is governor in all, but name."

"He is not! Your father is not cold in his grave! Or, do you wish that for him, too?"

"*Ummi*! You know I do not. Certainly, you don't suggest my brother feels that way?"

She swallowed and clasped her hands before her. "Of course not. I wish your brother had consulted with his father before making decisions about your future."

"I did, *Ummi*. Perhaps Father has not told you."

Fatima whirled in the direction of Ismail's voice, as he strode from his chamber in the harem and greeted them. She averted her gaze and bowed before him, which he greeted with a frown.

"When did you become so formal?" He raised her up and kissed her brow. Then he looked at Muhammad. "We must leave now."

Fatima stared in their wake long after both men had spoken their farewells and kissed her hands.

Baraka found her standing there. "I thought we were friends. You haven't come to see me." Resentment tinged her hollow tone. "Something troubles you, yet you do not speak of it. Unburden your heart, or have I not proved myself worth the effort?"

Silks swirling around them, Fatima dragged her out on to the belvedere by the sea. There, she confessed everything.

When she finished, Baraka nodded. "You must get away from this place."

"Niranjan said the same, but how can I leave? To go is to abandon my son."

"Prince Muhammad is a man!"

"No! I do not mean him. Don't you see? If I leave, I give up. I accept that Ismail has changed and turn my back on him forever. I cannot do that to my own son."

Unbidden, the memory of her last meeting with her late father came to mind. *'Have the courage to see your loved ones as they are, not as you would wish them to be.'*

Baraka gazed at her steadily. "You must leave Malaka. Go to al-Bajara. Ownership has reverted to Prince Faraj again, with the passing of your sister Alimah and her son. You must go with Faraj and your servants. If anyone else accompanies you, your son would be suspicious."

"I can't abandon Ismail's daughters, or you, Samara and Hayfa. Leeta and Marzuq."

"The children shall be well. I'll protect them. God shall watch over the rest of us."

"And keep you from Ismail's wrath? He'll know that you helped me."

"Nothing he can say or do would make me betray you or the master."

Fatima clasped her hands and kissed them. Baraka smiled at her.

"You must tell your husband the truth one day. For now, persuade him that the mountain air would do him well."

"Our son's disloyalty shall break Faraj's heart."

"The master is stronger than you know. He shall survive this. You both shall."

Niranjan died at the end of the cotton harvest in Al-Andalus. Fatima arranged for his burial beside his sister, her faithful Amoda. She witnessed the internment of his body from a narrow window overlooking the orchard.

In the cool days that followed, she lingered beside the newest mound in the *rawda*. The certainty that she would leave this warring world one day and see Niranjan again eased the pain of his passing. The burden of the past weeks dwelled upon her mind. Niranjan had once shouldered the travail with her, ever steadfast and true. For the first time since childhood, she would have to bear the troubles alone, without her shadow at her side.

Sunlight shimmered through the cloud cover. Its warmth offered no cheer. A mournful wind whispered in the trees. The scent of the sea mingled with the odors of pine and eucalyptus. She closed her eyes and inhaled deeply for a moment. When she opened them, Ismail stood beside her.

She jerked away, almost as a reflex. His eyes widened. "I did not mean to startle you, *Ummi*."

"What are you doing here?"

A frown marred his noble features at the undercurrent of annoyance in her tone. She could not help it. He dared intrude upon her now, in the only place that offered solace from the pain he had inflicted.

She returned his stare. "You're supposed to be touring the province."

Ismail nodded. "I returned because I have business here."

"With whom?"

"Oh, the market inspector. I must also speak to Uthman. One of his men molested a woman at an inn. I cannot allow the Marinids such liberties."

She nodded, although she did not believe the lie.

Last evening, Haniya had brought her a message. "The Sitt al-Tujjar's man has returned from abroad where all is well."

Fatima had sighed with understanding and wished Niranjan were alive to know that in his last service to her, he had discharged his duty.

Now Ismail had returned, possibly to contact the Marinid commander and learn why his treasonous letter never reached its destination.

Fierce anger swelled inside of her, as he stood silent at her side. His pride and bearing were the attributes of his father. She had always vainly assumed the cleverness of his mind was one of her gifts to him. Yet, good judgment had not guided him now, a path to despair and heartbreak for their family. He had betrayed his father. He had also deceived her. Yet, she could not hate him. How could she ever despise a child of her body and blood?

"Why do you look at me so, *Ummi*?"

"I was thinking of how much you remind me of your grandfather the Sultan."

The comment brought a wry smile to his lips. "I want to be like your father."

She nodded. "I do not doubt it."

He cleared his throat and looked away for a moment. "I am sorry Niranjan died. When I returned and saw you standing here beside a new grave, I realized he must have perished in my absence."

Then his stare returned to her face. "It is the fate of every man and woman."

"I know. Such knowledge comforts me. One day, I shall see him again."

"Thoughts of death comfort you?" Ismail frowned. "I would think you would rely on the living for your comfort."

"That is not always possible."

The wind receded and silence descended on the *rawda.*

Then she asked, "Did your brother return with you?"

"No, Muhammad is at Naricha. I shall rejoin him there, after I have concluded my business. He has met with the father of a girl he may marry."

"A woman of your choosing."

Ismail's stare narrowed. "You resent that I suggested her. Father trusts me to act in his stead. Don't you trust me, too?"

To answer in the way he expected would have given a lie to her lips. As Niranjan had predicted before his death, there would be many tests in this battle of wits between them. Could she prove herself smarter than her son?

"I am your mother, Ismail."

The curve of his smile dimpled his cheeks. The answer suited him. He bent and kissed her forehead.

She whispered, "I often think of the day that crazed assassin tried to kill your father."

When Ismail raised his head, his frown returned and with it, a sudden hard glint in the eyes and a thinning of the lips.

"Why do you trouble yourself with the memories of that day? Father has recovered. He may not have his full strength back, but he lived."

"Yes, by God's mercy alone. I know your father has rarely said so, but his pride in you knows no bounds. A father cannot help but love his sons. Parents are fated to see only the good in our children."

"Yes, I know this with my own daughters."

She continued, as if he had not interrupted her. "Faraj is a good man. We did not always love each other. Over the years, through trials and sadness, by devotion and mutual understanding, a bond forged between us. Even my betrayal could not destroy it. When we came to this place, your father vowed to erase the pain-filled memories of his parents' deaths. We made it a loving home and promised each other Malaka would be where our children would never know sorrow.

"I forsook those vows for the sake of another, but never again. I love your father still, as I once never believed it possible to love. I shall always love him, always protect him from anyone who would do him harm. Anyone."

Ismail stared, for the first time seemingly unsure of what he should say.

She stood on tiptoes and brushed her lips against his cheek. Then she left him.

In the afternoon, Fatima met with Baraka, Samara and Hayfa in the central alcove amid their rooms, at Baraka's request. Luxurious Baghdad carpets covered the floor. Silken cushions lined the walls.

Time had been as kind to Hayfa and Samara, as it had been to Baraka. Like glittering jewels, the *jawari* sat amidst their opulent surroundings. Hardly a wrinkle marred Hayfa, her opal-shaped eyes set wide in her dark rounded face, or her counterpart Samara, whose alabaster skin glistened like pearls. Baraka outshone them all, her hennaed hair pulled back to reveal a radiant emerald gaze. When the trio bowed, Fatima returned the respectful gesture.

Fatima said, "Your invitation surprised me. We have not always been sociable, though we share a common bond in our devotion to my husband."

Baraka snorted at this. Fatima and the others dismissed her pretense at outrage.

Hayfa leaned forward. "It is for love of the master that we help you."

Fatima stared at Baraka, whose smile widened. "I have entrusted them with your secret. I had to."

Fatima nodded. "My son Ismail has returned. I must wait until he departs at the end of the week before I leave Malaka."

Hayfa replied, "As soon as he is gone, you and the master must flee."

"Take only what you need," Samara added.

Fatima shook her head. The years of unease between them melted away, as if they had never existed.

Baraka asked, "Have you written to your father's queen?"

Fatima nodded. "Yes. It may be some time before Shams ed-Duna sends a reply. I cannot count on her. At al-Bajara, I shall get word to the Sultan."

Baraka clapped her hands. "At last! Justice shall fall upon your son's head."

"No! Nasr shall know only that I have left Malaka for my husband's health. I cannot tell him about Ismail's actions. It would ruin my son. Nasr would march against him and strip him of his birthright."

Baraka drew back, the disgust apparent in her flaring nostrils and the sneer on her lips. "How can you care about that after his betrayal?"

"You are not a mother, Baraka. I don't expect you to understand."

"You'll let him get away with this treachery?"

Fatima shook her head. "Baraka, he is my son."

Those simple words explained away all the turmoil she had experienced these last weeks. Despite her life lessons about the values of family and loyalty, Ismail had succumbed to the same temptations that destroyed the lives of her brothers Muhammad and Nasr.

She had been the instrument of Muhammad's ruin, so determined to avenge his cruel murder of their father. Yet in her recklessness, she had also paved the way for Nasr's destruction. She would not allow the same fate to consume her son. This time, there would be no vengeance, only regret. She would sooner harm herself than her firstborn.

Flustered, Baraka threw her hands in the air. Fatima reached for her fingers across the table. "I count you among friends. If you honor the bond we share, do not oppose me."

Her gaze flitted over the other women. "I must have the promise from each of you that you shall help me for love of Faraj alone, not to avenge the wrongs our son has done to him. When we leave this place, you shall live by Ismail's favor alone. Do not jeopardize your futures for my sake."

Baraka frowned, Hayfa sighed and Samara looked away, but then they each made the promise.

Then Hayfa said, "You must leave under cover of darkness, perhaps when the guard at *Al-Jabal Faro* changes the night watch."

Fatima nodded in agreement.

Samara cleared her throat. "We shall distract the men."

Her voice wavered, but resolve glowed in the Castillan Jewess' gaze.

Fatima frowned. "How?"

As one, the trio stood. Their fingers rustled silk and fastenings. Within minutes, their garments pooled at their feet. Fatima stood speechless, at the sight of their bodies. Each woman was at least the same age as her husband. Yet their bellies remained maiden flat, as neither of them had borne children. Their skin glowed with youthful vigor and health.

Baraka sensed Fatima's discomfort and laughed. "I told you, I'll never grow old!"

Fatima walked to her room before she planned to join the others at dinner. She met Ismail just outside her door. A crimson mantle swirled around his broad shoulders. His jaw slackened as he approached her and bowed. Reddened fury suffused his features.

"Are you unwell? Did your meeting with the market inspector and the Marinid commander go as intended?"

He snapped "It did not!" She raised her eyebrows at his clipped tone and he mumbled an apology.

"Forgive me. I am tired. I must go to the *hammam*. Shall I see you at dinner?"

"Of course, my son."

She entered her room and closed the door. Ismail's footfalls retreated. She stifled a sob behind her hand.

"Why do you cry, my beloved?"

Faraj stared at her across the room. She crossed the cedar floor and sank down beside him on the bed. There was so much she wanted to share. Love for him kept her silent. She kissed his brow instead.

He cupped her cheek. "Tell me."

"We have to leave this place for a time."

His free hand found hers. Their fingers interlaced, his gaze held steady. "If you say we must go, then we shall go. I trust you, Fatima."

She pressed her lips to his. She wondered at his easy acquiescence. Did he have an inkling of Ismail's betrayal? Had he overheard Haniya's confession? Whatever the reason, she would learn further in time. Only the immediate future mattered. If he stayed at her side, she knew she could withstand the dark days to follow.

An hour afterward, Fatima dined with Abeer, Leeta and her husband Marzuq. Basma and Haniya stood in the alcove behind Fatima. Over the rim of a cup of somewhat bitter pomegranate juice, Fatima smiled at the banter between Leeta and Marzuq. Long after she left Malaka, she wanted to remember her happy household as it had been. Whatever discord lingered between her and Leeta, she would never forget the treasurer's devotion.

When Fatima set down her cup and reached for an uneaten bowl of *'tharid*, Basma said over her shoulder, "My Sultana knows the spiciness of the lamb does not agree with her stomach."

Despite the truthfulness of her claim, Fatima did not appreciate the reminder.

Leeta looked up from her bowl of stew and glared at Basma. "How dare you speak so to your mistress? When I attended her, even I was never so bold. When I dared, I deserved the lash. The Sultana was always kind to me. She is still too good, I suppose, to have you whipped for your insolence."

Fatima stared at her in wonderment. She had never expected Leeta would speak a kind word of her again.

Then Marzuq clutched his belly and tumbled forward. He knocked the *'tharid* aside. His features reddened and contorted.

Leeta screamed as a crimson stain trickled from Abeer's nostrils. Then, Faraj's treasurer clutched her stomach, too. Blood dribbled from the corner of her mouth.

At once, Fatima understood the threat and knew its source. Poison.

Leeta's last breath escaped in a strangled whimper. She sagged beside her husband, who already slumped lifeless on the table. Abeer clawed at her throat before she screamed once, but never again.

Fatima tried to speak or stand, desperate to aid them. Her limbs would not cooperate. She fought for every breath.

Haniya appeared at her side and shook her. "My Sultana? What is happening? Please, speak to me!"

The room blurred before Fatima's eyes. Someone had poisoned her too, but with nothing as potent as the drug that coursed the blood of the others. Her fingers knocked aside the pomegranate juice. Basma had brought her the cup. Fatima swallowed and whispered the servant's name.

Heavy, distinct footfalls approached and another familiar voice sounded.

"You've always been so clever, *Ummi*. Yes, Basma's done exactly what I told her to do."

"Prince Ismail?" Haniya's voice seemed so far away. "Was it not enough that you betrayed your parents? You enticed my sister to do your evil work, too. Basma, the Sultana has ever been kind to us. She rescued us from cruel enslavement to the Ashqilula, yet you have deceived her. Why?"

"She deserves her fate. Our lives shall be better under Prince Ismail. He has promised me I shall be governess of his children, not that old whore Baraka. You don't know the things the Sultana has done to us, sister, the lies she has told."

The bitterness in Basma's voice did not surprise Fatima. She had lived with dread that this day would come for decades.

"What lies?" Haniya's voice exploded in agony.

"About our mother. She was the Sultana Fatima's spy. The Ashqilula killed our mother because of it. Our brother Faisal knew, he was old enough to remember how it happened. The Sultana did not take us in because of the goodness in her heart. She kept us close to hide her secret. Faisal told me, before his death. I killed him. He should not have kept silent, while we served the one who is responsible for our mother's death."

"You murdered our brother all those years ago? How could you, Basma? How could you destroy your own family? You're no better than Prince Ismail."

Prone, listless, Fatima could not prevent the horror unfolding around her. Haniya dashed for something on the table. A long glimmer of silver appeared in her hand, before she plunged it into her sister's chest. Basma crumpled at her twin's feet. Fatima's mouth refused to obey her mind. Her whimpered protest came too late. Haniya sobbed and stabbed the knife into her heart, too.

In the throes of her torpor, Fatima stared at the marble ceiling above. She remained silent, in the stillness of the room, among the dead.

# Chapter 27
# The Final Coup

## Princess Fatima

Malaka, Al-Andalus: Rajab 712 AH (Malaga, Andalusia: October AD 1312)

Fatima awoke in her room. Sunlight and cool wind spilled through the lattice. The spot beside her in the bed was cold and empty.

Ismail hovered beside her, a long scratch gouged into his cheek. Had she done that to him?

"I'm sorry it had to be this way, *Ummi.* I knew Leeta would remain loyal to you. Marzuq was devoted to my father. As for Abeer, I did not intend to harm her, but it would have looked suspicious if Basma stopped her from eating the *'tharid*, too. Still, she was only a concubine."

His callous tone, so reminiscent of Fatima's brother Muhammad did not matter now. She asked, "Where's your father?"

"He is safe, I promise you. I have sent a letter to my uncle in Gharnatah explaining how my father's recent troubles have left him incapacitated. I expect the Sultan shall confer the governorship upon me soon."

She gripped the bedpost and sat up. "You think I don't know what you've done. This was never about your father or the governorship of Malaka."

He bowed at her side. "You shall excuse me. There are other matters I must attend to."

"I'm coming with you." She swung her legs off the bed and stood. "What do you intend to do now?"

"As if you do not know. That harridan Baraka, she actually flew at me and started scratching my face. She and her companions shall pay dearly for uniting against me."

"They love your father as I do. You would not understand such love or sacrifice. You think only of your selfish interests."

He left the room and she followed.

"Get back, *Ummi*!" The snarl deep in his throat did not frighten her. Nothing could ever make her afraid again.

She glared at his back. "If you can murder those who have loved your father, then by the Prophet's beard, I have the strength to watch you."

They emerged in the full glare of midday. She shielded her eyes from the sun.

Baraka, Hayfa and Samara knelt under a pavilion, their hands tied at their backs. Behind them, men from *Al-Jabal Faro* stood, with bowstrings stretched taut between their fingers.

Baraka called, "You see, Sultana? I told you I would never grow old!"

At Ismail's signal, his men strangled the women. None of them struggled or cried out. Fatima refused to dishonor their courage with whimpers. Soon three bodies slumped on the marble.

When she sniffled, Ismail muttered, "I would have spared you this sight, *Ummi*."

She spat in his face. "Don't say it. *'Ummi'* – the word is meaningless to you! You've betrayed your father. You've killed his devoted servants! You're no longer my son."

Shawwal 713 AH (February AD 1314)

A year passed and a bitter, wintry chill descended on Malaka, the coldest in Fatima's long memory. Blustery currents tore the leaves from treetops and ravaged the flowerbeds, scattering their remnants through the unkempt grounds. The stench of decay and death lingered in the frigid air.

Then strange odors intermingled, a potent smell not unlike a mixture of ash and rotten eggs. Late in the evening torches burned bright, illuminating the faces of men who bustled to and from *Al-Jabal Faro*, sometimes with carts of white or yellow crystalline material. The sounds of metal against metal and men preparing for battle rang through Fatima's home. Cut off from the outside world with no one to trust, she languished as the months of loneliness crept by.

One day, the door creaked and faint footsteps padded across the wood. "I'm hungry."

At the plaintive voice of Asiya, Haniya's daughter Fatima looked up from where she sat on the floor. Strands of black hair almost concealed her almond-shaped eyes from view. Born almost five years earlier, Asiya was the image of her mother, but her quiet nature reminded Fatima of her father Khalid of al-Hakam also. With the death of both her parents, Fatima cared for the girl.

She reached for Asiya, who hugged her. "Aren't you hungry too, my Sultana? You haven't eaten today."

Fatima nodded. "You are good to remind me. We must both remain strong. Go to the kitchen."

Asiya did so. She returned with three slices of flatbread, lentils, and chunks of roasted lamb. Fatima broke each piece of flatbread in half and shared it with Asiya. It tasted like sawdust. She chewed and swallowed it, along with the rest of the meal.

Fatima pulled Asiya on to her lap and crooned softly to the little girl, who played with the rings on her mistress' fingers, until she tired and drifted to sleep. Fatima groaned and lifted her, placing her on the bed.

Ismail entered, for the first time in the months since he had shattered all Fatima's hopes for his future. He scanned the unkempt room, pillows strewn across the cedar floor, dust motes clinging to every surface including the rumpled bedding, before taking in her appearance. She ignored his gasp and turned to the window.

"*Ummi.* How do you fare?"

She did not answer.

"Forgive my absence. I have been with Father."

"Where is he?"

"He lives. I promised he would come to no harm."

She looked over her shoulder at him. "For once, since you turned to lies and folly, you have not deceived me. I know he lives."

She clasped her hands together and strolled toward him. He stepped back once and then again. Relentless, she kept coming. He bumped against the door behind him.

They stood close together. Each inhalation drew the scent of flames and gunpowder deep into her nostrils.

"The sights and sounds of men preparing for war have filled this place for weeks. You did not betray your father for Malaka. You are preparing to march on Gharnatah, to usurp my brother Nasr's rule. You seek the throne."

At night, dreams had tormented Fatima, remembrances of the past. The gypsy's tent and the tealeaves. A dire prophecy she had ignored.

*"You carry a son within your womb. One day, your son shall become the Sultan of Gharnatah. Such is the fate that awaits you, whether you would wish it or not."*

Ismail's gaze fell away before it met hers again. "Why shouldn't I have Gharnatah? Through you, the blood of Sultans flows in my veins."

She framed his face between his hands. "Yes, through me. Oh my Ismail, have you not learned the lessons of those kingly lives? My grandfather knew little peace before the end. Ceaseless struggles against Castilla-Leon and civil war nearly broke him. My dear father murdered by his favored son. Have you forgotten? I know you cannot forget Muhammad, the only son of my mother, driven to madness in his lust for power. Then poor Nasr, the last of my father's beloved heirs. I bullied him into seeking the crown. In the end, his love of strong drink ruled him. Has the tragedy of their lives not shown you the folly of what you seek? To wear the crown of Gharnatah is a heavy, perhaps perilous burden for any man. I would not choose such an end for you."

He wrenched himself from her hold. "Then why do you have so little faith in me? I am strong, just like your father. Do you not often say how I remind you of him, molded in his very image? I have ruled Malaka well. Don't you believe I can rule Gharnatah too? This is my destiny!"

"No, Ismail, it is a path you have chosen to walk alone."

He stabbed a finger in her face. "You're just jealous of my ambition! Look at you! You once told me your father said if you had been a man, you would have been a great Sultan. You could never aspire to such a goal and you want to deny me the power of it. It shall be mine!"

She shook her head. "How can you be so blind? Do you only see the lure of power now? Do you forget that no

Sultan since the time of my grandfather has borne his crown easily until the end?"

"I shall do it! You said it yourself, Nasr is unfit to rule. The people need a new, stronger leader. I am governor of Malaka, grandson of Sultan Muhammad *Al-Fakih*. If Nasr submits to me, I shall allow him a peaceable exile. If he rallies his army against my supporters, I shall destroy him."

"He is your uncle! Does the sanctity of family mean nothing to you?"

"My uncle Muhammad was your brother by the blood of your mother and father! Where was your concern for family when you conspired to remove him from his throne? Did you ever shed one tear of regret when Nasr blinded him?"

She drew back under his unforgiving gaze. Now, he advanced. "You recoil from me. Everything I have done is because of all I learned from you. Your machinations have led us to this point."

Her hands covered her ears in a vain attempt to drown out his incessant accusations. "Who was it that conspired with Nasr to destroy the rightful Sultan? Who put Nasr on the throne? It was you! If you cannot bear to hear where your lies and folly have led us, then you are a coward like him. From my childhood, you promised a great fate awaited me. Who taught me to seek a brilliant destiny except you?"

The backs of her knees bumped against the bed. "I never taught you this!"

"You are a descendant of Sultans. It is right that I, your heir, your firstborn son, should inherit their mantle of power. You were born a princess of Gharnatah. I shall make you a queen."

He clasped her hands in his rough grasp and kissed them. She wrenched them away and clutched at his shoulders. "No! I forbid it. Do not do this. Do not seek the throne. It shall be the path to tragedy and your undoing!"

Ismail shook his head. A somber expression darkened his downcast eyes. "I leave in the morning. I shall send word of my victory. You shall come to me in Gharnatah soon and celebrate my triumph."

Fatima crumpled on the floor and cradled her head in her hands.

Time passed, interminable without news of the ensuing conflict. Grief and seclusion returned. Every day, Fatima wept for fear of what Ismail would do. A great trial faced Nasr. Her brother had no heirs to follow him on the throne, just two golden-haired daughters sired on his Galician concubines. There would be no son denied his father's power, no princely blood spilled in Ismail's bid for the throne. She did not doubt Ismail would kill his uncle. His ambition knew no bounds.

His bitter words at their parting tortured her. She could not deny the inherent truth. What was it about the Nasrids that made their family so willing to war with each other? She recalled the past, where her grandfather and father had driven out the Ashqilula, once part of their family, bound by blood and ties of kinship. Her grandfather used her to thwart their ambitions and her father had gloried in their demise. The cycle of violence turned inward. Was there a curse upon her family? Were they destined to murder each other?

Unbidden, another memory sparked in her mind.

*"Your children shall destroy your grandfather's line of Sultans. Neither the Ashqilula, nor the Christians kings shall claim the victory over your family. No, that line shall end with the tyranny of the children you bear, and their sons, and the sons of their sons."*

Her grandmother Saliha had died with that promise of retribution on her lips. In Fatima's quest to avenge the death of her father, her grandfather's line of kingship had been broken. The blame that Ismail laid at her feet belonged to her.

Days later, Asiya scrambled into the room. "My Sultana, your son comes!"

On unsteady legs, Fatima rose. Her second son Muhammad rushed into the room and embraced her. She had forgotten for a moment that she had another son. Asiya left them, closing the door behind her.

When he drew back, she took in the soot and grime on his face.

He said, "The citizens of Gharnatah opened the *Bab Ilbira* to Ismail. He besieged *Al-Qal'at al-Hamra.* Our uncle surrendered and he has withdrawn to Wadi-Ash. Ismail has won. He bids you to Gharnatah for his coronation. He has sent word to our sisters and to his daughters in Aisha's care. He's also promised me the governorship of Malaka in his stead."

She pulled away from him. "So, you've betrayed your family, too."

Muhammad's hands alighted on her shoulders, but she shrugged off his hold. "I shall not go to Gharnatah."

"Ismail needs his family now."

"How could you support him? Don't you see all he has done? He betrayed your father and me."

Muhammad raked his hands through dark hair, so like his father's own. "I had to go with him. You must see that."

"Why? For riches and glory?"

"No, never. He's my brother. How could I fail him?"

Her anger abated at the tears in his eyes, the plea in his moon-faced expression. She touched his grimy cheek.

"I know you love him, but I must ask, do you love me and your father so well?"

"You should not have to ask. I quarreled with Ismail after he told me what he had done to our father and you. I only relented when he told me Father was safe and let me see him at *Al-Jabal Faro.*"

"He imprisoned him!"

"He remained there only for a short time."

"Do you know where your father is now?"

Muhammad's gaze darted away. She followed it. "Please, let me go to him. Your father needs me. I must be with him."

"But Ismail said I shouldn't tell you! He said you would try to escape with him."

"Muhammad, I am an old woman! Where would I go? Even after your brother's betrayal, I cannot take his father away from him. A mother cannot hate her son so much."

"You still love Ismail, after all he's done?"

His brows knotted together in a frown of disbelief, but she nodded.

"Yes, though he shall never hear of it. I want comfort and peace now. I cannot have those things when I am apart from your father. He is my strength and succor. I am his. If you love us, don't keep us away from each other anymore."

Muhammad shook his head. "Come to Gharnatah with me and speak to Ismail. I am sure he would relent."

She drew back. "You are governor of Malaka. Must you defer to your brother to decide the fate of those in your own household?"

Something flashed in Muhammad's eyes. She recognized it as the same pride that drove his brother, but her heart did not wrench at the thought. All she wanted was a reunion with Faraj. There would be time for sorrow and atonement again. As long as they were together, she could withstand the pain.

Muhammad clasped her hands in his. "Father's at Shalabuniya, up the coast. Prepare to leave, take only what you need. I know Ismail shall be angry with me at first. He shall forgive me. He is Sultan, but he shall pardon his brother."

Fatima remained uncertain that the bonds of brotherhood meant anything to Ismail. She did not burden Muhammad with such fears.

They left Malaka within the week on horseback, Asiya riding with Fatima. She halted at the outskirts of the city's walls and looked back. The escarpment topped by *Al-Jabal Faro* and the home of her children rose in the distance. She would miss the happy memories Malaka once afforded, the sounds of childhood laughter echoing through the gardens. A specter of betrayal and loss enshrouded the place again and tainted her remembrances.

Muhammad slowed at her side. "We shall escort you to Shalabuniya first."

"No. You would be late to Ismail's coronation."

"I cannot leave you! A woman and a child alone."

"I shall not be alone. I require the services of the Tuareg brothers, Bazu and Amud."

She trotted her mare down the line of soldiers, who bowed their heads respectfully. She came to the brothers near the end of the column.

She nodded to them. "I need you."

Both bowed their heads and nudged their horses on either side of her. She took her leave of Muhammad. Even as the distance grew between them, she felt his gaze linger, until the land dipped into a steep-sloped valley.

The whitewashed houses of Shalabuniya clung to a precipice above the shoreline, visible from the eastern outskirts. Atop the promontory, the citadel soared, framed in a backdrop of puffy white clouds and azure sky.

Fatima's mare sweated and snorted, as she struggled to find a proper footing in the craggy landscape. They climbed a maze of narrow, cobblestone streets as familiar as any in Al-Andalus.

At the gates that barred entry to the citadel, Fatima demanded entry.

"Who are you, woman?" A gruff, burly soldier glared at her from the gatehouse.

Bazu dismounted and she gave him the letter Muhammad had written and stamped with the seal of the governor of Malaka. He handed it to the guardsman. The man eyed them, suspicion echoing in his quizzical glance.

She stared back at him. "I am mother to the governor of Malaka. I'm a Sultana of Gharnatah, unaccustomed to being questioned by lowly guards."

The gatekeeper grunted and ordered the entryway unfurled. Fatima walked beside her horse and held the reins, while Asiya hugged the mare's neck, her spindly legs dangling. Bazu and Amud followed them. Palm, juniper and pine trees lined the cobblestone road. The citadel sprawled over the landscape.

A solitary figure leaned against a palm tree. He cradled a mewling kitten in his hands. Other cats played at his feet. His weathered hands smoothed over the kitten's coat. As it nipped at his fingertips, he laughed.

The horse's tether slipped through Fatima's fingers. She stood in silence, her heart full to bursting at the sight of her husband.

Then he set the small cat among the others and reached, hesitatingly, for a long length of wood beside him. He struggled to find it. When he did, he groped around with it. His furtive movements drew an angry hiss from a white-tailed cat.

"Sorry, I did not see you there. I can't see much of anything now."

Tears blurred Fatima's vision as Faraj shuffled forward. A glimmering sun beamed down and he raised his face to its glow. Light illuminated the opaque film obscuring his pupils. Then he sniffed and turned around.

"Who's there? Samir, is that you?" Then he chuckled. "Though I do wonder why my jailor should smell of jasmine...." His voice trailed off for a moment. "Who's there? Did Uthman send you to torment me? Or my son?"

She shuddered at the warble in his voice. Age and time had weakened him.

He wavered for a moment and cocked his head. "Come to laugh at the old blind man, have you?"

Fatima swallowed her tears. She would not greet him with tears. "No. I have come to find the man I love, whom I shall always love."

The walking stick tumbled from Faraj's gnarled grip. "My heart? Are all my dreams come true at last? Or do I imagine the sound of your voice again?"

"Your ears do not deceive you, husband. You may trust them, as you trust me."

Faraj opened his arms and at once, she was in his loving embrace again. She vowed never to leave it.

# Chapter 28
# The Last Farewell

## Prince Faraj

Shalabuniya, Al-Andalus: Muharram 720 AH (Salobrena, Andalusia: February AD 1320)

Faraj sat with Fatima on a smooth limestone boulder in the early afternoon. She watched the myriad ships leaving Shalabuniya under a brilliant sky with wisps of clouds, while he listened to her descriptions. Not a busy port akin to Malaka, yet the familiar sounds of Shalabuniya's sailors stirred his memories.

After almost seven years in this place, Faraj no longer thought of it as exile. Wherever Fatima remained at his side would be his home. Her familiar heat pressed against him, warming him against the coolness of a breeze from the White Sea.

He groped for her hand. Her fingers, which remained elegant in her later years, entwined smoothly with his. A gentle wind settled around their shoulders, enhancing the sensations around him. The aroma of the sea filtered through his nostrils. He stubbed and wriggled his toes in gritty, coarse sand beneath his feet. The serene wind briefly caressed his cheek, touching him with the same gentleness as the dear woman at his side.

Familiar footfalls crossed the sand behind them.

Fatima's reassuring squeeze preceded her subtle turn and soft greeting. "The peace of God be with you, Samir."

Their jailor answered, "And with you, my Sultana, my prince. I bring word from the Sultan of Gharnatah. A missive arrived just this hour."

Faraj winced as Fatima's nails dug into his hand. In his turn, he soothed her with a reassuring caress along the length of her fingers. "Our son is persistent, at least that has not changed in him."

Fatima did not chuckle at his poor attempt at levity. Tension coursed through her, radiating through her near painful grip and the rigidity of her form.

She said, "I have no wish to hear anything Ismail would say. My husband and I refuse to listen to more of his lies. You may go, Samir."

"Samir, you shall wait." Faraj leaned toward her, catching the rippling exhalation of her pent-up fury.

Seven years was a long time, perhaps not so long as to earn forgiveness. Their son still sought it. In the months after Fatima had come to Shalabuniya and remained with Faraj, their heir had written nearly every month with his fervent hope that his parents would join him in Gharnatah. He promised he would rescind the order that kept Faraj a prisoner and house them both in comfort and freedom at *Al-Qal'at al-Hamra*. Fatima, the prevailing decision maker between them, always refused.

"Dear heart," he began, though the waves of disapproval emanating from her made him pause for a moment. "My dearest heart, he is our son. Whatever he has done, he needs us. He needs you."

Her hand wrenched from his grasp. "How can you say that?" Her voice seemed colder than death, made bitter by resentment and regrets. "How can you urge me to listen to yet another of his pleas for forgiveness? He shall never have my understanding or comfort, for what he's done to you."

She cupped his cheek in a familiar embrace. He leaned into the warmth her touch offered.

He sighed. "My beloved. As soft as silk against flesh when you yield, but as fixed and unmovable as marble, when your mind is set against something. You know one day I must leave this world…."

"Faraj, do not say it!"

"My heart, heed me just this once. What shall you do, when I am dead? Can you return to Malaka, subject to the whims and wishes of our second son and his wife? He has been fairer in his dealings with us than Ismail. Yet he bends to his wife's will. She rules his heart now. Would she welcome a rival for her husband's love and devotion in his mother? Would you join your brother Nasr, in miserable exile in Wadi-Ash? He cannot support you.

From what we have heard of the poor state of his daughters' dowries, his excesses continue. He can hardly maintain his own household, much less the burden of your needs. I cannot bear to think of you living in such squalor at his side. Ismail is Sultan and you are the mother of the Sultan. Your place has always been in Gharnatah."

"I shall never go there as long as he holds the throne!"

"He has held it for seven years. Please, consider your future."

"I don't want a future where you are not at my side." Her lips pressed against his hand. "Dear husband, why must you ask me to do the one thing I cannot?"

"You have a great capacity to love. In time, your love for our son shall dull this pain. Then you shall go to Gharnatah."

Faraj craned in the direction where Samir's voice had sounded. "Are you still there, jailor?"

"I am here, my prince."

"Then I bid you place my son's letter with the others he has sent, in my chamber. She shall read it when she is ready."

Samir's footsteps crossed the sand and soon faded.

Faraj drew Fatima into his arms and marveled at the sweetness of her surrender. She clung to him, damp tears on his neck. Her fingers traced his features, with a languid sigh. He wondered how she could still take pleasure in his shriveled form.

"I am not the man you remember from our youthful days."

"No, but you shall always be my love."

Her lips pressed against his made him sigh. The second kiss with lips and breaths melded sharpened old desires. How perfect she remained. Truly, God had fashioned her for him. His finger slid beneath her mantle and smoothed over her waist and belly beneath the cloth.

She pressed against him and laughed into his mouth. "Faraj, the guardsmen from the citadel watch us. What must they be thinking of us, you caressing your wife so boldly?"

"I hope they are jealous to know that I still may have the pleasure of you. Take me back to our chamber."

"Now? It is hardly midmorning." Her husky tone belied her words.

He nuzzled her chin. "When did the daylight hours ever matter to us?"

She held both his hands and tugged him across the rough sands. Her murmurs and sighs guided him from the beachhead and up the rough-hewn, rock stairs. The wind billowed and carried the scent of jasmine in her hair.

"You remember, husband, just two more levels until we reach our room," she breathed in his ear, her voice ragged.

He reached for her. She escaped him in a whisper of silk, with a teasing chuckle. "Woman...."

Her merriment echoed to the rafters. Her fingers laced with his and she guided him. "I promise I shall not tease you further."

He tugged her close and held her immobile in his arms. "No, sweet wife. You may tease me as you wish, beloved."

She led him up the first flight and released him. He followed the siren's call of her scent and voice, as he held the bannister on the landing. Shafts of light warmed his face. Then she reached for him again. They mounted the second set of stairs together.

She drew him to their room. He gripped the railing and leaned against it, suddenly winded.

Fatima's trilling laughter died. "Husband, are you well?"

He wiped moisture from his brow. "The last few steps have undone me."

"Perhaps, you should lie down."

He groped for her hand. "I fully intended to do just that with you beside me."

"No, no, you look very pale. Come, you need to rest for a moment."

She led him into the chamber. The wooden floor creaked beneath their feet. Then he sank into silken comfort, their bed one of a few luxuries afforded to them at Shalabuniya.

Fatima's footfalls crossed the room again. "Asiya, I need you."

"I'm here, my Sultana."

"Please, a fresh pitcher of water for your master."

Faraj chuckled. "I can't drink a whole pitcher, Asiya. A cupful will be fine."

A soft gasp escaped the servant girl.

When the mattress shifted and Fatima settled beside him, Faraj asked, "Do I look so old to such young eyes?"

Her hands returned to his face and smoothed his brow. "Asiya worries for you. We both do."

"You should not. I am well. I have all I need here in this place with you."

"Who would have ever thought we would know such contentment in these days?"

"Indeed. Who would have ever thought I could make you so happy?"

"What are you talking about? Did you ever doubt I could know joy as your wife?"

"I may be ten years older than you, but I think my memory is sharper. Don't you remember our wedding day? You looked at me and frowned with such displeasure. I'd never thought myself so trivial."

"How can you consider that now? I was a sullen child, unsure about marriage and you."

"If I recall correctly, I did not always seek your good opinion of me."

"You were arrogant and thought too well of yourself to care for my estimation of you. Yet, you must have known how I loved you in all those years afterward."

He reached for her. "Remind me."

She giggled. "No, husband. Rest until Asiya comes."

The servant returned. At Fatima's gentle insistence, Faraj drank two cups of water before he settled against the pillows.

Fatima said, "Thank you, Asiya. I'll call you if I need you again."

The wooden door creaked before it closed.

Fatima asked, "How do you fare now?"

"I'm a bit weary. What did you have Asiya put in that water?"

Her soft chortle echoed around the room. "Trust me, husband."

"I do."

He yawned against the fatigue that seeped through his limbs.

"Is Ismail's last letter here, Fatima?"

"It is. Samir left it on the writing table in the corner."

"Promise me, you shall read all of our son's letters when the time is right. You'll know the moment."

"I promise, Faraj. Don't concern yourself. You should try to sleep."

The bed shifted slightly and her warmth receded. He groped for her hand. "Don't go. Stay with me, until I sleep?"

The full length of her body settled beside him. Her arm encircled his chest and her chin rested in the crook of his shoulder.

She whispered, "Don't you know, heart of my heart? I'll never leave you again."

He believed her. He knew only the peace and comfort her words offered, as he closed his eyes.

## *Princess Fatima*

Fingers of light streaked through the room's latticed windows. Fatima's eyelids fluttered. Warmth shone down on her face. Dust motes floated like faint wisps of clouds on beams of brightness. She snuggled beside Faraj. "We've slept past at least one prayer hour. I am certain of it."

With her head beside his, she became aware of the silence in the room. His barrel-chest did not rise and fall with breaths drawn in deep slumber. The rhythmic tattoo of his heart had faded beneath her touch. The grip of his hand on her shoulder had slackened and the gnarled fingers had fallen away from her.

She rose on her elbow and pressed her trembling hand against a vein in the neck that no longer throbbed with life.

"Faraj?"

No answer came nor would ever come again.

"Husband? Please wake, please."

She quivered and pressed her lips to his cool cheek. "Oh, my love, my dearest love."

The tears fell unrestrained.

Sometime later, shadows formed in the corners of the room. She stood and arranged her beloved's limbs so that his hands clasped together. Her fingers threaded through the smoky gray on his head and smoothed the wisps of beard on his chin. A ghost of a smile lingered on his mouth, upturned at the corners. She gently positioned his head to face the *Qiblah*. She kissed his lips for the final time, their last farewell.

"Wait for me, my heart, please wait. I promise I shall not tarry long in this life. We shall be together again."

She went to the window and unfurled the lattice. A pain-filled sigh racked her body and escaped her lips with a shudder.

Then a knock came at the door and Asiya's soft voice echoed through the wood. "My Sultana. It is nearly evening. I have brought the meal and candles for later."

"You may come, Asiya."

The servant's soft footfalls trundled across the floor. "Good evening. You missed a glorious sunset. Samir and I watched it together. The master still sleeps so soundly." Asiya's voice dropped to a whisper. "It is a wonder he can, with my chatter."

She approached the western wall where Fatima stood and placed a candle on the windowsill. A furtive glance from her took in Fatima's tear-stained cheek and she gasped. "Why are you crying?"

"The master, he is gone."

As Asiya sobbed, Fatima patted her shoulder. "Tell Samir. I want my husband prepared for burial tonight."

Before midnight, torches illuminated a small garden to the east of the citadel. Samir, Bazu and Amud, and the guards stationed at Shalabuniya interred Faraj's body. Fatima watched from a window, her arm draped over Asiya's shaking shoulders.

Custom dictated her absence beside the gravesite during the ceremony. It even forbade her from washing her husband's body, for everyone who touched a corpse remained impure until ritual cleansing. Yet, she had lingered in the chamber while the *ghasil* whom Samir had summoned performed the preparations for Faraj. The man attended to his body with care, anointed it with rosemary and lavender oils. Lastly, the *ghasil* draped Faraj in white linen before Samir and his men took the body to its resting place.

In the weeks that followed, she spent most of her days in the garden beside Faraj's grave. One evening, Samir interrupted her.

"The silk merchant has come to Shalabuniya."

She looked up from the ground. "Asiya manages our purchases. Why bother me with it?"

"The Sitt al-Tujjar said she has a fine length of samite meant only for your purview, an exclusive item for her most prestigious clients. She trusts no one else to handle it, except the eunuch who carries the cloth."

Fatima knew only one mistress of merchants who would insist on speaking with her. She stood and followed Samir to the indoor courtyard. The Jewess sat among her servants. Asiya inspected the textiles they proffered.

The family resemblance between the old Sitt al-Tujjar and this one, her granddaughter, struck Fatima in amazement. She exchanged greetings with the woman.

"I am told you have something to show me, Sitt al-Tujjar."

The Jewess replied, "Only you may touch it, in private."

Fatima glanced at the hooded man dressed in coarse woolen garments. He hovered beside the female merchant with a bolt of samite under his arm.

Fatima said, "Please follow me."

Samir cleared his throat. "Is that wise?" He jerked his chin toward the man.

Fatima said, "I trust the Sitt al-Tujjar and those with her."

Fatima took them to a large chamber at the end of the hallway. Shalabuniya served as a Nasrid prison, but the territory had been the seat of a governorship in the past, now vacant. The Sitt al-Tujjar and the man entered the room. Fatima closed the door behind them.

"What have you brought that is for my eyes only, Sitt al-Tujjar?"

"She brings a brother's grief at his sister's loss."

The hooded man set down his burden and revealed his reddened face, with puffy eyes and dark lips.

"Nasr!" Fatima embraced him.

Her brother kissed both her cheeks. Even with his blond hair cropped close to the skull, the hollows around his eyes and the leathery complexion that made him seem twice his thirty-four years, she would have known him anywhere by his resemblance to his mother.

"Forgive me for the deception." He kissed her fingers. "But your son has spies who cannot know I have left the safety of Wadi-Ash."

The Sitt al-Tujjar bowed and withdrew to the opposite end of the room.

Fatima hugged her brother. "Trickery is something you and I are familiar with, Nasr. You need not explain, for I believe that while our jailor is kind to us, he reports everything that happens here to Ismail. I'm so glad to see you, it has been too long."

"I wish I might have come under better circumstances."

Her arm looped with his, they walked the length of the room.

"Faraj loved you, sister."

"And I loved him. I often sit for hours at his gravesite and talk to him as when he was alive. My servant Asiya worries for me. She believes I am not grieving properly. No one knows better than I that my beloved is gone."

Nasr looked older than he should have, though she was thirty years his senior. She clutched his hand. "Can you forgive me?"

"For what, sister?"

"Setting you on the path to the Sultanate. I brought you to ruin and must accept my part in the fate that befell you."

"Fatima, my sins are my own. I followed the path without your guidance for some time. I wanted the power and prestige. I wanted to take Gharnatah from our brother Muhammad. Can you forgive me for treating him so cruelly at the end of his life? I broke my promise to you."

"Brother, let us forgive each other and start anew. My sins are your sins and your sins are mine."

"All but one."

She patted Nasr's hand. "You mean the battle of *Al-Fahs.*"

A year earlier, Ismail had fought the Castillans in a violent, bloody conflict. His army killed the regents of King

Alfonso XI of Castilla-Leon. Samir had recounted the details of the battle for Faraj one evening, while Fatima pretended not to listen. She did not miss her husband's gloating smile when Samir mentioned the death of Prince Juan, the child killer at Tarif. Faraj also seemed unsurprised to hear that Castillan mercenaries had appeared at the site in droves. He had actually chuckled. Many of the Castillan company became Ismail's prisoners at the end of the conflict. They swore the exiled Sultan of Gharnatah had bought their service.

Fatima sighed. "My son took your throne from you, Nasr. I understand your desire to avenge yourself against him. I regret all that he has done to you. You are my dear brother."

"And he is your son. Why are you here alone in this place?"

"I have my Asiya."

"You have other children who would welcome you. Your daughters...."

"Have their families. I am content to remain here, where I am closest to my husband."

"I worry for you." Nasr's chin drooped. His forehead touched hers. "I would bid you to Wadi-Ash, but my funds, well, I am not blessed with the fortune I had when I was Sultan. I can never return. One day, you must go back. You must go to the home of your heart, Fatima, to Gharnatah."

The next day, Fatima rose with the dawn. Asiya brought her the morning meal. She set the plate of flatbread and two hard-boiled eggs on a table at the foot of the bed. While Fatima ate, she tidied the chamber and removed the bedding for the wash.

Then she asked, "What shall I do with these letters Samir has left here each day?"

Fatima looked over her shoulder at the rolls of parchment. Each bore the unbroken seal of the Sultan of Gharnatah.

"Give them to me. I'll read them this morning."

# Chapter 29
# Queen of Queens

## Princess Fatima

Gharnatah, Al-Andalus: Sha'ban 720 AH (Granada, Andalusia: September AD 1320)

A chorus of applause and cheers welcomed Fatima home to Gharnatah. Its citizens lined the thoroughfares strewn with laurel boughs and palm leaves. The wind gusted through narrow cobblestone streets and scattered fragrant buds. From the balconies of Gharnatah's homes, silken gold, green and red pennons fluttered in the breeze, setting the bells affixed to them to a tinkling melody.

Fatima rode through the *Qaysariyya*, seated high atop a camel beneath a striped *hawdaj*. The beast snorted loudly, perhaps troubled by the noise and scents of the marketplace. The camel boy patted his neck. The Tuareg brothers Bazu and Amud rode at Fatima's side.

A portion of Ismail's personal guard at the forefront and rear had protected her on the journey from Shalabuniya. Now, they joined the soldiers at the base of the *Sabika* hill, who kept the mob at bay.

Asiya walked beside the camel, clutching bouquets thrown to her from the crowd. She looked up at Fatima with a wide grin, her cheeks pink.

Fatima shouted above the din. "You could have been at Shalabuniya with Samir."

Asiya laughed. "I would not miss your homecoming, my Sultana. Not even for Samir. He promised he would wait for me, even if I am gray and timeworn. I believe him. For now, I serve you, not the desires of my own heart."

At the age of twelve, Asiya possessed the beauty of her mother. Their former jailor Samir, who was old enough to be her father, had also noticed. In recent weeks, Fatima had hinted and then told Asiya outright that she was free to marry and establish her own family whenever she wished. Yet Asiya remained loyal.

The crowd surged forward even as they trekked past the gatehouse up the length of the *Sabika*. Ismail's captain, a Moor from Bilal as-Sudan, and his guards led them. They arrived at the royal precincts. A multitude of courtiers awaited Fatima's arrival.

Silks, linen and cotton fluttered in the breeze. More flowers and beribboned bells littered the marble grounds. She shook her head at the extravagant and unexpected welcome. She would have preferred to return to her birthplace without such ceremony.

The camel boy slowed the beast and lowered him to the ground. Stalwart guards lined the entrance to Gharnatah's palace. Fatima alighted and nodded to Asiya, who waited beside the camel.

Fatima proceeded alone to the cedar doors covered with brass. She recalled her childhood, when they had towered over her head. Courtiers lined the path and bowed, as she ambled past them. Incense, musk and ambergris greeted her. She passed through the gold-gilded antechamber just off the throne room. More wasted flower petals bedecked the marble walkways.

In the full glare of the midday sun, the splendor of her family's ancestral seat of power came into view. The profusion of multi-colored tiles and decorations incised within the marble walls glowed brighter than precious stones. Ismail sat on the gilded throne of Gharnatah in silken comfort. Her heart heaved. His green robe of state bore four *tiraz* bands and an ermine trim enhanced the majesty of the garment.

Other things were different, too. The puffiness beneath his dark eyes and lines scoring the olive brown skin did not exist the last time she saw him. Had he already learnt the great truth, as her father and brothers once had? All power came with a price. Yet, seven years on, she could not counsel her proud son against his mistakes.

The courtiers and ministers who milled about the room watched her nimble steps. She advanced past the square patchwork upon which no Believer would tread and prepared to make the obeisance required of those in the Sultan's presence.

Ismail stood and held up his hand. He brought all whispers and gossiping to an end by a simple gesture. Only the scattered bells littering the grounds dared shatter the quiet.

He began, "My ancestors ruled Gharnatah for almost a century before my coming. In that time, there has never been a queen mother. It is a great honor that my mother should be the first to bear the title in this court."

Ismail approached her. They stood an arms-length apart. He said, "In the name of God, bear witness and render homage to the presence of the *Umm al-Walad*, the Sultana Fatima bint Muhammad, daughter of *Al-Fakih*. She, who is like the life-giving water nourishing the earth in times of joy, and like the mighty pillar strengthening her family in times of sorrow. The magnificence of her deeds and the goodness of her heart shine brilliantly for all to see. She is the queen of queens, mother of the Sultan Ismail."

His gaze swept over the courtiers before he regarded her again. "From this day forth, the *Umm al-Walad* shall bow to no one, not even her son."

Ismail sagged to his knees before her, his hands clasped. He bent double until his forehead touched the marble floor, exposing his nape. The courtiers followed suit and abased themselves like him, before her.

She took in the spectacle, wondering what her proud father would have thought of men who knelt before a woman. He might have been amused, at best. She could not share the same sentiment.

She bent toward Ismail. "Did you enjoy that grand gesture?"

Her voice barely rose above a whisper. Ismail raised his head and winked.

"I hoped you might like it, *Ummi*."

She sneered at him. "You hoped in vain."

A scowl slashed across his features and then he stood. He tucked her hand under his arm. She forced herself to remain calm and not pull away. Even if she had tried, his grip held firm.

He said to the courtiers, "The *Umm al-Walad* and I shall retire. You may disperse."

Ismail led her outside. Sunlight glared at them. She shielded her eyes, as he led her down the length of a long courtyard. In a pool at the center, orange and blue fish darted through the clear water. Guards lined the walkway.

"What of my servant?" she asked. "Asiya is in that mob swarming the courtyard."

"My chief eunuch shall find her."

She expected to pass through gates and gardens before she reached the royal residence. Yet, he had altered her birthplace significantly. They moved westward beyond the sphere of the court to the harem, no more than thirty paces between the two. A new cistern fed water to the building ahead of them, with a red-bricked roof crowning the marble façade.

Beyond the open doorway, also unguarded, sunlight shimmered in a pool at the center of an indoor courtyard, ringed with columns. Every plant and flowering shrub in Al-Andalus crowded the space, including star thistle, sandwort, honeysuckle and chamomile intermingled with prickly junipers, hawthorn and flax-leaved daphne. Green, red and gold curtains fluttered above three cedar doors, at the north, west and south positions. The portals indicated rooms she could not see beyond the central space.

"What have you done here? No royal residence has ever so closely abutted the domain of the courtiers. You've destroyed my father's palace to build this?"

With a sweeping wave of his hand and a grin, he answered, "As you see."

"But it is dangerous! Even with guards to protect you. There has always been a clear demarcation of the sanctuary the harem offers, for the Sultan's sake."

"Careful. I might think you care about my safety. The people love me. All of Gharnatah is my domain and I walk without fear."

An arrogant presumption on his part, but Fatima ignored it. Instead, she tested his hold on her. "Release me, I pray. No one is here to see us. No further pretense is necessary."

"But you have always enjoyed pretense. I thought you might savor the delights of this moment. Here we stand a loving mother and her dutiful son."

"I prefer plain truths instead of deceit."

Ismail chuckled. "That was not always so. You deceived my father well when it suited your purpose. Who do you think I earned the talent for lies from, if not you?"

"You were always an apt pupil, perhaps too clever for your own good. One day, you must take responsibility for your faults and stop blaming me. Fortunately, I have never acquired your ease with lying to the people I loved. Each betrayal broke my heart. Such regrets as pain my heart cannot harm you, Ismail." Her nails sank into his forearm. Though he strove against it, he winced at the pressure of her hand. "You have no heart."

He released his grip and glared at her. "You dare to say such after what you've done? Not even my own mother would tell me my father was dead!"

"Did you care? You consigned him to his fate at Shalabuniya."

"I always cared!"

His countenance wavered for the space of a breath, before his lips thinned in a firm line. For a moment, he seemed like a small boy desperate for his mother's approval. She vowed he would never have it again.

Her gaze swept the courtyard, taking in the opulence of the space. "Your *Hajib* persuaded me to come here. He reminded me of what I was missing."

One week after she had read all of Ismail's correspondence, another letter had arrived. This time, the chief minister Ibn al-Mahruq personally delivered it. In his letter, Ismail promised that if she would come to him in Gharnatah, his men would exhume the body of his father and bring it to Gharnatah for re-burial.

Fatima wished nothing more than to be close to her beloved husband and father. She agreed to Ismail's terms with one goal in mind. Faraj's body went on to Gharnatah and she followed the next day.

"You mean to stay then? Now that Father's body is here?"

"Of course, but that is not the sole reason I came."

A boyish grin dismissed his downcast look. "Then, you...are you ready to resolve the past between us? Have you forgiven me at last?"

Her smile mirrored his. "Everything for you is so effortless, so swift, hmm? You believe that by the power you hold, all things are possible."

His features hardened, the lips pressed tightly together, but she would not relent. "One thing is not. I shall never lie to you, or pretend to approve of the evils you have done. You shall never have my forgiveness, not in this life or the world to come. You have wounded me to the core with your betrayal. You were beloved among all my children. My best and brightest, now my greatest disappointment."

This time he turned away. She turned from him too and closed her eyes. They did not look at each other again.

"You are a most unnatural woman, to hate your son so." His voice sounded wooden and distant. She kept her silence.

He continued, "If you have not arrived here to reconcile with me, why did you come?"

"I would like to meet my grandchildren."

"Very well. Wait here. I shall send the chief eunuch of the harem to you."

His footsteps departed, ringing against the marble tiles. When he was gone, she sagged beside a slender column.

The chief eunuch reminded her of a bumblebee, as he darted between the pillars in his haste. He offered the same humble prostration the courtiers did.

Fatima nudged him with the tip of her boot. "Please rise and tell me your name."

The simpering fool fluttered his long, golden lashes like a slave girl. "Abu'l-Qasim, o queen of queens. I am your most humble and devoted servant. For seven years, I have served the house of Nasr. It is my greatest wish to continue in your mighty favor."

"Get up, Abu'l-Qasim." When he did, she continued. "If you and I are to work together, please follow my requests."

"Anything the *Umm al-Walad* would wish...."

"Please do not use that title to address me. My son is not the legitimate ruler of Gharnatah. I have no right to the title of *Umm al-Walad*. You shall call me by my only title, Sultana. My father made me so and I shall always be thus. Further, those who are of use to me, recognize their worth, as well as my position. Mindless sycophants, bowing and scraping, shall not serve me.

"Now, if you have some wisdom in that head of yours, please use it. Arrange for my servant Asiya to meet me here. She is with the crowd in the courtyard. I need no one else. Then, take us to my quarters so we may rest. Last, arrange for me to see my grandchildren and their mothers within the hour. Can you do all this?"

"Yes, my Sultana." Abu'l-Qasim's patronizing tone vanished.

She patted his arm. "I think you and I shall work well together."

The chief eunuch attended to his task with speed and soon, Asiya stood beside Fatima, marveling at the opulent surroundings.

Fatima shook her head. "You should have seen *Al-Qal'at al-Hamra* in my father and grandfather's days."

Abu'l-Qasim led them to a room on the top floor. It spanned the width and breath of the entire harem. Here, Fatima could entertain guests, eat her meals and write her correspondences without leaving her chambers. Carved cedar furniture filled her bedroom and the bedding of damask silk fluttered in the breeze. Two of the windows faced outward to the gardens, with an open archway between them. It led to a small balcony that overlooked the willow, elm and cypress trees.

In the largest chamber, strewn with silk cushions and Damascene carpets, Abu'l-Qasim brought Ismail's children and their mothers.

He announced, "The Crown Prince of Gharnatah, Muhammad ibn Ismail and his mother, the Sultana Arub."

A pale, black-haired woman shuffled forward, her dainty feet in step behind the boy she followed. Both of them bowed, though the woman seemed more deferential than her son did. Then she coughed behind her hands.

She looked at Fatima sheepishly and murmured, "I greet you in the name of God."

Fatima nodded to her and stared at the sinewy boy who watched her beneath slits for eyes. Then he frowned. Asiya's gasp whistled through her teeth.

Fatima leaned forward. "Why do you make that face, boy? Do you know who I am?"

"*Ummi* said you are my grandmother. Why haven't I ever seen you before?"

Such an imperious tone for a child who could not be more than five years old. Fatima did not have to guess which parent he took after.

She replied. "I lived outside the capital for many years with your father's father."

"But now you shall stay here?"

When she nodded, the heir pronounced. "That is good. I wish to know my grandmother."

His mother tugged his sleeve and the glare reserved for Fatima swung to his pale-faced mother. Still, he moved aside and allowed another dark-haired boy and three girls forward.

"Prince Ismail ibn Ismail, and his sisters, the Sultanas Moraima, Zaynab and Saliha, also the children of Sultana Arub." Abu'l-Qasim said. The boy was perhaps one year younger than the Crown Prince was and much more pleasant. Each of his sisters seemed older than him.

Then a silk-clad, blonde-haired woman with dimpled cheeks approached, leading three jovial children who could not restrain their rambunctious tussling long enough to bow. Their mother chided them and looked at Fatima furtively before she snapped, "I said, be quiet!"

Asiya chuckled behind her hands. The blonde's dimples heightened her rounded face.

Abu'l-Qasim said, "The Sultana Jamila and her children, Prince Faraj ibn Ismail and his sisters, the Sultanas Hamda and Muna."

Ismail's second wife hustled her charges beside Sultana Arub and her family. She still chided them beneath her breath. Fatima viewed her with some sympathy, recalling how her daughter Mumina had been a tyrant as a child. Though Sultana Jamila's son was his grandfather's namesake, his mother's golden curls and dimples did not mark him as a Nasrid child. Fatima smiled as she remembered how she once thought the same of her brother Nasr.

A brown-haired woman approached clutching blue-black prayer beads. Her dark-skinned boy trailed in her wake. His large eyes and dark straight hair evoked lingering Fatima's memories. She clutched her chest, awed by the sight of him. A likeness of her husband stood before her again, reborn in the image of his grandson. The boy and his mother bowed low.

"The Sultana Safa and her son, Prince Yusuf ibn Ismail," Abu'l-Qasim said.

Asiya sighed and whispered. "He looks like the master. Do you see it, my Sultana?"

Fatima nodded and with some difficulty, focused her attention on the last arrivals, the two granddaughters she had not seen in several years. The Sultanas Leila and Fatimah bowed as prettily as their stepmothers did. Leila smiled shyly at her grandmother. When she straightened, Leila's bare feet peeked beneath her rode. Fatima realized with a pang that her namesake, the aunt she had never known, once did the same as a child.

Fatima reviewed the tender faces before her. Traces of her beloved father, her husband and even herself dwelled in her grandchildren's features. Her arms opened wide and she welcomed them. Leila and Yusuf approached her first, then all the children followed suit. Crown Prince Muhammad jostled his brothers and sisters, who did not give way to him because of his position. Fatima laughed at their antics and gathered them closed. She whispered a blessing upon each of the children's heads.

Asiya said, "The Sultana Fatima has brought you many presents, children, in her writing room."

She shepherded them next door. Their mothers laughed as the children scrambled for presents in the center of the chamber. They tussled with each other over dolls, board games, toy horses and balls. Only Leila, the oldest among them, showed any interest in the astrolabe. Fatima smiled at her, thinking that perhaps she would share the same penchant as Nasr for astronomy.

Little Yusuf, who had hesitated at the fringe of the group, also looked at the astrolabe with curiosity in his expression, until he settled on another choice.

He fingered the cover of the calligrapher's box, inlaid with tortoiseshell and ivory, mother-of-pearl and luminous gold leaf at the four sides. Fatima observed his fascination with a smile.

Wide-eyed, he turned to her. "May I have this?"

Yusuf could not have been more than two, but he spoke in a clear and pleasant voice that seemed to be that of an older child.

"Of course you may. Still, I wonder if you would not prefer something else. The last toy horse, perhaps." She gestured toward the spot where it remained unclaimed.

Yusuf shook his head. "I like this one. Thank you, Grandmother."

He traced the text inscribed upon the cover. "What does it say?"

Fatima recited the line from memory. "And God is most bountiful. He taught with the quill and ink. He taught His people that which they did not know." She paused and nodded to him. "It is a verse from *Al-Qur'an*. Have you heard of it in the princes' school?"

"There is no princes' school here, most honored Sultana," Sultana Safa said. "The children study with the imam of Gharnatah at the end of every week. Yusuf has not started the lessons."

Fatima frowned. "I began reading *Al-Qur'an* at his age. It was my first book. Before my childhood, there were always royal tutors who educated the sovereign's children. My son has not re-instituted this practice?"

In turn, the Sultanas avoided her eyes. Even the serene and pious Safa stared at the cedar floor.

Sultana Arub coughed, a deep rattling sound in her chest.

Fatima asked, "Are you ill?"

Sultana Arub shook her head, but continued coughing. Fatima sent Asiya for a pitcher of water.

Sultana Arub drank a cupful. "The *Umm al-Walad* is most kind, as her son says."

Fatima shook her head. "Is that what Ismail says? If he ever spoke of me in truth, with reference to my kindness, he should also have known I would never accept the new title. I have lived most of my life as a Sultana. I shall die as one. It does not please me that your children's full education suffers neglect. Studying *Al-Qur'an* is not enough. When I was a child, I learned the sciences and arts. Can any of my grandchildren write?"

Their mothers' silent stares answered her. She wondered if they were also ignorant of such an education.

She said, "Very well. I shall teach my grandchildren."

Sultana Safa gave her a dazed look. "What if the Sultan should wish otherwise?"

Fatima rolled her eyes heavenward. "His wishes are not my concern. These are my grandchildren. They shall be a credit to the name of my learned father, Muhammad *Al-Fakih.*"

# Chapter 30
# The Family

## Princess Fatima

Gharnatah, Al-Andalus: Rajab 725 AH (Granada, Andalusia: July AD 1325)

Beneath a sapphire sky, Fatima and her son's remaining wives ate the mid-morning meal of eggs and flatbread. Against Sultana Safa's protests, her counterpart Jamila had dismissed the servants. While Safa twisted blue-black mourning beads between her nimble fingers, Jamila whistled while she flavored steaming tisane with cardamom.

Fatima commented, "You're in excellent spirits today."

Jamila stopped whistling. Her sea-green eyes darted to Safa's pallid face before her cheeks flushed pink. Safa's lips widened in a smirk.

Jamila said, "Forgive me, I did not mean to offend."

"No, my daughter, you mistake me." Fatima reached for her hand. "We need smiles and great cheer in these miserable times. It does my heart good to see your dimples again."

Safa's breath escaped in a loud gasp. Her furtive gaze darted away and she sipped the tisane without comment.

Fatima did not have to guess how she felt about Jamila's cheerful nature, but Jamila's gaiety suited the morning better than dour expressions. Today was the first anniversary of the death of Sultana Arub, mother of Crown Prince Muhammad.

When Jamila offered Fatima the cup of brew, she asked, "Where are my grandchildren? I intend to resume our lessons after the midday prayer."

Jamila answered, "Abu'l-Qasim has not yet returned with the little Sultanas from the *Qaysariyya*. Leila is so excited at the prospects of choosing her own colors for the wedding. I doubt the chief eunuch can tear her away from the silk market."

Safa commented, "She should be well-pleased. It is a good match between her and the Hudayr clan in Qirbilyan. Leila's mother descended from that clan. It is just that the Hudayr should receive a Nasrid daughter."

Jamila glared at her counterpart before she cleared her throat. "I remember my own wedding. I was so frightened when I married and I was only a year older than Leila. I think she is a little sad, for though she is the eldest, her devotion to her brothers and sisters knows no bounds."

Soon, the youngest Sultanas returned to the harem, with Abu'l-Qasim leading them. The chief eunuch bowed and presented the textiles he had purchased from the *Qaysariyya*. When Fatima promised she would sew the *tiraz* bands for her granddaughter's *khil'a*, Leila preened with pride.

She asked, "Can I help you with the sewing, Grandmother? When can we get started?"

Fatima replied, "If you wish it, we may begin in a month's time, though the wedding is more than six months away. There is no need for haste, my lamb. *Tiraz* bands do not require the preparation your ceremonial robe shall entail."

Leila's eyes shone with pleasure. "I can't wait to marry! I shall miss everyone, but I long to have a husband of my own."

"Let me tell you a little of husbands, granddaughter. In His wisdom, God fashioned men and women to be a comfort for each other." Fatima paused. All nine of her granddaughters stared in rapt attention, even the last two who were born in the harem, Safa's three-year-old twins Tarub and Khalida. "But as my grandfather's sister Faridah taught me: Men plan and women endure."

Leila sat at Fatima's feet. "What does that mean, Grandmother?"

"The men in our lives wield great power, which pains the women they love. We must be strong for those whom we love, especially our men."

Leila blushed as she considered the explanation. Safa tugged at her lower lip with her teeth. Jamila's ever-present smile faded.

Fatima took her eldest granddaughter's hand in her own. "Before I married, my mother spoke words I have never forgotten. Words I wish you all to remember. Teach them to your own daughters someday." Her steady gaze swept the room. She held her granddaughters entranced. "Your mind has great worth, more than beauty. Your husband may rule your body and heart, but your mind is and always must be yours, where none but you rule."

She raised Leila's fingers to her lips. "Live by these words, my dearest, and may you have a long and happy union."

An hour before *Salat al-Zuhr*, the royal women readied for the *hammam*. Members of the harem had strictly scheduled times at which to attend their daily baths. The chief superintendent of the bathhouse observed the time.

He awaited Fatima and her son's wives at the white marble entrance of the bath, beneath a wooden ceiling with upturned eaves. From the center of the room, the swirling lantern cast silvery light over the ceramic tiles and the marble fountain, which spilled water into a circular basin.

At the entrance, Fatima pressed a hand to her chest, as she always did when she attended the palace baths. She could not forget the sight of her brother Muhammad and his violence in this place.

Jamila cupped her elbow. "Are you unwell, my Sultana?"

Fatima smiled at her. "No, no. Memories, that is all."

Jamila nodded. "The ugly ones fade with time."

The bath superintendent greeted them. His usual pleasant expression faded until he stood reddened in the face.

"My Sultanas, I pray, forgive me." He stammered and shook so badly, Fatima could not fathom what might have disturbed him. Then she looked past him, as did the other two Sultanas.

Beneath one of two tiled niches carved into the stucco wall, a black-haired beauty reclined. Bath attendants rubbed her hair with silken cloths. Moisture condensed on her alabaster flesh, rendering it an ethereal glow in the silver light. Her pale skin complemented black brows and lashes. She sighed languidly and arched her back for the masseur. Resilient muscle glowed beneath the flesh.

Safa muttered, "She does not dare intrude upon our pleasure!"

"Who is she?" Fatima asked.

"Our husband's new whore. A captive taken at Martus a few weeks ago."

Two years before, when the last treaty with the Christians ended, Ismail attacked strongholds along the Castillan border with Gharnatah. He concentrated on towns his forbearers had once claimed, including Martus.

Jamila frowned at Safa. "Your bitterness shall not bring our husband to your bed again. He has forsaken us for this girl, his Jumaana."

A fitting name, for the *jarya* possessed the luminosity of silver pearls.

Jamila continued, "She has been troublesome since her arrival. The *Shaykh al-Ghuzat* Uthman claimed her first, as did another. Until our husband saw her and desired her, too."

Fatima remembered Uthman well. After Ismail's ascension, he had rewarded the treacherous snake with one of the highest posts in the land, command of the Marinid and Berber Volunteers of the Faith.

She asked, "Who was the other rival for the slave?"

Jamila sniffed. "The young prince of Al-Jazirah al-Khadra, the eldest son of the governor."

Fatima cupped her mouth for a moment. "He is my grandson, the eldest child of my firstborn daughter. His father and Ismail were best friends when they were children. Do you mean my grandson quarreled with his uncle Ismail and the *Shaykh al-Ghuzat* Uthman over this woman, too?"

When Jamila nodded, Fatima studied the Ismail's new favorite. Her luminous blue gaze met Fatima's own between the slender marble columns.

Fatima entered the *hammam*. "Leave at once. The baths are reserved for the king's family now."

She spoke in the Castillan language. A flash of fury in the girl's eyes told her she had chosen well.

The girl, who could not have been more than fifteen, shoved her bath attendants aside and stood. With her hands on her generous hips, she tossed her ink-black hair. "Who are you to speak to me so?"

"If you possessed any wisdom in that head of yours, you would not question me."

"I am the favorite of the king, old woman."

"And I am his mother, the daughter and sister of kings."

Jamila touched Fatima's arm. "What does she say in such a haughty tone?"

Fatima advanced on the girl until they stood less than an arms-length apart. The concubine crossed her arms over her small, firm breasts. Her heated gaze radiated a challenge.

"You're so beautiful, hmm? You cannot compare to the favorite Nur al-Sabah, beloved of my father. She won the heart of a king. Her son became king in his father's stead. Do you think you shall be like her?"

The slave smirked. "I shall give my lord a son and then you shall see."

"And when the king is dead?" Fatima waved a hand to the Sultanas, who glowered at the girl. "The mothers of royal sons stand just there, but a few paces from you. Do you think either of them would allow the child of a slave to usurp the throne? Do you think I would set your spawn above my royal grandsons?"

Safa and Jamila's cold stares supported Fatima's words. The slave gathered her garments and fled.

Jamila came to Fatima. "What did you say to make her leave?"

"I reminded her that the true power of a Sultan's harem lies in his Sultanas."

After the bath, Fatima hurried through the avenue of cypress and juniper trees. At its center, Ismail reclined on golden cushions under a central pavilion. His lean fingers flicked the pert nipples of the slave whom he dallied with, before he pulled her against him. His hand slipped from her waist beneath the silken band of her trousers. Her ink-black hair spilled around his shoulders as she lowered her head.

Fatima nudged Ismail's heel with the tip of her kidskin slipper. He yelped in sudden fright and glared at her. Fatima's gaze fell on the slave, Jumaana. "Leave us. Now."

For the second time that day, the concubine scrambled off in disarray.

Ismail adjusted the front of his trousers. "I wish you would not send my slaves away!"

Fatima snapped at him, "I wish you would not cavort in the gardens where I played as a child!"

"What could be so important for you to interrupt my afternoon's pleasure?"

"You can see the *jarya* tonight or at any other time. I wish to speak of Yusuf, but I shall not do so until you're properly attired."

She turned her back on him. The rustle of silk and grumbled mutterings informed her that he dressed.

He tapped her shoulder. "I've given you everything you've required for Yusuf's education. What do you want now?"

She turned to him, satisfied with his respectable appearance. "The boy shows remarkable talents, especially in his interests in architecture. I believe he would benefit from a visit to the repair work on our summer palace, *Al-Janat al-Arif*. Your workers expect to be finished tomorrow. Yusuf must see them today. I would have your permission to tour the site with him."

Ismail cupped his forehead. "Bah! This is why you interrupted an afternoon's pleasure? A boy's whim! He would only be in the way, as would you."

She sneered at him. "Just because you spend your days idle, with your hands down the *sarawil* of your concubines, does not mean I want the same for my grandson! If you would leave a strong Sultanate to the Crown Prince, he must have learned men surrounding him within his own family."

"That is all you care about, the pride of this family!"

"It is the Sultan's duty as well." She tossed her head. "You have forgotten it. All because of this stupid slave, Jumaana."

"She has been here for two weeks! How can she have offended you already?"

"She offends your wives."

Ismail raked his hands through his dark hair, graying at the temples. "They are too easily affronted. I am Sultan of Gharnatah. If I wish to bed a thousand women, neither you nor my wives have any say in the matter."

"You care nothing for their feelings. You also risked the friendship you've enjoyed with your sister Leila's husband because of her."

"My friendship with my cousin remains unchanged. His son shall accept my decision. He shall learn of this, after we meet today. He is coming to Gharnatah, with his brothers, including young Ali. My nephew shall learn the slave is mine. I shall not give her up, no matter the cost."

"You are arrogant! It is your greatest shortcoming."

"And yours is to think you can bind everyone to your will with just a word. You may be the *Umm al-Walad*, but you shall never rule me again!"

She turned away, lest he glimpse how his careless words wounded her.

His mirthless snigger followed. "The predictable heart that never forgives. Won't you even pretend to it?"

"I have oft told you, my son, I shall never lie to you."

When he gasped, Fatima raced from the garden. She had broken her promise made years ago, never to call him her son again.

Before the evening meal, Fatima slumbered. When she awoke fitfully, Asiya hovered at her side. "You cried out in your sleep. I was frightened."

"I had a strange dream of my brother Muhammad. I had fallen and he was laughing at me...."

"Why should he come to you now?"

Heavy pounding sounded at her chamber door. A wavering voice cried, "Open in the name of the Sultan!"

Asiya put down the food tray and went to the door, while Fatima stood. Asiya's scream echoed. Fearful, Fatima gripped the stucco wall.

Ibn al-Mahruq burst into the room. The Sultan's bodyguards carried a bloodstained, prone form to her bed. Ismail, stabbed through the chest.

Fatima closed her eyes as if she could blot out the horrific sight forever. Her firstborn son's life and blood drained away in her bedclothes.

Ibn al-Mahruq bowed at her side. "My Sultana, your son and his nephews, Ali, Faraj, and Muhammad, sons of the *Raïs* of al-Jazirah al-Khadra, they have quarreled with Sultan this evening about a slave girl. The Sultan's nephews attacked him with daggers. I've called for the surgeon to bind the wounds."

Crimson stains discolored everything, including the bedding and carpets. Ismail's silken robe rent at the shoulders and torso. Wounds inflicted by his sister Leila's children.

The minister drew his bloodied sword. "The *Shaykh al-Ghuzat* had them trapped in the corridor. They shall die for this treason, my Sultana. Your son shall have justice!"

After he left, Fatima slumped on to the floor.

Asiya clutched her hand. "How can I help you?"

Fatima could not answer. Her grandsons had tried to kill their uncle. Ibn al-Mahruq said they had quarreled about the slave girl Jumaana. Fatima's family destroyed by greed and lust. Once more, the curse that had ruined fathers and sons, and turned brother against brother, had returned. Tonight, she would weep for her son and Leila's sons.

Abu'l-Qasim entered the chamber. His shriek startled her to full awareness. "Oh my Sultana, oh what has happened here?"

"Tell the Sultanas, tell the children to come to the Sultana's reception room," Asiya said to him.

"No, no, they must not see this." Abu'l-Qasim shook his head wildly.

"Find the *Hajib,* too! If the Sultan should die before he declares Crown Prince Muhammad...."

Asiya's warning penetrated Abu'l-Qasim's haze of grief. He dashed from the room.

Fatima stood and sought Ismail's right hand. Bloodied fingers dangled from the bed. His forearm disappeared beneath the ruined robe, connected to the shoulder where the silken material had torn away. A deep gouge exposed pink flesh beneath the skin, down to the bone. Thick red blotches trickled from the mouth and nose. His eyes were wide, fixed on Fatima's own.

"*Ummi,* I am dying."

His strangled whisper tore icy shards through her heart. "No, you shall not die."

He chuckled and coughed up blood. "You promised you would never lie to me."

Soft sobs followed by a deep wailing echoed from the next room.

When the surgeon arrived, he pried Fatima's fingers from Ismail's grasp, but her son would not release his grip until Abu'l-Qasim returned and restrained him.

Asiya stood at Fatima's side while the surgeon worked. Resignation etched in the lines of his leathery complexion, as he nodded to them.

"I can do nothing for the master, my Sultana. The wound at his right shoulder is particularly troublesome. I fear the blade has pierced his heart. I cannot staunch the bleeding."

"Who has done this to my father?" Crown Prince Muhammad bellowed from the next room. His hot fury chilled Fatima, for in his merciless tone she heard the voice of his predecessor and namesake, her brother. When the *Hajib* responded and tried calming him, Fatima summoned the minister.

The chief minister arrived and bowed beside his master.

Ismail whispered, "Gharnatah for my eldest son and heir, the Crown Prince Muhammad. Protect him."

The *Hajib* bowed again and withdrew.

Ismail reached for Fatima again. "*Ummi*?"

She came to him and took his hand in hers. "What would you have of me?"

"You promised never to lie to me. I ask you to break that vow. Lie to me for the last time."

She swallowed a sob and clambered onto the bed. She drew up her knees beneath her and held his head upon her lap. She swept back his dark hair. Her fingertips traced the familiar planes and angles of his features.

"It is warm and we are far from this place, riding along the shores of Malaka. Just the two of us as we used to do. The seabirds soar over our heads. Their cries echo through the wisps of clouds. Can you feel the wind in your hair, the golden glow of the sun on your back?"

"I...can see it, I see the light...."

His final, whispered breath escaped in a croaking sound, but she held him still. "The splendor of a new day rises to greet you. Its beauties are yours to behold. The sapphire skies, the waters of the White Sea, the golden sands, all of it as you remember. You are home again, my son."

She looked down at his sightless eyes. Her distorted image reflected in them. She kissed his cool brow and whispered, "It was not a lie, my Ismail. It was not a lie."

Someone touched her shoulder. "My Sultana, he is gone."

She shrugged off Abu'l-Qasim's hand, though he said, "Let his servants tend to him."

"No! They shall not touch him."

"But he…the Sultan is dead."

"Do you think I need you to tell me that? Leave us."

"But my Sultana, please."

"Get out!"

She held Ismail close, as if she could still protect him from the cruelties and pain the world offered. The chief eunuch ushered everyone from the room. They were alone.

Fatima rose from the bloodstained bed. Ismail's head lolled on the sheets. She fetched a basin of water and a towel. She blotted the crimson stains around his mouth and nose. She removed his ragged garments. The full extent of the cruelty done to him did not frighten her. She never recoiled from it, not even when the reddened towel smeared the stains, rather than cleansed him.

Memories cascaded through her mind with each touch against his cooling skin. The first fluttering of his life within her. His birth. His smile and first steps, all hers to treasure. The hours spent with him at the shores of Malaka. His skill with their family's horses, his father's pride in his leadership. Her admiration of his wisdom and intuitiveness. Then came the brutal betrayal, her heartbreak and their never-ending quarrels, all at an end now.

She completed her task, just as glimmers of moonlight flooded the chamber. Lastly, she arranged her son's limbs and turned his head to the *Qiblah*.

She kissed his brow one last time. "Go to them. They are waiting for you, your blessed father and mine. I pray you shall find the forgiveness of God, my son."

She opened the doors of the bedchamber with a creak. Ibn al-Mahruq knelt in front of her. She touched the coarse graying hair on his head. The minister bowed and wept in silence.

She asked, "Where is my family?"

"They are still in the *Umm al-Walad*'s receiving room."

Ibn al-Mahruq followed her. Ismail's widows had gathered their children around them. Fatima's granddaughters sobbed piteously, most of all Leila.

When Fatima entered, Yusuf looked up. His red-rimmed eyes glowed despite the dim lighting. With a wave, Fatima silently bade him to remain with his mother Safa. She sought the Crown Prince.

Muhammad stood apart from the group with Abu'l-Qasim at his side, his back to the wall. When Fatima advanced on him, his loud gasp filled the room.

She bowed low and grasped the hem of his robe between her fingers, before she brought it to her lips. "Long live the Sultan."

Her words echoed in a repeated murmur throughout the chamber. The fluttering of silk told her that everyone followed her example.

"Grandmother? What do I do? I don't know what to do."

Muhammad's heated whisper stirred her from the floor. "Go to your *Hajib* and place your hand on his head. Command him to rise."

Muhammad did as she said, then looked at her, "Was that right?"

"Now command your family to do the same."

"You may stand now." Muhammad closed his little fists at his sides.

Ibn al-Mahruq said, "We must proclaim the Sultan's death and the ascension of Abu Abdallah Muhammad the fourth."

"What about my father's murderers?" Muhammad asked. He looked at Ibn al-Mahruq expectantly.

The minister glanced at Fatima. "They are dead. All three of them. Uthman saw to it."

Ibn al-Mahruq's skin flushed as he answered, but Fatima did not avoid his gaze. Perhaps, it was for the best that her daughter had not lived to see this day. Whom would she have grieved for most, a murdered brother or her slaughtered sons?

Two weeks after Ismail's death, the Sultan and the *Shaykh al-Ghuzat* Uthman appeared at the entrance to the harem before sunset. Abu'l-Qasim walked with Fatima. She greeted the *Shaykh al-Ghuzat* and her grandson, before she reminded Muhammad of his calligraphy lessons.

"But Grandmother, I have scribes and ministers who can write my correspondence."

"Would you shame your forbearers? All of them wrote their own letters of state."

"But I wanted to ride in the hills this evening with Uthman and my guard." Muhammad stubbed the dirt with his red leather boots.

Fatima nodded to Uthman. "Surely the *Shaykh al-Ghuzat* has other matters of concern that occupy him."

He said, "I did wish to speak to the *Umm al-Walad* about something, if you remember, my Sultan."

Muhammad nodded. "Grandmother, I think Uthman should have a special reward for his service to us and my father. He has asked after the slave girl Jumaana from Martus."

Fatima met Abu'l-Qasim's gaze in a sidelong glance. She clasped her hands together. "I regret to inform the *Shaykh al-Ghuzat* and my Sultan, the slave Jumaana is dead."

At Uthman's incredulous look, she continued, "She drank bitter poison."

Uthman exclaimed, "She killed herself!"

Abu'l-Qasim said, "She was so sad after Sultan Ismail died, God preserve his memory."

Fatima added, "It is unfortunate, but the woman was responsible for my son's death. Without the rivalry for her, my son might still be alive."

Muhammad protested. "But Uthman rid me of Father's murderers!"

Fatima raised her eyebrows. "Did he?"

Her gaze lingered on the pale face of the *Shaykh al-Ghuzat.* She bent with some effort and raised her grandson's robe to her lips before she glanced at Uthman again.

"Then you shall have to find him another gift, my Sultan, or he shall have to prove his worth once more. I pray you may always rely on those who surround you for protection."

Abu'l-Qasim followed her, as she left the harem.

In the evenings, Fatima lingered beside the graves of the Sultans of Gharnatah. Her grandfather, father and brothers rested for eternity beneath the evergreen myrtles and cypresses. Nasr had succumbed three years before. At Fatima's behest, he had his final resting place among his ancestors, too. Now, Fatima's son had his grave beside his grandfather's own.

Abu'l-Qasim said, "You were right about the *Shaykh al-Ghuzat*'s desire for the girl. If you suspect his involvement in the murder of your son, why do you remain silent?"

Fatima hushed him. "I grow weary of the bloodshed. Leave me. I shall visit with my family."

The chief eunuch bowed and turned on his heels.

She roamed the hillside, leaving flowers at each gravesite. Moonlight gleamed through the trees before she finished. At last, she knelt between the graves of her father and her son.

She prayed, "Merciful God, is my father's legacy spent? Send me a sign of your mercy, some small measure of hope for the future. Please."

"Grandmother?"

Yusuf's plaintive voice drew her. His wide eyes filled with tears, illuminated by the torch he carried. He looked past her to his father's burial mound, covered in star thistle, chamomile and honeysuckle.

"I miss Father. You must miss him, too."

She nodded. "The call for *Salat al-Isha* sounded hours ago. Sultana Safa must have sent you and your sisters to bed before then. What are you doing here?"

"I had a strange dream, Grandmother."

She took the torch from Yusuf and led him away toward the palace. "Tell me of your dream."

"I became Sultan. A man lifted me high and crowned me. I don't want to rule. If I become Sultan, it must mean Muhammad shall die and I don't want my brother to die!"

Did Yusuf's dream foretell another bitter loss for their family? Could Fatima bear the pain again?

Her hand alighted on Yusuf's dark hair. "Tell no one of this dream. People can be very frightened of things they do not understand. Let's return you to your bed."

Yusuf asked, "You'll stay with me, Grandmother?"

She cupped his soft cheek. His words, so similar to the last her beloved Faraj had spoken, tugged at her heart. She answered him, as she had done with her dear husband.

"Don't you know? I'll never leave your side."

THE END

# Author's Note

I wrote *Sultana's Legacy* and its prequel, *Sultana,* after many years of research into the lives of the last dynasty of rulers who held the southern half of Spain, the Moorish family of Banu'l-Ahmar, alternatively known as the Nasrids in a later period.

## The Moors

The Moors were Islamic people of Arabian and Negro descent, who invaded the Iberian Peninsula, which encompasses modern-day Portugal and Spain, beginning in the Christian eighth century. They called the conquered land *Al-jazirat Al-Andalus,* but in later years, the term referred only to the south of Spain and became Andalusia in modern times.

The Moors penetrated the interior and brought three-fifths of the peninsula under their control. They gave their unique culture, rich language, and the religion of Islam to a land that welcomed them at first, for the valuable riches and social order they brought. Where superstition and ignorance once pervaded all elements of life, the Moors brought intellectual pursuit and reasoning. Their blood mingled with that of the Visigoths and produced a mixed race of individuals.

By Islamic law, Muslim men could marry or have relations with non-Muslim women. Periods of zealous anti-Christian and anti-Jewish views occurred and resulted in forced conversion, but mostly, Christians and Jews enjoyed religious tolerance under Moorish rule. Some families chose to convert willingly, for all the requisite benefits including the avoidance of certain taxes and the gains of political and social advancement, while others practiced their former religion in secret.

Spurred on by religious fanaticism, bigotry, and jealousy of the Moorish achievements, the people of the northern half of the peninsula began the *Reconquista*, a determined struggle against the Moors. Beginning in the Christian tenth century, the rebellion spread slowly southward, until only one Moorish kingdom remained, Granada, nestled within the Sierra Nevada Mountains. A complicated line of descent links each ruler and my protagonists, the Sultana Fatima and her prince, Abu Said Faraj ibn Ismail.

## Sultan Muhammad II

The second Nasrid Sultan, Muhammad II was born in the Arjuno region shortly after his father declared his suzerainty in 634 AH or AD 1237. His people called him *Al-Fakih*, "the jurist" or "Lawgiver" for his swift justice. During his reign, he added to his father's work at the Alhambra. His first cousin, Abu Said Faraj ibn Ismail, became a trusted and loyal advisor. Abu Said Faraj also married the Sultana Fatima, the daughter of Muhammad II (664 AH or AD 1265).

Sultan Muhammad II had at least three sons, Faraj, Abu Abdallah Muhammad and Abu'l Juyush Nasr. He married a princess of the Marinids dynasty to ensure peace with his erstwhile allies. He also created the *Diwan al-Insha*, his chancery, an institution that lasted almost until the end of the Sultanate. It produced some of the most brilliant thinkers in Moorish Spain's history.

Sultan Muhammad II died 2 Sha`ban 701 AH or April 8, AD 1302, after his son, Abu Abdallah Muhammad allegedly ordered Muhammad II poisoned, on the eve of a new campaign against the Christian kingdom of Castile. His doctor attributed his death to a poisoned cake that his heir sent to his house. Sultan Muhammad II was approximately 68 years old. The account of his death in the narrative is from period sources.

## Sultan Muhammad III

The third Nasrid Sultan, Muhammad III was born in 655 AH or AD 1256. During the first few weeks of his reign, Sultan Muhammad III negotiated peace treaties with the kingdoms of Castile and Aragon. The first treaty required the Nasrids to acknowledge their state as a vassal of Castile. Sultan Muhammad III was a detested figure and many of his own supporters eventually began to resent him. His erratically disturbing nature soon destroyed peace with Castile and Aragon.

Sultan Muhammad III inherited the refined tastes and upbringing, shared with his sister Sultana Fatima and their brother Sultan Abu'l-Juyush Nasr I. He combined his interests in learning and art with a sarcastic and cruel streak that made him unpopular. The references to his insults of his court poet at his own coronation and his cruelty to the prisoners in the Alhambra's Alcazaba are from period sources.

While he built up portions of the Alhambra, including the Palacio del Partal by day, he devoted his nights to reading and studying. However, his sadistic nature overwhelmed his heritage of learning. The feud with the Marinids that had begun during the reign of his father Muhammad II plagued Sultan Muhammad III. A revolt occurred on 1 Shawwal 708 AH or March 14, AD 1309 and Sultan Muhammad III went into exile, forced from his throne to the city of Almunecar. He died in 709 AH or AD 1310, after an abortive attempt to restore him to power failed. He drowned in a pool. Sultan Muhammad III was approximately 54 years old at the time of death. No record survives of his possible children. Historians accuse his successor Abu'l-Juyush Nasr I, of ordering the death of Sultan Muhammad III.

## Sultan Abu'l-Juyush Nasr I

Abu'l-Juyush Nasr who reigned as Nasr I, the fourth Nasrid Sultan, was the younger brother of Muhammad III. Sultan Abu'l-Juyush Nasr I was born 24 Ramadan 686 AH or November 2, AD 1287, the child of a union between Muhammad II and a Christian concubine. Nasr I continued the policy begun by his grandfather Muhammad I and paid tribute to the kingdom of Castile. Yet, during his reign, the Nasrids temporarily lost control of Algeciras and Ronda to the Banu Marin and Gibraltar to the Castilians.

For his losses and troubles, the aristocracy did not support Nasr. They believed he was a secret Christian, raised in his mother's faith. He preferred the clothing styles of Christians. He also employed a minister, Ibn al-Hajj, as his vizier whom his detractors believed was a secret Christian, too. Around a year after a coronation, Nasr's cousin and brother in-law Abu Said Faraj, the governor of Malaga, rebelled against him. In 711 AH or AD 1311, the two finally signed a truce. Abu Said Faraj later disgraced himself in a treasonous alliance with the Banu Marin, an act that resulted in his loss of control over Malaga, which his son, Abu l-Walid Isma'il claimed. Abu l-Walid Ismail deposed Sultan Abu'l-Juyush Nasr I a year later.

Nasr withdrew to Guadix where he later supported the army of Castile against his nephew Ismail at the Battle of la Vega on 7 Jumada al-Ula 719 AH June 26, AD 1319. Nasr suffered a stroke and died 6 Dhu al-Qa`da 722 AH or November 16, AD 1322. The Sultan was 36 years old. His nephew, Ismail, removed his body to Granada and re-interred him near the site of his grandfather, Sultan Muhammad I's burial on the Sabika hill. The historical record provides no evidence that Nasr had sons or that any such offspring survived him. With the death of Nasr, the direct male line of the Nasrid Dynasty ended and shifted to the descendants of the Sultana Fatima.

## *Sultan Abu'l-Walid Ismail I*

Abu'l-Walid Ismail, son of the Sultana Fatima and nephew of both Sultans Muhammad III and Abu'l-Juyush Nasr I, reigned as the fifth Nasrid Sultan. He was born in 677 AH or AD 1279. On his father's side, he was a cousin of Sultan Muhammad II and second cousin of Sultans Muhammad III and Abu'l-Juyush Nasr I, as well as his own mother Sultana Fatima. On his mother's side, he was also a grandson of Muhammad II, cousin to his own father, Abu Said Faraj, and nephew of both Sultans Muhammad III and Abu'l-Juyush Nasr I.

When Ismail rebelled against Nasr, the citizens of Granada opened the main gate of the city, now the Puerta de Elvira to him. He besieged Nasr until his surrender on 21 Shawwal 713 AH or February 8, AD 1314. In the Battle of la Vega on 7 Jumada al-Ula 719 AH or June 26, AD 1319, Sultan Ismail I defeated King Alfonso XI of Castile. His troops killed the regents, Alfonso's uncle Prince Juan (the murderer of Doñ Alonso Perez de Guzman's son at Tarifa) and the King's cousin, Don Pedro. He also raided along the border of Castile and Granada, taking slaves.

He added significantly to the Alhambra complex and the palace of Generalife. After the Battle of la Vega, he built the Alcazar Genil, which functioned as a residence for the elderly women of the Sultan's household. He also established the royal pantheon around the burial site of his grandfather, Muhammad II, perhaps to establish the legitimacy of his reign, by his descent through the Sultana Fatima.

Sultan Ismail I fathered at least four sons, Abu Abdallah Muhammad, Ismail, Faraj and Abdul Hajjaj Yusuf. Ismail died on 24 Rajab 725 AH or July 6, AD 1325, a victim of assassination. Ali, Faraj and Muhammad, the three sons of his first cousin, also named Ismail (only son of the Sultan's paternal uncle Muhammad) stabbed him to death over a slave girl taken during a raid on Martos. Servants carried the dying Ismail to his mother Fatima's chambers. The Sultan perished from his wounds, at 48 years old. His ministers ordered the perpetrators of the vicious attack executed. When

Sultan Ismail I died, his eldest son Muhammad who was born in 715 AH or AD 1316 reigned as Muhammad IV and succeeded his father as the sixth Nasrid Sultan.

## *Prince Abu Said Faraj & Princess Fatima bint Muhammad*

When Prince Abu Said Faraj ibn Ismail and Princess Fatima bint Muhammad married in 664 AH or AD 1265, it destabilized the kingdom of Granada and altered the perceived destiny of its rulers. Every Sultan from their son Sultan Ismail traced their descent through Fatima and Faraj, until the end of the Nasrid Dynasty. On his father's side, Faraj was a first cousin and son-in-law of Sultan Muhammad II, cousin and brother in-law of the Sultans Muhammad III and Abu'l-Juyush Nasr and cousin to his own wife, Fatima.

When the Nasrids defeated the Ashqilula, Faraj became governor of Malaga, which his father had held until his death. He and Fatima lived there for years, during which they had at least seven children, including Ismail and their second son, Muhammad, along with several daughters. Faraj was devoted to Muhammad II, whom his uncle Muhammad I, raised him alongside. He suggested several reforms and programs that the Sultan's court issued. His loyalty continued in the reign of Muhammad III.

Faraj changed after his brother in-law Nasr dethroned Muhammad III. The nobles of Granada approached him and begged him to depose Nasr, who they thought was an inefficient monarch, more interested in science, astrolabes and astronomical tables, and a secret Christian. When Faraj heard of the capture of Muhammad III, he rebelled against Nasr and attacked him at al-Atsha, in the Vega of Granada. Nasr lost his horse in a quagmire and ran to his capital on foot. Faraj besieged the city for several months, until the influence of Fernando IV of Castile persuaded him to seek a truce with Nasr.

Later, Faraj survived an assassination attempt, which many believed Nasr had ordered. In the end, Faraj lost power because of the discovery of a secret pact between Malaga and the Marinid Sultan, which would have allowed Faraj to claim the northern port of Chella in exchange for the wealth of Malaga's taxes. His son Ismail usurped his father's rule and assumed the governorship. He kept Faraj under close watch, first at the Gibralfaro, then in the castle of Cartama. After Ismail I took the throne from his maternal uncle Nasr, he had Faraj transferred to the fortress at Salobrena, where he lived out the intervening years until his death in 720 AH or AD 1320. Ismail had Faraj's body removed from Salobrena and re-interred in the royal pantheon of the Alhambra, near the burial site of Muhammad II. When the Nasrid Dynasty ended, the last of the family exhumed the bones of all their ancestors and took them out of Granada, including Faraj's remains.

Fatima did her duty as her grandfather Muhammad I commanded and married Faraj for political gain. History does not record anything about their marriage, whether it remained a political match or if they grew to care about each other. It also does not reveal anything of her perspective on the tragedies that embroiled her father, brothers, husband, and son. In writing about her, I have stayed as true to the sources as possible and to an understanding of human nature. Whatever the truth of her feelings, Fatima was a remarkable woman in a fascinating period of Spain's history. She lived a cultured and refined life, in the manner of her father and her brothers. She was well-educated, like her father, and possessed an interest in study that extended to her role as tutor of her grandchildren.

One can only assume how the turmoil between her husband Faraj and her brother Nasr in the later years must have torn her in two, as did her son Ismail's cruel actions toward his own father and his maternal uncle, Nasr. Fatima must have been a woman capable of extraordinary love and forgiveness. When the kinsmen of Ismail I attacked him, his servants brought him to Fatima's chamber, rather than his own. This gesture suggested, at least to me, the bond between Fatima and her son. She demonstrated further devotion to her family in the relationships with her grandchildren. She tutored them, especially the boys Muhammad and Yusuf. She did not overtly wield power, but another tragedy indicates the extent of her influence at court. When assassins murdered her grandson Muhammad IV's prime minister, Ibn al-Mahruq in 729 AH or AD 1328, he died in her suite of rooms after delivering his usual report to her on the affairs of the Sultanate.

The Sultana Fatima's legacy of wisdom flourished with the ascension of her grandsons, the Sultans Muhammad IV and Yusuf I. Muhammad's brutal assassination at the age of eighteen occurred in 733 AH or AD 1333, in his eighth year as ruler of Granada. Despite this tragic loss, Fatima remained the steadfast matriarch of her family. She died at Granada during Yusuf's twenty-one year reign, a period of intellectual and architectural brilliance, which sustained itself through the reign of Yusuf's eldest son Muhammad V.

Fatima's descendants continued to rule Granada for more than one hundred and fifty years after her demise. The last Sultan of Granada, Muhammad XII, surrendered to King Ferdinand of Aragon and Queen Isabella of Castile in Rabi al-Awwal 897 AH or January AD 1492, ending seven hundred years of Muslim rule in Spain.

Thank you for purchasing and reading this book. I hope you found the period and characters fascinating. Please consider leaving feedback where you bought this book. Your opinion is helpful, both to me and to other potential readers.

If you would like to learn more about the Alhambra and Moorish Spain during the Nasrid period, visit Alhambra.org. You may also email me at lyarde1175@gmail.com. I love to hear from readers.

# *Islamic Regions and Modern Equivalents*

| Muslim Town City Region or Country | Modern Equivalent |
|---|---|
| Al-Andalus / Al-Jazirat Al-Andalus | Spain |
| Al-Atsha | Lachar |
| Al-Bayazin | Albaicin |
| Al-Jaza'ir | Algiers |
| Al-Jazirah al-Khadra | Algeciras |
| Al-Maghrib | Northern Africa |
| Al-Maghrib el-Aska | Morocco |
| Al-Mariyah | Almeria |
| Arsiduna | Archidona |
| Aryuna | Arjuno |
| Fés el-Bali | Fez |
| Gharnatah | Granada |
| Jabal Tarik | Gibraltar |
| Jumhuriyat Misr | Egypt |
| Lawsa | Loja |
| Madinah Antaqirah | Antequera |
| Malaka | Malaga |
| Martus | Martos |
| Mayurqa | Majorca |
| Munakkab | Almunecar |
| Naricha | Nerja |
| Qumarich | Comares |
| Shalabuniya | Salobrena |
| Tarif | Tarifa |
| Wadi-Ash | Guadix |

# *Glossary*

**-A-**

- *Abu*: father of
- *Addahbia*: bridal trousseau
- *Al-Andalus:* the southern half of Spain
- *Al-Fahs:* the valley
- *Al-Fakih:* the Lawgiver
- *Al-Ghuzat*: the Volunteers of the Faith, the Moroccan soldiers billeted in Granada
- *Al-Hisn*: fortress
- *Al-Jabal Faro*: Gibralfaro citadel, which protected Malaga
- *Al-Laylat al-henna*: traditional henna night for brides, where their guests gather to feast and decorate their bodies with henna
- *Al-Murabitun*: the Almoravid Empire, which ruled North Africa and southern Spain, AD 1062-1150
- *Al-Muwahhidun*: the Almohade Empire, which ruled North Africa and southern Spain, AD 1145-1269
- *Al-Qal'at al-Hamra*: the Alhambra, a complex of palaces, residences, shops, mosques, etc. that served as the royal residence in Granada. Begun in AD 1237 under Sultan Muhammad I, each of his successors made improvements, especially Muhammad III, Ismail I, Yusuf I, Muhammad V and Yusuf III
- *Al-Quasaba*: the citadel within the royal residence in Granada
- *Al-Qur'an*: Muslim holy book
- *Al-Shaykh al-Ghuzat*: commander of the Volunteers of the Faith
- *Ashqilula*: one time allies of the Nasrids until AD 1266, known as the Escayola among Christian states

**-B-**

- *Bab Ilbira:* Puerta de Elvira, the main medieval gateway into the city of Granada during Moorish times
- *Bint*: daughter of
- *Burnus*: a Moroccan cloak

**-C-**

- *Carkenet*: a jeweled chain necklace or collar
- *Cortes*: the rudimentary Castilian parliament

**-D-**

- *Dinar*: coin bearing a religious verse, commonly made of gold or silver, or rarely, copper. They were minted in Granada with the Sultans' motto, "none victorious but God" and could be round or square shaped. Gold dinars weighed 2 grams, contained 22 carats of gold and were widely used for internal and external trade. Their value fluctuated over the centuries. Silver dinars were square and had a fixed value. Copper dinars were used for internal trade in the Sultanate and had a fixed value
- *Diwan al-Insha*: the Sultan's chancery of state

**-G-**

- *Galego*: the language of Galicia
- *Ghasil*: man who washes the Muslim dead

**-H-**

- *Habba souda*: a mixture of corn cockle seeds
- *Hadarro*: modern-day river Darro that flows through Granada
- *Hajib*: Prime Minister
- *Hakkak*: masseur
- *Hammam*: bathhouse
- *Hashishin*: Persian assassins
- *Hawdaj:* a leather canopy
- *Hijab*: a veil
- *Hud*: enemies of the Nasrids

**-I-**

- *Ibn*: son of
- *Insha'Allah*: God willing

**-J-**

- *Jahannam*: Hell
- *Jarya*: concubine, plural *jawari*
- *Jihad*: the struggle; a personal commitment to maintain the Islamic faith, to improve Islamic society and to

defend Islam and an Islamic way of life against its enemies

- *Jubba*: floor-length robe with wide sleeves, opening at the neck, worn by both sexes of the nobility

**-K-**

- *Kadin*: favored concubine, who has also had children for her master
- *Khanjar*: dagger
- *Khassa*: collective Moorish nobility
- *Khil'a*: ceremonial floor-length robe with wide sleeves, opening at the neck, decorated with *tiraz* bands, worn by courtiers on special occasions
- *Kohl*: black eyeliner

**-M-**

- *Madina*: a city
- *Marinids*: rulers of modern day Morocco AD 1248-1548
- *Mashwar*: the council chambers of the Sultan's chancery
- *Mihrab*: prayer niche

**-N-**

- *Naksh:* cursive style of calligraphy
- *Nasrids*: rulers of Granada AD 1232-1492
- *Nikah*: wedding ceremony
- *Niyyah*: declaration of the intent to perform prayers

**-P-**

- *Purdah*: room divider or screen

**-Q-**

- *Qadar*: pre-destiny
- *Qa'id*: judge
- *Qamis*: long shirt of white cotton or linen, worn as an undergarment by both sexes, in all social classes
- *Qaysariyya*: the central marketplace in Granada
- *Qiblah*: the wall of a mosque facing the city of Mecca, Saudi Arabia

**-R-**

- *Raïs:* provincial governor

- *Rak'ah:* prescribed series of movements and words during Muslim prayer
- *Rawda*: cemetery

**-S-**

- *Sabika:* the hill where the Alhambra was built
- *Salat al-Asr*: third prayer time, obligatory at afternoon
- *Salat al-Fajr*: first prayer time, obligatory at sunrise
- *Salat al-Isha*: fifth prayer time, obligatory at nighttime
- *Salat al-Maghrib*: fourth prayer time, obligatory after sunset
- *Salat al-Zuhr*: second prayer time, obligatory at noon
- *Sarawil*: trousers
- *Shahadah*: the Muslim Profession of Faith
- *Sharia*: the religious law of Islam
- *Shashiya*: skullcap

**-T-**

- *Tahini:* sesame paste
- *Talib:* apprentice or student
- *'Tharid*: dish of crumbled pieces of bread served in a meat or vegetable broth
- *Tiraz*: richly brocaded bands of cloth decorating the upper sleeves of a ceremonial garment, often bearing symbols, geometric motifs or script

**-U-**

- *Ummi*: my mother

**-W-**

- *Walima*: wedding feast
- *Wazir:* minister

# About the Author

Lisa J. Yarde writes fiction inspired by real-life events. She is the author of two historical novels set in medieval England and Normandy, *The Burning Candle*, based on the life of Isabel de Vermandois, and *On Falcon's Wings*, chronicling the star-crossed romance between Norman and Saxon lovers. Lisa has also written *Sultana* and *Sultana's Legacy*, novels set during a turbulent period of thirteenth century Spain, where rivalries and ambitions threaten the fragile bonds between members of a powerful family. She has written contemporary fiction including her first novella, *Long Way Home*, in which a young couple learns valuable lessons about love, loss and forgiveness, just before tragedy strikes.

Born in Barbados, Lisa currently lives in New York City. She is also an avid blogger and moderates at Unusual Historicals. She is also a regular contributor at Historical Novel Reviews and History and Women. Her personal blog is The Brooklyn Scribbler. Learn more about Lisa and her writing at the website www.lisajyarde.com. Discover bonus content on the website, including maps, genealogy tables, and photos of the Alhambra.

20093018R00209

Made in the USA
Charleston, SC
27 June 2013